The Warming

Also by Stanley Johnson

The Virus

The Warming

A Thriller

STANLEY JOHNSON

WITNESS
IMPULSE
An Imprint of HarperCollins*Publishers*

This book is a work of fiction. The characters, incidents, and dialogue are drawn from the author's imagination and are not to be construed as real. Any resemblance to actual events or persons, living or dead, is entirely coincidental.

This book was previously published by Cameron May in 1998, under the title *Icecap*.

EPub Edition JUNE 2015 ISBN: 9780062414908

Print Edition ISBN: 9780062414939

10 9 8 7 6 5 4 3 2 1

Preface

I FIRST THOUGHT *of writing this book early in 1984, when I had the good fortune to be invited by the British Antarctic Survey (BAS) to visit several of their bases in Antarctica. Most of the time was spent on the Antarctic peninsular or panhandle which juts up towards the Drake Passage and Cape Horn. On one occasion, however, we flew quite a long way south in one of BAS's Twin Otter aircraft towards the Transantarctic Mountains. In such circumstances it was not hard to visualize the scene on the Beardmore Glacier, over seventy years earlier, as Captain Scott and his companions gamely struggled to make their way back to their base at the edge of the Ross Ice Shelf.*

The tragic death of Captain Scott and his men has entered the national consciousness. Their heroism is legendary. What some people do not perhaps realize is that Scott's last expedition, besides being a race for the South Pole, also had serious scientific objectives and that the polar party, against all the odds, dragged back with them on their sledge a load of geological samples, which they had found somewhere near the top of the Beardmore glacier. Those geological samples were discovered next to the bodies inside the collapsed snow-covered tent on November 11, 1912, nine months after the polar party perished on the ice.

For years I have been fascinated by those bits of rock. What happened to them? Where did they go? Was the mineral content ever analysed? Why didn't the men who dragged the sledge, frostbitten and snow-blind and seared with the shattering disappointment of having been pipped at the post by Amundsen, simply jettison the load? Relieved of that weight, they might have been able to travel faster. Who knows, they might even have been able to reach the fuel depot which they missed by barely a mile.

By the time I actually started writing this book, four years ago, the debates about global warming were in full swing. I went to Rio de Janeiro, Brazil, for the Earth Summit when the first international convention on climate change was signed. That convention was followed in 1997 by the so-called Kyoto Protocol, which lays down specific obligations upon the nations of the world as far as the reduction of greenhouse or global warming gases is concerned. The Kyoto Protocol also provides for the possibility of increasing carbon sinks as well as reducing carbon emissions. Some scientists on the fringes of the Kyoto meeting argued that the oceans, as well as the forests, could under certain circumstances absorb increasing quantities of carbon, thus whetting my enthusiasm for completing an ecological thriller which could in some sense link the heroism of Britain's greatest Antarctic explorer with the solution to mankind's greatest environmental challenge - global warming.

I am extremely pleased that Cameron May, who are better known as the publisher of books on environmental law, have been ready to publish this, my ninth novel, as their first venture into the field of environmental fiction. I hope those who buy this book have as much fun reading it as I had writing it.

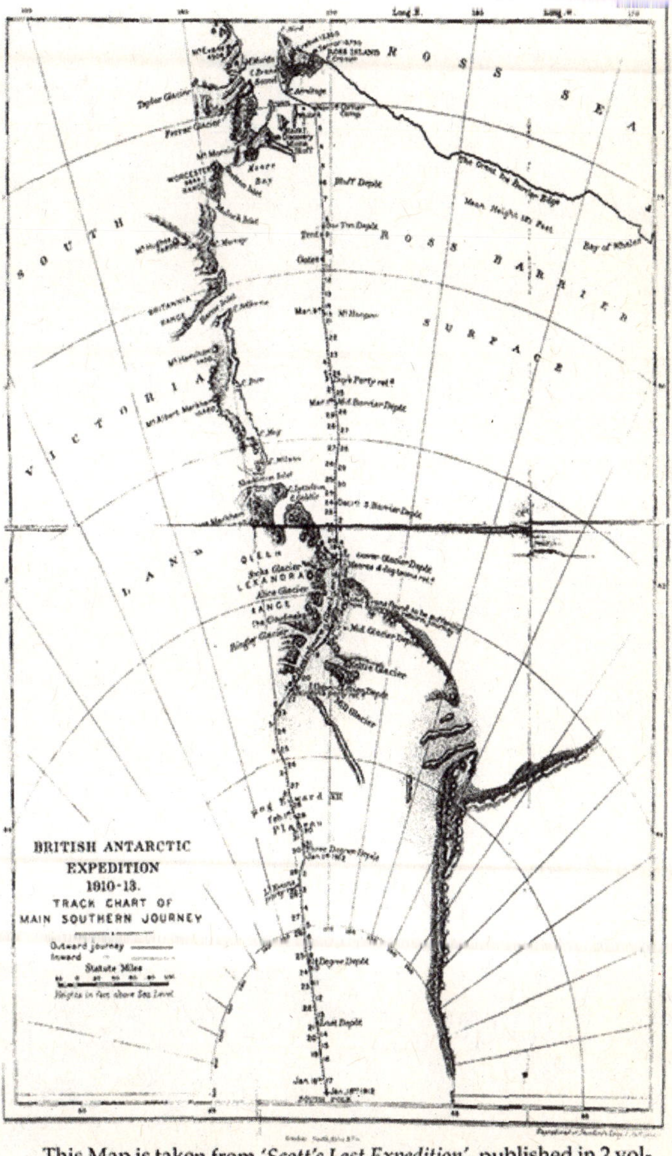

This Map is taken from *'Scott's Last Expedition'* published in 2 volumes by Smith Elder & Co., London 1913

I

London—Rio de Janeiro

I THINK I had better begin by saying a word or two about myself. The first thing to make clear is that I'm not a high-flyer. I'm thirty-five years old and, as a journalist, I reckon my career has probably peaked. Perhaps I should have been more adventurous, should have worked harder at adding spice and variety to the curriculum vitae. Looking back, I think I probably played it too safe. When I came down from Cambridge in the middle eighties, I was taken on by Reuters as a trainee and I've stayed at Reuters ever since.

My first posting was in Bonn. I was learning the ropes and I suppose that Bonn was as good a place as any to start. There aren't many distractions in Bonn, I can tell you. After that, I had a longish stint in Brussels at the end of the eighties and the beginning of the nineties, at a time when Britain's relationship with the European Community seemed to be going from bad to worse. For the last five years or so, I've been back in London on the general news desk.

When I say that I'm not a high-flyer, I don't mean to imply that I'm not good at my job. I'm a perfectly competent performer. But in Reuters nowadays that's not enough. The big story today is whether Reuters can beat Bloomberg, not whether we can still outrun AP or UPI. The reality is that old-fashioned wire-service reporters within Reuters are diminishing both in number and importance. The heavy hitters have moved on to the management side, particularly the ever-growing world of financial services. Or else they have taken jobs elsewhere. A couple of my former colleagues have become media pundits, with a photograph as well as a byline at the top of their columns. Another now heads a City bank.

I didn't quite have the nerve to leave what was a fairly interesting and well-paid assignment. I didn't jump ship when perhaps I should have done. I stayed put. At the time it seemed a wise decision. Now, when I see just how far some of my contemporaries have gone, I find myself regretting it.

There are of course some advantages to *not* being a high-flyer. Your life is more your own for a start. When I'm at home in my flat in the evening, for example, I often put the answering-machine on. If you're on the telephone most of the day, as I am, you can take a positive pleasure in *not* answering your calls. I watch television, write letters, listen to music. Above all, I try not to think about work. I leave the office at the end of the day and I put the job out of my mind. I may not have all the rewards, but I don't have all the grief either.

That particular evening I was watching a BBC *Panorama* report about the worsening economic situation in Russia. The price of bread had apparently quadrupled in the course of a month but that was just one symptom of more general chaos. According to the *Panorama* team, the hard liners in the Kremlin were getting ready for a showdown. The beleaguered Russian President Vladimir Cherniavsky was under tremendous pressure to come up with a solution to the crisis . . . 'Or else.'

Even though I was quite absorbed in the programme, when I heard her voice on the tape I knew who it was immediately. The rhythms and cadences were quite unmistakable. Nasreen once told me that at home in Teheran, before the wild men and the mullahs took over, her family had always spoken English when they were together rather than Persian. It was in a very real sense her native tongue. Her English vocabulary was more extensive than mine, and her grammar was text-book perfect. But the musical lilt in her speech was her own very polite way of reminding you that though she might look as though she had stepped straight out of the pages of *Country Life*, she had been born a long way east of the Bosphorus and was proud of it.

'Charles, this is Nasreen. I'm at home in Rio. I need to talk to you urgently. It's about Harry. Please call me back as soon as possible.' She gave her number in Brazil.

I don't have a large flat but I try anyway to keep the phone as far away from my desk as I can. I like to think that if I can't see it, it isn't there. Out of sight, out of mind. As a result, I'm constantly running into the alcove by the kitchen to grab the receiver just as the caller rings off.

Even if the phone hadn't been the other side of the room, I would probably have missed her. It had been five years since I last heard Nasreen's voice and it gave me quite a turn. As a matter of fact, I was rocked back on my heels. Literally, as well as figuratively. Instead of running to the phone, I sat transfixed at my desk. Just the sound of her speaking into the answering machine gave me goose bumps all over. Ten years ago Nasreen and I had been engaged. Two weeks before the wedding, she told me she was going to marry my brother Harry instead. I hadn't spoken to her since.

I ought to explain that Harry and I are twins though I apparently arrived first - by about two hours. Our father was a British diplomat and, as is the case with many diplomatic families, we were sent off at an early age to boarding-school. I'm always meeting people nowadays who complain about their school-days, particularly about being separated from their parents for so much of the year, as though there were something unnatural and inhumane about it. I don't believe that either Harry or I suffered from our years at Milborne School in the depths of the Dorset countryside, although we reacted very differently to the place.

I had a mediocre career at school, scraping into Cambridge with three 'A' Levels and a tutor's letter of recommendation which was probably friendlier than I deserved. Harry's time at Milborne was far more illustrious. We weren't in the same boarding house but it was impossible not to be aware of Harry's progress. He was a name, a 'blood', as we called it then, in a way that I never was. He played for the First Eleven at cricket, besides captaining the school tennis team and carrying off the debating prize two years in succession.

Truth to tell, from about as early as I can remember, in spite of the fact that we were twins, Harry and I went our separate ways. We didn't even look alike. Though we are both about the same height - around six foot - I am dark and narrow, while Harry is blond and broadshouldered. At school, he had his own friends and I had mine.

Oddly enough, we saw more of each other in Cambridge than we did at school. For a start, we were in the same college - Trinity.

Harry had always maintained that he didn't want to waste three years at university when he could be making a fortune in business but the school insisted that he sit the university entrance exams and, where I scraped in, he ended up with an open scholarship. We weren't on the same staircase but we both had rooms in Great Court and inevitably our paths crossed several times a week.

I met Nasreen in the Spring Term of my final year. Her full name was Nasreen Hassan. She came from a rich Iranian family which had fled Teheran after the fall of the Shah and had, I learned, established itself in leafy Surrey not far from Godalming. It was clear that the Hassans, though in a sense refugees, were far from destitute. Nasreen was always immaculately and expensively dressed. She floated into lectures with a chiffon scarf trailing from her lovely neck. Her almost pure-white skin contrasted with her thick, jet-black hair.

I fell madly in love with her at long distance. I found myself speculating about her life and loves and wondering how, if ever, our paths might cross. Then one day I found myself sitting next to her at close of play in the history faculty library. I was so tongue-tied that it was as much as I could do to suggest we might have a drink and a stroll by the river. I could hardly believe my luck at first. With the whole wide world to choose from, why did Nasreen select me?

We spent the rest of that term and most of the Easter holidays together. Nasreen took me to stay with her parents. They had an enormous mock-Tudor establishment with grounds of at least ten acres, swimming pool, tennis court and paddocks for the horses. Parvis Hassan - Nasreen's father - was a keen show-jumper in his spare time and Nasreen herself, as I soon learned, was a very competent horsewoman.

I said I fell in love with Nasreen. And I did. But we were not lovers. Nasreen explained quite matter-of-factly that her father and brothers would take a very dim view of any misbehaviour. She would love to go to bed with me, she said, but she didn't want to wake up in the middle of the night with a dagger in her back and she didn't suppose that I did either. I took her point. These rich Iranian families which fled to France, Britain and the United States when their country collapsed may seem westernised and sophisticated but, precisely because they have been uprooted, there are some customs they hold on to very dearly and pre-marital chastity at least as far as the girls are concerned is one of those.

Besides, I had another idea in mind. A better idea. At the beginning of the summer term I asked Nasreen to marry me. When she said yes - we were punting by moonlight along the Backs - I was overwhelmed with joy. Plenty of other men, I knew, had been sniffing around. Cambridge is nothing if not competitive. But somehow I had played my cards right. I told her that I had been offered a job with Reuters when I graduated. With my parents abroad, I explained that we would be able to live in a fairly well-appointed flat in Kensington while we looked for a place of our own. The future might not be scintillating, but at least it looked secure. Nasreen seemed content. She told me she loved me and I believed her.

And then, towards the end of that summer term, with the wedding only a few weeks off, Harry came into our lives. We bumped into him in Great Court one evening when we were going out to a concert. Up till then I had played my cards close to my chest. I hadn't brought Nasreen into college much. She was at Girton and I tended to pick her up there, or else we would meet in town. I think some instinct told me that it would be better if Harry and Nasreen didn't meet. Not until we were married, anyway.

But that particular evening the concert was actually in Trinity, so it made sense for Nasreen to come to my rooms. Harry was standing on the lawn, with a cigarette in his hand, surrounded - as was so often the case - by a small group of admirers.

Of course, I had to introduce her.

'Harry, this is Nasreen Hassan,' I said. And then I added, because it seemed the right thing to say, 'Nasreen and I are going to be married soon after the end of term. We'd like you to be best man.'

I can visualise the scene even as I write this. Harry was at his most glamorous. He had been playing cricket for some university side - the Penguins, I believe - and he was wearing a striped silk blazer, cream-coloured Daks and, would you believe it, a straw boater with a coloured headband like some Venetian gondolier.

As I told him the news, he swept the boater from his head and bowed theatrically before us.

'Good Lord! What wonderful news!' he exclaimed. 'I'm so pleased. So pleased for both of you. May I?' He took Nasreen's hand and raised it to his lips, looking into her eyes as he did so.

After that, something changed in our relationship. Nasreen seemed uncertain, confused. When I asked her whether anything was bothering her, she denied it. As a matter of fact, she became quite annoyed, accusing me of acting strangely. I put it down to stress - the wedding was only a month away.

We had planned to have a quiet civil wedding ceremony in Cambridge with just family and close friends present. Nasreen's parents intended to throw a big party for us at their Surrey home later in the summer. Paradoxically, as the pressure of exams mounted, I found that I was seeing less of Nasreen than I had been earlier in the year. In some ways, that wasn't such a bad thing. The offer of the Reuters job was conditional on my getting a decent degree.

Nasreen said she would come to meet me after my last paper. I finished early. As I emerged into the sunshine to join the crush of undergraduates on the pavement outside the examination hall, I couldn't see her at first. There was a good deal of shouting and cheering as the champagne corks popped. Mortar boards were being thrown in the air and it looked as though the proctors would be along at any moment to break up the party.

I clambered up onto the base of a lamppost to have a better view and suddenly I saw her at the edge of the crowd. She was with Harry. They were embracing. No doubt about it. I can't tell you what it felt like. Somehow, I think I had known from the moment Harry first met her that he wouldn't leave her alone. It was the way he looked at her that first evening. Was it the fact that Nasreen was so beautiful, that I was going to marry her and he wasn't? Or was he genuinely smitten? With Harry, you could never be sure of anything.

I didn't want them to know that I had seen them kissing. I got down off the lamppost feeling sick to the soul. I was, as a matter of fact, physically sick at that moment. I went back inside, found the toilets, and vomited into the basin. By the time, I had re-emerged, the crowd had thinned. Harry was nowhere to be seen.

Later that day, Nasreen told me she had made a mistake. It was Harry she loved, not me.

I drove down to London that night, stayed at the flat and tried - dumbly - to understand what had happened. I think the worst thing about it was that in a funny way I saw Nasreen's point. Harry had flair, he had poise, he had gaiety and charm. I could see what attracted her. But I knew there was a darker side to his character. There had been moments during our childhood and adolescence when I had seen him explode with anger at what seemed to be perfectly trivial incidents. For example, when we were both around fifteen and staying with an aunt in Cumbria, I saw Harry kick out viciously at a Labrador puppy which had peed on his suede shoes. When I remonstrated with him, he shouted at me: 'For Christ's sake, Charles, it's only a bloody dog!' I never forgot that.

Realistically, though, I knew it would be pointless to try to win Nasreen back by denigrating Harry. She wouldn't have listened to me.

I suppose I could have sued for breach of promise. But what was the point? I would only have made my own misery more intense. If ever there were a double whammy, that was it. Losing your fiancée to your brother! Nothing could be more certain to lower a man's self-esteem. And it wasn't just my pride that was hurt. I had loved Nasreen. More than anyone else, before or since. As for Harry, that brilliant, precocious, self-absorbed, charming, devious stinking rat, I wanted to kill him.

I came back to Cambridge the next day, packed my bags and left. I didn't see Harry. I didn't talk to him. I didn't even leave him a note.

As you can imagine, I didn't in the circumstances attend Harry and Nasreen's wedding. I wasn't even in England since Reuters posted me to Germany almost as soon as I joined. Graham Southgate told me about it, though. Southgate was at Trinity with Harry and me, though he was actually a few years older. He had already taken his PhD and held a junior lectureship in Geology, which was probably how he met Harry in the first place. Harry was also studying geology. Southgate, I knew, was close to Harry, but he had always been friendly with me as well. I had only been in Bonn a few weeks when I received his letter. Harry and Nasreen, he said, had been married at the end of the summer. He, Southgate, had acted as best man.

'I just want you to know,' Southgate wrote, 'that I think you have behaved admirably throughout this whole business. It must have been exceedingly painful.'

Southgate told me that Harry and Nasreen had left for Brazil. I later learned from various sources that Harry, with his Cambridge degree in geology under his belt, had set himself up in Rio as a dealer in rare minerals and precious stones. The first Christmas, Nasreen had sent a card signed - in her handwriting - with 'love from Harry and Nasreen'. I hadn't reciprocated. Since then, a decade had passed. I hadn't heard any more from them. They hadn't heard from me.

Then, out of the blue, a telephone call. The voice I knew so well, still with the same perfect musical diction. I felt as though I had been kicked in the stomach. As Nasreen rang off, I pushed myself out of my chair, walked stiffly over to the alcove and stood there staring down at the answering-machine. I hadn't written down Nasreen's number in Rio while she was speaking, so I pressed Play and heard her voice all over again.

I poured myself a stiff Scotch. Then I went back to the phone and stood there like an idiot, rattling the ice in the glass. I was paralysed with indecision. Should I call her back or shouldn't I?

One thing I knew for sure, even then, was that if I turned down the TV, then picked up the phone and dialled Nasreen's number, nothing would ever be the same again.

The next day, I told Reuters that I had urgent family business to attend to and that I would be out of the office for several days.

I packed some tropical gear and caught the British Airways overnight flight from Heathrow to Rio. Nasreen had told me that she would meet me at the airport. I came out of the Customs hall to find her standing, as we had arranged, at the information desk.

'Charles! Thank God you've come!'

Back in our Cambridge days Nasreen, as I've already mentioned, had the palest of complexions. She had once explained to me that the Iranians were a true Aryan race - indeed the etymology was the same. She had added that, contrary to the general supposition, pale skin was not unusual among the nobility. She had gone on to say, without any trace of self-consciousness, that her own ancestry could be traced back on her father's side at least a thousand years.

Be that as it may, ten years in Brazil had had an impact. Her hair was still as dark, still as lush but her skin had gone from cream to golden.

Beneath her tan, Nasreen looked pale and drained. There were dark rings under her eyes and her voice trembled as she spoke. My arrival seemed to have precipitated some release of tension because she fell on me and clung to me as though the world was about to end.

I wasn't sure I could handle it. Holding her in my arms like that brought back too many memories. I disentangled myself from her embrace.

'I think I had find better a porter,' I said.

Of course, it was an excuse. She knew it and I knew it. I could easily have carried my own luggage. I could sense her pulling back.

'I'm sorry,' she said. 'I've been so worried. So terribly worried. Nobody wants to know anything. Nobody wants to help.'

Her hair was cut so that it fell almost to her shoulders. She pushed it away from her eyes and with the back of her hand brushed away a tear.

There's something about a woman in distress that gets to me. Even if it hadn't been Nasreen, I would have been moved. As it was, I could barely hold back my own emotions.

'Don't worry, Nasreen,' I gulped. 'We'll sort it out. I'm sure of that.'

Calling her by name like that must have helped ease the tension of the moment. She smiled bravely at me through her tears.

'You're looking well, Charles.'

She was quite a tall woman. Five feet eight, I'd say. Perhaps more. When she leaned forward to kiss me on the cheek, she didn't have to stand on tiptoe or hang on to me for support. She just did it quite naturally, almost as though she had forgotten completely all that had happened between us.

Maybe she had indeed forgotten. Or maybe things didn't seem to her the way they seemed to me. Frankly, I'm not sure. One thing I'm quite clear about. The man who tells you he understands women is a liar, pure and simple.

There was something surreal about the next forty minutes. Less than twenty-four hours earlier, I had been in my flat in Little Venice, West London, watching the ducks and the barges on the canal out of my sitting-room window. Now I was cruising at 60 miles an hour along the new elevated highway which connects Galeao international airport on the Ilha do Governador to Rio de Janeiro, while Nasreen filled in the details of the bizarre story of Harry's disappearance.

'He drove up to Belo Horizonte last Tuesday,' she said as we joined the stream of *Cariocas* (which is what Brazilians call the inhabitants of the city) heading into town for another day's work or play. 'Belo Horizonte is the capital of Minas Gerais. It's about 300 miles north of Rio, up on the plateau in the interior.'

'What was he doing there?' I asked.

'Harry never told me much about his business activities. I think he was going to a meeting with CMG. That's the Compagnia Minas Gerais. It's a new mining company which some Brazilian entrepreneurs have established. Everyone's talking about it.'

I nodded. I'm not myself a financial specialist, but Reuters, as I've already mentioned, is heavily into financial news and services of every kind, and something rubs off even when, as I am, you're on the general news desk. In the back of my mind, I remembered reading something fairly recently about a new hot minerals stock on the São Paulo stock exchange. I also recalled seeing an article somewhere, probably in *Business Week* or *Fortune*, which described how CMG's boss, a former admiral in the Brazilian Navy, had been responsible for the rapid rise in CMG's fortunes by pursuing an aggressive policy of minerals exploration and exploitation in hitherto virgin areas of Brazilian territory.

'I read about that,' I said. 'Remind me of the name of CMG's CEO. Some ex-naval fellow, isn't it?'

'Alvarez,' Nasreen replied. 'Admiral Antonio Francisco Alvarez.'

'What went wrong?'

'Apparently, Harry never arrived in Belo Horizonte. Alvarez's office called to say that he had missed his lunch with the big man and what the hell was going on? Alvarez is not used to being stood up, as you can imagine.'

'Did you hear from Harry?'

'Not at all. Total silence. He's been gone five days already. Not a peep.'

'Is that unusual?'

Nasreen thought about that one. 'If he'd been off in the Amazon somewhere or Matto Grosso, I'd understand it. He makes trips to the interior sometimes and it can be quite a few days, sometimes even weeks, before I hear from him. They don't have telephones on every street corner up there. But Belo Horizonte is the third or fourth largest city in Brazil. If he arrived, why didn't he get in touch?'

'Did you try the police?'

Nasreen gave a dismissive shrug, changing down as she did so to overtake a truck laden with timber. Another bit of the Brazilian rain forest heading for oblivion.

'Of course I did. As soon as I knew he was missing I gave them the registration number of Harry's car, told them his itinerary as far as I knew it and asked them to make enquiries.'

'Did they?'

She shrugged again. 'Frankly, they weren't very interested. They rang back a couple of days later to say they had no reports of any accidents involving Harry or Harry's car. And that was that.'

'That's when you rang me.'

'Yes.'

'How did you know my number? I'm not in the book.'

'I tried Reuters but they wouldn't tell me your home number, so then I called Graham Southgate.'

I was surprised. 'Are you still in touch with Graham? What's he doing now?'

Nasreen seemed to hesitate for a second. 'Harry keeps up with him. Common interests, I suppose. Graham's a fellow of Churchill College now.'

'So he is,' I said. Graham Southgate was one of the few people I still knew from my Cambridge days.

We went through the tunnel under the mountains. As we emerged, I looked back and caught a glimpse of the great statue of Christ the Redeemer - Cristo Redentor - perched on the summit of Corcovado, with His arms stretched out over the city.

'When Harry and I first came to Rio after we were married,' Nasreen said, 'we lived in a hotel on Avenida Atlantica, that's the one which runs along Copacabana beach. Harry liked that. He found it easy for entertaining his clients.'

'Liked the bars too, no doubt.'

Nasreen shot me a wry glance. 'He certainly liked his *caipirinhas*. Likes, I should say.'

Odd, I thought, the way she used the past tense like that. Almost as though she feared the worst.

A minute or two later we hit the beach and drove west along the Avenida Atlantica. To the left was the great sweep of Copacabana beach, still empty - the sunseekers wouldn't arrive in strength until later. Beyond the white sand, the grey-green breakers roared and crashed. To the right, the tall facades of the fashionable hotels glinted in the morning light.

'I didn't much like living in a hotel, even on Copacabana,' Nasreen said. 'Besides, it was hideously expensive. Harry was always picking up the tab for all and sundry. You know Harry. Whatever his faults, he's not tightfisted.'

'When did you move?'

'About six months after we first arrived. I found an apartment just off Ipanema. Harry grumbled a bit but went along with it.'

'*The girl from Ipanema goes walking*,' I sang under my breath, '*and when she passes, each one she passes goes ah . . .*'

For the first time that morning, Nasreen smiled.

'Not quite that kind of girl,' she said.

At the end of Avenida Atlantica we cut through another short tunnel before, once again, hitting the ocean. The waves were even larger on Ipanema Beach than on Copacabana. In fact they looked distinctly nasty. It would be easy enough, I imagined, to be rolled head over heels or be pulled by the undertow out to sea. Apart from a couple of surfers riding the crests down the Leblon end of the beach, I couldn't see anyone actually in the water.

The flat which Nasreen and Harry rented on one of the side streets off the Ipanema seafront was a spacious affair; masterbedroom, study-cum-spare bedroom, kitchen, two bathrooms and a wide terrace from which you got an angled view of the beach and the great swirling breakers.

Nasreen showed me to the spare room.

'No point in your going to a hotel,' she said. 'We've plenty of room.'

I hesitated, suitcase still in hand. I felt that if I put it down and accepted her offer of hospitality without so much as a murmur or a quibble I would be devaluing, belittling, the hurt I had suffered. OK, I had picked up the phone that evening to call her back. OK, I had got on the plane to Rio to help her out in her moment of crisis. But that didn't mean, did it, that I was ready just like that to let bygones be bygones?

Of course it bloody well did! Just being with her an hour or so that morning, hearing her voice, watching her move, smelling the faint, subtle perfume that I remembered so well, made me realise that even after all that had happened, after all the hurt and bitterness - on my side at least - she still had me in the palm of her hand. She could - and would - set the terms of our encounter. That much was already clear. And there would not be a bleat of protest from me.

I released my grip on the handle of the suitcase and it plonked to the floor.

'I wouldn't mind a shower,' I said. 'I've been travelling all night.'

She had lunch ready on the terrace when I emerged, washed, shaved, and in a clean set of clothes.

As I sat down with my back to the wall so I could see the ocean, she said, 'I think the place to begin is with Alvarez's invitation. At least it makes clear where Harry was headed, even if he didn't arrive.'

She handed me an envelope containing an expensively embossed sheet of cream-coloured writing paper. The letterhead indicated that it came from the Chairman and Chief Executive Officer of the Compagnia Minas Gerais. It was addressed to Mr Henry Hodson, c/o J. R. Berg, Avenida Rio Branco 286.

'Who are J. R. Berg?' I asked.

'They're a big jewel company in Rio. In fact, they're probably the biggest in Brazil. Harry has an arrangement with them. They provide him with an office and a secretary and have a share in his profits. If there are any . . .'

Nasreen allowed herself a wry smile, but beneath it I detected a trace of unease. Moving out of the hotel might have helped the finances, but it seemed as though there were still some problems in that area.

Alvarez's letter, to which I now turned my attention, was brief and to the point. It was also, I was glad to see, written in English. Though I am a reasonable linguist, my Portuguese is pretty rudimentary.

'*Dear Mr Hodson,*' Alvarez wrote. '*This is to confirm that I am much looking forward to seeing you for lunch next week when you come to Belo Horizonte and to discussing with you matters of mutual interest.*'

The letter was signed with an expressive flourish, with the sender's name typed out beneath in full. As I put it back in the envelope, I noticed another sheet of paper inside. I glanced at it. Alvarez had kindly enclosed a sketch-map showing the location of CMG's headquarters in Belo Horizonte.

I pushed the letter back across the table.

'It doesn't say much, does it?' I commented. 'Who do you suppose fixed up this meeting? Harry or Harry's secretary?'

Nasreen looked vague. 'Harry's secretary, I guess.'

'Do you suppose I could visit Harry's office later?' I asked. 'I'd like to talk to the secretary. What's her name?'

'Letitia.'

'Does Letitia handle all his meetings and correspondence?'

'Supposedly. Of course, Harry is quite capable of fixing things up for himself without telling Letitia or me for that matter. That's the way he is.'

I nodded. To say Harry was a loner was an understatement. He was the original cat that walked by himself. Full of feline charm. And danger.

'Why do you think Harry brought Alvarez's letter home from the office?' I asked.

'I guess because he was leaving from here rather than the office. He must have left it behind by accident.'

'Exactly what time did he leave?'

'Tuesday morning. He said he was going to spend the night in Ouro Preto and drive on to Belo Horizonte in the morning.'

'And did he?'

'Did he what?'

'Did he spend the night in Ouro Preto?'

'I've no idea,' Nasreen replied. 'After he left here, I never heard from him again.'

There was a map of Brazil on the wall. I walked over and studied it for a few moments.

'Why would Harry have gone to Ouro Preto in the first place? It's not exactly on the direct route from Rio to Belo Horizonte, is it?'

'Harry didn't like being questioned about what he was doing,' Nasreen replied tensely. 'You know that, Charles. You were brought up with him. If he was in Ouro Preto, I'm sure he had a good reason for being there.'

I left it at that. I went into my room, took off my shoes, lay down on the bed and surrendered without a fight to the waves of sleepiness which overcame me. Through the open window I could hear the roar of the Atlantic as the surf pounded the beach.

II

Rio de Janeiro

TWO HOURS LATER, I awoke quite refreshed. Frankly, I would have preferred to have had a quiet cup of tea with Nasreen on the terrace before setting off on my Sherlock Holmes assignment but Nasreen told me that she had already arranged for me to visit Harry's office at the end of the afternoon.

'I talked to Letitia on the phone,' she said. 'She will be happy to see you though she's not sure she can be of much help. She says she already told me everything she knows.'

Nasreen didn't want to come with me so I set off by myself. J. R. Berg's main offices were in the heart of the business district. By the time I left the flat, the afternoon traffic had built up and the taxi took all of 30 minutes to cover a distance barely more than three or four miles. I'd missed the famous Rio Carnival by several months, but it didn't take much imagination to fill the streets with steel bands and swaying throngs. Even now, half the city's population seemed to be crowded onto the road and my driver progressed with one hand on the horn and the other gesticulating at the slightest provocation.

J. R. Berg, thank heavens, was air-conditioned and soundproof. Following Nasreen's instructions, I walked through the showrooms with their opulent display of gems and silverware. A single flight of stairs at the back of the building brought me out into a short, plush-carpeted corridor. Harry's office, two doors down on the right, was marked by a brass plaque which bore his name and the description 'Consultant - Gems and Rare Minerals'.

Letitia was expecting me. She was a middle-aged woman who in her youth must have been a considerable beauty. She stood up to greet me as I entered and after a few pleasantries she pointed to an inner sanctum.

'I sit out here, senhor. He sits in there.' Letitia smiled as she outlined the basic geography. 'Sometimes we keep the door open and shout at each other!'

She gave me coffee from a flask, one of those little cups of strong, sweet, black liquid they call *cafesinhos*, then she poured another for herself.

While Letitia went back to her desk, I sat down in a chair, perched my coffee on top of a glossy magazine entitled '*Gemstones*' and tried to pick up any clues, any hints or nuances, which might help to throw light on my brother's disappearance.

That Letitia was concerned, very concerned, was obvious. 'Almost one week now he is missing, senhor. I know the senhora is very worried. So am I. Senhor Harry has many things to attend to.' She pointed to a stack of papers and telephone messages on her desk. 'This is not good for business.'

She pursed her lips and it crossed my mind that, amongst other things, Letitia was probably worrying who would pay her salary at the end of the month if Harry remained AWOL.

While I drank my coffee, I tried to establish whether she had noticed anything unusual before Harry left on his trip.

'Did he receive any messages that could have accounted for a sudden change of plan? Did the pattern of his work change in the last few days?'

She thought about that for a moment. 'Senhor Harry did not really have much of a pattern. He came to the office most days, except when he was travelling, but I never knew precisely when I would see him.'

'Did he meet his clients here?' I glanced into the inner office as I asked the question. I could see that it was a sizeable room. Apart from a desk and a computer table, there was an expensive leather sofa and a couple of low-slung chairs of a fashionably futuristic design which clearly made up in style for what they lacked in comfort.

Letitia, understandably, was reluctant to talk in detail about Harry's business. I might be Harry's brother but that didn't mean I had carte blanche to pry.

'He met his clients wherever he needed to - in the Copacabana Hotel, at the Yacht Club, in their homes.' She paused. 'Of course, people also came to see him here.'

'What sort of people?'

Letitia shrugged. 'All kinds. Brazilians, Italians, Egyptians. Russians, sometimes.'

'Russians?' I was surprised.

'Why not? They need minerals too. At least the special ones.'

When I had finished my coffee, she showed me into Harry's office. 'I don't think you'll find much. Please call me if you need me.'

I sat down in Harry's chair. His diary lay open on his desk. I looked at the entries over the last few days. Most of them meant nothing to me. As Letitia had indicated, much of Harry's business seemed to be conducted at the Yacht Club over lunch or dinner. I didn't recognise any of the names, but then I didn't expect to. As Letitia had indicated, Harry's list of contacts seemed to be fairly eclectic.

I was about to turn my attention elsewhere when an entry for the previous week - just before Harry's disappearance - caught my attention. Unlike the others which were mainly pencilled notations, this one had been written in red ink. '*Oliveira*' it read. '*Meet at office - 12 noon*'. Next to it was scribbled a row of letters and dots '*http://www.mata-atlantica*'.

Curious, I picked up the diary and walked through to talk to Letitia. Putting my finger on the entry in question, I asked her 'Oliveira? Does that mean anything to you? October 28. That was the day before Harry set out on his trip. Did they meet as planned?'

Letitia took the book from me and examined it carefully. After a while, she shook her head.

'I wasn't in his office that morning. I had to go to the dentist.' She flashed a set of dazzling white teeth at me.

I tried again. 'What about this?' I asked, pointing out the scribble alongside. 'Does this mean anything to you? "*http://www .mata-atlantica*"?'

She gave me a withering smile.

'Senhor Harry was connected to the Internet. The Internet is very popular in Brazil.'

'Do you know his password?' I asked.

She shook her head emphatically. 'Certainly not, Senhor.' She looked shocked at the very idea. Gentlemen clearly weren't expected to read each other's e-mail.

'You don't mind if I play around with Harry's computer for a moment, do you?' I said. 'Mrs. Hodson - Nasreen - told me I should try to find out whatever I could.'

Letitia clearly wasn't too happy about leaving me alone in Harry's office, but she couldn't very well stop me. Nasreen had, after all, telephoned her earlier to give explicit authorisation.

I went back into the office, sat down again at Harry's desk, switched on the computer and double-clicked on the Internet icon on the desktop. A few seconds later, I was confronted by the message.

Name?

I typed 'Harry Hodson'.

The screen said: *Name incorrect. Try again.*

This time I typed 'H A Hodson', which was how Harry used to be known at school. HAH, for short. Or, as he sometimes put it, Hah, bloody hah!

The screen in front of me clearly approved.

Password? It asked.

I spent the next five minutes trying all the passwords I could think of, concentrating on topics which I thought might appeal to Harry - like 'Will Carling' and 'Manchester United' and 'Ronald Biggs' but none of them worked.

I was about to give up when another idea occurred to me. Harry and I as it happened both used the same Internet server.

I switched the computer off (just to make sure the machine didn't get suspicious), quickly rebooted, clicked on the Internet icon again and then, at the prompt, typed in my own name and password.

Bingo! Jackpot! The Internet explorer screen flipped up before my eyes. The cursor flickered enticingly over the empty box and the instruction just above the task-bar said in unambiguous language: *type in the address of the site to be visited.*

After that it was plain sailing. Of course, you've got to be careful to distinguish between the foreslash and the backslash and it took me a couple of goes to get it right. But after a while I typed in '*http://www.mata-atlantica*' without making a single mistake.

The chequered flag fluttered in the top right hand corner of the screen to indicate that we were in business.

'The golden lion tamarin,' I read, 'is one of the rarest species in the world. It is found in only one place in the world, Brazil, in coastal rain forests - the Mata Atlantica - now fast disappearing. The destruction of the Atlantic rain forest is one of the worst examples of ecocide to be found on the planet. A single hectare of Atlantic rain forest can be twice as rich biologically as a comparable plot in the Amazon and may contain 45 times the diversity of a North American hemlock forest. Most threatened of all are the tamarins (small monkeys), the black-faced lion tamarin *Leontopithecus chrysophygus* and the golden lion tamarin, *L. rosalia.*'

The words 'golden lion tamarin' were underlined and when I moved the cursor over them a ghostly hand beckoned me on. I clicked where the hand pointed and a few seconds later the screen was filled with an image of one of the most beautiful creatures I think I have ever seen. The animal which looked at me from the screen in my brother Harry's office had soft liquid brown eyes and a smooth hairless face almost like a baby's, surrounded by a great mane of golden hair. Its arms and feet and elbows were golden too, a veritable blaze of light and colour.

The caption under the photograph read 'Called King of the

Rainforest, the golden lion tamarin weighs about 13.5 oz when fully grown and is 8-14 inches long. Its tail length is an astonishing 12.5-16 inches, which is more than its whole body.'

At the end of the piece I read: 'For further information on the destruction of Brazil's Atlantic Forest contact Paulo and Josefina Oliveira. SOS Mata Atlantica.' The text gave an address and a telephone number.

I scribbled down some notes, then left the website, switched the computer off and went back into the outer room.

'I'm pretty sure Oliveira is the man who came to see Harry the day before he disappeared,' I said. 'Where is São Conrado?'

'A few miles down the coast. Half an hour in a taxi if you miss the evening rush hour. Would you like me to see if Mr Oliveira is available?'

I showed her the number I had noted down from the website but she seemed to know it anyway. She picked up the telephone and dialled. Then she spoke for a minute or two in rapid Portuguese. I didn't catch it all but I understood enough.

When Letitia put the phone down she explained, 'I didn't tell Mr Oliveira about Senhor Hodson being missing. I just said you were Mr Hodson's brother and you needed to have a meeting as soon as possible. Mr Oliveira will wait for you.'

I called Nasreen before I left.

'I think I'm on to something,' I said. 'Can't tell you now. I'll be back later, but in time for dinner. Let's go out.'

'What's later?'

'Around nine, I'd say.'

Nasreen laughed. 'Most people won't even be thinking about dinner then. This is Rio, remember.'

I said goodbye to Letitia, found a cab outside and gave Oliveira's address to the driver.

We were lucky with the traffic, which was thick but not unbearable. We went back past Ipanema and Leblon beaches, past the Sheraton and on down the coast. A few years earlier, the scenery must have been spectacular, a series of deserted beaches with nothing but golden sand and the blown spume from the gigantic Atlantic breakers. Now the highrise buildings and the vast condominiums were fast filling up the seashore areas road south of the city, blocking out the view of the ocean. Give it a few more years I thought and Brazil's coastline would resemble Florida's.

The Oliveiras lived in a spectacular cliffside house with its own private approach road on a still isolated stretch of coast. As we drove up, the taxi driver nodded his head approvingly and made a smacking sound with his lips. In Brazil, as everywhere else, the rich are different from the rest of us.

I rang the bell and told the driver to wait for me. In due course a middleaged man in crisp white shorts and a striped silk shortsleeved shirt appeared. He wore designer sunglasses and a heavy gold bracelet above the Rolex on his left wrist. The expression on his face was one of friendly interest.

'Senhor Oliveira?' I thought I had better come to the point directly. 'I am Charles Hodson, Harry Hodson's brother. Harry has been missing almost a week now. I believe you may have been one of the last to see him. I wonder if you might be able to help?'

Paulo Oliveira's suntanned face showed signs of alarm.

'Harry Hodson? Yes, of course - I know him quite well. Has he had an accident?'

We walked through the livingroom to the vast terrace which,

because of the curve of the coast, looked back towards the Bay of Guanabara and the distant Rio skyline. A woman was already sitting there, sipping a drink and watching the sun go down.

'My wife, Josefina.' Paulo Oliveira introduced me.

Josefina Oliveira was a few years younger than her husband. A bright smiling woman, expensively if casually dressed, whose mood rapidly changed as I explained the nature of my errand.

'This is too bad,' she exclaimed dramatically. 'We have gotten to know Senhor Hodson well in recent weeks. He has been helping us with the tamarins.'

Paulo interrupted. 'Perhaps I had better explain. Let me get some drinks first.'

Paulo Oliveira disappeared for a moment to fetch a couple of beers from the fridge. Then, when we were comfortably installed on the terrace with drinks in hand, he began.

'It could be my fault. I told him he shouldn't go into the forest alone and I thought he had listened to me. Perhaps I was wrong.'

'What was he doing in the forest?' I asked.

Oliveira took a pull at his beer. 'We believe one of the last surviving colonies of golden lion tamarins is up there in Minas Gerais. SOS Mata Atlantica has been running a campaign to save the forest and the golden lion tamarin is our flagship species.'

'Harry believed he could raise money for us in Europe,' Josefina Oliveira interjected. 'Paulo met with him last week in his office in Rio to discuss the matter. You knew that, didn't you?'

I nodded. 'I knew you had met with him. There was a note of the appointment in his diary. But I had no idea that Harry was involved in some environmental campaign.'

Frankly, I was puzzled by what I heard. To the best of my knowledge the only cause to which my brother Harry was truly dedicated was his own self interest. I couldn't imagine him acting as fund-raiser for some rainforest project. But it was ten years since I had last seen Harry and of course he could have changed. We can all change over the course of a decade. Sometimes we just don't realise it.

I noticed Oliveira give his wife an encouraging glance. For a moment it occurred to me that they might have rehearsed the dialogue in advance. But then I dismissed the speculation as absurd. Why on earth would they have needed or wanted to do that?

'Harry said we had to have photos,' Josefina continued, 'much better photos, if we were to attract the donations. He said he'd take his camera along and maybe he would be lucky. We assumed he would have an escort.'

Again, I was puzzled. Harry was a talented multi-faceted guy but as far as I knew, wildlife photography had never been a special interest. Still, I could sense I was getting warmer. Harry had obviously decided to kill two birds with one stone by photographing the golden lion tamarins in the forest on the way to his meeting with CMG in Belo Horizonte.

'Would you help me look for my brother?' I asked quietly. 'I'm not sure I'd know where to start.'

I wasn't surprised when Oliveira said yes. The man was clearly an activist, otherwise he wouldn't be Director of SOS Mata Atlantica. Moreover, somewhere along the line, as his current style of life indicated, he'd found the time to become a very rich man, and you didn't achieve that by gazing either at the stars or at your own navel.

'Of course, I'll come with you,' Paulo Oliveira said at once. 'I know the way. I've been there three or four times. We can take my jeep. You need a four-wheel drive vehicle up there. Shall we leave first thing in the morning?'

Oliveira said he would pick me up at Nasreen's flat at 6.00 a.m. the next day. He would bring all the equipment we might need.

'Thank God you came to find us,' Josefina said as I left. 'If we had known Harry was missing, we would have tried to track him down ourselves. Let's hope it's not too late.'

Once again I had this strange sense that Senhora Oliveira was repeating lines which she had learned in advance. It was almost as though the Oliveiras had actually been anticipating my arrival. Yet they had had only the briefest warning of my visit and Letitia had anyway not mentioned Harry's disappearance when she telephoned to say I was coming.

'I hope it's not too late too,' I said.

I rode back to Rio in the taxi that evening with my thoughts in turmoil. There was so much I didn't understand. Harry the nature-lover? Harry the charity-worker? Harry the photographer of wildlife? These were certainly sides of the man I didn't know existed.

And then, as we entered the outskirts of Rio, another thought struck me. As I left I had told Mrs. Oliveira that I too hoped that Harry would be found before it was too late. It had sounded a natural enough thing to say and I suppose I meant it at the time. But now I suddenly realized that I wasn't sure at all about hoping Harry would be rescued from wherever he was. If I was absolutely and entirely honest with myself, I had to recognise that part of me at least was quite comfortable with the thought that Harry might gone for good.

'Christ, Hodson,' I said to myself as we turned onto the Ipanema seafront, 'do you still hate him that much?'

Thinking that I had been addressing him, the driver half-turned his head.

'Si, Senhor?'

'Forget it,' I said.

III

Minas Gerais, Brazil

It was well after nine by the time I returned to the flat. Nasreen had given me a key. As I opened the door, I heard her talking - in English - on the telephone though I couldn't catch what she was saying. She hung up quickly as soon as she saw me and almost ran across the room towards me.

'Well? What have you found out? Please tell me, Charles. Tell me quickly.'

She had booked a table at a restaurant not far from the flat. I gave her a blow-by-blow account of my meeting with the Oliveiras. By the time I had finished, Nasreen was in a cheerful, almost exhilarated, mood. She seemed to believe that now we knew - or thought we knew - where Harry had gone he was as good as found.

'Harry's a survivor,' she kept telling me. 'I know he'll be OK.'

Looking at her animated face across the table, I couldn't help reflecting on the contrast with the tearstained visage that had greeted me at the airport that morning.

I didn't want to talk about the past. About Nasreen and me. Not then, anyway. But I couldn't help asking after her parents. I had liked Parvis Hassan and his wife. I hoped they had liked me.

'I know they've gone back to Iran,' I said. 'How are they finding life there?'

'I don't hear from them much,' Nasreen replied. 'I miss them, you know. They found it hard at first, going back like that but things are easier now. A new set of mullahs is in power. They're still maniacs but they're more moderate maniacs, if you see what I mean. My parents have got their old house back in Teheran and they still have the summer place on the Caspian, up in the mountains.'

Nasreen looked suddenly wistful. 'We had such a lovely house in the city. It was built around a great big courtyard with a fountain and fruit trees in the middle. As a child I used to sit out there for hours doing my lessons. We had an English governess actually and we would set up our desks in the shade of a giant fig-tree. I'm glad my mother and father have gone back. If you're going to grow old, it's better to grow old at home. I'd like to go back myself one day.'

I nodded without saying anything. I didn't actually quite know what to say. Under the present circumstances Nasreen's future plans must have been uncertain to say the least.

We didn't linger. Oliveira was going to present himself at the crack of dawn. Even without the prospect of an early start the next day I was ready for bed. Before we left the table I found a moment to quiz her about why she hadn't herself done what I had done, *viz.* rooted around in Harry's office, looking for clues. I had been bothered by that.

Nasreen seemed somewhat taken aback. 'Oh, but I did go

there,' she said. 'Of course I did. I don't enjoy going to Harry's office, since I know he likes to keep his business life separate. But I went to see Letitia as soon as Harry went missing.'

'Didn't you see the deskdiary?'

She shook her head. 'I don't think I did. Mind you, I was fairly distraught by then.'

I let it go at that, but I was still puzzled. When I had visited Harry's office, the diary had been lying in the middle of an otherwise empty desk. If it hadn't been on the desk when Nasreen went to the office, why was it there when I got there? Perhaps Letitia had been doing some tidying up in her boss's absence, had found the diary in another part of the room and had restored it to its rightful place.

It was only a small incongruity, but it bothered me.

Back at the flat, Nasreen offered me a nightcap, but I declined.

'I'm going to fold,' I said.

I could see her hesitate, as though looking for words. I walked over to her and put my hand on her arm. 'Don't, Nasreen,' I said. 'Don't think you have to explain. Not now. Not ever. I'm here because Harry's my brother. I don't think I'll ever forgive him for what he did but in spite of everything, he's still my brother. I'll help you find him. I promised that. As for the rest, I'll just have to live with it.'

'Can we talk one day?' She sounded almost pleading.

I forced back a surge of bitterness. My life had been ruined and she seemed to think we could just sit down and chat about it and all the hurt would disappear.

'Maybe,' I replied. 'When I'm ready. And I'm not ready now.'

I was waiting for Oliveira at the crack of dawn the next morning. His vehicle was a rugged Landcruiser. A Japanese model, probably manufactured under licence in Brazil. I noted the winch mounted at the rear.

'If you get stuck,' Oliveira explained, 'you usually have to pull yourself out.'

Nasreen had gotten up early to see us off. I couldn't help wondering how much sleep she had had. I had heard the telephone ring in the middle of the night, long after we returned from the restaurant. But looking at her, one would never had guessed that her sleep had been interrupted. She always had this ability to look fresh and fragrant, no matter what time of day or night it was.

She came down to the car with me. At dinner the previous evening she had seemed determined to join our little expedition, but I had managed to persuade her that she could be more use at home. 'We may need to contact you in a hurry,' I said. 'We should have someone standing by the phone.'

Of course, I was just being tactful. What I really feared was that Harry had indeed come to a sticky end up there in the mountains somewhere and, if so, it would be better to break the news to Nasreen gently rather than have her confront the ugly reality face-to-face. In fact I anticipated more of a problem in dissuading Nasreen from accompanying us than I actually had. I had imagined that she would protest vigorously at being left behind but when Oliveira too joined in arguing that we needed someone 'at base camp,' as he put it, she fairly quickly agreed to stay in Rio.

Leaving her standing forlornly on the pavement in the dawn light, we drove off through the still largely sleeping city, heading almost due north. It wasn't long before the road began to climb and the vegetation thickened.

'This is the beginning of the *Mata*,' Oliveira told me. 'Or what is left of it. A century ago, the Atlantic forest stretched in an unbroken sweep from Bahia to Rio Grande do Sul. Another few years and it could all be gone.' He pointed out of the window. 'See how they're clearing the hillsides? Cut the trees and you're halfway to a biological desert. It may look green for a while. It may even support crops or cattle for a time. But compared with what you had before, it's worthless. If only people would understand.'

Oliveira sighed and dropped his hand to the gear lever as the incline ahead of us steepened.

'You need to preserve the habitat to keep the wildlife, including the tamarin,' I mused. 'But I suppose it works the other way round too. Find a rare and endangered species like the tamarin and you may be able to generate enough public pressure to fight off the encroachments.'

Oliveira's spirits seemed to lift. 'That's what I *hope* anyway,' he said. 'If the tamarins are where we hope they are, we will not only fight to save them; we will try to save the whole forest.'

After about two hours we stopped for a few minutes for a coffee at a wayside cafe. As we sat at the table by the roadside I watched a great Volvo truck grinding its gears as it mounted the hill below us. Most of the trucks on this road would be heading for Belo Horizonte, but some would be going even further north, into Bahia or Amazonas.

We kept to the main road for another hour or so. With Belo Horizonte still over 100 miles ahead of us, Oliveira suddenly turned off to the right onto an unmarked track.

'We are really on the northern edge of the *Mata* here,' he explained. 'If we had kept going, we would have come out onto the great interior plateau, the *Planalto Brasileiro*. But we're going to curl back on our tracks now into that range of hills. That's where Harry would have gone.'

He pointed towards a distant ridge. There was a slight dip in the ground immediately ahead of us, but beyond that rose an unbroken vista of dense forest. It was clear to me that this was virgin land. No logging had taken place; no cattle ranches had encroached. I was looking at a landscape which could not have changed for hundreds, thousands of years.

'Awesome,' I muttered. 'Absolutely awesome.'

'Yes, isn't it?' Oliveira agreed. 'We want to make the whole area - 200,000 hectares - into a national park.'

'What are you going to call it?'

' "Parque Nacional do Vermelho." *Vermelho* is the Portuguese term for the golden lion tamarin.'

As we drove I kept an eye out for the tracks of other vehicles.

From time to time I could see tyre marks in the dust, but there was no way of telling whether they had been made by Harry's or some other vehicle.

Further into the forest the track began to twist and turn, following the contours. Once or twice Oliveira stopped to consult a large-scale map. Someone had stamped the word *SECRETO* on it in bold red letters. Rather a melodramatic touch, I thought.

'There are two copies of this map in existence,' Oliveira said. 'We drew it up so as to record precisely the area where the tamarins are thought to exist. I gave the other copy to Harry before he left.'

'So Harry had it with him?'

'Certainly.'

It took us another hour to reach the edge of what I now thought of as 'tamarin country'. The road by now had virtually petered out. Why was there a road here at all, I wondered?

'Who made this track?' I asked.

Oliveira, concentrating on following a sharp righthanded

hairpin, didn't reply, so I repeated the question. 'Who made the road? Logging companies? Prospectors? Cattle men?'

Oliveira turned to glance at me. 'Our people first explored this forest on foot from the other side. We hadn't even realised there *was* a road in from this side. That surprised us, I can tell you. And it worried us too. Roads mean trouble. It means someone else is interested in the area, and of course we would like to know who.'

'So you don't know?'

'No.' Oliveira frowned as the road dipped down into a dried up boulder-strewn watercourse. I held on to the edge of my seat as we bumped across. 'I doubt that it's the cattlemen. This land is really too steep for cattle. This isn't classic slash and burn territory.'

'Loggers?'

'Could be.' Oliveira nodded, pointing to the canopy of the forest which rose majestically at either side. 'There's certainly some valuable timber here. Without a road you'll never drag the timber out. Yes, it could be some of the logging companies are interested. I would be surprised if they weren't. They are always looking for more forests to destroy.'

'Would you rule out prospectors?' As I asked the question I had a mental image of giant earthmoving machinery uprooting trees and gouging out whole hillsides, converting a green paradise virtually overnight into mounds of rubble.

Oliveira nodded. 'Yes, that's another possibility. This state isn't called Minas Gerais - general mines - for nothing. Remember, Ouro Preto is not far north of here. The name means "black gold". At the height of the gold boom you had 100,000 people in Ouro Preto.'

'When was that?'

'In the middle of the 18th century. Did you know that the population of New York at that time was only 50,000, and Rio's only 20,000?'

I didn't know. Looking at the great sweep of the forest, so pristine, so undisturbed, it was hard to imagine that already two or more centuries earlier, the landscape of Minas Gerais not far north of where we now were had witnessed its first great transformation as men from all over Brazil rushed inland to seek their fortune in the hills. Yet what had happened once could happen again.

'So you don't rule out prospectors? What would they be looking for? Gold? Precious minerals?'

'God knows. They'll go for whatever they think they can sell.'

'And who are *they*?'

'Could be anyone. Even a small outfit could build a road like this. It doesn't take much.'

'Wouldn't you need permission?'

Oliveira laughed. 'In this country they don't ask for permission. They go in and find whatever there is to find and do the paperwork later. If at all.'

'What about the big companies, like CMG?' I felt a growing conviction that there could be a link between Harry's visit to the forest and his scheduled but unrealised encounter with Admiral Alvarez, Chairman of Brazil's new mining conglomerate CMG, with its headquarters in Belo Horizonte.

Oliveira laughed again but this time with an undertone of real anger, as though to indicate that, however unforgivable cowboy behaviour was in small operators, it was even more objectionable when the big boys were involved.

'CMG!' he scoffed. 'They are the worst of the lot. They'll cloak their actions with a veneer of respectability, but basically they know they can get away with murder!'

We drove on for another 40 minutes or so. Though I could still see occasional signs that other vehicles had also used the track, there was no hard evidence that Harry had himself passed that way.

Two miles farther on, the track petered out altogether. We parked the car out of the sun, took a couple of beers from the coolbox which Josefina Oliveira had thoughtfully provided, then spread out the map on the bonnet of the vehicle.

'If Harry came this way at all,' I said, 'this is about as far as he would have got, isn't it?'

Oliveira agreed with that assessment. 'Yes, from here he would have gone ahead on foot.'

'Where would he have put his car? We might find some traces there.'

'He'd probably have tried to hide it among the trees somewhere.'

'I'll take a look,' I said. It wasn't that I expected to find anything. More a question of stretching my legs after a long morning.

'Watch how you go,' Oliveira warned. 'It's easy to get lost. Try to keep me in sight if you can.'

Anticipating some hard trekking, I had kitted myself out that morning with a pair of Harry's tough hiking boots, as well as the denim trousers and khaki bushshirt that I had brought from England. Oliveira handed me a machete from the back of the Land-Cruiser. Feeling brave and purposeful I plunged into the forest.

I was slashing away at the creepers and underbrush with such gusto that I very nearly didn't see it at all. Harry had driven his vehicle deep into the undergrowth, about 40 feet away, so that only the rear bumper was visible beneath the dense foliage. I shouted to Oliveira.

'Come over here quick. I think I've found the car.'

I don't know whether we really thought that Harry might still be inside or whether we were just reacting instinctively to the situation. Oliveira and I thrust our way through the brush to peer inside the vehicle. It was empty and the doors were locked. We stood on either side of the vehicle, facing each other disconsolately.

'It's what I feared,' Oliveira said. 'Harry must have driven the car into the undergrowth to keep it out of the sun while he went off into the forest. I warned him about the dangers. I told him that if he left the track and went into the forest he should take a native guide with him.'

'So you think he's lost, do you?'

Oliveira looked me in the eye. 'Lost or dead,' he said.

That morning, as we were preparing for our departure, Nasreen had handed me a spare set of Harry's car keys. Maybe, deep down, she anticipated the situation in which we now found ourselves. Anyway, Oliveira opened the door, started the engine and backed Harry's car out into the small clearing which marked the end of the track.

Harry's travelling case was on the back seat. Oliveira lifted it out and we opened it together. Harry had packed a change of clothes - clean shirt, underwear, a couple of pairs of brightly coloured socks - but there was nothing to indicate that he had been planning anything more than a quick business trip upcountry. There was no sign - either in the case or the car - of the map which Oliveira had given him. There was, however, an open camera box on the passenger seat.

'No question but that he went off into the forest,' Oliveira said. 'He took the map and the camera with him.'

Oliveira turned out to be astonishingly competent. No man could have done more to find Harry, dead or alive. That morning, we made three or four extensive forays into the forest, heading out in different directions, then carefully retracing our steps to arrive back at the car. Oliveira swung the machete systematically, forcing his way first in one direction, than another. Later, when our own searches had failed to turn up anything of significance, he used his mobile phone to call in the police. He spoke to them carefully and authoritatively, explaining that a search party was needed. The police in turn called in the military from a local base and by the end of the day a small posse of vehicles had gathered in the clearing at the edge of the forest.

The first day we searched on foot. The authorities brought in a couple of trackers - *mestizos* who had obviously spent most of their lives in and around the forest - and they hunted diligently but without success for the faintest trace of my brother. The second day, they called in a helicopter, which made half a dozen fruitless passes above the canopy before heading back to base. Oliveira had to sign a paper guaranteeing that we would pay for the expense and I told him that, of course, he could look to me for reimbursement.

By the end of the third day, we had begun to give up hope. Wherever Harry was in the forest, we doubted he would still be alive. I didn't know as much as perhaps I should have about the fauna and flora of the Mata Atlantica - but I knew enough to realise that there were any number of nasties out there, ranging from tarantulas to jaguars. Even if Harry were lucky enough to avoid any hostile encounters with South American wildlife, I somehow couldn't see my brother living off berries and tree bark. It seemed only too obvious to me that he would by now have succumbed to hunger, thirst and exhaustion.

Apart from the car and what was in it, we found not one single trace of Harry. It was as though the forest had swallowed him up entirely. Like a giant sea anemone, it had stretched out its tentacles, folded him in and absorbed him so totally that, if it hadn't been for the car, we wouldn't have guessed he had been there at all.

All the time we were out there, I had kept in touch with Nasreen on the mobile telephone. I told her that we had found Harry's Mazda and that we were now searching for Harry himself. We didn't talk for long. The connection was not good and even though we could recharge the cellphone from the car battery, there was no point in being garrulous. Anyway, Nasreen knew that she didn't have to plead with us to do what we were doing. If Harry could be found, we would find him.

We made a makeshift camp at the edge of the forest. Oliveira had packed a tent and supplies in the LandCruiser. The Brazilian authorities had been enthusiastic enough at the beginning, but as time wore on it was clear that they had had enough. On the fourth day, instead of resuming the search at dawn, the squaddies packed their stuff onto their truck and departed unceremoniously, taking the two trackers with them. The police, whose presence throughout the search had been at best intermittent, went with them. It was clear that, as far as the host country was concerned, Harry Hodson, gemstone and rare mineral consultant, 44, married without children, British but resident in Rio de Janeiro, could officially be deemed 'missing presumed dead.'

After the others had gone, Oliveira and I mulled things over.

'How can a man completely disappear?' I asked. 'Without a trace, I mean. It's as though Harry fell overboard at night in the middle of the Atlantic and no one noticed.'

Oliveira didn't share my incredulity. 'I've known people get lost, totally lost, within a few square metres of forest. You've seen it for yourself. It can be so dense in there that even at midday the light barely penetrates. You can lose your way within seconds. You can become disorientated and panic. Nothing kills quicker than panic.'

'I don't think Harry would panic,' I said. 'That's not the man I know.'

For a time I stared at the fire. It wasn't easy to accept that Harry was dead, but that finally was what I had to do.

I called Nasreen that night. I knew that what I had to say would hit her hard, however much she might have been expecting it. 'We're calling the search off,' I said. 'I'm so sorry.'

Over the previous days, the telephone link with Rio had been patchy. Sometimes, communication had faded unpredictably, or there had been heavy static on the line. But tonight I could hear her clearly as she tried to fight back the sobs. 'Thank you so much, Charles. Thank you both. I know you could not have done more.'

'Oliveira has been fantastic,' I told her. 'He knew what to do. I just tagged along.'

I have to admit that I was feeling a bit tearful myself by the time our conversation ended. Nasreen's anguish touched me deeply. I longed to be with her, to comfort her, to share her grief. She seemed to sense what I was feeling.

'Please come back now, Charles,' she urged. She hesitated, then added: 'I'm going to need you.'

There was nothing I would have liked to do more than to return to Rio there and then. It had been a tough few days, that was for sure. The physical circumstances had not been ideal. The tent had been cramped and the nights sticky with heat. The mosquitoes had had a field-day as far as the softer parts of my anatomy were concerned. By day there had been a good deal of trekking and hacking in the forest and that too had taken its toll.

If anything, the mental stress had been worse. At any moment I had been expecting to see the half-eaten corpse of my brother, or some similar horror. In the event, the worst had not materialised. But in a strange way the lack of a corpse, of any clear indication as to how Harry had met his death, was hardly less traumatic. Uncertainty can be the most draining emotion of all.

However much I wanted to go back to Rio at this point - and I don't deny the idea was an attractive one - there were stones still left to turn, avenues to be explored.

'I can't come back now,' I told Nasreen firmly. 'Give me another day or two. I need to go on to Belo Horizonte. I want to talk to Alvarez.'

'Alvarez? What on earth for?' Nasreen sounded surprised.

'Harry had business with Alvarez. I want to find out what it was.' The line had begun to fade. 'I'll keep in touch,' I said. 'I'll call you from Belo Horizonte.'

The phone gave a beep to indicate that the battery had at last expired. I pushed in the aerial with a sense of finality. One chapter was over. Harry was dead, I was sure of that, and nothing would bring him back. But too many other things were still unexplained. I wasn't quite sure how much more I owed to my dear departed brother. In the circumstances, it seemed to me that I had already done quite a lot. Above and beyond the call of duty, you might say.

The reason I continued north rather than south at that moment was because, truth to tell, I was consumed with an overpowering sense of curiosity. I may not be quite top of the class but, by God, I'm a good enough journalist to know when to follow my nose.

IV

Ouro Preto, Brazil

As I explained at the outset, my career with Reuters has taken me to Bonn and Brussels. I have also visited the United States on several occasions and, when we were adolescents, Harry and I usually flew to join our parents during the school holidays. They were stationed successively in Rome, Canberra and Tokyo before the old man eventually retired from the heavy round of diplomatic cocktail parties and they went to live in the south of France. My mother died in a car accident in Provence while I was still at Cambridge. Some local on his tractor pulled out of a side-road without any warning. My father stayed on in the Luberon and died at the age of sixty-eight while I was on my Brussels posting. By then, of course, my rupture with Harry had already occurred. We might conceivably have achieved a reconciliation of a kind at my father's funeral but Harry quite simply failed to turn up. He sent a telegram to the housekeeper saying he couldn't make it and that was that.

Looking back, I think the fact that Harry hadn't bothered to come to the funeral merely served to compound the sense of grievance and of alienation from him that I felt. How many fathers did one have, for Christ's sake?

All that of course, is by the way. The point I want to make here is that, even though I've traveled a good deal in my life one way or another, mostly this has been in the so-called 'developed' countries. I have had very little of what you might call hands-on experience of third-world driving. When we visited our parents at their various residences, we tended to be driven around by the diplomatic chauffeur. Or else we used public transport for the longer forays. That being so I felt more than a little uneasy about the idea of driving on north by myself in Harry's car while Oliveira, who had already given generously of his time, headed back to Rio.

The moment I hit the main Rio to Belo Horizonte highway, I had to adapt very quickly to a whole new set of rules of the road. It may not be India in the sense that you don't have livestock of every kind wandering over the road; it may not be China, with its hordes of bicycles and rickshaws filling the carriageway from side to side. But Brazil has its own forms of bedlam as far as traffic is concerned. The great Volvo and Mercedes trucks and buses hog the crown of the road at 60, 70 even 80 miles an hour. If you don't give way, they simply crush you like a fly. By the time I had gone ten miles I must have seen the remains of at least six car crashes. One wreck was still smouldering as I passed.

Quite apart from the uniqueness, the sheer eccentricity, of the Brazilian version of the highway code, the terrain itself is challenging enough. As you drive up onto the *planalto*, the road describes an horrendous series of hairpins. There is one section, about sixty miles south of Belo Horizonte, where the ascent becomes positively vertiginous. On one particular bend, a section of the road has been roped off so that effectively you are on a single-lane highway. You are flying blind, as it were, since you are forced to negotiate the corners without any way of knowing whether or not another vehicle is coming from the opposite direction. All you can do is press the heel of your hand firmly on the horn and hope for the best.

Harry's Mazda was a snappy affair with airconditioning, bucket seats and a complicated dashboard like the cockpit of a plane. An electronic indicator told you how much fuel you were using per second as well as the optimum speed. I almost expected a sign to flash up in front of me saying '*Wrong direction*!'

As a matter of fact, in a sense I *was* heading in the wrong direction. I had told both Oliveira and Nasreen that I planned to go on to Belo Horizonte to interview Alvarez, the CMG Chairman. That much was true. What I hadn't told them was that I planned to visit Ouro Preto *en route*. As far as I knew, Ouro Preto - ancient capital of Minas Gerais and, as I now knew from Oliveira, 18th century boom town - was the last place Harry had been seen alive and I was determined to find out what had taken him there.

With Belo Horizonte still forty miles away, I turned off the main highway in a north-easterly direction on a minor, but still tarmacked, road. I guess it must have been noon or a little after when I turned the last bend in the road to see, spread out beneath, this extraordinary town which, for a few brief years, was probably home to the most intense concentration of wealth in the world. The houses below covered not one but several hills. They climbed up the surrounding mountainside in a rich architectural profusion, being interspersed with the gleaming domes and cupolas of some of the finest baroque churches to be found in Brazil, or indeed the whole of Latin America.

The bus station - or *rodoviária* as they call it - is located on a flat expanse of ground above the town. The cobbled streets twist and turn below, with steep stone steps providing shortcuts for pedestrians between the zigzagging terraces. I decided that I was probably better off without the car, so I parked it next to the bus station, locked it and set off on foot.

In spite of the fact that it was the middle of the day, the heat was not unbearable. Ouro Preto benefits from its location on the edge of the *planalto*. The altitude knocks the humidity as well as the temperature down a notch or two. Even though I walked briskly, I managed to stay cool by hugging the shady side of the road wherever I could.

I knew from Nasreen that Harry had stayed at the Grande Hotel. It took me about 15 minutes to find my way there. I was expecting some gracious colonial mansion, but instead discovered that the Grande, though it occupied a spectacular site with sweeping views across the valley, was of aggressively modern design.

A banner across the entrance of the hotel proclaimed that the Association of Brazilian Dentists was having its Twentieth Annual Congress there. My arrival had obviously coincided with a break in the proceedings as the lobby was crowded and it was some time before the young woman at reception was able to give me her attention.

'Si, senhor?'

'I'm sorry to trouble you when you're so busy,' I began politely. 'I'm making some enquiries about someone called Harry Hodson. He stayed here on Tuesday, October 29th, I believe.'

The woman looked up at me sharply. 'Senhor Hodson? Harry Hodson? The police have already been here.'

'I'm Harry Hodson's brother. I'm trying to find him. He's missing.'

'Yes, I know. The police told us that.'

The young woman was obviously trying to be helpful. She looked at me appraisingly. 'I remember your brother, senhor.'

'Do you remember anything particular about his stay here?'

By now the dentists had begun to filter into the diningroom for lunch and the lobby was quieter. The woman behind the counter had time to reflect on my question.

'I gave him a map of the town. He particularly wanted to visit the Museum of Mineralogy. I showed him the way. Actually,' - and here she blushed - 'I went with him. It was my afternoon off and your brother was, well, so charming.'

Of course, she said all this in fairly halting English and I've tidied up the presentation for the sake of the narrative. But, whatever linguistic difficulties there may have been between us, I had no trouble in imagining the scene. Handsome, debonair Harry, chattering away in his perfect Portuguese, had probably been at his most engaging. So what was he after, I wondered?

'You went with him to the museum?'

'Yes, it was on my way home. We had a coffee together afterwards in the Praça Tiradentes.'

'Did my brother by any chance explain what he was doing in the Museum?'

The lobby of the hotel was now completely deserted. From the restaurant came the distant clatter of knives and forks as the dentists got down to the most serious business of the day, eating. The woman stood up and came round the counter to join me and together we walked over to the terrace with its splendid panoramic view over the city. It was hard to imagine how, two or three centuries earlier, the hills had been alive with the press of humanity burrowing and scrabbling in the biggest gold rush the world had ever seen.

When she was sitting behind the counter, with her head down

tapping away at her keyboard, I had failed to realize what a striking beauty the receptionist was. Now, as she stood up, I could see that there was more than a hint of mulatto about her, as though somewhere in the distant past some Portuguese aristocrat had had his way with a local slave girl. The colour of her skin was a deep golden-brown, and her nose had a delicate but noticeable flair.

I repeated my question. 'Was there anything special about the museum?'

'It's a tourist attraction.'

'Harry wasn't much of a tourist. I think he came here for a purpose.'

The woman gestured to me to sit down. She smiled at me for the first time. 'Perhaps I should introduce myself. My name is Gloria Suarez.'

I held out my hand. 'Hello, Gloria. I'm Charles Hodson.'

She took my hand and shook it warmly. Just as I had with the Oliveiras, for a fleeting second I had the feeling that Gloria Suarez was in some sense prepared for this encounter with a dead man's brother. Maybe the police, when they came, had told her to expect further enquiries. Or maybe she had just assumed that sleeping dogs were seldom left to lie undisturbed, even in the depths of the Brazilian interior.

She spoke hesitantly at first, as though trying to remember accurately what it was that Harry had said.

'Your brother told me he was a businessman, working with rare minerals and precious metals.'

'Exactly.'

'He said he had reason to believe that a Brazilian mining company was planning a major new venture in the region of Ouro Preto.'

'Did he say what this mining company had discovered?'

Gloria shook her head. 'He said he didn't know for sure, but he thought he had an idea.'

'Was it gold? Another gold rush? I suppose it could make sense. If there was gold at Ouro Preto, there could be gold elsewhere in the region.'

'No, not gold. It was some other mineral. He didn't tell me the name.'

As Gloria spoke, I couldn't help thinking - again - how stunning she was. It wasn't just the rich colour of her skin and striking features. She had thick red-gold hair and the kind of brilliant gleaming smile that made you feel as though you were sole focus of her attention - at that moment at least.

'Did the museum have something to do with it, do you think?' I asked.

'I'm not sure. We went round the exhibits together. Your brother asked me to come with him and I thought, why not?' She laughed, showing her pearl white teeth. 'Senhor Hodson made a change, he had a different style, yes?'

I felt a mounting sense of irritation. Harry was dead, but even so he seemed omnipresent.

'If you went with him,' I said quite sharply, 'then I suppose you would remember if there was something special he was looking for?'

Gloria Suarez looked at me with some amusement.

'If you can wait till five o'clock, senhor, I shall be free to accompany you to the museum myself. If that is what you would like . . .'

Nothing could have pleased me better. By now I was convinced that Harry's presence in Ouro Preto was not simply a tourist's whim. He had come with a specific purpose and that purpose I felt sure had something to do with the Museum of Mineralogy.

Gloria had to get back to her desk. I wandered off into town to have lunch and then spent an hour or two visiting some of the magnificent baroque churches which are so much a feature of the town. On the whole I'm not big on baroque. It's too ornate for my taste. But there was no denying the splendour of the great Matriz de Nossa Senhora do Pilar or the Igreza de São Francisco de Assis, whose carved exterior represents some of Aleijadinho's finest work. The fact that such great art was constructed on the back of such extreme poverty made it somehow all the more poignant. It was as though the poor, having so little succour on earth, had to content themselves willy-nilly with their gilded visions of eternity.

The Museum of Mineralogy is located in the Federal University of Ouro Preto's Escola de Minás - School of Mines - which is in turn situated in the old Governor's Palace on Tiradentes Square.

I sat at a table on the edge of the square, sipping a beer and keeping an eye out for Gloria. A group of students had gathered in front of the monument in the middle of the square, strumming on guitars and singing.

A couple of them noticed Gloria's arrival before I did and waved to her. One of them walked over as she joined me at my table.

'Hello, Alfonso.' Gloria greeted the bearded young man with, I thought, a degree of reserve. 'I thought you still had classes at this hour?'

'No, we've finished for the day. The professor has had to go home early. His wife is expecting a baby.'

The young man sniggered as he spoke, as though to indicate that domesticity of whatever form did not rate high on his list of priorities.

'You must excuse us, Alfonso,' Gloria said firmly, seeing that I had finished my beer and was ready to leave. 'We have to visit the museum before it closes.'

As I paid the bill, Gloria explained. 'I'm still a student here at the university. I'm studying for my doctorate in the School of Mines. That's how I know Alfonso and the others. I do the job at the hotel to help pay the bills.'

I looked at the high spirited crowd of young men and women clustered round the statue. 'Who pays *their* bills?' I asked.

'Some of them work, like me,' Gloria replied, 'and some of them, like Alfonso, have rich daddies and spend their time getting drunk and fooling around. As you probably know, Brazil is a country where the rich are always getting richer.'

'Minas Gerais is one of the richest states, isn't it?'

'In the past, certainly. Now we're all waiting for the next gold rush. Or its equivalent.'

Gloria flashed her student card at the entrance to the museum but I had to buy a ticket. With only half an hour to go before the official closing time the place was deserted except for a couple of uniformed guards who lounged in a desultory manner against the wall.

'Was my brother interested in any particular exhibit?' I asked. I repeated the question I had asked earlier and, as I did so, I tried to imagine Harry as he must have been a week or so earlier, in precisely the same spot and with the same escort.

'Oh yes. Your brother knew exactly what he wanted to see.'

'Show me, please.'

We walked through the first two rooms, which were filled with glass cases of various sizes containing geological specimens. On the whole, the labels were self-explanatory. The exhibits referred to the history of mineral exploration in the Ouro Preto area from the time of the great gold rush at the beginning of the 18th century to the present.

We paused briefly to note the key exhibits.

'This is goldbearing ore from the first mine sunk in the district,' Gloria explained. 'See how black it is? That's why they called it Ouro Preto. Black gold.'

I stared into the case. How strange it was that these inanimate lumps of rock could be responsible for so much wealth - those towering gilded churches, for example - and, at the same time, so much misery.

'Was Harry interested in the gold?' I asked.

'No, not specially. I think he knew enough about the gold. He was more interested in the maps.'

Gloria glanced quickly at the guard as we moved on to the third and last room. The man seemed to be perfectly uninterested in our presence, but nevertheless Gloria instinctively lowered her voice.

'About ten years ago,' she said, 'the university received a grant from the government to conduct a mineralogical survey of the surrounding region. It was the first of its kind and it became quite famous. That's why it is featured in the museum. The university was asked to correlate satellite data with the available ground observations so as to produce a detailed classification of the mineral potential of the region.'

Against the far wall of the third room I could see a large map case.

Gloria pulled open the second drawer. 'Your brother seemed specially interested in this particular map where the satellite data are integrated. He spent at least ten minutes studying it.'

She began to close the drawer again, but I laid a hand on her arm to stop her. 'Wait a moment,' I said.

Suddenly I knew why Harry had come to Ouro Preto and why he had visited the Museum of Mineralogy in the School of Mines. *The second map showed the region due south of Ouro Preto as having the highest theoretical potential for containing rare and precious minerals. It coincided almost perfectly with the area of forest inhabited by the golden lion tamarin!*

Gloria sensed my intense interest. She studied my expression. 'You have learned something useful then?'

'Yes, I have,' I replied slowly. 'I think I'm beginning to understand.'

I said goodbye to Gloria when we left the museum. She took my proffered hand and clasped it earnestly with both of hers.

'I am so sorry about your brother, senhor. I hope I have been of some help.' She paused. 'And I am glad to have met you as well as your brother. You are the same but, yes, you are also very different.' She gave a little laugh and tossed her head so that her splendid red hair caught the late sun as it arched across the square.

'Well, I hope to see you again,' she said.

'I hope so too.'

She was still holding my hand and on an impulse I leaned forward and gave her a kiss on both cheeks, continental-style, before leaving her to join her student friends.

I drove on that night to Belo Horizonte. The first thing I did after checking into a hotel was ring Nasreen. I told her of my visit to Ouro Preto, dwelling not on the historical and artistic attractions of that town but on the clues which I had discovered relating to Harry's disappearance and presumed death. I explained about Gloria Suarez and how I had had the good fortune to be escorted to the museum by the very same person who had shown Harry round.

'What a coincidence!' Nasreen exclaimed.

'Not really,' I said. 'Harry asked the way to the museum and I did the same. Gloria was only too happy to oblige.'

'I'm sure she was.' Nasreen commented icily.

I sensed that Nasreen did not wish to hear too much about Gloria Suarez. Given her present mood and her all-consuming grief, she presumably didn't want to contemplate the fact that Harry on the eve of his disappearance had been chatting up the birds, as it were, and that, on the evidence, I had been doing much the same myself.

I came swiftly to the point. 'I'm pretty sure Harry was in Ouro Preto to check on the geological status of the area of forest where the golden lion tamarins are believed to exist. I think he was trying to establish whether they are under threat from mineral exploration or exploitation.'

'And are they?'

'They could be.' Over the telephone I explained about the survey carried out by Ouro Preto University School of Mines in the eighties.

Nasreen was sceptical. 'Why should Harry have known about the survey? How would he know where to go to find it?'

'Harry's job was precious minerals, wasn't it?' I countered. 'Even if he hadn't heard, specifically, of the 1980s' survey, Ouro Preto's School of Mines was an obvious place to start looking.'

There was a long pause at the other end. It was as though Nasreen had at last begun to follow the direction of my thoughts.

'You're linking a threat to the tamarins with CMG and Harry's appointment with Alvarez?' Nasreen still sounded sceptical, but I could detect a hint of interest in her voice.

'Let's just say I'm curious.'

We left it at that. I told her I would be going to CMG's headquarters in Belo Horizonte the following morning and that if Alvarez was there I should try to see him. If I learned anything important I would call her. I gave my telephone number at the hotel in case she needed to be in touch later.

'Take care,' Nasreen said.

'Oh, I'll take care all right.' I spoke with a confidence that I did not really feel.

V

Belo Horizonte, Brazil

After finishing my telephone conversation with Nasreen, I poured myself a Scotch from the minibar and glanced casually through the promotional literature provided by the hotel management. Belo Horizonte, I read, is situated at 850 metres of altitude on Brazil's vast interior plateau and owes its origin - as Brasilia itself does - to the architect's drawing-board. It was deliberately planned to replace Ouro Preto as the capital of the state of Minas Gerais. In the original blueprints, wide, carefully landscaped avenues criss-crossed the city's centre. The residential suburbs were laid out in neat geometrical patterns. A new generation of Brazilians was to grow up in airy, salubrious surroundings quite different from the crush and squalor of Brazil's older coastal cities.

In practice, things didn't quite pan out as the architects intended. With what I thought was commendable honesty, the author of the pamphlet went on to point out that though the basic elements of the blueprint could still be determined in the pattern of the city's streets and suburbs, Brazil's demographic explosion and the high rate of migration from countryside to town effectively negated the planners' vision. In the space of a few years, Belo Horizonte had grown to become Brazil's third or fourth largest city. At the latest count, its population numbered over 2.5 million inhabitants.

Most of that number - it seemed to me as I finished my drink and stepped out of the hotel lobby into the street - could be found in their cars or crowding the pavements in the early evening. I found myself assailed on all sides by the cacophony of traffic and the sheer press of humanity.

Belo Horizonte lies a few degrees north of the Tropic of Capricorn. By six p.m. the sun was already lying low on the horizon, a huge fiery-red ball. By seven p.m. the neon lights were already blazing from the cluster of skyscrapers which marked the city's centre. I planned to turn in early - it had been a busy day - but I wanted to have a meal first. I left Harry's car in the hotel garage and set out on foot. I had done enough driving for one day. Besides, one sure-fire way of ending up without a vehicle is to leave it unattended in the pulsing heart of Belo Horizonte.

I was staying at the Othon Palace on the Avenida Alfonso Pera. A block or two away, on the Praça Sete do Setembre, I discovered the Restaurante Praça 7. The place had a beer-hall atmosphere, but the music was good and they served the famous speciality of the region, *feijño tropeiro*, a mixture of cabbage, beans, maize, flour and pork.

Suddenly ravenous, I had one helping, then a second. As I sat there with a glass of cold beer in front of me, absorbing the sights and sounds of the place, I couldn't help reflecting that my well-ordered life in London was about as distant as it could possibly be.

Gray's Inn Road and the Reuters news-room seemed to belong to another planet.

I ordered another glass of beer to go with the second plate of *feijño* and surveyed my fellow diners. Restaurante Praça 7 clearly catered for the Brazilian middle class. At the table next to me, four young men in smart suits were entertaining two stylishly-dressed young women. Belo Horizonte's yuppies, I supposed. They could have been in the minerals business, since the gold, manganese and gemstones of the surrounding region were processed and traded in the city. Equally, they could have been in steel, automobiles or textiles - all burgeoning industries in Minas Gerais. When one of them produced a mobile phone and started talking into it loudly, my estimate was confirmed. Undoubtedly yuppies.

I must have scowled involuntarily, because the young man with the phone looked in my direction, cupped his hand over the mouthpiece and said in perfect English, 'Please excuse me. I hope I don't disturb you?'

'Not at all,' I muttered hurriedly. To cover my embarrassment, I picked up my beer and took a long cooling draught.

As I put the glass down, I had that strange sensation one gets sometimes of being observed. I glanced round to see a tall blond man standing by the bar and staring at me. In addition to his height and the colour of his hair - you don't see too many blonds in Brazil - the man had a deep scar on his right cheekbone. It was a bit like one of those duelling scars the German students used to wear in the old days as a badge of honour. As a matter of fact, I thought, the fellow did look rather German. I don't know whether it was the iced beer or a blast from the air-conditioning but I gave a sudden involuntary shiver. Not a man to meet in a dark alley, I thought.

I didn't linger long after that. I paid the bill, walked back to the hotel and was in bed and asleep before you could say Scola di Minas. As I drifted off into oblivion, rows of neatly-labelled minerals and gemstones floated before my eyes.

CMG's headquarters were in a smart modern skyscraper set among the cluster of high-rise buildings which dominates the centre of Belo Horizonte. I had called Alvarez's office from my hotel first thing that morning, had explained the situation to his secretary and had been granted an interview for 11.00 a.m. Once again, I had the feeling that my appearance on the scene was not entirely unexpected. CMG, I suppose, had already had to field a number of enquiries from the police and others about Harry's disappearance.

I parked Harry's car in the company car park. An attendant promised to keep an eye on it and I handed him a healthy tip. A few moments later I was waiting in the anteroom to Alvarez's office. The walls were decorated with large framed photographs of CMG's mining activities and there was a display case of minerals along one wall, not unlike the exhibition I had seen the previous day in the museum in Ouro Preto.

I had been sitting there less than two minutes when the door to Alvarez's office opened and Alvarez himself came out to greet me. About 60, he had an expensive well-oiled look. He wore a white linen suit, heavy gold cufflinks and a gold wristwatch. His hair was sleek and black with hardly a trace of grey and his smile seemed about as sincere as a TV talk-show host's. As we shook hands, it occurred to me that there was something familiar about the Admiral's face. Had I seen it on television, in the newspapers, in a magazine somewhere? I couldn't recall precisely. Perhaps it would come back to me.

Alvarez ushered me into his office. After inviting me to sit on an expensive cream leather sofa he installed himself in a matching armchair set at right angles. As a white-coated flunkey served coffee, he took a cigarette from a gold cigarette case, flicked a lighter, and leaned towards me, all concern.

'How can I help? You're looking for your brother? As you may know, I had an appointment to see him a few days ago. The appointment was made at his request. He never arrived. I have told the police this already, but of course I appreciate your interest.'

As Alvarez spoke, I had a chance to size him up. That the man possessed a certain magnetism couldn't be denied. His heavily-lidded eyes held me as he spoke. I found myself staring into two deep black pools which, so far from being windows into the soul, succeeded in concealing the inner man almost totally. They were pools of ice. You could freeze or you could drown and, frankly, I doubt whether Alvarez would have given a damn either way.

'It's good of you to see me at short notice,' I said formally. 'I'll try not to take up too much of your time.'

I explained how we had been combing the forest in our search for Harry.

'We think, quite simply, he got lost. His body is in there somewhere, but it may never be found.'

'That's probably what happened to your famous Colonel Fawcett in the Amazon,' Alvarez commented, somewhat gratuitously I thought. 'Fawcett's body was never found either, was it?'

I didn't want to get into a discussion on the fate of the legendary Colonel Fawcett. I wanted to pin Alvarez down if I could.

'Did Harry indicate what he wanted to talk to you about?'

'In general terms, yes.' Alvarez blew a ring of smoke towards the ceiling. 'When he called me he told me he was acting on behalf of SOS Mata Atlantica. He said he wanted to make a specific proposal which he thought would be of great interest to CMG.'

'Had you met him before?'

'Very briefly, I believe.'

The surface of those deep black pools which were Alvarez's eyes seemed to cloud over momentarily when he spoke.

'Why did you agree to see him?'

Alvarez looked surprised. 'My dear sir, your brother was an expert in minerals and minerals are CMG's business. More to the point, your brother was helping SOS Mata Atlantica - a respected Brazilian ecological society - and CMG's policy is always to co-operate to the maximum possible extent with such organisations. We are not cowboys, you know.'

As Alvarez talked, I thought of the environmental devastation wreaked by mining companies like CMG all around the world. Of course, the chairmen, the CEOs, would always talk a good game, but wasn't it all a show, a facade? In the end you had to get the minerals out of the ground. A company might mitigate the impact of its operations, but there was no point in pretending that a forest or a mountain or a hillside could remain pristine and undisturbed once the machines moved in.

While Alvarez was spouting his well-rehearsed spiel about corporate responsibility, the idea which had formed in my mind the previous evening as I was talking on the telephone to Nasreen began to grow into something altogether more substantial. Imagine, I said to myself, that Harry had somehow heard that CMG was planning a major minerals exploration in the region south of Ouro Preto. Imagine that such activity could threaten the colony of golden lion tamarins thought to be present in that same region. Might not Harry, in his typically impetuous fashion, have decided to raise the matter with Alvarez directly? I knew my brother only too well. He was a man of boundless charm and self-confidence, with a firm belief in his own ability to achieve results. Of course, he was a hard-headed bastard as well. I was sure he had calculated that an interview with Alvarez, one of the rising stars in Brazil's industrial firmament, might lead to other opportunities.

I decided to test my theory. 'One of the things that puzzles us, Admiral,' I said, 'is why there is a road into that part of the forest at all. It goes a long way in and it's definitely more than a rough track. The trees have been hacked down, the brush cleared and the ground levelled.'

Alvarez shrugged. 'Who knows? Some illegal loggers, probably. Sometimes a single high-value tree - like mahogany - can justify the incursion into the forest. Better still if they can find 20 or 30 such trees. Unscrupulous operators will always do it if they think they can get away with it. This is Brazil.'

He looked me straight in the eye as he spoke.

'Don't you think,' I asked, 'that some mining company might be interested in the region?'

Without mentioning that Harry had been there before me, I told Alvarez about my visit to Ouro Preto's School of Mines.

'I'm not an expert, of course,' I said, 'but it looks as though the survey the university mineralogy department carried out in the 1980s identified the region as being of considerable interest.'

Alvarez laughed scornfully. 'Academics! Pah! What do they know about real exploration? We've been over all that data. There's nothing there, I can assure you. Certainly not for a company like CMG.'

Alvarez paused and looked at me meaningfully. 'Maybe it

would have been better if we *had* been there. Perhaps your brother would not have got lost.'

While I had been probing him about CMG's exploration plans Alvarez had exuded a distinct sense of hostility. Now, as he shepherded me out of his office, he was all affability. He paused at the door.

'You never told me, Mr Hodson, what your own specialty is.'

'I'm a journalist in real life. With Reuters.'

I found a business card in my pocket and passed it to him. Alvarez looked at it with interest and then tucked it into his breast pocket.

'One day we must talk,' he laughed. 'Not now, of course. My lips are sealed.'

Alvarez was looking at me in what seemed to be a deliberately teasing manner. I was intrigued.

'Stock exchange rules, you mean?' I ventured, playing a hunch.

'Precisely. The BOVESPA - the Bolsa de Valores de São Paulo - is probably the busiest stock exchange in the world after London, New York and Tokyo. We can't afford a scandal. Foreign investors in particular - and they account for over half of the shares traded - have to be convinced that we stick to the rules.'

I've been around in the business long enough to know that when company chairmen start talking about stock exchange rules they generally have some ulterior motive.

'Quite so,' I said firmly. I wasn't wearing my Reuters hat that day and, even if I had been, the last thing I wanted to do was to tempt the chairman of a quoted company into an indiscretion. That's not the way we work. We try to deal in hard news, not innuendo. Of course, rumours can be hard news too if they move markets. Even unconfirmed rumours. But that's another story.

During our latest exchange of conversation we had moved across the anteroom towards the exhibit cases by the door. Alvarez, who at one stage had been anxious to get rid of me, seemed now to be in an expansive mood. He pointed to the various examples of CMG's mining activity in different parts of Brazil. Each rock sample was separately labelled. Tungsten, feldspar, molybdenum, platinum . . . most of the names were already familiar to me.

'This is tantalum,' Alvarez told me. 'Do you know that most of the world's tantalum is mined in Brazil?'

I didn't know, but I was quite ready to believe it. 'What do you use tantalum for?' I asked.

'Capacitors. Superconductors. That kind of thing. It's a key mineral for several high-tech industries.'

My eye fell on another lump of rock next to the tantalum sample. I noticed that it bore the label 'falconite'.

'What's falconite?' I asked.

Alvarez looked suddenly shifty. 'Just a geological curiosity.'

'Tell me more,' I said, my interest aroused.

Alvarez shrugged. 'It has only been identified very recently. When we found the sample our geologists weren't sure of their analysis. No known mineral seemed to correspond. But then they made a detailed search of the literature and came up with a paper some Cambridge scientists published not long ago. The Cambridge people have proposed the name 'falconite' after the famous explorer Robert *Falcon* Scott. It appears that Scott first found the mineral, without knowing it at the time, almost a century ago in Antarctica.'

'Where did CMG make its discovery?' I asked. 'Or is that a state secret?'

'I'm afraid that's not something I can reveal, Mr Hodson.'

I could sense that Alvarez did not want to be pressed on this point and I could understand the reasons. If CMG had discovered a geological anomaly, why should they shout it from the rooftops? They would want to assess the find first. No wonder Alvarez was being cagey. Still, I thought I would try him with one last question.

'Does falconite have any particular uses, as far as you know?'

I might as well have jabbed Alvarez with a needle. Putting his fingers to his lips dramatically, he said, 'All in good time, Mr Hodson. All in good time.'

As we said goodbye, he gave me a long thoughtful stare as though he had already said too much.

By now, it was over five days since I had left Rio with Oliveira and I wanted to get back to civilisation. Harry's Mazda was a more than adequate means of transportation for a man in a hurry. I fairly belted out of Belo Horizonte.

As I've already indicated, the road to Rio swoops down from the high interior plateau in a series of dramatic bends, with steep drops on the outside edge of the hairpins. To make matters worse, on this particular day, large stretches of the road seemed to be under repair and were single file only. There seemed to be no clear system for establishing priority and, in the space of just a few minutes, I witnessed some hair's breadth misses as macho drivers held fast to the wheel and attempted to stare down oncoming traffic.

Some instinct told me that, whatever aspiration I might have had up there on the plateau to emulate that great Brazilian driver Emerson Fittipaldi, it would be wise not to pursue it too far. Brazil may not be a Third World country in the strict sense of the word. It doesn't qualify for so-called soft loans from the World Bank, for example, and hasn't for many years. But, as far as driving is concerned, it very definitely *is* a developing region. It's easy to wind up in a ditch or dead or both through no fault of your own.

So I took it slowly and cautiously on the way down, keeping my speed around the 80 kph mark. It was on the third hairpin that I saw the blue Cherokee pick-up trying to overtake me. The driver came up close, sounding his horn and gesticulating as though to intimate that, by showing deliberate caution in the face of danger, I had broken all the rules of the road and didn't deserve my place behind the wheel.

The last thing I wanted was an argument. I didn't know whether Brazilians went in for 'road rage' the way Americans and now, increasingly, Europeans, do but I didn't propose to find out. I pulled over as far as I could, hoping to let the man pass. If he wanted to overtake me on the outside edge of a hairpin with traffic coming head-on in the opposite direction, that was his problem.

It didn't work out quite like that. I felt a terrific crash as the Cherokee barged past on the inside of the bend. The wheel spun in my hands and for a moment I wondered whether I would go over the edge. As a matter of fact, I think my front offside tyre did almost slip over. There was a spray of stones and a series of bumps as I wrestled with the wheel. By the time I had got the vehicle back under control, the Cherokee was out of sight. One image stayed in my mind. As he pulled past me, the driver of the pick-up turned to stare at me. Preoccupied though I was at the time in trying to avert imminent disaster, I was certain that I recognised the man's face. How could I fail to recognise it? The blond hair, the pale blue Germanic eyes, the duelling scar on the right cheekbone! I knew I had seen that face before!

There was absolutely no point in trying to catch the man up.

First, he was probably halfway to Rio already and I certainly wasn't going to try to match his speed on the bends. Second, Scarface - as I now mentally labelled him - didn't look like a man to be trifled with. I was a journalist, not a street fighter.

As soon as I could, I pulled over, got out and inspected the damage to Harry's car. It was not as extensive as I had feared. The Mazda's left-hand rear mudguard had been severely dented as the Cherokee barged past. But the tyre still had clearance and that was all that mattered.

I have to admit that I was shaken by the incident. Another foot or two and I would have been over the edge. Sometimes in these Catholic countries you see neat little crosses by the wayside to mark the site of some fatal accident. Occasionally you even see a posy of flowers, presumably placed by some loving relative. I doubted whether I would have rated any such memento. They probably wouldn't even have bothered to fish me out of the tangled wreckage hundreds of feet below!

I shuddered as I drove on, at an even slower pace than before. What an amazing coincidence that I had actually recognised the man! It had to be a coincidence, that was obvious. Scarface had been in the restaurant in Belo Horizonte the previous evening but he couldn't surely have been looking for me. Unless he had followed me from the hotel, he couldn't have traced me to the restaurant. I hadn't known myself that I was going to the Plaça do Setembre 7 that evening. And how could he have followed me from the hotel, since he couldn't have known where I was staying in the first place? I hadn't made a reservation at the Othon Palace ahead of time. I had chosen the hotel at random and checked in on arrival. Did Scarface receive some tip-off? If so, how? Apart from the hotel staff, the only person I had spoken to since my arrival in

Belo Horizonte was Nasreen. The whole thing was happenstance. I had just been in front of the wrong man at the wrong time.

I didn't see Scarface again that day, though I kept a wary eye out for blue Cherokee trucks. Absolutely nothing untoward occurred during the rest of the drive. The sun shone and the mountains and the forest were bathed in its golden glow. Traffic was light and the road, once those treacherous hairpins with their ubiquitous roadworks had been safely negotiated, gave way to a series of long, well-engineered curves as it worked its way down towards the coastal plain and the outskirts of Rio.

It could have all been fine and hunky-dory. I could have flown back to London with my conscience clear and a sense of duty done. My brother had gone walkabout in the jungle and had died somewhere - probably of heat exhaustion. I had done my best to find him, God knows I had tried to find him, but I had failed. Nasreen wouldn't get her husband back, but at least she would have his car. Slightly battered, but otherwise all in one piece.

Suddenly, in my mind's eye, I could see once again the blue Cherokee closing up fast behind me; I could see Scarface staring deliberately at me as he pulled past. No, I thought, goddammit! Everything wasn't fine and hunky-dory. I wasn't going to swallow the coincidence theory. Scarface had followed me to the restaurant. I was convinced of it now. He had probably followed me to the CMG headquarters building. And he had certainly followed me when I left Alvarez's office to drive back to Rio. The only questions were: 'how' and 'why?' How did he know my schedule? And why was he interested?

As I drove through the tunnel under Corcovado towards Ipanema, these questions repeated themselves insistently in my mind. How? How? How? Why? Why? Why?

VI

Rio de Janeiro

THERE IS A theory among the locals, that Ipanema beach is cleaner than Copacabana. On Copacabana, it is said, you can pick up HIV by stepping on infected needles which drug addicts have left buried in the sand. Ipanema beach is less frequented by vagrants and junkies. On the other hand, the breakers are more violent, the surf is treacherous and swimming as opposed to sunbathing is notoriously hazardous.

I decided that I preferred the risk of drowning to that of infection so I parked the car on the sea front by the Praia Ipanema hotel, changed into some swimming trunks and locked my clothes and valuables in the boot. Nasreen had already warned me to leave nothing on the beach if I ever planned to go swimming - not even a towel or a pair of shoes. I took her advice seriously, walking barefoot across the road which separated the hotel from the sea.

The tarmac was hot. So was the sand beyond it. Some Brazilian youths, the soles of their feet obviously inured to the high temperatures of the silicate, were playing beach football with all the skill of potential World Cup finalists. A couple of beach vendors were hawking their wares - scarves, gems, trinkets - before scattered sunbathers. One man led a donkey along the tidemark, panniers laden with melons slung over its back.

I ran quickly towards the water like some South Sea islander running over hot coals. The first wave knocked me off my feet and rolled me back unceremoniously onto the sand where, for a moment or two, I lay shocked and winded.

My next attempt was even less successful than the first. This time I was literally upended and tumbled like a cork this way and that in the surf. I had no sooner staggered to my feet than another wave caught me and thumped me down again. Instead of drawing breath, I gulped in a huge mouthful of sea water. This is just not my day, I thought, as I struggled upright.

I just had time to glimpse out of the corner of my eye an enormous breaker bearing down on me. It was as large as a mountain and it moved at the speed of a racehorse. The crest of this giant wave was already crowned in menacing white foam and I realised that if I didn't get out of the way there was a strong possibility that I would simply be rolled around in the surf long enough to drown. The fact that I would probably be knocked unconscious first was cold comfort.

At the last minute I stood up, lifted my arms above my head and dived at the base of the wave. For what seemed an eternity I could hear the sound of the water roaring overhead. I was buffeted and pummeled by the rush of water, but miraculously the strategy paid off. Several thousand tons of sea sluiced above me. And then a sudden peace descended. Surfacing at last, I looked round to see that I had managed to pass beyond the breakers into the much calmer grey-green waters of the South Atlantic.

I paddled on my back, with my head half out of the water, looking towards the now distant shoreline. What a magnificent spectacle it was! The hotels and apartment blocks which lined Ipanema beach were possibly not as dramatic as those along Copacabana's sea front. But, goodness knows, the contrast between the towering buildings, burning white sand and the thundering foam of the sea was striking enough. And high up on the mountains behind the city, His arms outstretched over this probably unredeemable city, I could - once again - see the mighty statue of Cristo Redentor.

Looking back, I've always believed there was something symbolic in the way I had to plunge through the turbulence in order to reach calm waters. There I was, swimming probably half a mile from the shore. The late afternoon sun was streaming down. A group of pelicans flew overhead and one of them plunged into the sea to rise again with a struggling silver fish in its mouth. I shook my head to clear the water from my eyes and as I did so I suddenly knew that even if I didn't have the answer to the 'how' question, I almost certainly had the answer to the 'why?'

I explained my theory to Nasreen at dinner that night.

We went to a Bahian restaurant on Rua Miguel Lemos, a couple of blocks from the seafront. The establishment is run by a former Brazilian soccer great called Toninho and his wife, Jacira, and the main diningroom is hung with soccer memorabilia, including, of course, numerous framed photographs of the proprietor in leaner fitter days. Footballs above the bar had been autographed by other soccer heroes of our time including the legendary Pelé himself.

Bahian food is hot and spicy - jumbo shrimps in *salsa piccante* and obscure peppers that can ambush you and take the roof of your mouth off if you're not looking out for them. You have to concentrate on what you're eating. In between cautious mouthfuls, I gave Nasreen a blow-by-blow account of the last few days. Of course, she had heard some of it already but I was able to fill in the gaps. In particular, I was able to outline the idea which had occurred to me with apocalyptic clarity as I had been swimming in the sea that afternoon.

'Murdered? What on earth do you mean?'

'Harry knew the location of the tamarins,' I began. 'And I suspect he also knew that CMG had found a truly exceptional mineral deposit somewhere in the area and was planning to exploit it.'

'How could he have known that?'

'Harry was in the business. However much companies try to keep the lid on these things, the word can get out. Harry may not have known precisely what the find was or precisely where it was, but he knew enough to be worried. I believe he arranged the meeting with Alvarez because he wanted to confront the man directly!'

'To talk Alvarez out of it?' Nasreen sounded sceptical.

'Yes, perhaps that's what Harry hoped. Perhaps he wanted to do more than talk Alvarez out of it. Perhaps he wanted to persuade Alvarez that CMG's best interest might be in working with, not against, the environmentalists. Instead of mining the forest, perhaps he hoped that CMG would put up funds to preserve it. Heaven knows! Harry could have gone green all of a sudden. People do. The Oliveiras could have been a powerful influence.'

Nasreen looked marginally less sceptical. Like me, she clearly had difficulty coming to terms with the idea of Harry as a wideeyed environmentalist but she was ready to make the effort to see things my way.

'So what went wrong?'

'Alvarez took him out. As simple as that.' I found myself using the military terminology without consciously wishing to. But then again, I thought, this was a kind of warfare.

'Oh, come on! That's absurd!' Nasreen protested.

'Is it?' I pressed the point. 'Alvarez could have known Harry was visiting the forest on his way to Belo Horizonte.'

'How?'

'Harry might have told him himself when they talked on the phone,' I replied slowly. 'Alvarez could have tipped off his people. CMG knows all about that road into the forest. My belief is that they made it themselves, probably when they were doing the initial prospecting. They waited for Harry to come along. Then they captured him and killed him. An object lesson, if you like. To CMG, organisations like SOS Mata Atlantica, and those who work for them or with them, are the enemy. Up in the Amazon, the mining companies have been massacring the Indian tribes for decades. They're still at it. The Yanomami are virtually extinct. They've been shot and tortured, or infected with the white man's diseases when they have no native resistance. It's worse than a massacre. It's genocide. What makes you think a man like Alvarez or a company like CMG is going to bow to the demands of a few bunny-huggers? Quite the reverse. If CMG wants something, it goes ahead and takes it - and heaven help anyone who stands in the way.'

I could see I had begun to make an impression on Nasreen. She pushed the remains of a jumbo shrimp to the side of her plate.

'You searched the forest. You found nothing.'

'There were tyre marks on that track that weren't made by Harry's car. I'm sure of that. Someone else was there. Someone followed him in. Or else was waiting for him.'

Nasreen shuddered. I could see the tears beginning to form in her eyes.

'You really believe he could have been murdered?'

'I do. As a matter of fact I wouldn't be surprised if the murderer wasn't the same thug who tried to drive me off the road today. I'll bet my bottom dollar that a blue Cherokee pickup was around in the forest somewhere the day Harry was there.'

'There were no police reports of other vehicles,' Nasreen said.

'No, of course there weren't. But I don't have much confidence in the police anyway. It wouldn't take much to put them off the scent. Not the way CMG operates.'

'I'm not sure I like any of this.' There was no mistaking the tears now.

I reached out across the table and took her hand.

'I don't like it either.'

I surprised even myself by what I said next. I had imagined I was going to utter some meaningless platitudes about how we had done our best to find Harry and how it was now time to give up and set about rebuilding her life. That kind of thing. In practice, nothing of the kind emerged.

Still clutching her hand, I found myself saying, 'We may not prove they murdered Harry, Nasreen. We may never prove that. But we can establish the motive. And that's a start.'

'What do you mean?' She raised her eyes to mine and I thought she would remove her hand from my grasp. But she left it where it was.

'I mean what I say,' I replied. 'We'll prove the motive. I'll make it my business to find out precisely what it is that CMG has found up there in the forest. What is it they have that's worth killing for?'

'And when you've found out, what will you do?'

I'm not on the whole a politically motivated man. I have tended to concentrate on the job in hand, leaving activism to others. I certainly haven't gone out of my way to espouse radical causes. If I surprised Nasreen at that moment, I surprised myself as well. I could hear the note of hatred, even fanaticism in my voice. 'We'll blow them out of the water. We'll go public with what I've found out. I'll confront Alvarez with the truth. I'll force him into a confession.'

It sounded like bravado, I know. But I meant it. I wasn't exactly sure what I was going to do. As a matter of fact, I wasn't exactly sure why I was going to do whatever it was. Partly I wanted to do the right thing by Harry. As far as I was concerned, Harry was guilty of a lot of things, including screwing up my life in a big way, but you couldn't be guilty of heroism. If he had met his end in the way I suspected, and for the reasons I surmised, that was indeed heroism of a sort and it deserved some recognition.

But there was more. I hated the ability of powerful men like Alvarez to lie and manipulate, and of powerful companies like CMG to have things their way no matter what the cost.

'You can count on me,' I said quietly. 'You know that.'

It was well after midnight by the time we returned to the flat. Nasreen poured us both a nightcap and we sat on the terrace with our drinks. Now that the din of the traffic on the seafront had died down, you could hear the roar of the breakers more clearly than ever.

'I often sit out here at night,' Nasreen said, 'particularly when Harry's away.'

'Is he away often?'

'Oh yes, very often.'

'Why did you marry him?' I asked.

'I thought you didn't want to talk about the past.'

'I said I didn't want to talk until I was ready.'

'Are you ready now?'

'Yes. Are you?'

There was a long pause. It was almost as though she was weighing things up, working out what to say.

'Try me,' she said at last.

It was painful but I knew I had to do it. Ten years ago, when she left me for Harry, I had been too shellshocked to say what I wanted to say, ask what I wanted to ask. Later, when conceivably I could have wished to talk, the opportunity had passed. Nasreen and Harry had left the country. It was different now. If ever there was to be a moment to set things straight or at least to throw some light on them, this was it.

'Why did you do it?' I asked. I didn't have to spell it out. She knew what I was talking about.

I waited for her to answer. It was almost as though she was turning the question this way and that, looking at it from all the angles. Finally she said:

'You have to remember how young I was then, Charles. You and Harry were in your last year at Cambridge. I was in my first. I had only just turned eighteen. I'd been brought up in Iran. Of course, ours was an advanced, intellectual household. We were the rich upper classes, no doubt about that. But that didn't mean that all the old traditions were thrown overboard. I didn't know any young men in Iran. And when my parents fled to England after the fall of the Shah, I went off to an all-girls boarding school to take my "A" Levels. It wasn't a convent but it might as well have been.'

'You looked pretty self-confident, I can tell you, when I first met you.'

Nasreen laughed. 'Bluff. Pure bluff. I was scared stiff most of the time.'

She took a sip of her drink, then set it down, turning to face me. Though we had turned off the lights on the terrace to avoid attracting mosquitos and other insects, there was still enough glow from the street below for me to be able to see her face clearly.

'I had never met anyone like Harry. He was so plausible, so convincing. From the moment you introduced me to him that evening in Trinity Great Court, I knew I was lost. I felt as though I was being sucked down a vortex. There was no point in struggling, because I wouldn't be able to do anything about it.'

She put her hand on my arm. 'I treated you abominably. I knew it at the time. I wanted to say sorry. I sent you a Christmas card but you never answered.'

'Big deal,' I said. 'Instead of a wife I get a card.'

'Don't be bitter. Things aren't always what they seem.'

I didn't quite know what to make of that. 'What do you mean?' I asked.

She took a step towards me and held out her hand. 'Let's go inside.'

It wasn't what I had planned. I can be honest about that. I've searched my conscience and I can truthfully say that I had absolutely no intention of seducing Nasreen that night. As far as I was concerned, Nasreen's bed was forbidden territory. Even if Harry hadn't been my brother, I would never have made the first move. I don't sleep with other men's wives. And I don't take advantage of widows.

I didn't seduce Nasreen that night. She seduced me. When, instinctively, I took her proffered hand, she pulled me to my feet, led me from the terrace to the sittingroom and then, when we were inside, flung her arms around my neck, pressing her body against mine as she kissed me on the lips.

For half a second I said to myself, 'Hold on, wait, there's something not right about this,' but then I was gone. We stood there with our arms about each other, embracing passionately. I hadn't kissed Nasreen for ten years. There was a lot of catching up to do. When I buried my face in her neck and smelt the same subtle perfume she used to wear in those far-off Cambridge days, I thought I had died and gone to heaven.

Yes, we slept together that night. As a matter of fact, it was the first time Nasreen and I ever made love. As I've already explained, when we were engaged we had both agreed, in deference to Islamic sensibilities, that we would wait until we were actually married before going to bed with each other! In the event, other matters intervened. More precisely, Harry intervened. Now, ten years later, for reasons best known to her, Nasreen was inviting me into her room and I, fool that I was, couldn't find it in myself to say no. I knew that it could all end in tears but I was powerless to resist. I wasn't sure whether she did what she did because she felt she owed it to me - her own way, however belatedly, of saying sorry - or whether she made love to me then simply as a means of turning back the anguish of the moment. I knew she needed comforting. And of course I hoped it was more than that. That said, when the one-time love of your life is in unmistakable terms inviting you to go to bed with her, you're not going to ask her to answer a whole series of questions like some sociological researcher armed with a pencil and clipboard. As far as I was concerned, at that particular point in time, questions could come later.

We made love with a passion and intensity that I had certainly not felt in the case of the half-dozen girlfriends I had had in the decade since I left Cambridge. This was a wholly new experience and it took me totally by surprise. Afterwards, we lay naked on the bed together.

'I needed that, Charles,' Nasreen said. 'After so much, I needed that.'

'I still love you, Nasreen,' I said. I wasn't sure that I meant it - how could I possibly be sure? It had all happened so fast. But I wanted to say it anyway.

She put her finger to my lips. 'Don't say that, Charles. I don't deserve it.'

Suddenly she turned and buried her face in the pillow. When at last she fell asleep, I lay there listening to the gentle rhythm of her breathing.

Much as I wanted to stay all night, instinct told me to leave. I wasn't expecting Harry to walk through the door and surprise us - Harry was history - but I didn't exactly feel comfortable either. As I mentioned a moment ago, making love to another man's wife is not really my scene; as a bachelor, I've always regarded the matrimonial bed with the greatest of reservations.

Not wishing to wake Nasreen up, I tiptoed to the door carrying my clothes in my arms. As I walked across the room, I couldn't help glancing at the photographs on the dressing-table. There was a framed picture of Harry and Nasreen at their wedding and another, to my surprise, of Harry and me on a fishing holiday in Scotland. (I remembered the occasion well - Harry had all the luck. Or else he was a much more competent angler.) The third photograph particularly caught my attention. Looking at it, I realised that I had seen precisely the same print in Harry's office, hanging on the wall behind his desk. I remembered now why Alvarez's face, when I met him the previous day, had seemed familiar. The picture on the dressing-table - and in Harry's office - was of a group of people gathered round a table in what was clearly the Rio Yacht Club. Masts and pennants featured in the background. The party was in festive mood. Harry was nearest to the camera, glass in hand and an expansive grin on his face.

He had his arm round the shoulders of the man sitting next to him, who seemed to be in a similarly relaxed and friendly frame of mind. What surprised me was that the man on Harry's right, the man Harry had his arm around, was none other than Admiral Antonio Alvarez!

For a moment I stood stock-still in surprise. Why on earth had Alvarez written to Harry in formal terms to confirm a meeting ('Dear Mr Hodson . . .') if they were already close drinking partners? Was that the way they did things in Brazil? Sticklers for etiquette when it came to sending letters? None of that sloppy American familiarity with first names which nowadays seems to be so all pervasive.

Behind me, Nasreen stirred, breaking my train of thought.

'Are you still there, Charles?' she moved her head on the pillow. 'Don't go. Stay with me tonight.'

She held up her arms to me. I hesitated by the door. I had already decided to catch the early flight out of Rio next morning. I had no idea when I would see Nasreen again. Suddenly I couldn't bear the idea of not spending the whole night beside her. I wanted to trace the lines of her face with my fingertips, kiss her breasts and navel, make love to her again. Then I wanted to hold her like a child while she slept in my arms.

'Yes, I'm here, darling.' How long had it been since I had called her 'darling'?

I put my clothes back on the chair and slipped into Nasreen's outstretched arms.

VII

Cambridge, England I

On the long flight back from Rio to London I had time to re-examine the theory that I had put to Nasreen over dinner the previous day. Assume Harry had got wind of CMG's plans to exploit the tamarin zone (as I now mentally codenamed the critical area of Atlantic forest where the golden lion tamarin had been found). Assume he had actually stumbled upon some CMG operatives, caught them redhanded as it were, or in any case bent on exploitation. Assume they had got rid of him somewhere to stop the news getting out . . . But what news? What was it that CMG could have discovered? Gold? Silver? Gemstones? Tantalum? Was tantalum really that valuable? How important was the world's demand for capacitors and superconductors? Or was there some other mineral there vastly more significant and vastly more valuable? Something that could potentially transform CMG's fortunes overnight.

As the Varig 747 roared onward through the night, I paced up and down the aisle. Dinner had long since been served and the movie screens had been retracted. Most passengers were asleep. A couple of stewardesses were enjoying a break in the galley and one of them offered me a coffee when I poked my head round the curtain looking hopeful.

I accepted the drink gratefully and stood for a few minutes by the window looking out. It was a clear cloudless night. Far below I could see occasional lights of seagoing vessels. Towards dawn, I imagined, we would be skirting the coasts of Western Europe. An hour or two later we would be touching down. What was I going to do?

The choice, as I saw it, seemed clear. I could forget about the last few days, forget about Harry, forget about Nasreen. I could go back to work, get on with my job and put Brazil, with all its stress and turmoil, behind me. I could honestly say to myself that I had done my best. The call had come from Nasreen that fateful night, and I had responded to that call. No man surely could have done more, particularly given the circumstances.

I lifted the cup of coffee to my lips and as I did so I knew there was another option. It wasn't the easy option. Professionally, it was risky. It would mean taking time off work, possibly jeopardising my position. As I explained at the beginning, the highflyers at Reuters seem nowadays to concentrate on the management and financial side but even workaday writers like me can still be under a lot of pressure. Journalism is a pretty cutthroat business. There's usually someone after your job and if you don't watch your back, they'll have it. In personal terms, too, I knew there were risks involved. I had been badly shaken when Nasreen walked out on me. I didn't want to risk any more emotional upheavals. I still wasn't sure exactly what had happened between Nasreen and me the previous night. Deep down I think I had been a bit surprised by her behaviour. It had been so, well, deliberate. The more I thought about it, the clearer it seemed to me that it was Nasreen not I who had set the pace. What if I allowed myself once again to fall under her spell and once again she kicked me in the teeth?

Over the Tannoy the captain announced that there was one hour to go before landing. I came to a sudden decision. Whatever the personal and professional risks involved I knew I couldn't give up now. I also knew that if I were to make any progress in pinning down a motive, a reason, a probable cause, for Harry's disappearance, I had to probe much deeper. I had to follow up all available clues.

I went back to my seat, put it as far into the reclining position as it would go, leaned my head back against the cushion and shut my eyes, trying to review all that I had learned during my few days in Brazil.

I suppose it was the mental image of avenues being explored and stones not being left unturned which set me thinking about the display cabinet I had seen in Alvarez's outer office. Alvarez, I recalled, had seemed uneasy as I examined the specimens. He had shifted his body in an attempt to block my view. I replayed the sequence in my mind, freeze-framing the images. As I looked back, I realised from my recollection of Alvarez's body-language, when I was looking at the falconite sample, that he obviously hadn't wanted me to probe too far. Certainly he didn't want me to ask questions about where CMG might have found a falconite deposit or what it might be used for.

By the time the seatbelt sign came on, I knew what I had to do next. Alvarez had spoken about some Cambridge scientists being involved in the analysis and identification of falconite. Graham Southgate was at Cambridge. He was a professional geologist with a growing reputation. I knew that, in addition to holding a fellowship at Churchill College, he was a senior member of the staff of the Scott Polar Research Institute in Cambridge. He was obviously still on friendly terms with Harry, or had been until Harry's disappearance, otherwise Nasreen wouldn't have called him when she was trying to get hold of me. And, as I had told Nasreen, I was still in touch myself with Graham, if only intermittently. Contacting Graham Southgate was an obvious and logical step.

I rang Reuters as soon as the plane landed and left a message with the newsdesk to say that I was back from Brazil but wouldn't be coming into work till the following day. Then I caught a cab to my flat in Little Venice, picked up the accumulated mail from the mat, and headed for the shower.

My hair was still wet and I had a towel round my waist when I got through on the phone to Graham Southgate in Cambridge.

'Charles? Charles Hodson?' he exclaimed. 'Good to hear from you.'

I told him about Harry as succinctly as I could.

Southgate sounded shocked. 'I'm so sorry. This is terrible.'

'I need to see you, Graham. Today if possible. Have you got time?'

'Yes, of course I've got time. I'll *make* time.'

By midday I was on my way to the station.

Unlike some people - Mrs. Thatcher, for example - I have never had any problem about travelling by train. I've always regarded it as a practical way of getting around. Trains to Cambridge leave every half-hour from King's Cross mainline station. When you arrive, you're virtually in the town centre.

The Scott Polar Research Institute is in Lensfield Road, only a few minutes from the station. When I gave my name at the reception desk, Southgate came quickly down to collect me and took me back with him to his office on the first floor.

It had been a year or two since I had last seen Southgate. As I have already explained, the three of us (Harry, Graham and I) had all been at Trinity together though Graham was already doing post-doctoral research when we met him. Harry and I had embarked on our own separate careers as that cataclysmic summer term ended, but I had never lost touch with Graham. We had met up at college reunions and from time to time I had rung him up when I needed a short, sharp quotation from a knowledgeable scientist for some story I was writing for the agency.

I almost didn't recognise Southgate at first. A copious beard obscured virtually the whole of the lower half of his face.

'Spent last winter in the Antarctic,' Southgate explained. 'Grew the beard there. When I came back, I never got round to shaving it off.'

I took the point. If you're faced with a temperature of minus 30°F and a howling gale to go with it, you may as well use all the protection you can get.

'What on earth were you doing down there?'

'I was working with BAS actually. The British Antarctic Survey.' Southgate sounded offhand, matter of fact.

I had already given Southgate the bare bones of the story over the telephone. Now I outlined my own theories regarding Harry's disappearance and presumed death. I was gratified to see that Southgate was ready to take my speculations seriously. Very seriously indeed.

'What do you need from me?' he asked quietly. 'You know I'll do anything I can to help.'

I had had plenty of time on the plane to work out what I wanted to ask.

'Alvarez spoke about some Cambridge people writing a paper about falconite, about how the mineral was originally discovered by Captain Scott, though he didn't know about it at the time. I want to find out more.'

Southgate looked at me quizzically. 'Something to do with Harry's death?'

'I think so,' I nodded. 'But I'm not yet sure precisely what.'

Southgate didn't merely have a beard. He smoked a pipe as well. When he had finished tamping the tobacco, he pulled out a box of Swan Vestas, cupped his hand over the bowl and puffed away until clouds of acrid blue smoke billowed out into the room.

'I'm surprised you don't set off the fire alarm,' I said.

'Sometimes I do,' he laughed. 'How much time do you have?'

'I'm not in a rush.'

'Well, the first thing you ought to know,' Southgate said, 'is that the Cambridge source Alvarez is referring to is actually sitting right here in this room. I did the research on the rock samples Scott brought back from the Pole, I wrote up the results and, of course, I was delighted when the editors of the *Journal of Geological Studies* decided to publish it. It's not always easy getting things published nowadays. There's tremendous pressure on the scientific journals because every Tom, Dick and Harry likes to rush into print nowadays otherwise they think they're going to lose their research grant. But I guess the story of falconite is particularly fascinating. Do you want to hear the whole thing?'

'Anything that can help.'

Southgate stood up from his desk, put the matches back in his pocket, walked across to the bookshelf and took down a thick paperback volume.

'This is Roland Huntford's best seller,' he explained, returning book in hand to his desk. 'It was first published in 1987. It's called *Scott and Amundsen: the race for the South Pole.* A lot of people round here hate Huntford, as you can imagine, believing he set out to debunk, to demythologise Scott. But he tells a good tale. Do you mind if I read you a passage or two? If you want to know more about falconite, Huntford is a good introduction.'

'Go ahead.'

Southgate flipped through the pages until he found what he was looking for.

'Huntford is describing the journey back from the Pole,' he explained. 'The chapter is entitled *The race lost.* Amundsen has beaten Scott to the Pole and all Scott and his men can do now is retrace their steps.'

He sat back in his chair, put on his spectacles and began to read.

' "*That day,*" ' he began, ' "*they started the descent of the Beardmore Glacier, reaching the upper glacier depot the same evening. They now had five days food with five days to the next depot, the mid-glacier depot according to the outward journey, with icefalls, crevasses and all kinds of potential delay.*" '

Southgate paused. 'You get the picture don't you, Charles? Scott had to climb the Beardmore Glacier on his way up to the Antarctic plateau and he had to go back the same way on the return journey. He had cut things incredibly fine.'

He continued his reading. ' "*Scott had left himself no safety margin. The following day he found lee under Mount Buckley, with sunshine and calm after weeks of cold winds on the plateau. It was a moment to seize and cover distance while the going was good."* '

Southgate paused again as though to emphasise the point he was about to make. 'This is where Huntford delivers the hammer blow,' he said looking at me over the top of his spectacles. ' "*Scott, with grotesque misjudgement, stopped for the afternoon to collect geological samples and thenceforth dragged thirty pounds of stone on the sledge. Geology cost him six or seven miles and time when time was against him.*" '

Southgate turned over a few more pages. 'Listen to how Huntford describes the scene when Scott's frozen tent was eventually found, when they dug out the bodies and uncovered the sledge with its load of geological specimens. Huntford writes: "*They had dragged those thirty pounds of rock to show themselves martyrs to science, a pathetic little gesture to salvage something from defeat at the Pole and the wreck of their hopes. Half the weight in seal meat would have saved them. A pint of paraffin or a tin of pemmican would have been worth more to them that the most valuable stone in the world.*" '

Southgate put the book down on his desk.

'Ten years ago, five years ago, two years ago,' he said quietly, 'I would have agreed with Huntford. Not with the way he put it, of course. That was needlessly wounding to a dead man's reputation and I'm not surprised people don't forgive Huntford for it. But I would have agreed with Huntford on the substance. Until very recently, I, too, would have taken the view that Scott wasted precious time and energy collecting those samples. I would have said he should have concentrated on saving his own life and those of his men and let science go hang.'

'What made you change your mind? What do you know that Huntford didn't know, when he wrote the book?'

'It was when I analysed the samples Scott brought back with him,' Southgate replied, 'That's what's made me change my mind.'

He could see that I was by now totally intrigued. 'Let's take a walk,' he said.

We left his office, walked down a flight of stairs hung with the portraits of the great Antartic explorers - I recognised Scott and Shackleton immediately - then made our way to the main exhibition room on the ground floor.

'This is the museum,' Southgate explained. 'It's fairly quiet this afternoon. Let me show you round.'

As Southgate walked me through the Museum of the Scott Polar Research Institute he explained the basis of the collection.

'The permanent exhibits include material from seven of the so-called "Heroic Age" Antarctic expeditions from Britain. Captain Scott's expeditions - as you may know there were two - are particularly well-represented. The museum also exhibits material from British voyages to the Canadian Arctic which took place in the 19th Century. And we show a selection of Eskimo and Lappish artefacts.'

I wasn't quite sure where Southgate was heading, literally or figuratively, but I was content to follow him for the moment wherever it was. We walked past a display of scrimshaw in one glass case and a collection of official-looking documents in another.

'That's a copy of the Antarctic Treaty, signed in 1960,' Southgate told me, pointing at one of the exhibits. 'It reserves Antarctica for peaceful purposes.'

I nodded. I've never been much of an environmentalist but I knew - as any competent journalist would - that the nations of the world had agreed a hands-off policy towards Antarctica in the sixties and, amazingly, appeared to be still sticking to it several decades later.

'What's in here?' I asked, looking at a third display cabinet.

'That's the famous Scott journal,' Southgate replied. 'The one they found in the tent where he and his men died. Actually, it's a photocopy. The original is in the British Museum.'

I gazed with something akin to reverence at the document. Even though it was a facsimile, I felt strangely moved. The journal lay open at the final page. The handwriting was easy enough to follow. Even during those last desperate hours, Scott's orthography was still clear and bold, the words cramming the pages to avoid any waste of space. I read the words that I, and thousands of schoolboys of my generation, already knew by heart. '*We shall stick it out to the end, but we are getting weaker, of course, and the end cannot be far. It seems a pity, but I do not think I can write more. For God's sake look after our people.*'

Southgate could see how affected I was.

'Would you like to see more?' he asked.

When I nodded, he slid back the bolt on the case and brought out the volume. He turned to some of the earlier entries.

'Huntford pokes fun at the expedition's scientific claims, but that is completely unjustified. Scott may have lacked the tools we have today but the expedition's scientific observations are still extraordinary acute. However tired and hungry he was, no matter it was blowing a howling gale, Scott made his notes and wrote up the diary.'

I took the facsimile of the journal from him - it was a loose-leaf collection in a simple ringbinder - and flicked through the pages. I could see what Southgate was driving at. Almost every day there were precise indications of latitude and longtitude, as well as a detailed record of events.

Southgate had allowed the suspense to build so that by the

time we walked over to the last display cabinet in the room he had me well and truly hooked.

'In here,' he said, pointing to a small collection of rocks inside the case, 'are some of the geological samples actually found in Scott's tent. The ones they found on the Beardmore Glacier and dragged back all that way.'

I could see at once that one or two of the rocks looked similar, if not identical, to the specimen I had seen in Alvarez's outer office. They had the same dull metallic sheen, the same purple-brown texture.

We were still the only people in the room, but I found I lowered my voice instinctively. 'Is that falconite?' I whispered.

'Oh yes, that's falconite all right,' Southgate replied. 'Or rather that's what I proposed it should be called when I wrote the paper for the *Journal*. Official recognition may take some time, of course. It's a bit like naming a saint in the Catholic Church. But there's no reason why it shouldn't go through in the end. We have Curium after the Curies, Rutherfordium after Sir John Rutherford - a Cambridge man, of course. We have Laurencium after Laurence. Why not *Falconite* after Robert Falcon Scott? After all, Scott was one of our great national heroes.'

I could not drag my eyes away from that small pile of rocks nor put out of my mind the image of Scott and his men battling heroically through snow and ice, hauling their prize behind them, no matter what the cost.

'Why hasn't this become known before?' I asked.

Southgate turned to face me. He looked coy, almost bashful.

'When I first came to the Institute, Scott's rocks, as I call them, were still buried in the basement along with a whole lot of polar mementoes such as discarded snowshoes, Nansen sledges, whalebones and heaven knows what. Scott, as you know, died in 1912. The First World War began shortly thereafter. The institute was founded in 1920 as a memorial to Scott. The rock samples and other material from Scott's last journey were transferred there from temporary storage in London. Somebody bunged them in the basement and there they stayed for decades, absolutely undisturbed.'

I could hardly believe what I was hearing.

'Are you saying that in spite of the scientific importance Scott claimed for his expedition, thereby - as I understand it - distinguishing himself from the adventurer Amundsen, nobody for seventy or more years actually bothered to check what he had brought back in terms of its scientific interest?'

'No, I'm not quite saying that,' Southgate replied. 'Let me go back a bit. It was Edward Wilson, the naturalist, who actually found the specimens. Wilson was intrigued by the presence of fossil plants in the specimens. Indeed, if you read Wilson's notes - his journal, like Scott's, was discovered with the bodies - it's clear that this was the feature which attracted him to the samples in the first place. Wilson, of course, died on the way back from the Pole. The specimens were first submitted for analysis to one of Wilson's colleagues, actually Frank Debenham, who served as the expedition's geologist. Debenham confirmed that the specimens collected by Wilson and Bowers were - and I quote - "*perhaps the most important of all the geological results.*" '

'Why was that?' I asked.

'According to Debenham, the presence of fossilised plants shed important light on the long-standing controversy between the geologists of the day as to the nature of the former union between Antarctica and Australia. Subsequently, the specimens were sent back to Cambridge. Mr A. C. Seward, who was Professor of Biology here at the time, confirmed their significance from the botanical point of view. He identified the fossils plants as leaves of glossopteris and described the discovery, in terms of palaeophytogeography and of geological history in the strictest sense, as being of the greatest interest.'

'So they didn't look in detail at the *mineral* characteristics of the samples?'

Southgate shook his head. 'In practice, the rock samples weren't the only things that escaped a proper evaluation. There was biological material too. The Terra Nova expedition brought back three Emperor penguin's eggs, for example, but no one identified them correctly at the time, though it could have caused a sensation if they had.'

'I guess the war threw everything into a turmoil.'

'That's right,' Southgate agreed. 'From this distance, it's hard to realise the impact the First World War must have had. The geologists, the physicists, who might have gone to work on the samples died in the trenches of Flanders. And you have to remember, of course, that the analytical methods they had were quite primitive compared to those we use today.'

When I had telephoned Graham Southgate that morning, I had wanted to learn the answer to two questions. First, I had wanted to know what falconite was, how and where it had been discovered. Well, now I knew.

The second thing I wanted to know was what uses the mineral might have, assuming just conceivably that it had been discovered to exist in commercial quantities outside Antarctica.

'I realise, of course,' I said, trying to sound as casual as possible, 'that you've been concentrating on the geological characteristics of falconite, as an historical curiosity if you like, and it may be too early to give a definitive answer. But, assuming that somewhere in the world you could actually mine the stuff, would that be of any interest? I mean, might there be some vital uses for falconite in some industry? Computers? IT? That kind of thing.'

I could see that Southgate was intrigued by my question. In fact, he seemed more than intrigued. It was almost as though I had come in right on cue.

'Indeed there are,' he replied. 'We could use a cup of tea, don't you agree? Why don't we get a bit of fresh air?'

VIII

Cambridge, England II

We went to a café down the road. The place was full of students - skipping lectures, I presumed - but we managed to find a table in the corner away from the blare of the piped music. Southgate ordered a pot of tea for two with muffins on the side, and, after a commendably brief interval, our order arrived.

Southgate poured for both of us. The tea, I was grateful to note, was a healthy brown colour, not the usual gnat's piss you so often find.

'I have to tell you,' Southgate began, 'that it wasn't purely intellectual curiosity that led me to reanalyse, after so many years, the geological material which Scott brought back with him from the Antarctic. Of course, curiosity played a part. Any good scientist is naturally curious. But there was more to it than that.'

Southgate drained his cup and poured himself a refill. 'How much do you understand about global warming?' he asked.

For a moment I was irritated. 'Whatever I may know, I'm sure I don't know enough,' I said somewhat frostily. 'Fire away.'

'I'll put it in a nutshell if you like,' Southgate said. 'Global warming is probably the most serious problem the world has ever faced. Manmade emissions of carbon dioxide and other so-called greenhouse gases have increased dramatically this century. Atmospheric concentrations of carbon dioxide are almost double their pre-industrial levels and are set to double again within the next few decades. We could be looking at an increase in global mean temperature of over three degrees Celsius, perhaps as much as five degrees. Unless we can do something about it - and soon - we shall almost certainly see a melting of the Antarctic icesheets - in fact that process has already begun. We shall see a rise in sealevels world wide and the devastation of coastal communities. And, in parts of the world, we shall see a vast increase in the rate of desertification, hunger and starvation on an unprecedented scale. We're talking millions. Hundreds of millions maybe.'

'I thought the United Nations was trying to do something,' I said. 'The politicians keep on going off to meetings and making speeches.'

'Puff and flannel!' Southgate exclaimed. 'Of course, governments have programmes for reducing emission of greenhouse gases. There are international treaties and agencies by the score looking at the issue. But none of this even scratches the surface of the problem. The only thing that is likely to make any difference to our prospects would be a total change in the world's patterns of production and consumption. And how is that going to happen? Even if the West cuts back on some of its worst excesses, which is unlikely, do you think the Indians, the Chinese, the South Americans, the Africans aren't going to go for what they can get, just as we did? It's already happening. The greatest rise in carbon dioxide and other greenhouse gas emissions over the next century will come from rapidly developing Third World countries and frankly they don't want even to think about the implications of climate change if it means cutting back on their development programmes.'

'So what do we do?' I said.

He leaned across the table towards me with the light of excitement in his eyes.

'There's a group of us up here in Cambridge who believe that trying to change the way the world is, is a waste of time and effort. It can't be done. The patterns are too entrenched. We believe we should be putting all our energies into looking for the technical fix. The basic chemistry of the world's carbon cycle is very simple. *We just need to find a way of taking the carbon out of the atmosphere at a faster rate than we're putting it there.*'

'What do you mean by that?'

'I'll explain what I mean,' Southgate said. 'The key issue relates to the productivity of marine plankton and the rate of carbon uptake by the oceans. Mathematical models are being developed to relate field observations and the function of upper-ocean plankton in carbon, nutrient and mineral cycles. The biological parameters are being studied too. One thing has emerged very clearly from all these studies and that is that the biological productivity of the plankton, the rate at which plankton is able to absorb atmospheric carbon, is crucially linked to the level of micro-nutrients received. *The models show that, theoretically at least, if you found the right micro-nutrient, you could speed up the carbon absorptive process to such an extent that you could quite possibly by this action alone reverse global warming trends and haul the world back from the brink of disaster.*'

'Do you have any empirical evidence or is it just a theory?' I asked.

'As a matter of fact there is some empirical evidence. Not conclusive, but interesting,' Southgate replied. 'In 1990, an American oceanographer called John Martin, from the Scripps Institute, put forward the idea that iron could be used to boost the carbon-absorptive capacity of marine plankton. An international team of thirty scientists from the US, Mexico and the UK took a ship to the Pacific and fertilised the equatorial oceanic waters with a cocktail of iron filings. For a short period, they achieved the effect on plankton which they were looking for. But it didn't last. There was no permanent absorption of carbon dioxide by the plankton, no reduction in atmospheric CO_2. The other problem was the logistics. Even if it had worked, very large quantities of iron would have been needed. Probably hundreds of thousands of tonnes. If you were lucky enough to find the right spot on the surface of the ocean to achieve the permanent absorption of carbon, you would still have to mount an operation of enormous complexity. You'd have to dose a large area of the ocean within a very short time-frame, using a large fleet of aircraft, and enormous international complications could arise.'

'What you're saying, then, is that at the present time we simply don't have the micro-nutrient we need.'

Rather self-consciously, I thought, Southgate canvassed the immediate neighbourhood for potential eavesdroppers, as though even in an empty restaurant he was afraid of being overheard. In fact, most of the tables were empty by now, the students having drifted off to other more pressing engagements.

Southgate nonetheless dropped his voice. 'Cambridge University, as you can imagine, is very well equipped with computer facilities. We have access to one of the Super-Krays which can compute at the rate of several million calculations per second. One of my colleagues has worked a unique programme which is, if you like, the reverse of predictive chemistry.'

'What do you mean by that?'

'Let me explain. With predictive chemistry, you look at the molecular or chemical structure of a substance or mineral compound and you say what you expect the likely impact on the environment will be. Here it's the other way round. We know the environmental effect we wish to achieve - let's say in this case a quadrupling of carbon uptake among plankton communities - and then we work back from that to estimate the nature of the mineral or the chemical we need.'

I could see where Southgate was leading. I was more than intrigued; I was absorbed.

'Go on,' I said.

'A few weeks ago we loaded the model with all the data we could come up with. We asked the computer to tell us the properties and molecular characteristics of the mineral or chemical, if it existed, which could achieve an impact on global warming through increased carbon-uptake in marine plankton. Basically, the computer works through every known chemical compound and comes up with a short list. It's a very efficient and versatile programme. A Norwegian scientist called Johannsen invented it up at Trondheim University. They'll probably give him the Nobel prize one day. You could ask Johannsen's model how to make grass greener and it would give you a short list of potential substances in no time at all.'

'Such as nitrogen fertiliser?'

Southgate laughed. 'You've got the point.'

To prove I had got the point, I asked, 'Did the computer give you a short list of potential substances when you asked it how to increase the carbon absorptive capacity of marine plankton?'

'As a matter of fact, it didn't give us a short list at all. We put the request in several different ways, using different parameters - time-scale, dose rate, area to be covered, effect desired and so on. Every time we ran the programme it came back with the same answer - it profiled the chemical which would achieve precisely the result we were looking for. It even drew a detailed diagram of the molecular structure for us, but at the same time the computer observed that its response should be considered only "theoretical" because *no chemical at the present time having the necessary characteristics was listed on its basic inventory.*'

'What did this chemical look like?'

Southgate took out a felt tip pen, plucked a paper-napkin from a glass in the middle of the table and started to draw on it. 'Basically,' he said, 'the molecule has a fairly compact body but with an immensely long tail.'

It took him a moment or two to complete the drawing. As I looked at it, I had the feeling that I had seen something similar quite recently but I couldn't work out where.

'You know what this is, don't you?' Southgate said.

'The molecular structure of falconite?'

'Exactly. But the computer maintained the substance we needed was non-existent because falconite has not yet been added to the basic chemical inventory! At the same time, I personally happened to know that falconite as a potential climate modifier fulfilled the requirements in every respect.'

'Only theoretically, surely,' I said. 'You don't have any empirical evidence that falconite will act as a growth-enhancer as far as marine plankton are concerned, do you?'

'Oh, but we do,' Southgate replied. 'I'll show you.'

As we left the cafe, I picked up the paper napkin on which Southgate had drawn his diagram of the molecular structure of falconite, folded it and put it in my wallet as a memento of a memorable conversation.

We had to walk back to the Scott Polar Research Institute to pick up Southgate's parked car before driving to the British Antarctic Survey's local research station, a modern building situated on the outskirts of Cambridge on the fringes of the science park.

'We've been running some tests in the laboratory,' Southgate said. 'You may find them interesting.'

The walls of one of the large rooms on the ground floor of the building were lined with glass-fronted tanks. Two white-coated technicians, both female, were busy checking the printouts from the computer.

'We want to test the actual results, as opposed to the predictions, of using falconite as a plankton micro-nutrient at different dosage levels,' Southgate explained. 'Each one of these tanks contains samples of plankton-rich seawater as collected last season by BAS research vessels operating in the Antarctic. We took just one of the falconite samples from the Museum, ground it to a powder and then dosed each tank at different rates.'

'Did you ask permission?' I asked.

Southgate laughed. 'The samples have been sitting there undisturbed for the best part of a century. Nobody's going to notice if a small piece of rock goes missing.'

He pointed to the printout. 'What we are seeing is exactly

what we hoped to see. At certain dosage levels, plankton activity increases almost exponentially resulting in a dramatic increase in the uptake of atmospheric carbon. In a real life situation that carbon is going to be taken out of circulation permanently and stored in various carbonaceous forms on the ocean floor.'

I looked in awe at the row of tanks. As far as I was concerned, I don't think I could tell the difference between them. They all seemed to contain a murky green liquid of varying complexion, putting me in mind of the original primordial soup from which all life on this planet is supposed to have evolved. Yet I knew that what I was looking at was a scientific experiment which could turn out to be in its own way as significant as the splitting of the atom.

'If you increase the dose of micro-nutrient, do you increase the carbon uptake?' I asked. 'Is there a simple linear relationship?'

'Good question,' replied Southgate. He pointed towards the first three tanks. 'What we are finding is that there is a straightforward correlation between dose and effect up to a certain point. Plankton which have absorbed falconite at increasing levels of concentration show an increasing degree of carbon-absorptive activity. What's more, they appear to be able to transmit the carbon-absorptive property, whatever it is, to neighbouring plankton even if that particular collection of plankton has not in fact received the micro-nutrient. In other words, a kind of chain reaction is set up. However, we don't yet know for sure what happens if we go beyond a certain dosage rate. *It could be that, after that point, we're going to witness a perverse or negative correlation.*'

'Such as?'

'An overdose of falconite might actually have a toxic effect. So far from enhancing the carbon-uptake rates, it could send them into reverse. In other words, as far as global warming is concerned, the effect achieved would be precisely contrary to the effect we wish to achieve. We would actually be impairing, not improving, the capacity of the oceans to modulate climate change.'

'And with the chainreaction you spoke of a deliberate or accidental overdose of falconite could be calamitous?'

Southgate pointed to the fourth tank in the row. The water in the tank appeared dull and lifeless. All traces of biological activity, to the naked eye at least, appeared to be absent. It was as though all forms of existence had been snuffed out.

'If we got it wrong,' Southgate said, 'it could be the end of all marine life as we know it. Of course, in practice the whole thing's hypothetical anyway. Falconite may be the ideal substance to stop global warming dead in its tracks and save Planet Earth. On the other hand, it's the one substance we just do not have, apart from a couple of samples in the museum and that's certainly not enough to do the trick.'

We walked back to the car and drove down to the river, parking by the meadow which runs along the Backs. I'd almost forgotten what a beautiful city Cambridge is. A few hundred yards away King's College Chapel soared majestically heavenward. Even without being there, I could imagine the pure treble voices of the choristers rising up through the great fluted columns to caress the marvellous fanvaulting of the ceiling. I remembered I had come here once with Nasreen during our brief ill-fated engagement. It was a weekday afternoon and the choir was practising. We sat in one of the pews at the back, holding hands as we listened.

Damn Harry, I thought. Damn him to hell!

As I sat there in the car, contemplating the Cambridge skyline and willy-nilly reliving the past, I suddenly knew the question I had to put. I chose my words with care.

'Is it at all conceivable,' I asked, 'that falconite might actually be discovered in South America, say Brazil?'

Southgate looked at me curiously.

'The short answer to your question - could a geological anomaly found in Antarctica also be found in South America - is yes. How much more do you want?'

'A bit more.'

'Very well,' said Graham. 'Go back to the beginning of this century. Have you heard of the great German scientist, Alfred Wegener?'

'Vaguely,' I lied.

Southgate let it pass. 'Wegener first came up with the theory of continental drift and by now it is generally accepted. Some two hundred million years ago all the continents were joined together in one vast land mass known as Pangaia, which if you remember your Greek, as I expect you do, means the whole earth. Some time after that, say one hundred million years ago, the southern part of that great land mass split off from the northern part to form a super-continent known as Gondwana and that super-continent in turn split up into the several continents which we have today - South America, Africa, Australia and, of course, Antarctica. It's a bit like a jigsaw puzzle. Even now, if you cut out the shapes of the continents and jiggle them around a bit you can recreate Gondwana without much difficulty. There is a lot of geological and biological evidence to prove the Gondwana hypothesis. The presence of fossilised *glossopteris* leaves on the Beardmore Glacier in Antarctica is part of that evidence. So, yes, it's entirely possible that Antarctica was linked to Brazil and that certain mineralogical phenomena could occur in both places. Indeed, I'd say it's more than possible. It's probable. Does that help?'

Did that help?! Was the Pope Catholic?! Southgate had told me precisely what I needed to know. It was all so obvious now. CMG must have been prospecting in the tamarin zone. That was not surprising. After all, the basic survey which I'd seen summarised in the Ouro Preto museum had identified that zone as being geologically promising. CMG's surveyors must have discovered a new mineral which they had identified as falconite on the basis, presumably, of the report which Southgate himself had published in the scientific literature. And, somehow, someone in CMG must have got wind of the results of the computer modeling which proved that a mineral substance having falconite's known characteristics could be the answer to global warming. They must have informed Alvarez who in turn would have realised the enormous potential value to CMG of a falconite deposit. CMG probably already owned the mineral exploitation rights in the region. If they didn't, Alvarez would have taken immediate steps to acquire them. The diggers and the excavators would have been ready to move in. And then what happens? A bunch of crackpots - from CMG's point of view - claim that the area in question may be the habitat for a tribe of endangered monkeys and thereby seems set to throw a monumental spanner in the works.

I remembered that one tiny fish known as the snail-darter had for years, decades, held up the construction of a vital dam in the Tennessee valley because that particular species was protected under US environmental legislation! And we weren't talking about snail-darters here. We were talking about one of the rarest and most beautiful creatures on earth! Once word got out that one of the last living colonies of the world's most endangered monkeys lay in the path of the bulldozers and the earth-movers, CMG's prospects of exploiting the deposit could sink to zero. The lawsuits would fly thick and fast. Organisations like SOS Mata Atlantica, and men like Oliveira, were no fools. I imagined that they would find allies inside Brazil as well as outside, notwithstanding the potential importance of the falconite deposit in terms of global warming. That's the way things are. The good guys are not always on the same side. At the very least, the prospects of working the deposit could be held up for years while they sorted out which set of environmental priorities was more important. For CMG, for Alvarez, Harry must have spelt tremendous trouble. Harry knew about the tamarins; he may not have known specifically about the falconite but he knew that CMG was planning a major exploitation in the *mata*. He was linked to Oliveira. From Alvarez's point of view the best thing to do was to get rid of Harry before it was too late.

As I sat there in the car looking out at the river and the colleges beyond, I was more than ever convinced that Harry's disappearance in the forests of Brazil had not been accidental. Harry had been liquidated, eliminated, removed, taken out, zapped (take your pick) and I was convinced that Admiral Antonio Francisco Alvarez himself was personally responsible. The question was, could I ever prove it?

In any event, I didn't make it back to London that day. Southgate was a fellow of Churchill College and he invited me to dine with him on high table. I accepted with pleasure.

Southgate went home to change, arranging to meet me later.

'Will you be all right on your own?' he asked. 'I've booked a room for you in college. Just ask at the lodge.'

'I'll be fine,' I said. 'Since I've a bit of time on my hands, do you think I might potter around the museum again? I'd like to take another look at some of those exhibits.'

Southgate glanced at his watch. 'The museum will probably be shut now,' he said. 'Tell you what, take my key. You can let me have it back later.' He took out his keyring, removed a key and handed it to me.

When Southgate left, I walked back to the museum which, as Southgate had suspected, had now closed for the day. I used Southgate's key to get in and found my way easily enough to the exhibition hall where Southgate had shown me the facsimile of Scott's diary. Whereas, earlier that day, I had only been able to skim through the entries, I now had the chance to make a more thorough study of that last fateful journey to the South Pole.

I took the facsimile over to a table and sat there for at least an hour reading through the entries. If I had been moved that morning, I was almost overwhelmed now. Sitting there in that magical room, surrounded by the mementoes of the past, I found myself totally absorbed in recreating in my own imagination Scott's painful pathway into legend. How stupendous, how fitting it would be, if looking back we could finally say that, thanks to their extraordinary discovery on the Beardmore Glacier, Captain Scott and the rest of his heroic band had not died in vain.

Before I left the museum, I found a photocopier in a nearby office and Xeroxed two or three pages of the Journal before putting it back in the glass case.

Later that evening, I met Southgate in Churchill College lodge as planned and gave him back his key.

'I'm glad you had a second crack at the museum,' he said. 'It's probably the best Antarctic collection in the world. Well worth the effort.'

I had the feeling that Southgate was burning with curiosity to know precisely why I had wanted to visit the museum a second time. I deliberately chose not to enlighten him. There might come a time for that later, but now was definitely not the moment.

'I had a fascinating time,' I said. And left it at that.

We went in to the college dining-room together. I've always enjoyed the ritual of high table - the long polished oak surfaces, the gleaming silverware, the food and wine - and of course the conversation which, if sometimes rather esoteric for a workaday journalist such as myself, generally manages to be entertaining and informative.

Churchill is one of the newer Cambridge colleges. It opened for business in 1960. Its statutes require that seventy percent of students study natural sciences, mathematics or engineering and that about one-third should be postgraduates. With its high reputation for science, Churchill attracts a number of distinguished Visiting Fellows from other countries.

As we filed into the hall, Southgate murmured that he had arranged for me to be sitting next to Professor Boris Kalinin.

'Kalinin has a Visiting Fellowship at Churchill,' Southgate explained. 'He's an extraordinary man. The doyen of Russian climatologists.'

After the Provost had said grace, I turned to the burly white-haired gentleman who sat on my immediate left.

'Professor Kalinin?' I asked.

'The same,' he replied, turning his huge head towards me like a great shaggy bison on the North American plains lowering its head to sniff a change in the wind.

I can remember even now the sense I felt of being in the presence of a towering personality. I've seldom met someone with such immediate magnetism. Partly it was the sheer size of the man. He must have been easily six feet four and he seemed almost as broad as he was tall. Partly it was his deep booming voice which I was sure, even unamplified, would have made the largest lecture hall reverberate. Most importantly, Kalinin seemed to have an extraordinary natural authority. He was the kind of man, one felt, who if he had pursued a political rather than an academic career would have dominated by the sheer force of intellectual ability all those mediocre careerists who nowadays seemed to people the Kremlin.

I almost hesitated to talk to him lest he find my conversation unworthy. But with my neighbour on the right being otherwise engaged, I decided - after that first exchange - that it would be more rewarding and more courageous to plunge ahead rather than to retreat.

'I'm Dr Southgate's guest.' I said, banally. You have to start somewhere and it seemed a safe enough opening. Pawn to king four, as it were.

Kalinin's English was perfectly comprehensible, if thickly accented.

'Ah, Dr Southgate,' he said. 'A brilliant man. A credit to the science of geology. Have you read his recent piece in the *Journal of Geological Studies?* An extraordinary piece of detective work.'

'You mean the article about the discovery of falconite? I've not read it, but he told me about it. How did you come across it?'

'He sent it to me for peer review although of course I'm more of a climate man than a geologist.'

'What are you doing in Cambridge?' I asked, changing the subject. For reasons I couldn't really explain, I felt uneasy talking to Kalinin about falconite.

'I'm visiting Cambridge for a few weeks,' Kalinin replied. 'I'm a member of the Russian National Academy of Sciences. As a matter of fact I'm Chairman of the National Scientific Panel on Global Warming. The work which is being conducted on this topic in Cambridge is, as you can imagine, of great interest to us.'

As he spoke, Professor Kalinin drained his glass of claret. Almost instantly, one of the college servants, cut-glass decanter in hand, arrived with a refill. The second glass rapidly went the way of the first.

'Which particular aspects are you interested in?' I asked.

For the next twenty minutes, as we worked our way through the meal, Kalinin talked with dazzling lucidity about global warming. He was, so it seemed, interested not so much in the causes of climate change but in the impact it was likely to have.

'Regional variations will be crucial,' he told me towards the end of the exposition. 'Global warming may be bad for some regions, but it may be highly beneficial for others.'

'Which region in particular?'

'Ah,' Kalinin said mysteriously. 'That is what we need to find out.'

I hoped he would say more. Already, his remarks had whetted my curiosity. The way Southgate had presented it that afternoon, global warming was going to be a global disaster. Did that view have to be modified?

Unfortunately, Kalinin at this point seemed to lose interest in our conversation. He turned abruptly to the guest on his left and shortly thereafter excused himself from the table.

I watched his huge figure shamble from the room. Where was he going, I wondered? Outside the college, what kind of life did he have? Did he stay in contact with Moscow? Who called the shots? It was hard to imagine Kalinin, with all his stature and authority, dancing to someone else's tune.

Later that evening, when we had moved to the senior common

room for coffee and brandy, I found myself repeating to Southgate some of the elements of the conversation I had had with Kalinin.

'He spoke of regional variations in the effects of global warming,' I said. 'Are there going to be winners as well as losers?'

Southgate looked at me sharply. 'Possibly,' he said. 'According to some computer models, vast areas of Russian permafrost could turn into productive land. The arctic ice could melt, opening up the north-east sea route to Japan with enormous potential benefits for the Russian economy.' Southgate paused to allow his words to sink in.

'Let me make sure I understand this correctly,' I said. 'Global warming may be a disaster for most of the world, *but for the Russians it could conceivably be precisely what they need.*'

'More than that,' Southgate said. 'Given certain assumptions, global warming could shift the geopolitical balance completely. As the great prairies of the United States turn into dustbowls, Siberia becomes the granary of the world. Clearwater ports in the Arctic will permit worldwide exports.'

'Where does that leave falconite?' I asked quietly.

Southgate looked at me puzzled. 'I've told you, Charles. Falconite is purely theoretical. A dream, a fantasy. The alchemist's stone. Of course if falconite were ever discovered to exist in quantity, there would be such a scramble to dig it up that the Klondyke and Ballarat goldrushes would look like picnics. Such a deposit, wherever it is, would overnight become the most valuable the world has ever seen.

'One side - our side, presumably would be rushing to dig it up because it represents that quick simple technical fix to global warming that I was talking about. If you can bury giga-tonnes of carbon in the ocean at minimal expense, who needs the massive economic and social disruption that would be caused by cutting back on greenhouse gas emissions from cars and factories and all the other sources? But let's be clear: the Russians would be in that scramble too. Their interests, though they may be different from ours, are no less real, no less vital. To them at least.'

'Can you clarify that?'

'Of course. If falconite turns out to be the answer to global warming, and if the Russians by some crazy process of scientific jingoism have determined that they want to *accelerate*, not reduce global warming, then they'll try to stop us getting it. Or else they may try to acquire the falconite and then try to sell it to the rest of the world for an exorbitant price. We may be living in a new era, Charles, but we're still playing the same old games, only with different pieces.'

'What if your overdose theory is correct? What if falconite at certain dose rates could actually destroy the carbon-absorptive capacity of the ocean?'

'All the more reason for the Russians to want to get their hands on it.'

I wanted to tell Southgate about the falconite sample I had seen in Alvarez's office, about the deposit in the forest, about CMG's mining prospects or whatever. I knew I had a scoop, perhaps the largest scoop I was ever likely to have in my life. But I'm a professional journalist. You don't tell people about scoops ahead of publication. Not even friends.

As we lingered over our drinks, the room emptied.

'Most of the fellows have to get home to their wives,' Southgate explained. 'It's not like the old days when the dons lived in college and would stay up half the night pushing the port around.'

It was clear to me, from the affable way in which his colleagues bade us good evening, that Southgate commanded considerable respect in the senior common room. In due course, I imagined, he would be a senior figure in the college and the university. Maybe, as so many dons from the ancient universities did, he would fish in even wider pools. As a matter of fact, it occurred to me as I looked at him that over the last few years Graham had acquired an air of substantial authority. From our discussions that day, and particularly from his remarks after dinner, I realised that his concerns ranged far beyond the narrow confines of a Cambridge college or university institute. He was clearly versed in matters of state. This in itself was not surprising. The universities of Oxford and Cambridge have always been part of the establishment in Britain. But I could see that Graham's progress and contacts were rather special. For example he told me, quite casually, that he had recently been elected a Fellow of the Royal Society. To be FRS before you are 40 is a remarkable achievement. It means you have been weighed in the balance by people who count and have not been found wanting.

There are moments, late in the evening, when the decanters are lined up on the polished mahogany sideboard and the flames of the log fire are flickering in the grate, when reminiscence is almost inevitable. In spite of the fact that we had been quite close at the time, I had never spoken to Southgate about the events of that summer term at Trinity, ten years previously. At the time, I hadn't wanted to talk to him - or to anyone. And after I left Cambridge the opportunity hadn't arisen. But now, as all the memories came flooding back, I suddenly wanted to know how Southgate had seen things then.

'What did you make of us?' I asked, 'Harry and Nasreen and me? What did you make of what happened?'

'I thought you were all mad, quite mad,' Graham replied. 'You were all much too young. Good God, Nasreen was barely out of her teens. That said, I think she treated you abominably. And you behaved extremely well. As I wrote to you at the time. As for Harry, his behaviour was unpardonable.'

'Nasreen was in love with him.'

'She thought she was,' Southgate commented. 'Anyway, that's no excuse.'

Once we began to talk about Nasreen, we somehow found it hard to stop. Graham wanted to know how she had fared during her long stay in Brazil, what she looked like, what kind of life she was leading. I gave him as many details and as many insights as I could.

'I don't think she's happy,' I said finally. 'Leaving aside the question of Harry's disappearance or death - if we *can* leave it aside - I'd say she's suffering some kind of inner anguish. As a matter of fact, I think she's homesick.'

'What do you mean?'

'I think she misses her family, her country. Her parents have gone back to Iran now, you know.'

'Oh, have they? You think Nasreen will want to visit them in Teheran?'

'She may well,' I said.

'That's most interesting,' Southgate said.

I said goodbye to Southgate in the college lodge.

'You must come and meet my wife and the family one day,' he said. 'We're living in an old rectory in a village about ten miles outside the city.'

'I'd love to,' I said as I turned to climb the stairs to my room. I meant it. At that moment I envied the stability, the fullness, the *relevance*, of Southgate's life.

IX

London

As I waited on the platform at Cambridge station early the next morning to catch the train to London I was surprised to see Southgate again. He was standing facing the track with a briefcase in one hand and an umbrella in the other.

'Hello, Graham,' I said, walking up to him. 'Great evening last night.'

'Good heavens! You're up bright and early.'

'I've got a story to file.'

He smiled at that. 'I shall read it with interest.'

The train was crowded and Graham and I found ourselves sitting at different ends of one of the first-class compartments. I caught up with him again at King's Cross.

'Do you want to share a cab?' I asked. 'I'm heading for Gray's Inn Road. Where are you going?'

'Whitehall. I think I'll take the tube. Thanks anyway.'

I looked at the umbrella, the briefcase, the pinstriped suit. 'I thought you were looking smart,' I smiled.

I watched him disappear down the steps into the underground. As I waited in the queue for a cab, I wondered precisely what official business had brought Graham into town that morning. Networking of some kind, that was obvious. But what kind of networking? Which part of Whitehall? The Foreign Office? The Ministry of Defence? Both of those? If you were one of the youngest and brightest Fellows of the Royal Society, doors tended to open.

I was still idly speculating about Graham Southgate's mission when the taxi reached the Independent Television News building at 200 Gray's Inn Road.

The Reuters news room on the seventh floor of the ITN building has a very special flavour. The electronic message is all-pervasive. There must be at least two hundred screens up and running at any one time and each one will contain a veritable mosaic of information. A screen will be split up into boxes. You've got a political box, a bonds box, a companies box and God knows what else - all changing by the second as the various feeds come in from around the world.

ALERTS and URGENTS are red. If you read in the press some story that begins '*Traders' screens were red today*', that is an accurate description of the reality. The news room literally changes colour as the terminals light up. Share prices move on an ALERT. Fortunes are made or lost. I've seen it scores of times.

I wasn't actually thinking about share prices when I reached my desk in the news room the morning after my return to work. I was thinking of the story I had to write.

It was obvious that I couldn't quote Southgate by name. I hadn't asked him for permission and he hadn't given it. But, apart from that, I reckoned I had everything I needed. I typed in my access code, pulled down a blank document and then paused for a second with my fingers over the keys. What slant was I going to use? What priority was I going to give it? Putting out an ALERT is not something you do every day of the week. The ALERT is Reuters top priority. It breaks into the general news services. It's flashed onto dealers' screens. You've got to be pretty damn sure your story's important before you use the ALERT tag. You've also got to be pretty damn sure you're right.

According to the rules, I had eighty characters to play around with. Eighty characters is not a lot, but it's enough. Most messages worth communicating can be communicated in eighty characters.

I decided to suck it and see. 'CMG,' I typed, 'MAKES NEW MINERALS FIND IN BRAZILIAN FOREST.' I clicked on the Word Count icon and learned that I had written eight words for a total of forty characters. I tried again, this time giving CMG its full title and adding the necessary caveat. 'COMPAGNIA MINAS GERAIS BELIEVED TO HAVE MADE NEW MINERALS FIND IN BRAZILIAN FOREST.'

I clicked the mouse again and this time learned that I had fourteen words for a total of seventy characters. I decided to put 'vital' in place of 'new'. If falconite wasn't vital to the future of humanity, I didn't know what was.

I could sense my pulse racing as I looked at the screen in front of me for the last time, re-reading what I had written. I clicked on the Save icon and then I paused again. I'm one of Reuters' senior journalists. Relatively speaking, I've been around a long time. I have filing rights. If I click the Send button, the story goes out on the wires without any bureaucratic interference. It doesn't have to be subbed. It doesn't have to be seen by the editors. It goes out on my responsibility and my responsibility alone. Of course, if you get it wrong, it's your ass that's on the line.

I clicked the Send button anyway. Then I really got down to work.

The Reuters house rules are quite precise. If you put out an ALERT, you have to follow it with a NEWSBREAK within three minutes. Generally, the first two paragraphs repeat the ALERT, which gives you a further three paragraphs to develop the story, making a five paragraph story in all.

I wanted a coffee badly but I didn't have time to get one. A journalist is no different from anyone else. You're never so good you're indispensable. Seconds ago I had just taken the biggest risk of my career. I'd put out a headline at the highest level of priority which, in my heart of hearts, I knew might not stand up against the most rigorous tests of journalism. For a start, there had been no explicit confirmation from CMG of the new minerals find in Minas Gerais. And, in spite of what Southgate had told me, falconite's crucial role in the battle against global warming might need further confirmation. Basically, I was going on a gut feeling about this one. And that gut feeling was all to do with my brother Harry and his disappearance up there in the rain forest. That was the clincher.

I looked at my watch. Forty five seconds had already elapsed since I had sent out the ALERT. If I didn't get on with the NEWSBREAK I'd be out on my ear. That was another of Reuters' nice little house rules. Any journalist who failed to sequence an ALERT with a NEWSBREAK had broken the most sacred rule of wire service reporting. You might just get away with it if a major heart attack left you slumped over the keyboard, but even that wasn't certain.

Once more, I began to type, trying to establish beyond a shadow of a doubt that my ALERT had been fully justified and that CMG's minerals find in Brazil could truly transform the prospects for humanity.

As prescribed, my first paragraph more or less repeated the flash. It was wrong of me, I knew, but the second time round I dropped the qualifier 'believed', beginning instead with a clear bold statement. '*Compagnia Minas Gerais (CMG) has discovered a major deposit of a mineral of vital importance for the future of mankind. The new discovery is thought to involve a rare earth known as falconite. Independent sources last night confirmed that falconite may play a major role in preventing climate change and forestalling global warming by dramatically increasing the carbon take-up of the key ocean-atmosphere interface.*'

Southgate would probably tell me that I had got it all wrong. Or else had over-simplified horrendously. But Southgate didn't have to tell a complex story in five short paragraphs.

I decided to end the piece with a couple of handy information notes for editors. 'CMG,' I wrote, '*is Brazil's fastest growing minerals company. Brazil is already a major exporter of minerals and precious metals, including aluminium, nickel, tin, manganese, titanium and tantalum.*'

Then, just in case anyone had any doubts as to the story's priority rating, I added: '*On current trends, global warming could result in a melting of the polar icecaps and massive flooding of coastal areas, leading to the death or dislocation of hundreds of millions of people, as well as transformation of the world's grain-belts into dustbowls.*'

I ran a quick spellcheck on the piece, then did a word-count. The story was well within the prescribed limits for a NEWSBREAK follow up to an ALERT. I looked at my watch. Twenty seconds to go.

There was one last adjustment to make. I typed in Rio de Janeiro, Brazil, as the dateline and my own name underneath. Strictly speaking I was breaking the rules, but it was only the teeniest fiddle. Journalists were always flying back to base, then filing their piece as though they were still in Timbuktu or wherever. That was accepted practice, only considered unethical if you hadn't actually been to Timbuktu or wherever at all.

Precisely two minutes and fifty-eight seconds after transmitting the first ALERT, I clicked on the Send icon for a second time. My machine whirred and clicked. I checked in the outbox to see that the message was safely on its way. Then, to be double sure, I brought up the general news box.

The story was already there. That's how fast the system is nowadays. It was good to see my name at the top before the Rio dateline. It was even better to see that the screen was red. This was one news item which had scooped the pool. Suddenly that long frustrating mission to Brazil seemed worthwhile. I hadn't found Harry but I had come back with a bloody good story.

House rules said that a NEWSBREAK has to be followed by a longer piece - say sixty lines or four hundred words - within twenty minutes. Twenty minutes! At the speed I had been working so far that morning it seemed like as though I had all the time in the world.

I pushed my chair back and headed for the coffee machine by the door. Arne Van Meert, the general news editor, who sat in his own glass cubicle just outside the news room, looked at me curiously as I passed.

Let me tell you a bit about Arne. As far as I'm concerned, he's a fat Dutchman who has been brought in by the senior management to make our lives hell. He's always talking about 'cost centres' and 'profit centres'; I don't think he has actually written a story himself in his life.

I've had a couple of run-ins with Arne in the recent past, most recently over the matter of expenses. I put in for the price of a round of drinks at El Vino's one night and Arne came back and said I had to submit a receipt for Christ's sake. Whoever heard of asking for a receipt when you buy a round of drinks in a pub? Arne backed down in the end when some of the colleagues joined in and told him in no uncertain terms that this was London not Amsterdam and that penny-pinching could only be taken so far. But I know the defeat had rankled with Arne. He was looking for ways of getting his own back.

I could see him now on the other side of the panel. He was clearly wondering what brought me in so early and why I had been typing so furiously. He looked suspicious. I am sure he thought I was wasting my own and Reuters' time. Leaving any personal animosity aside, I'm sure Arne was profoundly convinced that Reuters should concentrate almost exclusively on providing financial services. That after all was where the profits lay. As far as Arne was concerned, an old-fashioned generalist was as near to a wino as you could get and still pull down a monthly pay cheque.

I lifted a hand to him as I passed his box. Just keep watching the screens, Arne, I thought. Wait till my Brazil piece feeds across into your beloved financial news, as I knew it would. Though I'd given my story a general news coding, I'd also made sure it went across to the economic news boxes as well as the business and financial pages.

I must have passed Arne's cubicle at exactly the right moment because I saw him start and give a scowl of annoyance. They probably bleeped out the Tokyo stock market report to make way for my piece.

I tapped in my PIN number on the coffee machine. Some management consultants, brought in at vast expense by the Reuters management, had dreamed that one up, but for once I didn't mind. For an old-fashioned journalist, nothing is as sweet as a good old-fashioned scoop. I lifted the plastic cup of coffee to my lips.

'Cheers,' I murmured to the still half-empty news room.

It was strange, I reflected as I stood there sipping the nauseous black liquid, how powerful one's basic journalistic instincts were. The urge to file that morning was the result of a knee-jerk reaction. If you think you've got a good story, you go with it. Simple as that. That's the rule I've followed all my professional life and it has seldom, if ever, let me down.

But I knew there was more to it than that. Some purely personal factors were involved. If I were to prove that Alvarez, as I now believed, was implicated in Harry's disappearance and death I needed to show a motive. From my brief encounter with Alvarez, and from the accounts others had given me, I knew that he was an immensely skilful operator who would have done whatever was necessary to cover his traces. But once it was public knowledge that CMG planned a major minerals exploitation in a protected zone, the wildest conspiracy theories might look plausible. I realised, of course, that insofar as I had allowed these more personal considerations to colour what I had written that morning, I might have been guilty of a journalistic indiscretion. I might have departed from the strict norms and canons of objectivity.

Well, too bad, I thought as I tossed my coffee cup into the bin. To paraphrase Barry Goldwater, sometimes a little extremism in the pursuit of truth is entirely defensible.

Back at my terminal, I rapidly wrote up, as required, the sixty line or four hundred word follow-up to the NEWSBREAK. You can say a lot in four hundred words, and believe me I did. I set out as clearly as I could the basic dilemma. On the one hand, CMG had discovered probably the most important and the most valuable minerals deposit ever to have been found in the history of exploration. On the other hand, exploitation of that deposit was almost certain to result in the destruction of a major chunk of the fast disappearing Atlantic forest - the *Mata Atlantica* - and to involve a critical loss of biodiversity, including the disappearance of the golden lion tamarin, one of nature's greatest glories.

Since I was purporting to write a purely factual piece, it was not up to me to suggest how this dilemma might be resolved. To conclude my piece, I resorted to traditional journalistic sleight of hand. '*Informed sources last night commented,*' I wrote, '*that it would be virtually unthinkable for a deposit of such vital importance to remain unexploited, whatever the consequences for the forest and its wildlife.*'

As soon as I had finished, I sent the article out over the network. After that I left the office as quickly as possible. Though no one could have stopped the story hitting the wires since, as I've already mentioned, I have filing rights, it was not inconceivable that questions would be asked by the management and those questions would come back to me since my byline was on the piece.

In the circumstances, I didn't want to be around, not for the time being, anyway. Let the story build, I thought. I didn't even take my cellphone with me as I headed for Kent to follow up yet another uninspiring item about the route of the much delayed high-speed rail-link from London to the Channel Tunnel.

I spent an hour talking to officials in Maidstone, then caught the late afternoon train back to Charing Cross. On arrival, I walked along the Strand for a drink at El Vino's. I didn't return to the Reuters news room until around 7.00 p.m. My plan had been to write a paragraph or two about new developments in Britain's transport policy, as seen from a mid-Kent viewpoint, then call it a day. I was still jetlagged and I was looking forward to getting back to the flat and having an early night.

As soon as I walked through the door of the news room I knew something was wrong. Arne van Meert was shouting into his telephone. I could hear him bellowing behind the glass door of his office.

'Of course, we'll run a correction if we have to,' he said as he slammed the receiver down.

He caught sight of me as I made my way across the room to my terminal and rapped hard on the window, beckoning me into his office.

'Where the hell have you been?' he asked angrily. 'We've been looking all over for you.'

Most of us just have the screens in front of us but Arne, as befitted his superior status, had the tapes as well. He now angrily thrust a pile of printouts towards me. He tapped the top of the pile accusingly with the middle finger of his right hand.

'You can't file a story like that and then just bloody disappear,' Arne spoke with a thick Dutch accent but there was nothing wrong with his grasp of English idiom.

I looked over his shoulder to the monitor on his desk. Generally, Arne watched what we call the 'useful screen'. In the top left-hand corner you have a box called 'glance' which rounds up all market-moving news from around the world and presents the stories in a concise and fluid way. You just click on the headline to view the story. The top right-hand box surveys world stock market indices. Middle right, you have a box for breaking equity news.

Arne swivelled rapidly on his chair to face the screen. 'Take a look at this, dammit,' he snarled, pointing to the middle-right box.

He clicked with the mouse a couple of times to bring up the detail. Two out of the ten items running in the last half-hour in the equity news box referred to the 'CMG share price explosion' or the 'dramatic rise in CMG futures'. I glanced at my watch. The latest item had been logged at 6.45 p.m., barely twenty minutes earlier, which was 12.45 p.m. São Paulo time.

Arne checked with the mouse again and brought up the full text of the flash. I read the message over his shoulder. The Reuters São Paulo office reported: '*CMG officials have not so far been available to comment on speculation that the company has made a major minerals find in the state of Minas Gerais. CMG shares have risen dramatically on BOVESPA, the São Paulo stock exchange, and in other South American markets when they opened today, matching gains posted elsewhere.*'

'What other gains are they referring to, Arne?' I asked. I didn't like being shouted at, certainly not by this obese sweating Dutchman, but at the moment I wasn't going to make an issue of it.

Arne went over to the 'equities useful' screen, which gives quotes for any and every market when a share is traded. London, New York, Tokyo, Singapore, São Paulo - you name it, the 'equities useful' screen has it. As a Brazilian stock of growing importance, CMG was traded in a dozen markets around the world and all of them were showing massive gains.

By now the markets had long since closed in the Far East and trading was virtually over in Frankfurt, London, Paris and Brussels. But the United States stock exchanges and the South American bourses were active. CMG stocks were still climbing rapidly on the other side of the Atlantic.

'Bring up New York, Arne,' I said quietly, keeping as cool as I could in the circumstances. 'Let's see the detail.'

Arne clicked again to get the complete listing of trade on the New York Stock Exchange involving CMG shares. The screen in front of us detailed the date and time of each transaction, the volume of shares traded and the price at which the trade took place.

It wasn't the time or the place to look at the detail of individual movements, but the broad picture was clear enough. For the last five hours CMG stock had been rising steadily upward at around ten points an hour. There had been a blip in the curve twenty minutes earlier, around the time the Reuters report from São Paulo had hit the screen, but in the last few minutes the upward trend had resumed.

'Let's see São Paulo as well,' I requested.

'Coming up now,' Arne, still furious, spat out the words as the screen in front of him started pulsing.

'Christ almighty!' I exclaimed.

I'm not particularly knowledgeable about how the world's stock exchanges function. As I've said before, my beat is general news stories rather than specifically financial items. But you can't work for Reuters for over a decade, as I had, without acquiring some insights into the working of individual markets. Financial stories often *are* general news stories. And vice-versa. Like now.

Though there are nine stock exchanges in Brazil, the São Paulo one is by far the most important. There are 544 companies listed on BOVESPA - Bolsa de Valores de Saõ Paulo - with a total market capitalisation of 149 billion US dollars. As with the other main trading centres in the world, most of the trades on BOVESPA nowadays are performed electronically through a sophisticated electronic trading system known as CATS (Computer Assisted Trader System).

CATS, as I could see at a glance from Arne van Meert's screen, had been performing frantically so far that day. Trading in CMG shares had been more than four times their average level and activity in the market as a whole was well up, as though the boost given to CMG's fortunes by the publication of my story on the Reuters wire had galvanised the whole economy. I checked the list quickly for familiar names. Petrobras - Petroleo Brasileiro - was up a quarter. Telecomunicacoes de São Paulo up one-fifth. Compagnia Vale do Rio Doce up an eighth.

As with the NYSE, trades were being posted as we watched. Each trade seemed to have a ratchet effect on CMG's share price.

'You did that, Hodson,' Arne van Meert told me accusingly, pointing his chubby index finger at the screen. 'I hope to hell you didn't just report a rumour! And you bloody well better not have invented it! Well, I can tell you something. If you have, the chickens will come home to roost sooner than you think.'

By now quite a little crowd had gathered in Arne's office. Hacks who had been heading for home paused, sensing a drama in the making.

'I resent that, Arne,' I retaliated. 'The story's solid. I believe in it. I wouldn't have written it if I hadn't. And I certainly didn't invent it!'

'Then get a confirmation,' Arne shouted, almost beside himself with rage. 'If the market discovers that all this activity is based on unconfirmed speculation by one Reuters journalist there'll be hell to pay. If you can't get confirmation, we'll publish a correction and that's final. I told the MD that and I'll stick to it. You've got fifteen minutes. Now get out!'

I have to say I worked pretty hard in the next fifteen minutes. I called our São Paulo office first and spoke to the bureau chief, a tough professional woman called Christina Markham.

Christina was witheringly sarcastic. 'Jesus, Charles,' she said when I got through. 'You byline the piece Rio when you're not even there; you don't check the story with me; you don't even have the courtesy to tell me you're going to file. You just leave me to read it on the wire and now you expect me to bail you out!'

'I don't expect you to bail me out,' I protested. 'The story is solid. It's cast-iron. It would take too long to tell you why. You'll just have to take my word for it. Van Meert's threatening to put out a correction if we don't get a confirmation. Can you help?'

I could hear the explosive hiss at the other end.

'What the hell do you think we've been doing all day? We've been trying every hour on the hour. Alvarez is apparently on his yacht somewhere in the South Atlantic - out of contact, or so they say. And no one else at CMG is prepared to make a statement. What else can we do? Sorry, partner, no dice.'

The line went dead as Christina banged down the receiver.

I looked at my watch. Ten minutes left. Maybe Southgate would still be in his office. A statement from Southgate might not be as authoritative as a statement from CMG confirming the find, but it was better than nothing.

Luckily, Graham Southgate was still at his desk. I quickly explained the problem. 'I believe the story holds up,' I said. 'Strictly copperplate. But the powers that be here at Reuters want confirmation.'

There was a nasty pause the other end. Some instinct told me that this wasn't going to be as easy as I had hoped. The trouble with academics in my experience is that they hate clear unqualified statements which can later be held against them. I guess there's nothing worse than being sniggered at in the senior common room.

I pressed on regardless. 'It's just a matter of confirming the existence of a major deposit of high-grade falconite in Brazil,' I said, 'based on the Gondwana hypothesis.'

'My dear Charles,' I felt sure I could hear Southgate tamping the tobacco in that ghastly pipe of his, 'the Gondwana hypothesis, as you call it, might lead one to expect the presence of certain minerals in the eastern regions of Brazil, but that could certainly not be taken by itself as a positive indication of a substantial find of falconite. No indeed. Sorry, Charles, I must run. Professor Kalinin is my guest at high table tonight. He's already waiting for me. You remember Kalinin, don't you?'

This time it was I who slammed down the receiver. I felt as though I had been punched in the gut by a giant fist. What a pompous fucker. And what an almighty liar too! I tried to remember word-for-word the conversation I had had with Southgate the previous day in Cambridge. Surely he had confirmed the existence of the falconite deposit? Or had I got it wrong? Horribly wrong.

I was still sitting there wondering whom to call next when the internal phone rang. It was Arne. 'Look at the screen,' he said. 'There's a message coming in from São Paulo.'

As Arne spoke, I located the message. It was from Christina in the Reuters São Paulo office. While I was talking to Southgate she must have been beavering away trying to help out in spite of her protestations of righteous anger. Good old Christina I thought, massively relieved.

'*1412 hours São Paulo*,' I read. '*Compagnia Minas Gerais officials say they will be making statement at 1500 hours local time.*

Though no indication has so far been given as to the nature of the statement, market here expects CMG to confirm major minerals find. Meanwhile hectic trading in CMG and other shares continues in Saõ Paulo and other South American markets, with CMG equities hitting new highs.'

I read the text on the screen in front of me with a mounting sense of relief. In all my professional career, I had seldom felt so exposed, so vulnerable.

'Thank God for that,' I murmured to myself. I pulled a handkerchief from my pocket and wiped the sweat from my brow.

By 7.55 p.m. London time - 2.55 p.m. São Paulo time - the whole news room was on tenterhooks waiting for CMG's announcement. Half-a-dozen reporters, myself included, drifted into van Meert's office and clustered round his screen. There was a palpable sense of crisis in the air. If my own professional reputation was on the line, so too was Reuters'. Though the story had gone out over my byline, it had still been issued with the full authority of Reuters behind it. And since - several hours later - no correction had been published, the markets were entitled to conclude that Reuters still stood by the account I had provided. Reuters did not risk its reputation lightly.

That said, I noticed a couple of surprised glances aimed in my general direction from one or two of my colleagues and I understood why. If one thing is drummed into a Reuters journalist time and time again it is: be objective and verify the facts. If you are going to print a rumour, make sure it is labelled a rumour.

In my heart of hearts I realised I had been pushing at the edges of the envelope when I wrote the CMG story the way I had. I had treated my meetings with Alvarez and Southgate as confirmation of a minerals find because, frankly, I was convinced that's what the story was. Deep down I knew that if it hadn't been for Harry - and what had happened to him - I would never have strayed from the straight and narrow path of journalistic propriety.

Somewhere a clock struck eight. I found myself mopping the moisture from my brow.

Instinctively I joined the small group in van Meert's office. Though Reuters has a no-smoking rule on the seventh floor, van Meert himself lit a cigarette and a couple of my colleagues followed suit. I hadn't smoked for years, but when old Jo Symonds, the doyen of the Reuters news room, pulled out a pack of Marlboro and offered me one, I gladly accepted.

Arne had the São Paulo's equity box running next to the general news box. While most of my colleagues kept their eyes on the news box I watched the equities. As I saw it, whatever CMG said would move the markets. If CMG confirmed my story we would see a further rise in the CMG share price, as well as an increase in trading volumes. If I had got it wrong, the local São Paulo market, which certainly had its own direct links to the CMG press office, would react even before the Reuters São Paulo office ran the story. Reuters prided itself on being fast, but it wasn't that fast.

At precisely five minutes past three in the afternoon, Brazil time - five minutes past eight in the evening, London time - I watched the still rising CMG marker on the São Paulo equity screen make one last tiny lurch upwards before beginning to slip, first slowly, then quicker, then dramatically as a wave of selling hit the market. As I watched, shell-shocked, the news flashed up in pulsing red on the screen. '*CMG management totally denies any new minerals find in Minas Gerais.*'

I could feel the blood draining from my face and the bile mounting in my throat. I wanted to scream. I wanted to smash the screen. I wanted to run from the room, curl up in a corner somewhere and die.

But I didn't do any of that. Somehow I managed to remain preternaturally calm. Keeping half an eye on the still-plummeting price of stocks on BOVESPA, I read the full text of the report. '*Reached on his yacht this afternoon off the coast of Bahia, Admiral Antonio Francisco Alvarez, Chairman and CEO of CMG, this afternoon categorically denied that CMG had discovered any new miracle mineral in the Mata Atlantica rainforests of Minas Gerais. He attributed today's spectacular rise in CMG share prices on BOVESPA and other stock exchanges to unconfirmed and entirely speculative rumours emanating from Reuters' London office.*'

There was a pause and then the tape started running again. We were clearly reading the story in real time - in other words we were getting it just as Christina Markham, or whoever was on the desk in São Paulo, typed it in.

The delay was less than ten seconds long. Still outwardly calm, however much I was churning inside, I read the follow-up. '*BOVESPA authorities suspended trading in CMG stocks at 1515 hours local time.*'

Over in the equities box, I saw that CMG's price on the BOVESPA had fallen to, and was now frozen at, precisely the level it had started the day. Lesser volumes were still being traded on other exchanges, including New York, where CMG dealing shares had not been suspended, but here too share values were hovering at or around traditional levels.

I've never known Arne van Meert to turn off his screen during the course of a working day. Normally it's the last thing he does at night, and even then you can sense he just hates to flick the switch.

He'll stand there, briefcase in hand and ludicrous porkpie hat on his head, staring at his beloved boxes for one last time like some teenage girl saying goodbye to her lover on a station platform. But tonight, right in the thick of the action, he hit the button hard so that the screen flared and went blank. Then he swivelled round in his chair to face me. He didn't bother to get up.

'You're fired, Hodson,' he said. 'Clear your desk now. And don't come back.'

I couldn't believe what I was hearing. There have to be rules about this kind of thing, I said to myself. You can't throw a chap out just because he gets it wrong once in his life. I looked at the faces of my colleagues, hoping to find sympathy and understanding or at least some sense of solidarity. On the whole I get on fairly well with my colleagues. I'm not a hail-fellow well-met kind of guy but we are all friendly enough in the office or out on the beat.

I knew I'd lost when I saw them turn away. They may not have agreed with Arne's way of running the office, and I don't suppose they liked him any more than I did, but I could see from the expression on their faces, that they basically agreed with him. I had screwed up and I had to pay the price. It was as simple as that.

So in the end I didn't argue. There was no point in arguing. Deep down I knew if a firm like Reuters loses its good name it loses its most precious asset. Arne was right to fire me. If I had been sitting where he sat I would have done the same. That said, I can tell you I wanted to hit Arne full in the face, ram his teeth down his throat.

Mustering what dignity I could, I stubbed out the still smouldering cigarette and tossed the stub into the wastebin. Most of my colleagues had prudently slipped away when the crockery started to fly, but old Jo Symonds was still there - I guess he'll last us all out. I wasn't really sure whether the look on Jo's face was sympathy or stupefaction. But I shook his hand anyway as I left the room.

'Sorry, Jo,' I said. 'I guess I called that one wrong.'

'Sure did, son,' he said, shaking his head. 'Talk about the South Sea Bubble! Talk about Bre-Ex!'

'Clear out both of you,' Arne snapped. He swung through 180 degrees on his chair and switched his screen back on. 'You've got ten minutes.'

It took me less than ten minutes to clear my things. We don't work on the hot-desk principle at Reuters. On the whole you know where you're going to sit when you come in in the morning. Usually it's where you sat the previous day. But you're not encouraged to personalise your workstation or to clutter the area with a lot of bric-a-brac. I had some personal items in a desk drawer. Letters. A spare cheque book. An A-Z of London. That kind of thing. It didn't take long to sort that lot out.

I gathered all the debris together and stuffed it in a paper folder. As I did so, a photograph fell to the floor. I saw that it was a picture of Nasreen, taken ironically outside Trinity on the day she told me she was going to marry Harry. I'd kept it with me all those years.

I took one look at it, tore it up and threw it in the wastepaper basket. If I hadn't answered that telephone call from bloody Nasreen, I thought bitterly, I'd still have a job and a life ahead of me.

X

Luxembourg

I WAS UP early the next morning, well before seven a.m. I felt dazed, punch-drunk, unable to realise fully what had happened. One thing I did know was that since this was going to be the first day of the rest of my life I'd better get on with it.

My flat overlooks the Regent's Canal in one of its few salubrious phases. Instead of the usual flotsam and jetsam - dead dogs, rusty bedsteads, plastic containers and so on - the area is rather picturesque. Gaily painted houseboats, decorated with hanging flower baskets and pot plants, line the canal banks and the cast-iron railings have been newly painted.

Normally I'm rushing to make it to the office before some busybody like Arne van Meert starts making a note in his little black book. I don't really have time to admire the scenery. Now, I had all the time in the world. Or at least I thought I did.

I made myself a cup of tea, donned a tracksuit, did a few li bering up exercises and then set off at a trot along the car path until I came to the zoo. Just beyond the zoo, I turned off into Regent's Park, circled one of the football pitches a couple of times before shifting down a gear so as to power my way, more winded than I would have cared to admit, to the top of Primrose Hill.

There is something magical about Primrose Hill. You are less than a mile from Oxford Circus, yet you can see virtually the whole of London. A few years back, the dominant feature of the skyline would still have been the mighty dome of St Paul's cathedral. Now you can barely distinguish Wren's masterpiece. In its hectic determination to remain one of the great centres of the financial world London has thrust its tower blocks ever higher into the sky.

There was an old boy practising Tae Kwon Do at the summit of the hill. He slashed rhythmically at the air, then followed through with a couple of hefty kicks aimed at the distant skyline. He watched me panting up the last fifty yards of track.

'Great morning, isn't it now?' he called.

I didn't have enough puff left to disagree with him, but as far as I was concerned, it wasn't a great morning at all. What good was the best view in London when you were over forty, unemployed, with your professional reputation in tatters?

For a minute or two I stood with my hands on my hips next to the old martial arts fanatic, wondering what it was that kept him so full of pep and fizz. What did he use this carefully honed aggression for? Did he still put on a suit and head off to work each morning? An hour from now, would he be arriving, like so many thousands of others, at an office in the Barbican, or Broadgate, or Canary Wharf?

I didn't have any difficulty visualising the scene. After all, for the last ten years I had been one of that crowd. I might have bitched about it - the travelling, the long hours, the stuffy atmosphere in those air conditioned buildings, the office rivalry and the tittle-tattle - but, by God, it had provided a framework. It wasn't just the fact that you got a pay cheque at the end of the month, though that helped. It was the whole damn thing. Working with a firm like Reuters gave a structure to your life. Even the married men admitted that basically they were wedded to the job. For my part, the job in many ways *was* my life. I didn't have a wife and kids to go back to at the end of the day. I didn't have a partner, as they are called nowadays. After the bust-up with Nasreen, I had had a series of girlfriends, three or four at least, but nothing permanent, nothing you could even call steady. That was the way it was. Well, unemployment could give a whole new twist to the bachelor life. I could learn new skills. Like cooking. Like Tae Kwon Do, for example.

'How long did it take you to learn that stuff?' I asked my companion of the moment.

'About twenty years,' he said. 'Mind you, I've still got a long way to go before I get it right.' He released a quick backhand chop in the direction of the British Telecom tower. 'Never too late to start, mind.'

The postman had been by the time I returned to the flat. I picked the letters up from the mat and put them on the hall table without looking at them. After taking a shower, I squeezed myself some fresh orange juice, which I don't normally have time for, whipped up some scrambled eggs and bacon, and finally felt ready to take a look at the mail.

Most of the letters were standard everyday stuff. New offers of PC software, communications from estate agents saying the market was booming, and did I want to sell? An invitation to join the newly born Regent's Canal Cleanup Society. One item, however, took my eye. The envelope was of the heavy ivory variety.

There was no return address on the outside, but from the stamp and postmark I saw it had been mailed express the previous evening in Luxembourg with guaranteed next-day delivery.

There was a single sheet of paper inside, with the sender's name and address heavily embossed in black letters. 'Banque de Graaf,' I read. '16 Côte d'Eich, Luxembourg.' The message itself was brief.

'*Dear Mr Hodson,*

'*We have received a communication for you which we would hope to be able to discuss with you in person. Would it be possible for you to call in to see Mr Jan Visser at the above address at your convenience, preferably within the next two or three days? It would be helpful if you could let us know when you are likely to be here so we can make the necessary arrangements.*'

The signature was indecipherable, but the words '*Managing Director*' appeared as a subscript.

I poured myself a cup of coffee, spread butter and marmalade on the toast and took a couple of bites. Then, laying the toast on my plate and wiping my fingers on the napkin, I held the letter up to the light. There was no watermark, no other distinguishing characteristics as far as I could tell. By now, I have to admit, I was intrigued. I knew nobody in Luxembourg, certainly no bankers. Why should a Luxembourg bank have received a communication for or concerning me? What kind of communication?

I took the train that afternoon to Luxembourg. It seemed the only sensible thing to do. What more did I have to lose?

As far as I'm concerned, the opening of the Channel Tunnel has transformed the journey to the Continent. The Eurostar trains are fast and comfortable. You can sit back with a respectable bottle of wine and a tray of good food and watch life slide by at a high speed. The only minor annoyance is the constant announcements over the loudspeaker, usually repeated in two or three languages.

I felt particularly irritated by the Tannoy that afternoon. I needed a period of calm reflection if I was to sort out in my mind what had happened over the last few days. I didn't need to be advised every few minutes about the train's current location and speed or the availability of duty free purchases. In reality, of course, I doubt whether even the silence of a hermit's cave would have helped me much. As the train emerged from the tunnel at Calais and gathered speed across the plains of northern France, my mind kept on returning fruitlessly to the same question. How, with all my years of experience as a writer, had I misjudged a story so totally, so comprehensively?

Using my mobile phone, I rang the Banque de Graaf from the train soon after we left Lille. Jan Visser was not available but I left a message with his secretary to say that I expected to call on him at 10 a.m. the following morning.

When I arrived in Luxembourg, I checked into a hotel near the station, had dinner in the local brasserie and was in bed before midnight.

Luxembourg is one of those solid attractive little cities which you don't hear much about during the normal course of events but which somehow manages to exercise a disproportionate weight in world affairs. Partly this is to do with its membership of the European Union. Tiny Luxembourg's representatives confidently take their seat at EU meetings alongside heavyweight countries like Germany, France and Britain.

More importantly, Luxembourg's influence stems from the muscle it wields in Europe's financial affairs. You hear a lot about Swiss banks, you don't hear a lot about Luxembourg banks; yet the reality is that Luxembourg's banking sector is almost as rich and powerful, and certainly just as secretive, as its Swiss counterpart. The heavy stone buildings which line the Côte d'Eich, for example, with their thick wooden doors and discreet, highly-polished brass plates, look remarkably similar to the structures which line the Bergdorfstrasse in Zurich. They have the same air of bourgeois solidity. Politicians may come and go but bankers, at least those of the Swiss and Luxembourg variety, seem to go on for ever.

At precisely five minutes to ten I rang the bell outside the Banque de Graaf. A uniformed flunkey ushered me into a panelled, richly carpeted, waiting room. Almost immediately, a middle-aged well turned-out secretary emerged from a nearby office to inform me that Mr Visser would be available very soon. She took my coat and invited me to read the day's newspapers while I waited.

Both the *Financial Times* and the *Wall Street Journal* were still covering the CMG affair, as they had the previous day, though by now some of the steam appeared to have gone out of it. The FT reported on an inside page that the Brazilian Securities and Exchange Commission had rejected the call for a special enquiry into recent trading in CMG shares, though apparently some questions were still being asked about the methodology used to calculate the influence of individual share prices on the BOVESPA index in the light of recent events. The *Wall Street Journal*, in a diary column, dismissed the CMG affair as another example of the sensitivity of mining shares to unsubstantiated rumours, while praising CMG's management for their rapid efforts to set the record straight.

Mr Visser still hadn't made an appearance so I put the newspapers aside and picked up a glossy brochure from the coffee table. The Banque de Graaf, I read, had been incorporated in Luxembourg on August 16, 1991 with a share capital of 25 million US dollars. Its products and services, according to the brochure, included capital market, private banking and trade finance. Its stated purpose was 'to facilitate the approach to the Brazilian market as well as to other markets over the world with the efficiency you need'.

I riffled through the pages quickly. Under the section headed 'Private Banking', a series of bullet points indicated that the bank offered:

- call and time deposits in all convertible currencies
- sale, purchase and custody of securities
- fiduciary investments/loans
- secured loans and guarantees
- foreign exchange transactions.

Underneath, as a contact person, appeared the name of Mr Jan Visser together with a photograph of the gentleman in question. Just as I was examining the photograph, the door of the waiting room opened and the secretary reappeared.

'Mr Visser will see you now,' she said.

I followed her back into the hall, up a wide flight of stairs with large carved stone eagles at either side, to a spacious office on the first floor. The photograph which I had just inspected failed to capture the air of rich affability which Mr Visser exuded as he rose from behind his massive desk to shake my hand.

'Ah, Mr Hodson!' he beamed. 'How good of you to come so promptly. Did you have a good journey? You came by train, yes? The Channel Tunnel? What a difference that must make!'

Visser ushered me across the room to a conference table and for a few minutes we made polite conversation.

'Coffee perhaps?'

'Thank you,' I replied.

'Thank you "yes" or thank you "no"?'

By the time we had sorted that one out and had been served coffee in porcelain cups by yet another flunkey, Visser was ready to get on with the business in hand.

'I'm afraid I shall have to see some identification,' he said.

Puzzled, I produced my passport which he examined carefully before handing it back to me.

'What's this all about?' I tried, without success, to keep my sense of growing bewilderment out of my voice.

Visser tapped the outside of a large buff folder with a long manicured finger. Then, with slow deliberation, he opened it. There was only one document inside the folder, a single sheet of white paper on which I could see a brief typed message.

'What I have here,' Visser said, taking out the document, 'is a copy of the instructions my bank has received to pay you a certain sum of money.' He paused, then - as he handed the paper to me - continued. 'You will understand when you read this message why I was anxious to see you in person.'

I put the paper on the table in front of me and scrutinised it carefully. The message appeared to originate from Curaçao in the Netherlands Antilles. I noted the date and the time of the communication - October 30, 2000 hours. I glanced quickly at my watch to check. October 30 was last Tuesday, Black Tuesday as far as I was concerned, the day all hell broke loose on the Saõ Paulo stock exchange and I lost my job into the bargain. I tried to remember which time zone Curaçao was in. Was it the same as Saõ Paulo, Brazil? I thought so, but I wasn't sure.

I looked at the text of the message itself.

'*Please pay the sum of one hundred thousand pounds sterling to Mr Charles Hodson on production of satisfactory identification. Signed Cornelius Brokke, Managing Director, MinFin Holdings NV, Curaçao.'*

It's hard to describe the shock I experienced on reading those few lines. What got to me was the sheer size of the sum involved. I know that nowadays millionaires can be numbered in their thousands and that even billionaires are not uncommon. I know that in the City people trade in seven figure sums without batting an eyelid and at the end of the year pocket bonuses which most of us wouldn't earn in decades of hard slog. But frankly, I'm not in that league. For me, a hundred thousand pounds is a great deal of money.

'Are you feeling all right, Mr Hodson?' Visser sounded solicitous.

I found it hard to speak. There was still too much I didn't understand, too much to be explained. I wasn't even sure that I wanted to know.

I took a deep breath, trying to stay calm. I hoped I managed to sound nonchalant, like your average run-of-the-mill client engaged on a run-of-the-mill banking transaction.

'I wouldn't mind knowing more of the background,' I said.

'Background?' Visser raised an enquiring eyebrow.

'Who is Mr Cornelius Brokke?' I asked. 'What is MinFin Holdings? Why the Netherlands Antilles?'

Visser froze visibly. 'As you can imagine, I am not at liberty to discuss a client's affairs. We act for MinFin Holdings, which has been properly incorporated in the Netherlands Antilles. Mr Brokke is known to us as the responsible officer of the company and the instructions are fully authenticated.'

'Authenticated how?' I asked sharply.

'All of our clients have agreed codes for communication with the bank. As I say,' Visser repeated, 'we have no doubt at all of the validity of the transfer instructions. What we need to know now, Mr Hodson, is how you wish us to proceed. Shall we prepare a banker's draft? Would you like us to arrange an onward transfer of funds?'

Visser paused and smiled ingratiatingly at me across the table. 'Or perhaps you would like to think about it for a while. We would be happy to hold the funds on deposit, or even to invest them for you, while you make up your mind. We would need your signature of course on the necessary authorisation.'

Visser glanced quickly in the direction of his desk. I had no doubt that he had the papers already prepared and that it would be the work of a moment for me to sign them. But still I hesitated. I am not a naturally suspicious person. I don't on the whole look gift-horses in the mouth and I certainly don't kick them in the teeth. But I'm not ready to see one hundred thousand pounds transferred into my bank account without making an effort to find out where the money is coming from and the reason it is being paid.

'I'd like to get in touch with Mr Brokke in person,' I said at last, trying to sound businesslike. 'Do you have his address?'

'Of course.' Visser clearly knew the MinFin address in Curaçao by heart. He wrote it down for me on a piece of paper.

'And the money?' he asked.

'Ah yes, the money. Please keep it here on deposit. I think that's the best thing for the moment.'

As far as Visser was concerned, I had obviously given the right response. There's nothing a Luxembourg banker likes better, I imagined, than handling someone's nest egg. I had little doubt that my one hundred thousand pounds (I admit I was already thinking of it as my money) would be reinvested by the bank at a tidy profit for Mr Visser and his colleagues.

'We will open an account for you at once,' he said. 'We have the strictest rules, of course, about revealing the identity of our clients or any other information. Many people don't realise it,' - again he smiled ingratiatingly - 'but Luxembourg's banking laws are even tighter than Switzerland's.'

'I expect there are quite a few who *do* realise that, Mr Visser,' I said quietly, 'otherwise you wouldn't be here.'

For a second, the smile left his face, as though I had committed some grave breach of etiquette in hinting, however obliquely, that not all the reasons for holding numbered accounts in Luxembourg were wholly kosher.

He stood up abruptly. 'I will prepare the necessary document at once, Mr Hodson. We shall need your signature for the record and you will receive other relevant information.'

By the time I left the Banque de Graaf half-an-hour later I was the proud possessor of a numbered Luxembourg bank account. My identity, so Mr Visser assured me, was known only to himself and one other duly authorised official. Neither he nor any other employee of the bank were allowed by law to divulge my name - or the details of any financial transactions - to a third party.

As the heavy door of the Banque de Graaf closed behind me I took a deep lungful of the crisp November air. The sky was clear and bright. The sun shone. Across the ravine the ramparts of Luxembourg's famous castle soared majestically. As I stood there, absorbing the scene, I felt like doing a victory dance and shouting war whoops from the rooftops. One minute I'm an unemployed journalist whose prospects of finding another job look seriously bleak. The next, out of the blue, I'm sitting on a personal pension fund worth a hundred thousand, with interest clocking up by the hour.

As I say, I wanted to let rip, but something held me back. In retrospect I guess I had had my doubts the moment I opened the letter from Visser back in my London flat. I probably scented something fishy even then. My suspicions had grown minute by minute during the morning interview with the oily and obsequious banker. Should I have held up my hand and said, 'No thank you very much. I want no part of this?' Should I have told Visser to send the money back where it came from?

Perhaps I should have done just that. Heaven knows, it's easy to be wise after the event. In self-defence, I can honestly say that it was curiosity, not greed, which brought me to Luxembourg that morning. I genuinely believed - at the time at least - that I could walk through the mud without getting it on my boots.

XI

Willemstad, Curaçao I

I REACHED ZURICH in time to catch the evening plane to Miami with an onward connection to Curaçao. On the long flight west I tried to make some sense out of recent events, but failed dismally. If answers were to be found, I felt sure they would be found in Curaçao. MinFin Holdings NV was obviously a real company, at least in the legal sense. And Cornelius Brokke was apparently its authorised representative. Brokke had sent me the cheque. Brokke, whoever he might be, could tell me in person what the cheque was for.

Willemstad is the capital of Curaçao. It has grown up around Curaçao's natural harbour, a narrow channel deep enough to allow even the largest ships to dock in safety. The Dutch, the English and the French have all battled for control of the town over the centuries, largely because of its strategic value. Today, of course, the Netherlands Antilles in general - and Curaçao in particular - is famed mainly as a tax haven, a place where companies can be legally based with the minimum of interference by the authorities. As long as you pay the incorporation expenses, the annual management fee, and a tiny withholding tax, you can lie back and enjoy the sunshine and the sea air without any other cares in the world.

After checking in to a hotel on the front, I went looking for MinFin Holdings NV. The address Visser had given me was J B Gosiraweg 36, a pleasant street set back from the harbour and lined with a mixture of old Dutch colonial buildings and more modern concrete constructions. Number 36 was a new block, five stories high, almost a skyscraper by Willemstad standards. The foyer was clean and bare, with no visible occupants. A noticeboard beside the lift listed the companies which, notionally at least, had their world headquarters in the building. There must have been over a hundred of them.

MinFin Holdings, so the board told me, was on the fourth floor. Room 406 to be precise. I didn't expect to find the lift working, but it was. A few moments later I walked along the corridor and stopped in front of a door labelled 'Cornelius Brokke'.

I knocked at the door.

'Come in.' There was something familiar about the voice.

I opened the door and went in. Cornelius Brokke was sitting in a chair behind his desk. He had his back to me and appeared to be staring out of the window at the yachts in the harbour. When he heard me enter, he swivelled round and placed the cigar he had been smoking in an ashtray.

The man walked round the desk with his hand held out in greeting. 'Hello Charles,' he said. 'I wondered how long it would take you to get here.'

I now know what people mean when they speak of seeing a ghost. That's how I felt then. It was the weirdest experience you can imagine. Here was someone I'd given up for dead walking towards me with outstretched palm and a self-satisfied smirk on his face. Every feature was familiar. I knew him as well as I knew my own brother. It *was* my own brother. Of course, the passage of time had had its impact. When you haven't seen someone for ten years, you notice the changes - the deepening of the lines about the mouth, the thinning of the hair, the slight thickening of the neck. But on the fundamental issue of identity - was this man Harry Hodson or not? - no mistake was possible.

'Harry!' I gasped at last. 'What the hell are you doing here?'

It's hard to describe my emotions at that moment. On the one hand, I experienced a sense of overwhelming relief. That which was lost was found. Harry was safe. The man was my own kith and kin after all. We had grown up together, been to school and university together, had friends and - yes - a fiancée in common. You can't write all that off. And yet, at the same time, I felt a sense of revulsion. Whatever else I knew or didn't know, it was clear to me that Harry yet again had been playing games. Looking at my brother's sleek, debonair appearance - his natty tropical suit and brightly coloured tie, his bronzed face and trim haircut - I realised at once that this was not a man who had somehow miraculously managed to survive weeks in the forest living off nuts and berries. I found myself doubting whether he had ever been in the forest at all, apart from parking his car for us to find so conveniently in that benighted clearing.

'Harry,' I repeated - and I didn't even try to keep the note of bitterness out of my voice - 'I need to know why you're here. And why I am too.'

Harry, as long as I have known him, has always had a sense of fun, of drama. He could always milk an occasion for what it was worth, and this was no exception.

'Don't let's talk here,' he said. 'I've booked a table at *The Clipper.* Best restaurant on the harbour. It's the least I could do after bringing you all this way.'

I realised then that Harry completely failed to recognise just how appalling his behaviour had been. He had put us through the wringer and I don't think he cared. He had apparently got what he wanted and that was enough. The fact that Nasreen had endured the mental agony of believing he was dead, the fact that I myself had spent days on a wild goose chase looking for him, were for him wholly nugatory considerations.

I was so angry that I almost walked out then and there. Whatever scam he might have been up to, I didn't want to know about it. And I wasn't just angry. I felt used and humiliated as well. When I thought of the miles I had trekked through that fucking forest wondering whether the termites were already gnawing Harry's bones white; when I relived my conversation with Alvarez and realised just what a patsy I must have seemed; when I thought of the deeply-flawed story about CMG I had filed, I found myself blushing to the roots of my hair.

'Jesus Christ, Harry!' I shouted, giving full rein to my anger. 'Why did you do this to me?'

'Calm down, Charles.' Harry smiled his wide innocent smile. 'For heaven's sake calm down. I'll explain everything.'

If there'd been a plane back to Miami that afternoon I think I would have caught it. But I knew the next flight out of Willemstad didn't leave until the following morning. I'd been on the road for ever, or so it seemed. Plus lunch at *The Clipper* sounded like a nice idea.

'You had better bloody explain, Harry.' I sounded - and meant to sound - menacing. 'And it'd better be good. Otherwise, I'm out of here and that's the last you'll see of me. Period. I mean it. We're finished.'

He put his hand on my arm. 'Have a drink first, Charles. Things will look better after you've had a drink.'

He did the talking over lunch. I did the listening. I watched him carefully as he spoke, analysing the changes in his appearance. Harry's face was fuller, coarser somehow than when I last saw him; his blonde hair was beginning to go grey around the edges. He laughed a lot - he had always laughed a lot. But behind the laughter I detected a slightly frantic tone.

'Frankly, Charles,' he said, leaning across the table to pour himself another glass of wine. 'I was literally on my uppers. Nasreen and I were broke. We couldn't even afford the rent on our apartment. I simply wasn't hacking it. Brazil is full of minerals dealers and fine gemstone consultants. They didn't need another one. Certainly not a Brit. And not me anyway. The reality was I had to make money fast. Lots of it. Otherwise it was back to Blighty and a life of poverty for both of us.' Harry shuddered as he envisaged the prospect of having to return to England with his tail between his legs. 'God, I hate England,' he added in parenthesis. 'Ghastly, grimy little place.'

'Get on with it, Harry,' I said sharply. For the time being, at least, I was conscious of my moral superiority.

'Sorry, Charles. Don't mean to digress. Where was I?'

'In Rio. Broke.'

'Exactly. More than broke. Seriously in debt. In fact likely to go to a debtors' prison, and I can tell you in Brazil that's no joke. You tend not to come out alive. Of course, I might not even have made it to prison. There were people out there looking for me whose habit is to shoot first and ask questions later. I bought a gun to keep in the flat. For self protection. We even took shooting lessons at the Rio Gun Club. As a matter of fact, Nasreen turned out to be a natural. She could shoot the pips out of the three of spades at twenty five yards. But none of that was much help really. Those people could get you anywhere if they wanted to. In the car, in the office, on the beach, even in prison . . .'

'So what was the scam, Harry?' I interrupted icily.

'You were, Charles. You were the scam.'

'You'd better explain.'

It took him the best part of a second bottle of wine - a fine Chilean red as I recall - to go through the whole thing and by the time he had finished I don't think I'd ever been so angry in my life.

I wanted to shout and scream and hurl things about the room, but we were in a public place so I contented myself by hissing furiously, 'Let me get this straight. I want to be sure I understand it all. You and Alvarez were in on it. Was Nasreen in on it to?'

Harry looked me in the eye as he answered and I was pretty sure that, for once, he was telling the truth. 'No, Nasreen wasn't in on it. She had to believe I was dead. If she hadn't believed I was dead or dying, truly believed it, she would never have convinced you to come and look for me.'

'What gave you the idea of using me in this way?' I asked.

Harry shrugged. 'It's been done before. Journalists have been used to influence share prices. Ivan Boesky made 80 million US dollars once planting a story in the newspapers about an upcoming merger. And the way that phoney gold strike in Indonesia - Bre-Ex was the company, wasn't it? - was written up in the press, with the fake gold assays and so on, probably earned someone ten times as much as that. The journalist doesn't need to know he's being used. In fact, he mustn't know. Otherwise it's illegal.' He laughed, as though he found the idea of doing something illegal rather funny.

'You're such a shit, Harry,' I said quietly.

I sat there in silence for a while after that, inwardly seething. I could see now clearly, oh so clearly, what had happened. As a Reuters journalist, I had been in a key position. Reuters stories have triple A ratings. They move markets. No question of that. That's why we're trained to be so bloody careful about what we write.

Once again, I found myself blushing with shame and anger. 'Couldn't Alvarez be indicted for insider trading?' I asked at last.

'In Brazil?' Harry scoffed. 'You must be joking. Besides,' he went on, 'Alvarez never asked you to write the story. You put two and two together and came up with five.'

'What about the falconite in Alvarez's office?'

'What about it?'

'Was it real or not?'

'Of course not. Alvarez just stuck a label saying "falconite" on a suitable rock and made sure you saw it.'

'And the geological map in the museum at Ouro Preto, was that phoney as well?'

'No, that was real enough. As a matter of fact, that geological survey in the museum at Ouro Preto was what gave me the idea for the whole business in the first place. I'd been to Ouro Preto a couple of months earlier and I had actually visited the museum. I said to myself, "what if there's an amazing new find somewhere, in this mineral-rich zone? What if there are some rare animals in precisely the area where a mineral company would need to destroy the forest? What if a journalist wrote a story and unwittingly puffed the share price of the company?" I got thinking and one thing led to another. I knew you would follow me to Ouro Preto. I knew you would meet Gloria. She took you to the museum, didn't she? Rather a stunner, don't you think?'

I wanted to punch him, to wipe the grin off his face, but I managed to restrain myself. There were still too many things I needed to understand. I can't remember who it was - a Frenchman, I think - who said 'to understand all is to forgive all'. That certainly wasn't the way I felt. I needed to understand, yes. But forgiveness at that particular moment in time was a long way from my mind.

'So you suborned Gloria too, did you?'

'Not suborned, Charles. Certainly not. Gloria is an old friend. I met her years ago, before she went to the university up there. Her father and I used to do business together. I knew she was working part-time at the hotel. She was only too happy to help. I simply told her you'd probably be along in a few days and that you might want to visit the museum. I've never been to bed with her, by the way, if that's what you're thinking.'

'I suppose we should be grateful for small mercies, then,' I said sarcastically.

'Oh come on now, Charles.' Harry leaned across the table. 'It's not such a disaster, is it? You acted in good faith as a competent professional journalist. You had all the elements of a terrific story and you wrote that story as you saw it. Any other journalist would have done the same. You have nothing to reproach yourself with. You genuinely believed that CMG had made a major minerals find. That belief sprang, in part at least, from your assumption that I had met a sticky end in the forest.' He smiled. 'I have to admit you picked up all the clues absolutely brilliantly. You found the reference to Oliveira's home page on the Internet. You tracked down Oliveira himself, as I knew you would.'

'So Oliveira was part of the scam as well?'

''Fraid so. We had fun, as you can imagine, constructing that particular website. As a matter of fact, Oliveira is convinced there could actually be tamarin in that part of the rain forest, but I'm afraid it may be wishful thinking. The habitat of the golden-headed lion tamarin is down to less than two percent of its original size. I don't believe there have been any clear sightings, either there or anywhere near. But that's not the point. The main thing was that you believed in the tamarin angle. That was vital. I wanted to build up the story, the motive, don't you see? You had to be convinced that I had been murdered.'

'So Harry Hodson, the brave eco-warrior helping out the locals, is a fiction too, is it?' I couldn't help adding a dig of my own. 'I must say I was a bit surprised by that aspect. You'd never shown much interest in wildlife before to the best of my knowledge, except for the hunting, shooting and fishing aspects.'

'*Touché*, old boy,' Harry laughed. 'You're dead right there. I knew you might have your suspicions; that's why I involved Oliveira. Oliveira is a rich man, of course. You will have seen that, but he's genuinely interested in ecology and SOS Mata Atlantica is a genuine organisation. Oliveira and I met up years ago, when I first arrived in Brazil. He was quite ready to help. He and Alvarez led you on and then Southgate clinched matters.'

'Southgate? Graham Southgate? Christ, Harry, you disgust me. Are you telling me that Southgate was in on this too. I'll, I'll . . .' I was speechless with indignation.

'Don't blame Graham. I talked him into it. I picked up a reference on the Internet to some article he had written about falconite, a super-rare mineral Scott was supposed to have discovered in Antarctica and I flew over to England to see him. We worked out the details over a long boozy lunch in the King's Head. Southgate clinched it in your mind, didn't he, with that Gondwana business and his explanation of how a rare mineral configuration found by Scott in Antarctica might, in fact, plausibly be replicated in Brazil. And, of course, the link with global warming was tremendously helpful. It meant that falconite would have a vital role as a climate modifier and on that basis would be of almost incalculable value to mankind.' Harry chuckled. 'I remember him soon after he got the fellowship at Churchill. He was complaining then about how difficult it was to live on an academic's salary. And it hasn't got any better since or so he said.'

I didn't want to think about Graham Southgate. I didn't want to believe that a man of honour - or so I saw him - would be contaminated by Harry's dirty tricks.

'Did you pay Southgate, too,' I fumed, 'as well as Oliveira, or did you just offer them a piece of the action?'

Harry took offence at that. 'I don't like your tone, Charles. As you know, Graham and I are old friends. He got me into the minerals business in the first place when I came down from Cambridge. I simply asked him if he would have a chat with you. I never asked him to lie. And by the way, I don't think he *did* lie to you. Graham wouldn't do that.'

I was amused at how much concern Harry had for Graham Southgate's honour and how little he seemed to have for his own or mine for that matter. 'But still you paid him?' I persisted.

Harry ducked that one. 'We have made a contribution to his research,' he said rather grandly.

I still couldn't quite take in the sheer effrontery of the scam which Harry had perpetrated.

'Why didn't Alvarez officially contradict my story the moment it appeared? Why did he wait almost a whole day before putting out the denial?'

Harry smiled with patent insincerity. 'Oh, come now, Charles. We needed the time. Alvarez agreed that he would be on his yacht when your story appeared. Unreachable. In theory at least.'

I saw it all now. 'You mean you and Alvarez were both trading your pants off that day, weren't you? You both went long in CMG shares before the price rose and then, when the stock was at its peak and the official denial was coming, you sold them short. You made a killing both ways, didn't you - you and Alvarez. I understand now. God only knows why I didn't realise all along. If the authorities know what to look for they'll find a record of all your trades that day. You may think you've covered your tracks but they'll sort you out in the end.' I banged the table as I spoke, working myself up into a fit of righteous indignation.

Harry frowned at me across the table. 'Don't do this to me,' he warned quietly. 'And please don't underestimate your own part in this affair. Don't forget *you* filed the story. Not me. Not Alvarez. Your name is on the byline. Yours alone. Did you check with the Reuters office in São Paulo before you filed? Apparently not. Did you take any other steps to verify the information, apart from talking to Southgate? Again, apparently not. Your fingerprints are all over this one, Charles. If anyone is going to be done for insider trading, you are.'

'What the fuck do you mean?' I spluttered.

'Don't be naive,' Harry snapped. 'I've had reports on all your movements over the last couple of weeks. I know when you visited Oliveira and Alvarez, when you visited Cambridge. I knew when you visited Luxembourg too. And how do you think this will look when the Serious Fraud Office in the UK or its equivalent somewhere else starts to investigate?'

He pulled some sheets of paper from his breast pocket. One of them, I saw, was a copy of the letter which Jan Visser had sent me from Luxembourg a few days earlier. The others - still more damning - were copies of the papers I had signed at the Banque de Graaf the previous day instructing them to hold one hundred thousand pounds for me in a numbered account until further notice.

'These were faxed to me this morning,' Harry said. 'One of Mr Visser's assistants has been most obliging. Funny how leaky these places can sometimes be.'

After he was sure I had taken a good look at them, Harry slipped the papers back in his pocket. 'Well then, Charles,' he asked. 'Are you in or are you out?'

'You bastard,' I replied. 'You fucking bastard.'

Finally, I had had enough. I left him sitting there at the table and stormed off to my hotel. For an hour or more I lay on the bed in my hotel room, staring blankly at the ceiling. I felt as though I was being sucked down into a pit of molasses and there was nothing I could do about it. Eventually, however, sheer exhaustion set in and I drifted off into a deep and dreamless sleep.

I was still asleep when, hours later, the telephone rang. The room was dark. I turned the light on and looked at my watch. Half past seven. Christ, I had been asleep for hours!

I picked up the phone. 'Hello,' I said groggily.

'Charles, this is Harry. I'm downstairs in the lobby.'

'Go away, Harry. I don't want to talk to you.'

There was a pause the other end. Then Harry said, almost pleadingly, 'I've got a message from Nasreen for you. Come down and we'll talk.'

'Oh shit,' I said. 'OK, I'll be down.'

I met him in the bar twenty minutes later. He looked sober and contrite, a bottle of mineral water placed conspicuously in front of him as though to proclaim that, this once at least, he was going to keep off the booze.

I helped myself to a glass of Perrier and stared frostily at my younger brother.

'What did she say?' I asked.

'She said to tell you she's sorry she put you to so much trouble. She had absolutely no idea I was still alive. She said it was good to see you anyway in Rio.'

Harry's eyes narrowed as he spoke and I wondered for a second if he knew or guessed that I had slept with his wife a few days earlier. Then I put the thought from my mind. I felt convinced Nasreen would not have told him and I sure as hell wasn't going to. In a funny way, knowing what I did made me feel better. I had managed to even up the score.

'When did you tell Nasreen you were still alive, then?' I asked. 'I can't believe you waited till now.'

'I had to,' Harry replied. 'If you had had the slightest suspicion that the story of my disappearance wasn't kosher, you wouldn't have fallen for the scam. And if Nasreen herself hadn't believed it, you would have sensed it immediately. Nasreen's a woman of many qualities - we both know that - but she's not Sarah Bernhardt.'

'Did you call her collect?' I asked. ' "I have a call for you, Mrs Hodson. This is Harry Hodson, calling from Hades." '

Harry took a gulp of his mineral water. 'You can do better than that, Charles. What I said to Nasreen and when I said it is my business. I hope she understands that I did what I had to do, however painful it was for her. Please believe that.'

I didn't at that moment know what to believe. I was totally confused. Though I had not admitted it to myself, deep down I guess I had been hoping that when all the fuss to do with Harry's disappearance was over, Nasreen and I might get together again. I could envisage a situation where, Harry having been declared officially dead, Nasreen and I actually got married, thus completing the business which ten years earlier had been so rudely interrupted. The time we had spent in Rio together, particularly that last night, had seemed some kind of earnest of the future.

Now such hopes had been thrown out of the window. For the second time, Harry had managed to screw up my life and this time he had not limited himself to wreaking havoc in the personal life. He had destroyed my professional integrity as well.

What Nasreen must have made of it all I couldn't imagine. One moment she is grieving for a lost husband; the next he rings her from the Caribbean to say it's all a hoax. How could she live with a man who treated her like that? Whatever the motives which had led Harry to stage his extraordinary disappearing act, how could she ever forgive the personal hurt and distress he must have caused her?

Even if, at the emotional level, my life had once again been thrown into disarray, in other respects I was in much better shape after the few hours' sleep which I had had in the afternoon. The germ of an idea which had occurred to me when I visited Southgate in Cambridge had been quietly sprouting. The anger, the bitterness, the sense of revulsion which had gripped me during the course of my long lunchtime conversation with Harry had been replaced with a feeling of steely determination. I am not a religious person myself but I have heard people talk about experiencing sudden illuminations or sudden conversions and I think I can understand now what they mean. I decided that evening to get a grip on my life. I wasn't going to be mucked around by Harry any more. I wasn't going to be mucked around at all. Period. If there was any mucking around to be done, I was going to do it.

One of the practical consequences of this new attitude to life was that I was now able to look at my own situation clearly and objectively. Circumstances which the previous day seemed confused and threatening now seemed much less so. To put it succinctly, by the time I joined Harry downstairs I saw a way of emerging from the whole fiasco with my honour intact. And more.

'Harry,' I replied magnanimously, after he had made his plaintive little plea for my understanding and forgiveness. 'Only you and Nasreen can know what has passed between you. For my part, I'm ready to let bygones be bygones. Not least in view of some of the observations you made at lunch about my own apparent complicity in the business. It's my turn to talk now, if you're ready to listen. I've had an idea.'

I could see at once that my positive, almost jaunty tone took him by surprise. For the whole of his life, Harry had been used to being known as the star of the 'Hodson twins'. He was the one who had shone at school, at university; the gilded youth who had turned into the flamboyant and charming entrepreneur, while I was the careful plodder, moving step by step along a sad preordained career path with assignments in dull, worthy places like Bonn and Brussels. He was the one who had walked off with my wife-to-be simply by bending the crook of his little finger and saying 'here, girl, here' as a man might address a dog. It was as though there was some unwritten contract between us.

But that evening our roles were reversed, like the earth's magnetic poles doing their once-in-a-while flip-flop. I don't think Harry liked it much but he knew he had to listen anyway.

'Go ahead, Charles,' he said reluctantly.

I knew that if my plan succeeded, I would have achieved something of global importance, while Harry's sordid little scam would rate nothing more than a footnote in the history of the São Paulo stock exchange. So I ordered a bottle of champagne and poured us both a glass. After that, I started to explain to Harry what I had in mind. He, Harry, might think he had scored a coup with the CMG business, and of course he had if the evidence of a bulging bank balance was anything to go by. But my ambitions went far beyond commercial or financial gain although, realistically speaking, the practical rewards, if my plan succeeded, could be very large indeed.

'Far larger than anything *you've* ever contemplated, and I include in that the stunt you've just pulled off,' I told him smugly.

I lifted the glass of champagne to my lips. 'I'm going for the big one, Harry. Thanks to you, I've got time on my hands, no professional ties to bother me. Bye-bye Reuters. Thanks to you, I've got money in the bank. I've got the leeway I need. So I tell you, I'm ready to run with this one. Now you tell me something, my dear younger brother.' I fixed him with a beady eye. '*Are you ready too?*'

'What do you mean?'

'I don't know want to know how much money you made from the CMG affair. I'm not asking and I'm sure you're not telling. But what I do want to know, Harry, is are you ready to take the next step, this time with me in the driving seat?'

I don't think Harry much liked the idea of letting me do things my way for once. It put our relationship on a new footing. But I could see he was intrigued by what I had said.

'What the hell do you have in mind?' he asked.

'Falconite,' I replied quietly. 'The *real* deposit, not the pretend one. That's what I have in mind.'

XII

Willemstad, Curaçao II

'Harry,' I said, 'do you remember one evening ages ago, when we were still at Milborne School, they showed us the film *Scott of the Antarctic* with John Mills in the title role? Remember those shots of Scott's defeated band struggling back from the Pole through the blizzard?'

Harry nodded. 'Of course, I do. Great film.'

'Then do you remember at one point they find some rock samples and Scott insists on dragging the samples all the way back on the sledge at a time when both he and his men were faint with exhaustion, when they must surely have been desperately anxious to lighten, not add to, the load?'

When Harry nodded again, I drove my point home. 'That wasn't fiction. That was based on reality. We know Scott found the falconite on the Beardmore Glacier - Graham analysed the samples. What's more I think I know precisely *where* they found the mineral.'

It turned into a long evening. On the whole, I kept the initiative.

I think that Harry was impressed at the way I had thought it all out. He was certainly surprised.

'How do you know where to look?' he asked.

'The idea came to me when I was in Graham's office,' I replied. 'He was reading me a passage from Roland Huntford's book on Scott and Amundsen. Huntford makes it clear Scott collected the samples on his way back from the Pole, somewhere near Mount Buckley at the top of the Beardmore Glacier. Later that day Graham showed me the facsimile of Scott's diary in the Scott Polar Institute Museum. It occurred to me when I was looking at the diary that, just conceivably, Scott might have indicated where the samples were found and, if in fact, he had done so, that might be an extremely interesting piece of information.'

'Yes, indeed,' mused Harry. 'Most interesting. What did you do?'

'Graham invited me to dinner in college that evening. He went home to change, but since I had a room in college I had some time on my hands. So I went back to the museum at the end of the day, got the facsimile out of the exhibition case and studied it in detail. It wasn't difficult to work it out. Scott reached the Pole on January 17–18, 1912 and turned back again more less straight away. They reached the upper glacier depot on February 7. Huntford mentions Mount Buckley, which is at the top end of the Beardmore Glacier, so I knew I should be looking for an entry somewhere around February 8, 1912. And that's precisely where I found what I was looking for.'

I took a piece of paper from my pocket.

'This is what Scott wrote on that day. I copied it down word for word.' I read him the passage exactly as I had transcribed it.

' "***Thursday, February 8*** *- R 22. Height 6260. Start Temp -11°; Lunch Temp -5°; Supper, zero. 9.2 miles. Started from the depot rather late owing to weighing biscuit, etc., and rearranging matters. Had a* *blustry morning. Wind very strong and cold. Steered in for Mt Darwin to visit rock. Sent Bowers on, on ski, as Wilson can't wear his at present. He obtained several specimens, all of much the same type, a close-grained granite rock which weathers red. Hence the pink limestone. After he rejoined we skidded downhill pretty fast, leaders on ski, Oates and Wilson on foot alongside sledge - Evans detached. We lunched at 2 well down towards Mt Buckley, the wind half a gale and everybody very cold and cheerless. However, better things were to follow. We decided to steer for the moraine under Mt Buckley and, pulling with crampons, we crossed some very irregular steep slopes with big crevasses and slid down towards the rocks. The moraine was obviously so interesting that when we had advanced some miles and got out of the wind, I decided to camp and spend the rest of the day geologising. It has been extremely interesting. We found ourselves under perpendicular cliffs of Beacon sandstone, weathering rapidly and carrying veritable coal seams. From the last Wilson, with his sharp eyes, has picked several plant impressions, the last a piece of coal with beautifully traced leaves in layers, also some excellently preserved impressions of thick stems, showing cellular structure. In one place, we saw the cast of small waves on the sand. Tonight Bill has got a specimen of limestone with archeo-cyathus - the trouble is one cannot imagine where the stone comes from; it is evidently rare, as few specimens occur in the moraine. There is a good deal of pure white quartz. Altogether we have had a most interesting afternoon, and the relief of being out of the wind and in a warmer temperature is inexpressible."*'

When I had finished, Harry was silent for a while. Then he said, 'Fascinating, absolutely fascinating. What you have there, without doubt, is an account of how they found the rocks. But the February 8 entry doesn't give you the coordinates, the map reference, does it? Have you really got enough to go on?'

'I think we have. Scott writes that they started out that morning - February 8 - from the depôt. That's the Mount Darwin or Upper Glacier Depôt as the entry for the previous day makes clear. I agree with you that there are no geographical coordinates given in the February 8 entry for the Upper Glacier Depôt. Scott didn't bother with them *because he had already accurately noted the position of the Upper Glacier Depôt on the way up the glacier.* We know the precise location of the Upper Glacier Depôt and thus of the starting point for the march Scott and his men made that day.'

I took another piece of paper from my pocket.

'I copied these down,' I said 'from the diary entry for *Thursday December 21.*'

This time I passed the notes over to Harry.

' "***Thursday, December 21***",' he read. ' "*Camp 43. Lat. 85° 1′ Long. 163°4′. Height about 8000 feet. Upper Glacier Depôt - Temp. –2°...*" '

He studied the paper for a moment then handed it back.

'I think you've got it,' he said.

Harry insisted that I should call Southgate personally.

'Ask him to fax you the pages from the diary. Both entries. December 21 as well as February 8. I want to see them. You may not have written down the coordinates correctly. We can't afford to make a mistake.'

I wasn't sure at first that I wanted to call Southgate. I was feeling pretty sore about the way in which Southgate colluded with Harry.

But Harry insisted. 'We're going to need Graham,' he said. 'He knows Antartica, he knows the background. Hell, Graham analysed the falconite in the first place. It's not as though we're letting him in on a secret. And, anyway, we're going to need some sort of backing if this thing is going to get off the ground. Graham can open doors. He knows all the right people.'

We left it at that for the time being. While Harry went back to his hotel and - I suspected - a few more nightcaps, I turned in after arranging an early wakeup call. If I was going to talk to Southgate - and I hadn't finally decided - I wanted to do so as soon as he arrived in his office in Cambridge, which meant I would have to rise well before dawn Caribbean time.

When the bedside telephone rang and reception informed me that it was four-thirty a.m., I decided that Harry was right. At the very least, we had to be sure about those coordinates.

I hadn't spoken to Graham since that fateful evening when I telephoned him from my desk at Reuters seeking confirmation of my story of a massive falconite discovery in Brazil. He had not, to put it mildly, been altogether helpful then. If he had come through with a firm - and quotable - endorsement of my own version of events I might just have hung on to my job. But of course he hadn't been able to verify my tale of a new South American El Dorado based on rich deposits of falconite, because no such deposits existed. Not there anyway. Academics may indulge in a few terminological inexactitudes from time to time - like the rest of us they are only human. But on the whole they try not to lie. Like hell they don't!

Such are the wonders of modern technology that I was able to dial through to Cambridge direct from my hotel room.

'Good heavens!' Southgate exclaimed when he heard my voice.

I decided to forget about the strained circumstances of our last conversation. Southgate certainly knew that he had helped to land me in the deep doo-doo, as ex-US President George Bush so charmingly put it. He would have to live with his conscience even if I didn't remind him.

'Graham, good to hear you,' I said, accentuating the positive.

Over the next few minutes I told Southgate as much as I

thought he needed to know. I didn't tell him that I had been fired by Reuters. Instead, I tried to give the impression that I was still following the falconite story, in spite of getting my fingers badly burnt.

'I want to confirm the references in Scott's own journal. The one you have on display in the museum over there. Can you fax me a copy of the relevant pages, Graham?' I gave him the dates.

'I don't see why not.' Southgate sounded both puzzled and intrigued. 'Give me your fax number.'

I gave him the hotel's fax number and the telephone number too just to be on the safe side.

I thought he was going to hang up then, but I was wrong.

'What the hell are you really up to, Charles?' Southgate asked.

There are times when you have to make a judgement about people. Do you trust them or not? Deep down, in spite of his obvious collusion in Harry's nefarious schemes, I still believed in Southgate. If my plan was going to work I needed support, and Graham's help would be as good as any and better than most. Harry was right about that. Having Graham on board could make all the difference between success and failure.

I came at it in a roundabout way.

'Would I be correct,' I asked, 'in thinking that a mineral located by Scott in Antarctica over ninety years ago will still be there today?'

I don't think Southgate realised immediately what I was getting at, but he had clearly decided to humour me.

'Yes, you would,' he replied. 'Of course you can pick up a few geological samples here and there, as Scott did, but mineral exploitation in Antarctica is strictly forbidden under the terms of the Antarctic Treaty. So, yes, that deposit will still be there. No one could or would have removed it.'

'What if the future of the planet was at stake?' I asked. 'Would exploitation still be illegal?'

There was a long silence the other end. Then I heard Graham say, 'Oh my, we are getting into deep waters, aren't we?'

We talked for another twenty minutes at least. I told him what I knew already, although I didn't tell him how I had worked it out. I told him what I was planning. I told him I needed his help. I invited him to join us.

He wouldn't commit himself then and there. 'I'll call you back. I can see where you're coming from.'

'Can you see where I'm headed?'

'That too,' Southgate replied.

'Then you ought to know I'm serious,' I said quietly. 'Deadly serious. I'm going ahead with this anyway.'

'And Harry? He's with you, isn't he?'

I laughed. 'A Mr Cornelius Brokke, Managing Director of MinFin Holdings, Curaçao, is part of my team.'

Graham was amused by that. 'I shall look forward to meeting Mr Brokke in due course.'

Southgate was as good as his word. Twenty minutes after I had put the telephone down there was a knock on the door of my hotel room.

'Message for you, sir,' said the bellboy.

I took the envelope, thrust five dollars into the still-outstretched hands, unfolded the sheets of fax paper and spread them out on the desk.

I compared the text in front of me with my own transcription, noting with satisfaction that I appeared to have copied down the relevant entries in Scott's diary with one hundred percent accuracy. I checked the documents once, then checked them again just to make sure.

It was on the second read-through that I spotted the slight discrepancy. When I transcribed the journal entry for December 21, I had noted down the coordinates of the Upper Glacier Depot as being latitude 85°1", longitude 163°4", but the fax Southgate had just sent me which was an exact photocopy of Scott's manuscript entry gave the latitude as 85°7". In other words I had misread the last digit of one of the map references.

I have to admit I was puzzled. I don't usually make that kind of mistake, but this time I clearly had. To remove any shadow of doubt in my mind, I noted Scott had actually put a horizontal penstroke through the trunk of the seven as they do on the Continent.

'*Tiens!*' I exclaimed to myself as I stared at the fax. 'How did I miss that one?'

As I put the fax back in the envelope I reflected how fortunate it was that Harry had insisted on seeing the manuscript pages rather than my own transcription.

I was about to take a shower and order room service breakfast when the telephone rang again. Southgate's sudden change of tone surprised me.

'I can't say too much on the phone, Charles,' he said. 'This is a pretty sensitive area. We may have said too much already. I've been checking around since we last spoke. There are some things you ought to know.'

'What on earth . . . ?' I began to protest, but Southgate cut me short.

'I'm sending a message through now to your hotel. Make sure you grab the fax off the machine yourself so that no one else sees it. Then destroy it when you've read it.' He paused. 'We're not playing games any longer. You understand that, don't you?'

'I realise that, Graham,' I said quietly.

Five minutes later, I removed the single sheet of paper as it emerged from the fax machine downstairs, almost ripping it in half in my anxiety to read the message.

'*Meet me in the Upland Goose, Stanley, Thursday 12 noon,*' the message said. There was no signature, no header at the top of the page nor any other indication of the message's provenance. But I had not the slightest doubt that Graham Southgate had sent it.

'Presumably he means the Falklands?' I heard a voice behind me say.

I whirled round to find Harry standing there, reading the faxed message over my shoulder.

'I thought I would come and have breakfast with you. But I see you're up and about already. Won't you join me for coffee anyway?'

'Christ, you startled me,' I said.

'Oh dear,' Harry sighed insincerely. 'I seem to be making quite a habit of that. I'm so sorry.'

Over coffee, I told him about the telephone conversations I had had with Southgate earlier that day and showed him the fax from Scott's Diary which I had received less than an hour earlier. Before I could stop him, Harry called a waiter over and asked for some photocopies.

'Just to be on the safe side,' he said. 'Heaven knows, we might get split up again.'

When the waiter returned, Harry gave me back the original fax and put the copy in his pocket.

I hadn't expected to see Harry so early that morning but since he was there, I decided to make the most of the opportunity.

'We are going to have to charter a plane,' I said. 'We can pop down to Rio and then across to the Falklands.'

'Who's going to pay for it?'

'How about the Banque de Graaf?' I smiled but Harry knew

I was serious. The least he could do was bankroll the expedition. Compared with what Harry must have netted with the CMG scam, the sums involved were paltry.

To do him justice, Harry didn't hesitate.

'No problem about chartering,' he said. 'But I think we had better give Rio a miss. Much as I'd love to see Nasreen, that happy reunion may have to be delayed. And by the way,' he added, 'officially, I'm still dead.'

'So you'll be travelling under a false passport?'

'Harry Hodson's not the best handle to have at the moment.'

I didn't want to know too much about Harry's reasons for wanting to remain incognito. The fact that he had been reported dead, and wasn't, was clearly part of it. But I suspected that there was more to it than that. Harry had said as much. There could be some big beasts out there looking for my little brother.

'Anything you say,' I said. 'Perhaps I could take a look at your documents now, just to avoid surprises later?'

Harry fished inside the breast pocket of his natty white tropical suit and showed me his passport.

'Where's the real Mr Brokke?' I asked.

'Let's just say he's lending me his identity for a while.'

I checked the photo. The substitution looked perfect. The stamp was clearly professional. I couldn't help smiling. 'Harry, you're incorrigible.'

He shook his head and a wistful look came over his face, almost as though he wished he could, after all, have stuck to the straight and narrow. 'Needs must when the devil drives,' he said.

XIII

En route to the Falklands

WILLEMSTAD, CURAÇAO, BEING the kind of place it is, chartering a neat little Jet Cruiser with space for half a dozen passengers and fuel tanks large enough for the South American run was simplicity itself. Curaçao's main *raison d'être* is keeping rich men happy and, by most standards, we were rich.

Of course, even in Curaçao, you have to file a flight plan. And so we did: Caracas, Lima, Santiago, Stanley. It was the long way round, but it meant we missed out Brazil, which was what mattered.

'Brazil's so bloody large isn't it, when you look at the map?' Harry commented to the pilot, a forty-year-old American with a neat black moustache called Jack Irving, who both owned and flew the Jet Cruiser.

'It sure is, Mr Brokke,' said Irving. 'Certainly bigger than Holland.'

Harry winked at me. I could see he was enjoying his alias.

We arranged to leave at midday. Harry disappeared for an hour or so, telling me he had business to take care of. It didn't surprise me. Though MinFin Holdings NV was clearly a flag of convenience for Harry, even in Curaçao there were, I imagined, some minimal formalities to take care of when a company's managing director went walkabout.

At five minutes to twelve, Harry reappeared looking somewhat agitated.

'Anything wrong?' I asked.

'Actually, yes,' he replied. 'Nasreen hit the roof. She said that now that I was back in the land of the living she wanted me to come home. Or else. She sounded pretty fierce.'

Though I had never witnessed it at first hand, I could well imagine that Nasreen in a bad mood would be an impressive spectacle, something like a volcano erupting. Still, Harry's relationship with Nasreen was not my concern. Not at that moment anyway.

'You didn't tell her where we were going, did you?' I asked.

'Why on earth not?'

'We're playing for high stakes. We have to be vigilant.'

I noticed a look on Harry's face. A kind of naughty boy look.

'You trust me, old boy, don't you?' he smiled at me.

'Ah, Harry,' I sighed, 'I wish it were that simple.'

We had time to talk on the long flight south. Somewhere on the Caracas to Lima sector, I asked about Scarface. I felt bitter about Scarface. I told Harry what happened on the road from Belo Horizonte to Rio de Janeiro.

'You damn well nearly got me killed,' I said. 'Why did you do it?'

'I had nothing to do with that. Ask Alvarez, not me. Scarface, as you call him, must be one of Alvarez's heavies. I guess Alvarez wanted to demonstrate how rough CMG could play. Enhancing the storyline, that's how I see it.'

I wasn't certain I believed him. I was pretty sure now that Harry had worked out every last detail with Alvarez. On the other hand, though they had clearly decided to scare me, neither Harry nor Alvarez would have wished to see me killed in a car crash. That wouldn't have suited their plans at all. In fact, it would have scuppered them comprehensively since at that stage I still had to file my story and make them millionaires.

In the circumstances, I decided to give Harry the benefit of the doubt. I could come back to Scarface later, if I needed to.

Somewhere on the Lima to Santiago sector, with the snow-capped Andes on the port wing and the Pacific Ocean to starboard, I pressed Harry on some of the other details which still puzzled me.

'It's the timing I don't understand,' I said. 'How could you get the timing so pat?'

'What do you mean?'

We had a bottle of champagne in an ice bucket on the table in front of us. From time to time the agreeable Jack Irving put the plane on autopilot and came back into the cabin to check that we had everything else we needed by way of refreshments.

Before repeating my question, I topped up Harry's glass. I wasn't sure if I would ever get the answers I was looking for, but the present occasion seemed as favourable as any that was likely to occur in the foreseeable future. Loosen him up first, I decided. Get him talking. Keep him talking. Let one thing lead to another.

'I mean, how the hell did you know I was going to file my story precisely when I did file it? As I understand it, you and Alvarez built up huge long positions in CMG stock before the story appeared. How could you take the risk?'

'Watch it, Charles,' Harry looked warningly towards the cockpit.

Frankly, I doubted whether the pilot could hear our conversation, given that the cockpit door was closed. Nor did I believe that anyone had bugged the cabin since we had only decided at the last minute to charter a plane. But I took Harry's point.

I lowered my voice. 'I need to know, Harry. I think you owe it to me to tell me.'

Harry obviously wasn't keen to go into all the details. 'Graham Southgate called me the afternoon you saw him in Cambridge. While you were doing your detective work in the museum - brilliant, I admit - Graham went home to change. But before he did so, he picked up the telephone. That was part of the deal. He promised me he would do that. I made him go over the conversation he had with you. I knew you would file your story as soon as you got to the office the next morning. So we started buying straight away. That very afternoon. Remember the time difference was in our favour. New York was still open. So was Mexico City, Caracas, São Paulo. We bought up whatever CMG shares were to be had that day on the American exchanges. We even picked up some stock in the Far East overnight. Tokyo, Hong Kong, Singapore. I tell you, anywhere CMG stocks were trading, we were there waiting for them. We bloody well cornered the market, Charles.'

Harry drained his glass of champagne and poured himself another before continuing. 'And then you filed. I stayed up all night, as you can imagine. I had my eyes glued to the Reuters screen. I kept checking my watch. You came in bang on cue, 9.00 a.m. London time, 3.00 a.m. Curaçao. Of course you coded the story for the general news desk. I knew you'd do that. That's what you are. A general news reporter. Christ, if you had been specialising full time in financial news you might have smelt a rat. But you gave your piece a financial as well as a general news coding. For us that was vital. It ensured the markets took note. We even had an hour or two's good trading in London before the price explosion. Not that many CMG shares traded in London.'

Harry's face was beginning to look flushed and he pulled at his collar to loosen his tie. He looked at me with sudden suspicion.

'You're not wired, old boy, are you?'

I must admit that the idea of fitting myself up with a bugging device had fleetingly crossed my mind. I go to the movies too.

'Don't be absurd,' I said. 'I thought we had been over that. I don't approve of what you and Alvarez have done, Harry. Frankly I think it's criminal. Insider traders are criminals. But I'm not going to press the point now.'

Harry couldn't let it go at that. 'There was no insider trading. There was no insider knowledge. The only story was the story you invented. OK, it was a scam. But it wasn't insider trading.'

I seemed somehow to have hit a raw nerve. I could see that in his own mind, at least, Harry didn't really believe he had crossed the line. He appeared still to believe that what he and Alvarez had done was a prank, a scam, a caper - good clean fun which incidentally had netted both of them a fortune and provided comfortably for the hangers-on such as the Oliveiras and, I presumed, Harry's Brazilian secretary, Letitia. Maybe even that pretty young woman, Gloria Suarez, who worked in the hotel in Ouro Preto, had received a little sweetener. Tuition fees for the term at the University of Minas Gerais?

I tried to calm him down. 'For Christ's sake relax, Harry,' I said. 'I'm not raking over the past. As you have taken the trouble to point out, I'm implicated in this too. I just needed do know some of the details.' Suddenly Harry smiled at me, that bright winning smile that I remembered so well. 'Jesus, Charles,' he said. 'I thought you'd be pleased. You've been working your butt off for years. I thought you could use a hundred thousand pounds. As a matter of fact, I felt I owed it to you.'

Watch out, I said to myself. This could be paydirt. This could be the moment of truth.

I pretended I didn't understand. 'Owed it to me?'

'The business over Nasreen,' Harry said. 'She was going to marry you and then married me. We never talked about it.'

'We never had a chance,' I said.

'We have a chance now.'

I could have been wrong, but I thought I detected a hint of tears in Harry's eyes. 'I think the moment she married me,' he continued, half swallowing his words, 'she knew she had made a mistake. I don't know what she thought she saw in me, but whatever it was I think she realised quite soon she got it wrong.'

Fuck you, Harry, I thought. Don't do this to me. I didn't want to sympathise with the bastard.

'She didn't get it wrong,' I said, far more gently than I intended. 'Nasreen saw the brilliance and the gaiety. That's what counted.'

'Some brilliance, some gaiety,' Harry sniffed. 'There wasn't much that was brilliant or gay about our life in Rio I can tell you. We were stretched to the limit. And I was drinking too much. But that wasn't the problem.'

'What was the problem?'

For a moment, I thought Harry was going to draw back.

'Don't say anything you don't want to say,' I said. 'I don't need that. You don't need it either.'

I've never been quite sure how Harry's mental processes work.

He operates far more by intuition than I do. His reflexes are combative, mercurial.

'I'll tell you what the problem was,' he said, deciding after all to take the plunge. 'Not money. Nor the lack of it. Not my job. Not even bloody Brazil. We could have handled all that.' He looked me in the eye. 'The real problem, old boy, is that Nasreen, even after she married me, never stopped loving you. She never said so. But I knew. A chap can always tell these things.'

It's hard to describe what I felt at that moment. At one level, I felt an overpowering sense of relief. In the ten years that had elapsed since she went off with Harry I doubt if a day had passed without my thinking of Nasreen, without my missing her. There had been a gap, an aching void at the centre of my life. I had tried to fill it with work, with travel, with the hard grind of a professional career. Yes, I had tried to fill the gap, but deep down I knew that I had failed. To hear now from Harry that Nasreen still loved me was sweet indeed. And I needed to believe that when Nasreen that last night in Rio had taken me into her arms and into her bed, she had done it from the heart.

But at another level, I felt a sense of gloom and foreboding at the sheer complexity of it all. And that sense of feeling was compounded when Harry, visibly moved, confided, 'Christ knows, I want to give her what she needs. I've tried so bloody hard.'

I let him ramble on. He talked about how struck he had been the first time he met Nasreen, that evening in Trinity Great Court. About how, even when Nasreen and I were engaged, he couldn't leave her alone, kept pestering her with his attentions.

'I usually knew when you were seeing her, old boy. I made it my business to know. Once I followed you when you walked her back to Girton. She knew I was there, I could tell. I knew she would be waiting for you when you came out of your finals, so I made sure I was there too. You came out early and saw us then, of course, but it wasn't the first time. I didn't do it to hurt you, Charles.' His cheeks were moist. 'I did it because I loved her.'

I'm not sure I believed everything he said - Harry could spin a web of gossamer lies so fine you could be trapped even without noticing - but I believed a lot of it. In a strange way I found it comforting to believe that Nasreen's defection a decade earlier was not a capricious move on her part but an almost self-defensive reaction to Harry's overwhelming barrage.

'Truth to tell,' Harry burped as he spoke, 'I think she knew I wasn't going to give up. Even if she *had* married you, I was still a fact of life. I would have kept up the pressure. I think she realised it was better to surrender sooner rather than later.'

'Better for whom?' I asked icily. 'Better for her? Better for you? Or better for me?'

When there was no reply, I glanced across the aisle to see Harry had fallen into a deep sleep. His head had toppled back against the seat; his mouth was half open and he was snoring gently. The champagne glass was on the floor at his feet.

The pilot opened the cockpit door and poked his head into the cabin.

'Everything all right?'

'Everything's fine,' I replied, 'absolutely fine.'

XIV

Falklands I

THE RAIN STREAKED the windows of the plane as we flew in low over the West Falklands. From the air, the landscape reminded me of the Scottish highlands on a wet day. Bleak, barren, treeless, miserable. I caught a glimpse of a penguin colony on a rocky promontory. That was one difference: you don't get penguins in Scotland.

Harry was still out to the world, so I had time for my own thoughts. What was it, I wondered, that Britain had really fought for during that brief bloody Falklands campaign in the early eighties? Not these desolate uncluttered hills, surely. Not the wool produced by the handful of sheep stations dotted around the island with names that awoke echoes of the grim battles of the Falklands war: Darwin, Goose Green, Fitzroy and so on.

I doubted, frankly, whether the conventional political arguments were any more powerful. In the space of fifty years, Britain had rushed to give away an empire which encompassed at least a fifth of the human race. Were we really so exercised by the need to preserve the right of a handful of Falkland Islanders to self-determination? We hadn't bothered much about the people of Hong Kong, when we handed them back to China, and there were four million of them.

In my view, you had to look elsewhere. I had long believed there was one reason, and one reason only, why Margaret Thatcher decided to send the fleet south that fateful Saturday in August, 1982. *The Falkland Islands are Britain's gateway to Antarctica.*

Britain is one of the claimant nations to Antarctica. We have half a dozen bases down there in what we call British Antarctic Territory. And the vital supply point for the whole of Britain's Antarctic presence is the Falklands. Without the Falklands as a logistical hub, as a jumping off point to the south, Britain would have no Antarctic ambitions. It is as simple as that. The fact that Britain, at vast expense, has now constructed a spanking new airport outside Stanley only reinforces the point.

'Christ, Harry,' I exclaimed, as we came into land. 'Look at this bloody great airport.'

In truth, it wasn't so much an airport as a vast tarmac airstrip. The Mount Pleasant airfield might not be able to handle a jumbo 747, but it could certainly take your run-of-the-mill long-haul jet, your C130 or anything else RAF Transport command decided to throw at it. If the Argies ever tried it again, our men could be on the ground in less than eighteen hours.

Harry had some difficulty waking up.

'Oh God,' he groaned. 'Are we there already?'

We settled up with the pilot there and then. Harry had paid half the fee for the charter in advance. Before we disembarked, he gave Irving the rest, laboriously counting out hundred dollar bills onto the table in the cabin.

Some sixth sense had told me that it was a bad idea to arrive in a place like the Falklands without at the same time knowing how you were going to leave. I seemed to remember that a ship came out from Cardiff twice a year to pick up the wool. Or else you could try to persuade the RAF to run you back on a Hercules via Ascension. But we might need to do better than that.

'Just hang on till you hear from us, Jack,' I said. 'We'll contact you as soon as we can.'

I'm not quite sure how the authorities knew we were coming, but they did. As we walked into the little airport building, a uniformed officer stepped forward and saluted smartly.

'Mr Hodson, Mr Brokke? I'm Major Willoughby. James Willoughby. Good to have you with us. This way please, gentlemen.'

An army Land-Rover was waiting for us outside with its engine running. The driver put the vehicle into gear and set off at speed.

'It's fifteen miles to Port Stanley,' Major Willoughby informed us, removing his hat and smoothing back his sandy-coloured hair. 'This is one of the few stretches of tarmac in the whole island. Otherwise it's mainly sheep tracks across the bog.'

'How did you know when to expect us, Major?' Harry asked.

Major Willoughby laughed. 'Can't tell you that I'm afraid, sir. Let's just say we've tracked you down half of South America.'

The road to Stanley followed the coast. A few minutes after leaving the airport Willoughby pointed to a group of whitewashed houses clustered round the head of an inlet.

'That's Bluff Cove,' Willoughby said. 'That's where they blew up the *Tristram* and the *Sir Galahad*. Sitting ducks, they were. The Argies had spotters on Tumbledown Hill.'

I kept staring until we rounded a bend and the little hamlet dropped from sight. Men had died at Bluff Cove, I remembered. Many of them had been burned alive or hideously disfigured. Those men hadn't been playing a game. They had paid with their lives.

'Where are we going, Major?' I asked. 'Mr Brokke and I are expected at the Upland Goose by noon.'

Willoughby glanced at his watch. 'The Goose may have to wait, I'm afraid. We're going straight to Government House.'

'And Dr Southgate?' Since the Army appeared to know so much about us, I assumed they knew about Southgate as well.

'Dr Southgate is with the Governor now, sir,' Willoughby said.

'Ah, I see,' I said. As a matter of fact, I didn't see at all.

'Has he been here long?' I asked.

'Who?'

'The Governor.'

'The Governor is not a "he",' Major Willoughby said. 'The Governor is Dame Pauline Fairweather. No, she has not been here long. A couple of months only.'

The surface of the road degenerated noticeably when we reached the outskirts of Stanley, the small town that is the capital of the Falklands. As we clattered over the potholes I dredged through my mental card index. I seemed to recall that Pauline Fairweather had been number two in the British Embassy in Washington and then had returned home to chair the Joint Intelligence Committee. Now, she had reemerged in the Falklands. On the face of it, it was an odd assignment. There were several hundred thousand sheep in the Falklands and a few million penguins, but not much else. Did they really need to send a high flyer like Pauline Fairweather?

We rattled along the seafront, past West Store, the town's main shop, a monopoly still run as in past decades by the Falklands Island Company. We continued on, by the massive arch of whalebone erected in front of the cathedral, towards a large and graceful white house with a red roof and trim green lawn set on a low hill at the far end of the bay.

We swung up the hill and turned into the gravel drive. A London taxi, maroon in colour and with the royal crest emblazoned on the doors, was parked on the forecourt.

'The Governor's official transport,' Willoughby explained. 'Makes more sense than a Rolls.'

By now Harry looked as though he was well on the way to recovery. A couple of stiff ones, I thought, and he would be right as rain.

'I still think I'd prefer a Rolls,' said Harry, as we got out of the car.

We were ushered straight into a large room whose windows gave out on to the lawn at the side of the house. In the middle of the lawn, the Union Flag flew proudly on its pole. I recalled that after the invaders captured Stanley at the beginning of the Falklands conflict, an Argentinian flag had replaced the British one. When the British recaptured the islands, the first signal sent back to London had stated simply, 'The Union Jack flies once more over Stanley'.

I glanced briefly beyond the flag towards the harbour. It wasn't hard to imagine the tension and drama of the battle for Stanley and, indeed, for Government House itself.

While we were waiting, Major Willoughby explained.

'Normally, this is the diningroom, but the Governor uses it for conferences as well. The Argies fired from outside into the room. You can still see the holes in the walls.' He pointed to a line of holes over the glass-fronted sideboard.

'When Menéndez occupied the house, the Argies had dinner parties in this room.' Willoughby pointed to a splendid lifesize portrait of the Queen. 'They kept that portrait in place all the time they were here.'

The Major's exposé was interrupted by the entry of a handsome grey-haired woman of medium height followed by two men, both bearded. I recognised one of the beards immediately. It was a thick bushy affair, grey about the edges. Southgate looked me straight in the eye and gave an almost imperceptible nod of his head.

'Do sit down, gentlemen.'

Dame Pauline Fairweather took her seat at one end of the mahogany table beneath the portrait of the Queen. Graham and the other beard sat to her left, facing the window. Harry and I had our backs to the ocean. Willoughby placed himself at the foot of the table, directly opposite the Governor.

Dame Pauline glanced around the room. 'Perhaps we should all introduce ourselves.'

I was sitting to her immediate right, so when the Governor fixed me with her steely eye I said at once, 'My name is Charles Hodson, former Reuters journalist.' I gestured towards Harry. 'This is a Dutch colleague, Cornelius Brokke.'

'Welcome to you both.' Dame Pauline turned to the man on her immediate left. 'Mr Munro, why don't you tell us who you and your colleague are? Then we can get on with the business of today.'

Munro had a craggy weather-beaten look about him. His face - or at least those parts of it which were not covered with hair - was a deep red-brown colour of the kind induced by exposure to a combination of sunshine and strong biting winds.

'My name is Steve Munro.' He spoke with a pronounced Scottish burr, a bit like Sean Connery on an off day. 'I'm base commander of the BAS base at Rothera which, as you may know, is Britain's largest Antarctic establishment. BAS, of course, stands for the British Antarctic Survey. I flew up yesterday to meet you two gentlemen.'

The way Munro said it left me in no doubt that he was sceptical about the relevance of the instructions he had received, clearly at the last minute, to drop whatsoever he was doing and attend this hurriedly organised briefing.

'I believe you, Mr Hodson, already know Dr Southgate,' Munro continued.

'Yes, I do,' I said quietly. 'We have known each other for some time.'

I kicked Harry sharply under the table. Given his alias, I wasn't expecting Harry to remind the gathering that we had actually known Graham at Cambridge, but it was as well to be on the safe side.

Southgate, I noted, gave me the barest of nods when my name was mentioned, but otherwise kept his eyes firmly fixed on the horizon.

'Pray continue, Mr Munro,' Dame Pauline commanded.

I hadn't heard anyone use an expression like 'pray continue' for years but Munro took it in his stride.

'Thank you, Governor, I will,' Munro nodded gravely. 'We must all recognise,' he sounded almost resentful, 'that we owe Mr Hodson and Mr, er, Brokke, a debt of gratitude. Somehow it takes an idiot to see the obvious. No offence meant there, gentlemen.'

'Perhaps you should explain a little more clearly.' The Governor dropped her voice to a whisper, but it could still have sliced a penguin in half at a hundred paces.

Munro raised an eyebrow. 'May I take it that our visitors are cleared?'

Dame Pauline didn't answer that one directly. 'You may take it that you are authorised to undertake a full briefing, Mr Munro.'

'Thank you.'

Munro went on without further pause.

'When I say "we failed to explore the obvious," I mean quite simply that we failed to think of Scott's diaries and the clues they might contain. We are, of course, aware of Dr Southgate's work. We are aware of the potential significance of falconite in the battle against global warming. Down there in Antarctica we actually witness the effects of global warming on a day to day basis. We see the icesheets breaking up, the pack ice shrinking, the icefree areas expanding. So, yes, we knew about the vital importance of falconite as an ocean nutrient enhancer. But we have all been working on the assumption that for practical purposes falconite is simply not available. We failed, perhaps inexcusably, to look at the *historical* evidence. We failed to recognise that a viable falconite deposit was to be found right there under our very noses!'

Graham Southgate, speaking for the first time, interrupted. 'I don't think BAS should be too hard on itself. Let's face it. I'm the one who actually did the work on the samples Scott and his men brought back from the Beardmore Glacier. I wrote the piece in the *Journal of Geological Studies.* As far as I was concerned, I was just looking at some lumps of rock. I didn't, I admit, imagine that the precise coordinates of the find would be noted in Scott's diary. I never even looked for them then. It took a rank amateur to do that. I wish I had thought of it myself.'

Graham Southgate beamed in my direction and I felt the warm glow of satisfaction.

XV

Falklands II

While Southgate was speaking, Munro went over to the wall and pulled down a large map.

'What we have here,' he said, continuing with the briefing, 'is a map of the route of Scott's Southern Journey in 1911. As you can see, they had first to traverse the Great Barrier Ice Shelf, otherwise known as the Ross Ice Shelf, and the Transantarctic Mountains. Like Shackleton before him, Scott used the Beardmore Glacier as a way through the mountains and up to the Polar Plateau.'

He pulled down another chart. 'This is the detailed map of the Beardmore Glacier. The Beardmore is a great river of ice. In its most swiftly moving part, the flow is probably not more than three feet a day. The length of the Beardmore from Mount Hope at the base to Mount Darwin at the summit' - he flashed the pointer at the screen - 'is about one hundred miles. Its breadth varies from about eight miles near the bottom to twenty-five miles at the top. The slope of the glacier also varies considerably. It is steepest opposite Mount Buckley in latitude 85° South and opposite Mount Hope in about latitude 831/2° South.' Again he pointed.

'The Polar Plateau itself,' Munro continued, 'is at around 10,000 feet, so this is no mean climb for men on foot hauling sledges behind them.' Munro turned for a moment to face us. 'You have to remember, of course, that the Beardmore is frequently heavily crevassed. You should also remember that by the time they reached the entrance to the Beardmore, at a place called the Granite Pillars, the last of Scott's exhausted ponies had been shot. The motorised sledges had long since packed up. What got Scott and his team up the glacier was willpower and sheer muscle. Each four-man team at this point would have been dragging around five hundred pounds in supplies.'

I glanced quickly in Dame Pauline Fairweather's direction and could see at once that she was deeply absorbed in Munro's presentation.

'This is fascinating,' she said. 'Do go on.'

Munro pulled down one last map. 'What we have here,' he explained, 'is a large-scale map of the region at the head of the Beardmore Glacier. As you can see, both Mount Buckley and Mount Darwin project upwards through the ice and the glacier flows around them. Several other rocky outcrops, or nunataks, jut out of the ice in the general area and not all of these have been charted. Mount Buckley is, of course, mentioned by Scott as the area where Wilson and Bowers collected the geological samples from a nunatak. The trouble is: how do we find the nunatak we're looking for? We're talking about a pretty large area. We know the coordinates of the Upper Glacier depot which is where they began the march that day. Latitude 85.7, Longitude 164.4. But we can't be sure of the precise route they took.'

I noticed that Dame Pauline had left her seat and walked over to a bookshelf in the corner. She came back to the table with a large brown leather volume in her hand.

'Major Willoughby and I did a little research before this meeting,' she told us. 'I think we may be able to shed a little more light on the matter. As you can imagine, successive Governors have built up quite a good library here, particularly of Antarctic material. You know this volume, do you not, Mr Munro?'

Steve Munro walked down the room to take the book from her. 'I know it,' he said. 'This is a pretty rare volume. It's Frank Debenham's account of Scott's Antarctic Expedition, 1910–1913. Debenham was the expedition's geologist.'

'Exactly. But it's not Debenham's account which we're interested in, Mr Munro.' The Governor smiled complacently. It clearly amused her to be able to talk to these old Antarctic hands in their own language. 'Debenham, as you know, was not on the final polar party. That was limited to Wilson, Bowers, Oates, P.O. Evans and of course Scott himself. So Debenham never witnessed the descent of the Beardmore when Wilson and Bowers collected the samples. Why then do I think this volume could help us?'

Dame Pauline milked the suspense for what it was worth. She looked around and, seeing blank expressions on the faces of her audience, including even Munro, decided to answer her own question.

'This particular volume' - she held it up for all of us to see - 'was published in 1923 in London for the Committee of the Captain Scott Antarctic Fund. It contains reproductions, not only of some of the photographs taken by the Scott expedition but also of many of the actual drawings made by the expedition's naturalist at the time, E. A. Wilson. These drawings, like Scott's journals, were found with the bodies in the tent.'

I couldn't help looking at the woman with amazement. How much notice had she had of this particular briefing? More than Harry and I had, certainly. But how much? What feat of lateral thinking had led her to rummage through the bookcases to find this faded volume?

'Let's not be amateurs,' she said. 'You won't have much time up there on the glacier. You don't know what the weather's going to be like. Scott had to survive some fearful blizzards as I recall. You may get caught in a storm. Even if you don't, you will have to work under pressure. If I understand Mr Munro correctly, there are a lot of nunataks sticking up out of the ice around Mount Buckley. We have to find the right one quickly. That is where, I believe, this volume may be of some help.

'Major Willoughby,' she commanded imperially, 'can you bring out the epidiascope?'

I'm not sure when I last saw an epidiascope. In this computer age, when you tap out transparencies and overheads on your laptop and they come out of the printer complete with your own personalised logo, epidiascopes have gone out of fashion. But Willoughby jumped to it. He plugged in the big brass machine, looking a bit like the old harpoon gun mounted on the quay, while Munro rolled up the various charts and maps and pulled down instead a large white screen.

Willoughby reverently placed the book on the epidiascope. 'The beauty of this old-fashioned device,' he reminded us, 'is that you don't have to make a transparency. You just project the image in whatever form you have it.'

Of course, the first couple of photos came out back to front or upside down but Willoughby soon got the hang of it.

For the next fifteen minutes we sat there entranced. We were suddenly miraculously transported back into the great heroic era of Antarctic achievement. We were looking at the very photographs Scott and his men had taken as they set off up the Beardmore. Those photographs, I suspect, more than anything else, gave us a feel for what we were looking for. We knew, if we were to be successful, that we had to see the scene through Scott's eyes and we would never get closer than this.[36]

I suspected that Major Willoughby had prepared the presentation in advance. He rattled through the first photographs quite quickly.

'Here we have the party at the Gap, the entrance to the Beardmore. The photographs show the view looking south from the Ross Ice Shelf; in other words we're looking up the glacier. And here we see the Granite Pillars, with the Queen Alexandra Range behind. The expedition's tents are in the foreground. You can see the skis stuck in the snow. Bowers took this picture as well as the previous one.'

Image by image, Willoughby took us in the footsteps of Scott as the great explorer and his party climbed, slowly and painfully, up the great glacier towards the Polar Plateau. Plate 11, for example, showed the view looking east from Cloudmaker depot to the Commonwealth Range. Plate 14 showed the Cloudmaker itself.

'The peak was first named by Shackleton,' Willoughby told us. 'The top is at about 10,000 feet. It's flat and snow-covered, with persistent cloud.'

It wasn't until plate 25 that we had the first image of Mount Buckley.

'This is the south-east side of Mount Buckley, showing the dip of strata to the north. And here,' Willoughby turned the page and placed the book back on the epidiascope, 'is Mount Buckley, with part of the Wild and Marshall Ranges behind.'

'Take a good look, gentlemen,' Dame Pauline intervened. 'This is the terrain you will be searching.'

Dame Pauline looked expectantly at the sandy-haired young major. I could see the gleam in her eye. There was obviously more to come. For a second the thought crossed my mind that the relationship between the Governor and the young major might go a little further than the purely professional. Dame Pauline was a good-looking woman and Major James Willoughby probably had a few wild oats still to sow. It wouldn't be the first time a young officer had answered the call of duty, particularly when you considered what the options were down here in this desolate land.

My thoughts were interrupted as the epidiascope threw up the next breathtaking image. It wasn't a photograph. It was one of Edward Wilson's drawings.

'Look at the date in the top right-hand corner,' Willoughby instructed. 'Wilson drew this sketch on February 8, 1912. *That is exactly the same day as Scott made the crucial entry in the diary.*'

Willoughby fell silent, letting the image on the screen speak for itself.

I have to admit it was a weird sensation. There we were, half a dozen of us, sitting around the polished table in the Governor's diningroom, looking at a beautifully executed pen and ink drawing made by a man who had been on the march for months and who, even then, was suffering the agonies of snow blindness.

It was a moving moment. No doubt about it. Willoughby himself seemed to be overcome with emotion but fortunately Dame Paúline herself intervened, picking up where her aide had left off.

Taking her stance behind the epidiascope, she told us, 'In the background, you can clearly see Mount Buckley. You will recognise it from the photograph we saw earlier. In the distance you can see Mount Darwin.

'In fact,' she continued, 'Wilson has labelled most of the key features.' She read out some of the notes. '*Lunch camp Mount Buckley, February 9. Snow deposits showing well the different gradient of erosion. Black rock scarp.*' As she spoke, she moved the stub end of a pencil over the page, thereby throwing up a black pointer on the screen.

'In front of Mount Buckley, on the glacier ice, you can see Wilson has written "*heavily crevassed.*" ' Again she moved the stub of the pencil. 'And here he was written "*bare scooped blue slate and red ochre rock face*".'

Like a picky eater, she had saved the best bit till last. 'Look what Wilson has drawn over here, to the right of the crevassed area, with Mount Buckley in the background. Look at the shape of that outcrop. And see Wilson's written comments "*Geological samples taken from pear-shaped nunatak*".'

We could see immediately what she meant. The rocky outcrop which Wilson had sketched appeared to emerge from the glacier with a large rounded base which then tapered to a narrower, but still substantial, neck.

I glanced across at Harry. Up till then, he had taken no part in the proceedings apart from scribbling the occasional note or doodle on the pad in front of him. However, as Wilson's sketch was projected onto the screen, I noticed that he converted one of his doodles into a more than passing resemblance to the pear-shaped nunatak. My brother, I remembered, had always been something of a draughtsman. If he hadn't been so bloody anxious to make money, he could have been an artist.

Dame Pauline closed the big leather-bound book and switched

off the machine. 'You're the scientists, gentlemen,' she said. 'I'm just an interested spectator. But don't tell me you're not going to be able to locate that nunatak. If you start from the right place and line up Mount Buckley and Mount Darwin the way Wilson has drawn them, you're surely going to find what you're looking for. How can you go wrong?'

The last was clearly a rhetorical question. Dame Pauline had the light of battle in her eyes.

For most of the meeting up to this point she had virtually ignored Harry's and my presence. Certainly she had not directed any questions at us, nor sought to include us in the discussions. But now, very deliberately, she turned to Harry.

'Before we break up, Mr Brokke,' she said, 'let me put on record how much we owe to you.'

When Harry looked genuinely puzzled, she continued:

'What I'm talking about is your sponsorship of this vital expedition.'

'I'm not sure I follow,' Harry said in what I imagined he thought might pass for a Dutch accent.

Dame Pauline threw Harry a wryly amused glance. I imagined she had a substantial repertoire. 'Oh, but you do, Mr. Brokke. I'm sure you do. Let me explain. The British Government as such cannot become involved in any activities which would result in a breach of our international obligations under the Atlantic Treaty and, more specifically, under the protocol which bans all exploitation of Antarctic minerals - a protocol which the U.K. has itself ratified. We are all clear about that, gentlemen, are we not?'

The Governor of the Falklands looked rapidly around the room. Willoughby, Munro and Southgate nodded in unison.

'That being said,' Dame Pauline went on, 'no signatory to the Antarctic Treaty, including the United Kingdom, can control totally the activities of purely private parties. We can discourage, but we cannot forbid. We could not, for example, stop those two young Britons - Roger Mear and Robert Swan, I believe they were called - from trying to walk in Scott's footsteps to the Pole, even though the Americans wanted us to. And we certainly couldn't stop Sir Ranulph Fiennes from attempting his solo trans-Antarctic walk. We don't have the legal powers to do that. Do you follow me now, Mr Brokke?'

'I'm beginning to,' Harry mumbled.

Dame Pauline swept on, remorseless, like the advancing tide.

'Excellent,' she continued. 'You do understand then, Mr Brokke, that you and Mr Hodson here are the sponsors of a purely private expedition. The purpose of that expedition is to construct a suitable monument to Scott and his party at the top of the Beardmore Glacier. A preliminary reconnaissance is clearly necessary, and that is what we are discussing at the moment.'

The Governor obviously relished driving the message home. 'As I said, the United Kingdom cannot stop or impede a private expedition to Antarctica, whose purpose is to reconnoitre a suitable site, being launched from British territory or from a British base in the Antarctic. We can even cooperate within certain limits. The British Antarctic Survey has a mandate, indeed an obligation, to undertake work on a customer-contract basis. The wind of privatisation blows even down here. In the circumstances, BAS is, I understand, ready to make its services available to the Scott Memorial Expedition on a cost-only basis. And I must say I think that is a very generous offer.'

There was a chorus of assenting grunts around the table.

I think Harry realised by then that he had been painted into a corner. It was quite amusing to see him try to wriggle out of it.

'How much are we talking about?' he asked grudgingly.

Dame Pauline turned to Steve Munro. 'Mr Munro? Do you have a rough idea?'

'I'd say we're looking at between one hundred and two hundred thousand,' Munro replied without batting an eyelid.

'Pounds, dollars, escudos?' Harry sounded truculent.

'Pounds,' Munro said firmly. 'We have to run the Dash 7 down to Rothera. Then we have to fly a Twin Otter over to the Beardmore Glacier and that will mean fuel depots en route. Then there are the personnel and equipment costs.'

'What if I don't want to sponsor the expedition?' said Harry menacingly. 'I've got a plane waiting at the airport.'

'Not any more, you haven't,' Major Willoughby said quietly. 'Take a look behind you.'

I don't know how they managed to time it so precisely. That staggered me, I must admit. I suppose they gave the pilot his marching orders and somehow timed his departure to coincide with the crunch point of the briefing. Anyway, when Harry and I turned in our chairs to look out of the window over the Falkland Sound we could clearly see our Jet Cruiser banking after takeoff before passing almost directly overhead.

Harry still hadn't given up. 'How are you going to make me pay?' he asked.

Dame Pauline sighed. 'Your recent financial activities are no particular concern of mine, Mr Brokke, but they may indeed be of concern to the authorities in London. I understand that companies in which you have an interest, such as' - she consulted a paper in front of her - 'MinFin Holdings NV, based in the Netherlands Antilles, may recently have been engaged in illegal trading on the London market. Not to mention other markets which might, I'm sure, be interested in the information we could provide. There may even be a warrant out for your arrest in the United Kingdom. At the very least, you may be wanted for questioning.'

Dame Pauline Fairweather kept her eyes firmly fixed on Harry as she spoke and I was grateful for that. As Harry himself had been pleased to point out, my own role in the CMG affair would not bear too close a scrutiny.

'If they want to arrest me or question me,' Harry growled, 'they'll have to wait till I reach Britain.'

Dame Pauline stood up at that point and drew herself up to her full height. How splendid she would have looked, I thought, in a full-dress uniform - with a plumed hat and a ceremonial sword dangling from her belt. I was expecting her to say something like, 'Sergeant-at-Arms, arrest that man!' And she came pretty close.

'I need hardly remind you, Mr Brokke,' she thundered, 'that the Falkland Islands *is* British territory and that my writ runs here. Major Willoughby,' she commanded, 'you will see to it that if Mr Brokke does not cooperate he is detained forthwith.'

With that, the Governor of the Falklands stormed from the room, leaving behind her a stunned silence.

I could tell Harry was a shaken man. I think seeing the Jet Cruiser fly off like that had something to do with it. Harry is the kind of man who always likes to have an escape route organised. Now the obvious route out of Stanley was closed off and he didn't have an immediate backup plan. I could sense his brain working overtime.

At last - and with obvious reluctance - he creased his face into a smile. 'I am honoured to be able to sponsor the Scott Memorial Project. Mr Hodson and I will look forward to cooperating to the fullest with the British Antarctic Survey, and indeed with any other party in order to ensure that this expedition achieves a resounding success.'

To give Harry his due, it was a nice formal little speech. Glancing round the table, I could sense the relief. I doubted whether they wanted to lock Harry up. What they needed were the funds, the financial resources, that Harry could provide.

It was, if you like, a straightforward cynical deal. Without anyone saying so in so many words, Harry was being offered immunity from prosecution, in the UK at least, in exchange for a whacking contribution to a new and highly speculative venture.

Of course there was more to it than that. By bringing us down to the Falklands, a place which is about as near to the end of the earth as you can possibly get, the authorities were able to keep effective control of us. We had already proved conclusively that we were loose canons. We knew too much and we could go off at the wrong moment.

What would they do with us, I wondered, once Harry had signed the cheque? Knowing what we knew, would they trust us to keep quiet? How would they ensure that we didn't go blabbing to all and sundry? They could put us in gaol, I supposed. I felt sure that the Governor of the Falklands legally possessed that kind of power and from what I had seen of her she would not hesitate to exercise it.

I was just about to come forward with some interesting alternative suggestions of my own when Steve Munro saved me the trouble.

'Well, gentlemen,' he said briskly. 'Now that we've sorted all that out, I had better check with the stores to make sure we can get you kitted up properly. Once you're out on the glacier you'll need a full set of clothing, even if it *is* coming up for midsummer down there.'

I couldn't help smiling. So Harry and I were not only the official sponsors of the Robert Falcon Scott Memorial Project. We were to be fully-fledged expedition members in our own right.

Well, I thought, that was one way of keeping us out of trouble!

XVI

Falklands III

I MET SOUTHGATE in the bar of the Upland Goose around seven o'clock that evening.

'Where's Harry?' he asked.

'Down at the communications centre,' I replied, referring to the up-to-date telecom facilities which had been installed in Stanley following the Falklands war. 'He's still on the phone to his bank, I expect.'

Given the time difference between the Falklands and Europe, I imagined Harry could be having some difficulty in ensuring the rapid transfer of funds from Luxembourg to the Falklands. He had probably had to track down the egregious Mr Visser at home.

Southgate took advantage of Harry's absence. We took our beers - Penguin Ale, as I recall - into a quiet corner.

'I want to apologise,' he said. 'You must feel used in all this. Harry used you. Then I used you. Quite deliberately and, I suppose you could say, cynically. But it was the right thing to do.'

Southgate took a long reflective pull at his beer. Bits of froth attached themselves to his beard, but he didn't seem to notice.

'Let me explain,' he continued. 'Harry first came to me with his scheme a few weeks back. He was on a visit to England. He rang me from London saying he wanted to come up to Cambridge to see me. Of course I said yes. I hadn't seen him since he went to Brazil and he is an old friend, as you know. Harry had a quite specific objective. He said he had read my piece in the *Journal* about how I had identified the mineral structure of Scott's geological samples and called it 'falconite'. And he said he'd heard through some other sources, which he wouldn't specify, that provided it could be actually discovered to exist in quantity somewhere, falconite might be vitally important as a climate modifier. Frankly, I was quite surprised by this as you can imagine. How the hell did Harry know all this? I guess more of this stuff gets onto the Internet than we realise. Be that as it may, when Harry started talking in detail about his plan that afternoon I thought he had taken leave of his senses. Frankly, I was minded to tell him to get out there and then. But I didn't. And do you know why?'

'No, why?'

'I didn't kick him out because he was so bloody convincing. He had it all worked out. The golden lion tamarins in the forest, the geological survey in the Ouro Preto museum, the split-second timing you needed if you were to run a scam involving stock exchanges on three continents. It didn't take me long to realise that, even without me, Harry was determined to go ahead.'

'Why didn't you warn me?' I asked. 'Do you think I wouldn't have played ball if I had known what was going on?'

'I'm not going to question your role in this affair, Charles,' Southgate said quietly. 'I'm trying to explain mine.'

Southgate's demeanour at this point took me back to the last time I had seen him - that day in Cambridge. There was the same deliberate fumbling with pipe and tobacco, the tamping of the weed into the bowl, the first puffs of smoke, followed by the deliberate melodramatic glance around the room to make sure that no one was listening in.

'Do you remember meeting Professor Kalinin when you came to see me in Cambridge?' he asked.

'I certainly do. I sat next to him at dinner in College.'

'Ah, I thought so,' Southgate sucked audibly at his pipe. 'What did you think of him?'

'Very smart, very impressive,' I replied. And I meant it. However much wine Kalinin had consumed that night, I had no doubt that the white-haired professor was totally and utterly on the ball.

'He's a key man in Moscow, no doubt about that. He carries a lot of weight. Harry came to see me soon after Kalinin took up his visiting fellowship at Churchill and I suddenly realised that there was a way of turning Harry's self-serving scam to our advantage.'

'You've got to do better than that, Graham,' I said. The whole thing sounded to me like a tissue of lies. Frankly, I was disgusted.

I stomped off to the bar and came back with two more beers. The place was beginning to fill up with off-duty soldiers. Quite soon, I imagined, the noise level would make further conversation impossible. I banged the beer down on the table.

'Well?' I asked.

'For Christ's sake, Charles, give me the benefit of the doubt,' Southgate implored. 'You've known me long enough. You don't really think I was in this for money, do you?'

'Harry was. Harry is.' I glanced around. I imagined that any second now Harry would be coming to join us.

'I'm not Harry,' Southgate said. 'All right, let me be more specific. When Harry came to see me, I told you that my first reaction was to dismiss the whole idea, but the more he talked about it, the more I realised that here was a golden opportunity to put the Russians off the scent. Men like Kalinin, as we were saying a moment ago, are not stupid. We have to assume that they know what we know about falconite. Kalinin read my piece in the *Journal of Geological Sciences.* He's on the Editorial Committee. He was bound to see it at an early stage, long before publication. He certainly read it even before Harry did. And as soon as he got to Cambridge, if not before, Kalinin was likely to have found about falconite's potential role as a marine micronutrient. *So we had to assume, if falconite was indeed a critical factor in global warming, then the Russians would start looking for it pretty damn soon, either to use it for their own purposes or to stop us getting hold of it.*'

'So you set up a decoy using Harry and me?'

'Exactly. I can't, you realise, go into all the details. Let's just say, that I am in pretty close touch with the authorities and those authorities took the view that Harry's scam could just conceivably be turned to us. The Russians would be on the trail of the mineral but once your story about the discovery of a major falconite deposit in Brazil appeared, Russian interest might focus on South America. We have reason to believe that's exactly what happened.'

'But the story died a death,' I protested. 'Alvarez put out a total denial. CMG denounced it as a fabrication, a journalistic speculation.'

'In Russian eyes, that would have made it even more credible,' Southgate said. 'Don't forget they are masters at the game of disinformation. They expect others to play that game as well.'

'So that's why you went along with Harry's scam. That's why

you allowed me to make a fool of myself.' If I sounded bitter, it was because I still felt bitter.

'I've told you I'm sorry, Charles,' Southgate said quietly. 'I'm not sure I could have done any differently. We're talking global politics here. Committees take these kinds of decisions. Powerful men and women sit on those committees. Like Dame Pauline. People are bound to be used. Or to feel used. And sometimes, however regrettably, they are going to get hurt.'

'Means and ends?'

Southgate nodded. 'It's always means and ends, isn't it?'

I found myself wanting to laugh at the sheer incongruity of the whole thing. Setting up a decoy for the Russians! Encouraging them to look for a possibly nonexistent mineral in Brazil to prevent them looking for the same possibly nonexistent mineral in Antarctica! It was like a game played by kids on computers. Indiana Jones and the Temple of Doom! That kind of thing. It was hard to believe this was the real world.

And yet, it *was* the real world. No doubt about that.

'How come you reacted so fast?' I asked. 'I call you one morning saying 'let's find the nunatak' and the next thing I know we have a neat little expedition all ready to go.'

'I think our people would have been on their way even if you hadn't called me that morning,' Southgate said. 'They hadn't worked out where to go, but they were ready to start looking. You gave them the focus they needed. All I can say, once again, is congratulations. You were spot on!'

Flattery, as they say, will get you anywhere.

'How much time do you think we have?' I asked.

'Not a lot. When the Russians realise they've been tricked and that there's no falconite in Brazil, they may start looking elsewhere. In the Antarctic, for example. After all, you worked it out for yourself. Why shouldn't they?'

'I hope you've taken Scott's dairy out of the display cabinet back there in Cambridge,' I said.

'We thought of that,' Southgate replied. 'We've also asked the British Museum to place the original in storage for the time being and not to let anyone have access to it without specific authorisation. However, let's not panic. We have a clear head start on the Russians. What's more, we know the coordinates of the deposit and they don't.'

'Another race for the Pole?'

'Exactly,' Southgate nodded. 'But this time we should get there first!'

Southgate finished the last of his beer and stood up. 'Let's go and find Harry. He must be through by now.'

As we walked along the front towards the signals station we bumped into Harry coming out of the cathedral. He seemed surprised to see us and hovered uneasily under the giant arch of whalebone which we had driven past earlier that day. Now that there were just the three of us I imagined Harry was trying to work out whether to stick to his alias or revert to his old identity.

Southgate solved the problem for him. He obviously recognised that Harry had his own reasons for wishing to maintain his alias.

'Ah, Mr Brokke?' Graham said jovially, 'We meet again. Have you been at prayer? It's not the Dutch Reformed Church, I'm afraid, but it's the best we can do.'

Harry laughed nervously. I couldn't help wondering whether the strain was at last beginning to tell.

'I thought, since I'm here, I might as well see the sights,' he replied. 'Just nipped in for a moment.'

We walked along the waterfront towards the great grey pontoon dock which serves as a hostel for some of the troops still stationed on the island. Looking out into the Sound, I could see half a dozen vessels riding at anchor. Since they opened up the fishing, the Falklands' commercial prospects have seen a modest transformation. Trawlers of several nations put into port here on their way down to harvest the rich waters of the southern ocean. One of the boats in the harbour was showing the Spanish flag. There was a Japanese vessel moored not far from the pontoon. And out in the middle of the bay two trawlers stood at anchor, flying a blue, white and red flat which I didn't recognise.

'What's that flag?' I asked, pointing.

Southgate stared for a moment out to sea. 'It's the Russian equivalent of the Red Ensign, if I'm not mistaken,' he replied. 'Russia dumped the old hammer and sickle when the Soviet Union split up.'

'About time too,' grunted Harry. 'Bloody Soviets.'

He gave the Russian vessels the briefest of looks, then turned back to talk to us.

'I got through to Luxembourg in the end,' he said. 'The money will be deposited in the BAS account tomorrow. The full amount. Two hundred thousand pounds. All above board.'

'That's great, Mr Brokke. An excellent decision,' Southgate commented drily.

'Any time, Dr Southgate,' Harry permitted himself a smile. 'You know my motto. In for a penny, in for a pound. You chaps ready for another drink?'

We went to the stores the next day. Steve Munro, with years of experience behind him, made an educated guess as far as our weights and dimensions were concerned and fished in his lockers to produce what I imagined was a standard armful of Antarctic clothing. Key items included: bright orange anorak (the colour to stand out against the ice and snow, thereby assisting rescue parties in the event of mishap), woolly Balaclava helmet and gloves, waterproof trousers, Antarctic boots and two pairs of long thermal underwear.

'We'll take this lot down with us on the plane,' Munro said, 'but you may as well try it on for size now.'

When we were all togged out, Munro inspected us fore and aft. 'You'll do,' he said.

Before letting us go, he checked the front pocket of our anoraks.

'When you're out on the skidoos,' he said, 'you'll be clipped on with a line. If you get thrown off, for example when the skidoo goes down a crevasse, the line will hold you. In here,' he said, patting each front pocket in turn, 'there's a homing device, a miniaturised navigational beacon, a bit like the ones those solo round-the-world yachtsmen have in case they fall overboard. When the line jerks taut the beacon is activated. If you're lucky enough to take a tumble when there's a satellite overhead, they might pick up the signal back in BAS headquarters in Cambridge. And if you're really lucky, you may even be rescued. But I wouldn't count on it.'

Munro laughed. He'd obviously been through the spiel before. And Southgate, of course, was no novice. He'd seen a few crevasses in his time.

But for Harry and me, the idea of being out there on the icecap with only a beeper for company was more than a little alarming. I didn't even know how to drive a skidoo. There aren't many skidoos around in my part of England.

After that it was all a bit of an anticlimax. We were raring to go when word came that the weather had closed in at Rothera, the BAS base halfway down the Antarctic peninsula, and the Dash-7 wouldn't be able to land even if it did take off from the Falklands.

'It's a bit manky down there,' Munro explained laconically. Antarctic professionals have developed their own vocabulary. Some enterprising soul has even published a dictionary of Antarctic slang. 'Manky' is one of the easier terms to understand. As Munro explained, it meant anything from 'poor' to 'bloody miserable'.

We hung around the Upland Goose for three days, biting our nails. We weren't really expecting an invitation to dinner at Government House and none materialised. Growing restless, Harry and I hired motorcycles one morning from a local entrepreneur - two 250cc Suzukis - and set off to visit Darwin, the tiny sheep station on the other side of the Island where 2 Para had fought its uphill battle and Colonel H. Jones had so gallantly met his death.

It wasn't just curiosity which impelled us. In our own way, we wanted to pay tribute.

It poured with rain. Our new Antarctic clothing was soon soaked and splattered with mud. We tried to stick to the road but the tarmac rapidly turned into a muddy track which ended in a bog a few miles out of town. The only signs of civilization were the noticeboards which warned us, ominously, that we had entered a danger zone.

We squelched to a halt beside a solitary noticeboard. A message had been pinned to the board which said:

'The map below shows three categories.

'**1.** Green. These areas have been exhaustively checked by the Royal Engineers and are believed to be safe.

'**2.** Blue. There is no evidence at all that these areas contain minefields or booby traps. However, they may contain unexploded bombs, ammunition, missiles etc.

3. Red. These areas are known to contain mines or booby traps. Do not enter.

'YOU ARE NOW IN A RED AREA!'

'Harry,' I called back through the driving rain. 'I think we ought to turn back.'

Harry and I ended our brief unprogrammed excursion by turning tail and trying to ride our motorcycles back through the bog to Stanley on precisely the tracks we had made coming out. Easier said than done, I can tell you, in those conditions. All the while we were waiting for the explosion.

'What the hell are we doing?' Harry shouted at one point. 'Are we mad?'

Willoughby asked the same question when, shaken, we finally arrived back in town looking as though we had yomped across half a continent.

'You could have been killed,' he shouted at us when he found us still shivering at the bar of the Upland Goose.

Actually, I don't think Willoughby was especially concerned for our safety. His job was to make sure that the Scott Memorial Project left the Falklands as planned *en route* for Antarctica. He would not be truly happy until he saw the Dash-7 take off from Mount Pleasant with a full complement on board and he could go back to being ADC to the Queen Bee.

Apart from that failed attempt to ride motorcycles across the 'camp' (which is what the locals call the island's interior), the hours passed uneventfully. Harry spent a good deal of his time in the Goose or, alternatively, when he was bored with the Goose, at a nearby rival establishment known as the Globe Hotel. If the Goose was for other ranks, the Globe was largely for officers. Harry, one of life's born mixers, moved easily between the two.

Spanish, Japanese, Russian and Norwegian seamen came ashore at regular intervals to sample the few attractions that Stanley had to offer. Anything would make a change from the dull grey ocean and the stink of fish.

Harry mingled with most of the visitors whenever he encountered them.

'What do you talk to them about?' I asked him one night when he staggered back into the Upland Goose after carousing elsewhere with some Spanish trawlermen.

'I practice my Dutch,' Harry laughed. 'Fortunately they haven't a clue what I'm saying.'

In spite of his instinctive readiness to fraternise, I noticed that Harry gave the Russians a wide berth when they showed up at the Goose one night. Thank God for that, I thought. The last thing we wanted at this point was the Ruskis cottoning on to what we were up to, even if they were paralytic most of the time.

Oddly enough, that brief interlude in the Falklands (particularly the mad motorcycle ride), brought me closer to Harry than I had been for years. We didn't talk about Nasreen. There wasn't much more to say really on that subject when you got down to it. He had won and I had lost. Or we had both lost. Anyway, as far as I was concerned, those particular scars would never disappear. You just had to forget about them.

There was another reason we didn't talk about the past. Somewhere, our relationship had moved into another plane. Nasreen was a long way away. There were other things to attend to now. It sounded corny. It is corny. But the truth is that the prospect of shared endeavour had brought, was bringing, us together.

It even seemed possible that Harry and I could be friends again. I was glad about that.

XVII

Rothera, Antarctic Peninsula I

We finally took off for the Antarctic on the morning of the Friday of the first week of November.

The Dash-7 circled once over the sea, then headed almost due south. Looking down, I could see the white-capped waves. These, I knew, were some of the roughest seas of the world. Forty, fifty, even eighty feet swells were not uncommon. You don't want to fall overboard in that kind of sea, even if you are wearing a homing device.

We kept well out of Argentine airspace as we headed for the Drake Passage. It was one of those amazingly clear days when you can see the whole curvature of the earth. Behind us and to the east was the long pointed tip of the South American continent; over to the west, we could see the outline of South Georgia and the South Sandwich Islands; ahead of us lay Antarctica. Pilots down here call it 'The Big White'.

I don't think I will ever forget that first view of Antarctica. As we flew south, the ocean, which had seemed so fearsomely choppy as we left the Falklands, began taking on a frozen glacial appearance. Around one o'clock, with our arrival time still an hour or so ahead of us, we saw the first big iceberg. It gleamed white and majestic in the sun and trailed in its wake half a dozen smaller acolytes.

'What you're seeing here is not an isolated phenomenon,' Munro said, as Harry and I stared out of the windows. 'A couple of years back an iceberg the size of Oxfordshire broke off from the Larsen Ice Shelf. BAS headquarters in Cambridge alerted us and we flew down in the Dash-7 from Rothera. I've never seen anything like it. For the first time in recorded history, James Ross Island has become circumnavigable. In the short term, the retreat of the ice shelves is probably irreversible.'

Soon after that, Munro pointed at the horizon over the starboard wing.

At first it looked like a thin white line rising out of the pack ice, which had by now accumulated below us until it seemed to be a single solid sheet.

As we flew closer, that thin white line grew and grew until it seemed that we were approaching great towering cliffs of ice.

'That's Anvers Island,' said Munro, 'still about twenty miles ahead of us. See the peak rising up behind the ice-barrier? That's Mount Fosse - it's over nine thousand feet high. There aren't many places in the world where ice-covered mountains rise sheer out of the water like that.'

I don't know how many times Munro had made an Antarctic landfall, but it was good to see that, even for a veteran, the last continent had lost little of its wonder.

Rothera - the Antarctic base where Britain conducts most of its geological research - lies at sixty-seven degrees south and sixty-eight west. Or, more precisely, 67°34'S, 68°08'W. The reason I know this particular point of detail is that I had bought some postcards in the Falklands - of seals and penguins, as I recall - and on arriving in Antarctica I asked Steve Munro to stamp them with the official Rothera postmark. In addition to being base commander, Munro acted as the Queen's postmaster. In the old days, apparently, the Rothera 'postoffice' did a roaring trade, even if the outgoing mail did pile up waiting for the yearly supply ship to heave its way through the ice. More recently, the 'Fids', as they are known (after the Falkland Islands Dependency Survey, which was the UK's first official 'cover' for her early, largely clandestine, Antarctic activities), have taken to the Internet. The number of customers at Britain's most southerly post office has fallen sharply.

'I'm sure you'll get back to Britain long before these will,' Munro said as he stamped my postcards.

Now that we were officially 'on board' as it were, Munro's attitude had softened. When we first met him he had seemed to regard us as a nuisance, a regrettable necessity foisted on him by a higher authority. I suspect that the arrival of a large cheque in the specified account had done much to improve our image in his eyes.

Graham Southgate didn't need any rapid Cooks' tour of the base. He had actually spent not one but two winters at Rothera in the past, almost twenty consecutive months in all. From talking to some of the Fids, I quickly came to realise that 'wintering' in Antarctica is what separates the men from the boys. Southgate had earned his spurs. If you can survive six months of total darkness down south and come back with body and soul intact, they give you a special Antarctic tie. Southgate, as far as I could see, was entitled to two of them. A kind of DSO and bar.

'I'm going to find a terminal somewhere,' Graham said. 'I need to check my website.'

Steve Munro shook his head. 'Sometimes I wish the Internet had never reached Antarctica. Some of the lads get messages when the wife runs out of cornflakes. I'm not sure all this communication really makes for sound science.'

While Southgate found his computer terminal, and Munro picked up on his duties as base commander, one of the Fids, a young rather earnest meteorologist called Colin who was on his third tour of duty, showed us round.

We started with the bunks where the men slept two and sometimes four to a room. We saw the library, well-stocked with novels for the long dark Antarctic winters, but with a good selection of the classic Antarctic literature - books by or about the Big Four - Scott, Shackleton, Amundsen, Mawson - as well as lesser heroes such as Fuchs and Fiennes.

Upstairs was a large, light airy room, which served both as a canteen and as a general dayroom for the Fids. Fire-extinguishers were prominently displayed along the wall.

'In this ultra-dry Antarctic environment,' Colin told us, 'fire is a very real danger. Everybody has to have fire training.'

It was not hard to understand why. Much of the base was constructed of combustible material. Once a fire started, it could be very difficult to control. You can't dial 999 and call the fire brigade.

At the far end of the room was the bar. 'I won't show you that now,' Colin joked. 'I expect you'll be visiting it later.'

They'd found a two-man room for us. 'Bags I have the top bunk,' said Harry, reverting to the language of our school days together.

We changed into our Antarctic gear. Colin was waiting for us outside. 'I'll run you up the ramp.'

He drove us in a Tucker Sno-Cat up the ramp to the ski-way, which in turn led up to the glacier where we had landed earlier. It was a smooth easy ride. The Sno-Cat had automatic transmission so there was no loss of momentum as you changed gear. On that brilliantly sunny afternoon. I still found it hard to realise that I was in Antarctica.

Rothera is actually located at the south-eastern corner of Adelaide Island. Looking down at the base as we drove up the ramp, I could see seals basking on the ice floes.

'What kind of seals are they?' I asked.

Colin took his eye off the ramp to glance down at the ice floes below. 'Weddells,' he said. 'And a couple of crabeaters. Look over there.' He pointed to another ice floe where I saw a large black seal stretched out on a ledge. 'That's a leopard seal. Watch out for him. He'll have your leg off if you let him.'

When we reached the top of the ski-way, Colin switched off the engine of the Sno-Cat.

'Listen.' In the sudden total stillness, the sound of an aircraft was clearly audible. 'There she is,' he said.

BAS actually operates four de Haviland wheel-ski Twin Otter aircraft out of Rothera, as well as the de Haviland Dash-7 which had flown us in that morning. Three of the Twotters were parked up on the glacier, the bright vermillion of their wings and fuselage contrasting starkly with the glaring white landscape.

As the plane which Colin had pointed out in the distance came nearer, I assumed at first that this was the fourth Twotter in the BAS stable. I imagined it had been out on duty somewhere and was now returning to base.

But as the skis touched down on the ice and the plane came to a halt a hundred yards from us I realised I had got it wrong. This particular Twotter was totally bereft of any BAS markings. Even the colour was different. Instead of the standard vermillion, the wings and fuselage were painted a snappy green, exactly the same colour, I recalled, as the huts down below at Rothera.

'The boys had to use whatever paint they could find,' Colin explained, switching the engine back on so we could ride over to the plane. 'There were some cans of paint to spare from last time they spruced up the base. Pity to waste it.'

As we approached, I was stunned to see the legend, stencilled in large black letters on the fuselage just behind the wing, 'SCOTT MEMORIAL PROJECT'. They'd even included a special logo for the expedition - a stylised man standing in front of a stylised nunatak with some kind of measuring tool in his hand.

'Brilliant job, don't you think?' Colin said.

'It's terrific, absolutely terrific,' I replied. I felt elated. We had a bird. We could fly.

'They might have consulted us about the logo.' Harry pretended to grumble, but I could tell he was as thrilled as I was.

'Shall we go and take delivery of your machine?' Colin asked.

'You bet,' Harry and I answered together.

We climbed out of the Sno-Cat and stood on the packed ice of the runway, next to the plane, gazing at it admiringly. I understood now why - apart from uncertainty over the weather - we had been delayed in the Falklands. The Fids had had to repaint the BAS Twotter and that must have taken some time.

Another reason for the holdup, as far as I could understand, was simple logistics. While the pilot was shutting down the engine and making the routine post flight checks, Colin explained the problem.

'They've had to set up fuel depots for your trip to the Beardmore Glacier. You're going to be flying over fifteen hundred miles there and the same distance back again. That's way beyond the range of a Twotter. You'll be picking up fuel at Fossil Bluff and a couple of other places on your way south. The drums had to be put in place. It's slow work. All the time you're using fuel to carry fuel, if you follow me.'

I nodded. One thing you begin to understand after just a few hours in Antarctica is the sheer size of the continent. It covers 5.5 million square miles, which is one-tenth of the earth's surface. The Ross Sea Ice Shelf, just by itself, is the size of France. There aren't any handy little airports dotted around if the fuel gauge runs low or the weather gets bad. Planning and preparation, that's the name of the game. Otherwise you can get caught out in a big way.

The pilot eventually climbed down from the cockpit of the Twotter and a couple of Fids emerged from the fuselage.

'How did it go, Gary?' Colin asked.

Gary Lawson, the Twotter pilot, was a tall, deeply tanned Australian. He had worked for BAS for seven seasons as a contract pilot and appeared to enjoy every minute of it.

'Piece of cake, man.' He gestured towards the empty interior of the plane.

'This is the Scott Memorial Project,' Colin introduced us.

We all shook hands. 'Good on yer,' Gary said. 'Glad to be of service.'

'Gary's going to fly you down,' Colin explained.

'And bloody well back I hope,' Gary said.

We all laughed at that.

The pilot and the Fids drove back to Rothera in the Sno-Cat, leaving Harry and me with Colin.

'We're going to have a practice run on the skidoos,' Colin said.

A skidoo is a motorised sledge and it is the workhorse of Antarctic travel. In the old days, when the various nations of the world established their bases in Antarctica, dog teams were still being used and seals were killed to feed them. Only a decade or so back, Rothera still had dogs. But skidoos were more practical and they didn't need seal meat. Some of the old hands regretted the loss of companionship which the dogs had provided, but the world had moved on.

'At least we don't have to shout "mush",' Harry joked as he mounted his skidoo.

Colin frowned. I could see that he had already marked Harry down as a potentially awkward customer, the kind of guy who could risk lives out on the ice. Other people's lives as well as his own.

'Let's run through the drill,' he said. 'The two skidoos, as you can see, are roped together. The driver is tied on to the skidoo. If the skidoo goes into a crevasse and the driver is thrown off he'll fall up to fifteen feet, but it's quite a comfortable fall since the ropes have sixty percent "give" built into them. The skidoo's engine is automatically turned off if you fall, as long as you remember to clip on the line which throws the switch.'

'Are there any crevasses round here?' Harry asked.

'No,' Colin replied. 'This area is free of crevasses. Crevasses occur mainly when the snow is stressed, for example where the glacier is moving over rocks or humps. You'll find plenty of crevasses up there on the Beardmore.'

Harry and I exchanged glances. We were both thinking the same thing.

'When were you last in a crevasse?' Harry asked Colin.

'A month or two back actually. I was probing a bridge and the bridge went. I had to climb back up the rope. Normally, if you can't see the crevasse, the bridge ought to be strong enough to take you. Visibility is important. Today there's good contrast because there's bright sunlight. When you have cloud and there's no sun, you can't tell which way you are going except by the angle of the sledge.'

We were feeling a bit uneasy by now.

'Let's hope the weather holds,' I said.

We spent an hour up there on the airstrip driving the skidoos around. Sometimes Harry rode the lead sledge; sometimes I did.

'Just make sure you're roped together at all times, no matter what,' Colin said. 'Avoid sudden changes of speed or direction.'

We got the hang of it fairly quickly.

We arrived back at the base in time for dinner. After shedding the bulkier items of our Antarctic clothing, we went upstairs to the bar. It was almost eight in the evening, but the sun was still streaming into the room. At this southerly latitude, if it dipped beneath the horizon at all it would be for the briefest of intervals. For the next few months, there would be no such thing as a dark night. And nearer the Pole, of course, you had to adjust to perpetual daylight during the Antarctic summer, the counterpart of winter's long total darkness.

Steve Munro was already sitting on a bar stool by the counter with a bottle of beer in his hand. On the walls were various Antarctic mementoes - photographs of ships held fast in ice, a coat of arms presented by USAP, the United States Antarctic Program, on a fraternal visit to their British colleagues a few years back, a peaked cap from one of the crew of a Russian ice-breaker. On these remote research stations camaraderie is important. These men are left to their own devices for so much of the time that visits from the outside world can be welcomed, if only to break up the monotony. So when the Americans, or even the Russians, drop in, it's doubles all round.

Munro must have warned the Fids not to probe too deeply into the Scott Memorial Project. I suspect there had been a little in-house briefing session while we were up at the airstrip practising our U-turns. At all events, though the Fids we met that evening in the bar, and later at dinner, were friendly enough, their questions concentrated on the trivial: football results back home, the survival of the government, the latest films, etc.

'The old "need to know" principle. Works both ways,' Harry whispered to me as we moved from the bar to the canteen.

Dinner was quickly over. There's no 48-hour or 40-hour per week rule in Antarctica. Not yet anyway. When the scientists had finished their meal, they pushed back their chairs and went about their business.

'I guess if you're shut down half the year,' said Harry, 'you have to make up for it during the other half.'

There had been no sign of Southgate at dinner.

'Maybe he's in the radio room, I'll see if I can find him,' I said. 'I'd like to have another look around anyway.'

XVIII

Rothera, Antarctic Peninsula II

I LEFT HARRY nursing a beer while I went on another (this time unescorted) tour of the facilities, looking for Graham. Climbing up to the top floor of the base-hut, I passed one room stuffed to the roof with cartons of breakfast cereal (enough to last two consecutive winters in the worst case scenario of the supply vessel not making it through the ice) and then another filled, or so it seemed to me, with spare parts for skidoos and other vital equipment. At the end of the corridor I saw a handwritten sign on a door saying 'Radio Rothera'.

I knocked and, when there was no reply, pushed the door open. The small cramped room was occupied by a dark-haired woman in her late twenties. She was sitting in front of her microphone with headphones on. Stuck on the wall in front of her was a large scale map of West Antarctica, including the Antarctic Peninsula. Coloured pins were placed at various points of the map. Most of them were clustered in the general area of Rothera, but a few others were scattered more widely to the east and south.

'Sorry to disturb you,' I said, introducing myself. 'I'm visiting the base on the way south. Actually, I'm looking for one of our party, Dr Southgate. Man with a beard. I thought he might be here.'

The radio operator took her earphones off and swivelled round.

'My name's Maggie Ormerod, generally known as "Sparks". I've not seen anyone for the last few hours. I've had the headphones on. There are plenty of men with beards around here though.' She laughed, looking at me appraisingly. 'You're with the Scott Memorial Project party, are you? I've been tracking the Fids as they've been putting in fuel depots for you over the last few days. Good luck!'

We chatted for a while. I could see that Radio Rothera served as a kind of control centre, enabling the base to keep track of the field parties. I asked Sparks what the coloured pins meant.

'Those are skidoo parties out in the bundu at the moment,' she explained. 'We've got a two-man unit at Fossil Bluff and another team at Sky Hi, a group of nunataks about two hundred miles farther south.'

Concentric circles had been drawn on the map, with Rothera at the centre. I had the feeling that Sparks would welcome a break from the headphones, so I seized the chance to ask a few more questions. I was a novice. I needed to understand the basic logistics.

'What's the scale?' I asked.

'It's sixty miles for every degree of latitude,' Maggie said. 'Here at 67° South we are 1,380 miles from the Pole.'

I studied the map closely. 'Where's the nearest Russian base?'

'They've got a base up here,' she pointed to an island off the tip of the Antarctic Peninsula, 'at Bellingshausen, which is right next to the Chilean Antarctic base called Rudolfo Marsh. And then the Russians also have a base at Druzhnaya, at the edge of the Ronne Ice Shelf.'

I noticed some coloured pins stuck on the Ronne Ice Shelf, where it joined the Wedell Sea.

'Is that a skidoo team from Rothera?' I asked. 'They're a hell of a long way from base!'

'They are indeed. I sometimes have difficulty keeping track of them. That particular two-man team is travelling about 1,500 miles over the ice-shelf on skidoos, and that's no mean feat.'

'How do they know where they are?'

'They have satellite surveyors with them on their sledges. You use them in much the same way as a ship uses its own satellite navigation system. You can achieve pinpoint accuracy, and when I say "pinpoint", I mean within yards.'

'What are they doing?'

'I don't know the detail,' Sparks said. 'You'd have to ask Steve.'

I didn't press the point. I don't think it would have done much good if I had. But I couldn't help feeling that it was more than a coincidence that a British skidoo party was right over there at the edge of the Ronne Ice Shelf within hailing distance of the Russian base at Druzhnaya at this particular moment. Something was clearly going on.

'Can I listen in for a while?' I asked.

Sparks passed me a set of headphones and I pulled up a chair.

'The air waves are getting pretty crowded down here nowadays,' she told me. 'You've got the usual US activity. That's mainly from their big base at McMurdo over on Ross Island, where the Ross Ice Shelf merges into the Ross Sea. But they've also got a base at the South Pole itself as well as at Siple and we get some traffic from both of those stations too. The Americans tend to chatter away quite a lot. Nothing like as bad as the Argies and the Chileans though. They've got bases further up the peninsula. They're on the air half the day. Listen.'

Through the headphones I could hear a gabble of Spanish.

'Most of the time they seem to be talking either to or about their wives or girlfriends. Or football.' Sparks laughed. 'I suppose I should say *futból*!'

'Do you speak Spanish?' I asked.

'You pick it up,' Sparks replied. 'Once you know what you're looking for.'

'And the Russians? How often do you hear them?'

'Depends on the ionic conditions. But, yes, we hear the Russians from time to time. Mind you, they're quite hot on radio discipline. On the whole they don't chatter away like some of the others.'

'Have you heard them recently? I mean more than usual?'

'Yes, as a matter of fact,' Sparks looked at me sharply. 'In the last few days there seems to have been quite a lot of Russian activity. Their big supply vessel, the *Leningrad*, which is ice-strengthened, has come in early to their base at Druzhnaya. From what I can make out, the Russians have been running quite a few helicopter sorties inland, as well as missions with fixed-wing planes. They appear to be setting up - or to have set up - some kind of fuel supply line towards the deep south.'

'Actually to the Pole?' I asked.

'That or thereabouts,' Sparks replied. 'They had a bit of a scare the other day, from what I could make out. One of their pilots missed a fuel depot and found himself running low. Found it at the last minute, I imagine, because the next day the panic appeared to be over.'

I listened, fascinated. Russian supply vessels, helicopter sorties, fuel depots laid in for long-distance flights. It all added up, didn't it?

'How do you know what they're saying on the air?'

Sparks pointed at a recording machine set on a table next to her desk. I could see that the spools were turning.

'We tape all transmissions twenty-four hours a day. When the Dash-7 flies back to the Falklands, the tapes go with it. Then they're flown back to the UK, where they're transcribed. The juicy bits anyway.'

'Isn't that a bit slow?' I asked. 'What if there is something on the tape Rothera ought to know about in a hurry?'

'That's what I'm here for.'

'Are you a Russian speaker?'

'Fluent.'

'Can you pick up the Russians now?'

'I'll have a go. Can't tell what the reception will be like this evening.'

We both put our earphones back on. Sparks fiddled with the dials, running through the frequencies.

'Normally you find the Russians on the upper reaches of the short waveband,' she explained. 'But sometimes they switch to the lower frequencies. They obviously have some pre-arranged patterns for their transmissions - different frequencies at different times - but we're not sure what they are. Ah!' She gave a sharp exclamation as over the air came the unmistakable tones of a male voice speaking Russian.

Even though the static distorted the sound, I felt sure that I had heard those cavernous base tones before. Kalinin! What the hell was he doing here?

Sparks listened intently for the next few minutes, from time to time jotting notes on the pad in front of her. I'm not a Russian speaker myself, but once I could make out the word 'Leningrad' and then I heard Kalinin say 'Druzhnaya'.

A few seconds later the transmission was over. 'What was all that about?' I asked.

'Routine stuff, as far as I could tell,' Sparks replied. 'We were picking up a ship-to-shore conversation between the *Leningrad* and the base. As far as I could understand, the *Leningrad* has completed her resupply mission for this year and is about to head back to her home port of Vladivostok.'

'Do the Russians know we monitor their transmissions, even down here in Antarctica?'

'I'm sure they do. I expect they listen to ours too. That's why on-air discipline is important. You must always assume you're being overheard. Of course, that's not always a disadvantage. If you're stuck down a crevasse and calling for help, you're not going to mind who picks up the transmission. We keep the SOS channel clear at all times. All of the nations down here use the same frequency for emergency calls. We may all have conflicting claims to Antarctica, but at least we can agree about that!'

'I thought I recognised the speaker,' I said. 'Professor Boris Kalinin. I met him in Cambridge not long ago.'

Sparks looked at me blankly. 'Not a name I know.'

After I had said thanks and goodbye, I left 'Radio Rothera' to resume my interrupted search for Graham Southgate. I found him eventually in the library with Harry.

'I've already been over the problem with Mr Brokke' - Southgate stuck punctiliously to the rules even though there was no one else around. 'I can tell you we're in big trouble.'

He pointed to a sheaf of papers spread out on a table in front of him. 'It took me a while to get through to my email messages. That's why I wasn't at dinner. The modem was playing up, but I succeeded at last. I've had a very disturbing message from some of my collaborators back in Cambridge.'

'What kind of message?'

It was obvious that Southgate was dying to smoke, but since Rothera, given the fire hazards, operated a strict no-smoking policy he had to content himself with pulling ferociously at his beard.

'I'll summarise what they said.' Southgate's air of gloom deepened by the second. 'Remember those tanks I showed you at the BAS Research Laboratory outside Cambridge? Well, it's a question of the dosage rate. The marine biologists, the plankton wallahs, have been taking another look at the role of falconite as a micronutrient. They have been able to confirm empirically that at the dose rates I postulated falconite will trigger a population explosion in those tiny ocean plants we know as phytoplankton. However, *when they increased the dose rate beyond a certain point, they found that the impact on phytoplankton was precisely the reverse.*'

'The fourth tank?'

'Exactly. Above a certain threshold, *you would be destroying, not enhancing, the ability of the plankton to absorb carbon from the atmosphere.* What is more, if you overdose the phytoplankton, you not only achieve a complete kill-off of the phytoplankton in the marine area in question. *You apparently set up a chain reaction in surrounding areas. You might even trigger a global plankton crisis, which could be the end of all marine life as we know it.* I can't think of a single marine organism, from the largest whale to the smallest crustacean, which at the end of the day doesn't depend either directly or indirectly on the existence of plankton. And just think how many human resources, including our food supplies, depend on the sea!'

'Jesus,' I exclaimed. I'm not a scientist, but even I could understand the horrendous implications of the scenario Southgate had just outlined. 'This isn't science fiction, Graham, is it?' I asked.

Southgate shook his head. 'I'm afraid not. We're dealing with a two-edged sword here. In the right hands, falconite could help the world win the battle against global warming.'

'And in the wrong hands?'

'In the wrong hands, it could have precisely the opposite effect. It could lead to a rapid acceleration in global warming. It might even result in global ecological catastrophe. We have no way of telling at this moment.'

'What do you mean by the wrong hands?' I asked quietly.

'I mean the Russians, of course,' Southgate replied. 'I told you back in Cambridge that if there was one nation on earth that stands to gain, in the short term at least, from global warming, it is the Russians. Vast tracts of so far frozen Siberia would be opened up to production. Russian ships will be able to go from the Baltic to the Pacific, transforming Russia's prospects as a trading and industrial nation. Meanwhile the US suffers a cataclysmic shock as dustbowl conditions return, this time irreversibly. We all thought the cold war had ended, didn't we? Well, let me tell you something,' - he banged for emphasis on the table - 'the cold war hasn't ended at all. It is simply being fought by other means!'

'The Russians must know their advantages could disappear if there was a global ecological catastrophe,' I said.

'Russia's politicians are like any other politicians,' Southgate replied gloomily. 'There may be a battle going on in the Kremlin over this. President Cherniavsky has his back to the wall. Did you see that BBC *Panorama* programme the other day?'

I nodded. I remembered I had been watching the *Panorama* report on the disintegration of the Russian economy the night Nasreen telephoned me from Rio.

'I saw the programme,' I said. 'Pretty frightening stuff.'

'Then you'll realise that short-term gains are probably good enough, no matter what the long or not-so-long term risks may be. This is a way of saving Cherniavsky's bacon and the Russian economy at the same time. Besides the Russians haven't had a chance to do the scientific work on falconite that we have. They haven't run the experiments so they will probably suspect us of fabricating the overdose theory to suit our own purposes. If they knew where to find a major falconite deposit, they'd go for it like a shot. Not just to stop our side from getting it. No, they'll want to use it themselves.'

At this point, Graham Southgate lapsed into a long silence. He stared out of the library window towards the ice-filled channel that separates Adelaide Island, on which the Rothera Station is situated, from the Antarctic Peninsula proper. I could see a group of Adelie penguins pitching one after another off an ice floe into the water. Not far away, half a dozen Wedell seals were lying in the sun.

Southgate stood up from his chair and walked moodily over to the window. When all the Adelies had disappeared from the ice floe, he turned back to face me.

'I wish I'd never analysed those damn rocks,' he said. 'I would have done better to leave well alone. Those rocks should have been buried in the tent with Scott and Wilson and Bowers. They should never have been brought back to England.'

He came back to his chair.

'There's one good thing anyway,' he looked at Harry. 'Thanks to Mr Brokke's ingenious little scheme, with any luck the Russians are still tramping looking for a mystery falconite deposit in the forests of Brazil. We're days if not weeks ahead of them.'

Once again, I couldn't help recalling the film *Scott of the Antarctic* which Harry and I had watched with the rest of the school one cold winter evening in Dorset. Scott's ship, the *Terra Nova* is about to set sail from Christchurch, New Zealand. Captain Scott, alias John Mills, has just said a stiff-upper-lip farewell to his wife on the quayside when someone brings him a telegram to inform him that the dastardly Norwegian Amundsen, who has apparently promised Scott his interest lies in the Arctic not the Antarctic, turns out to have headed south after all and is actually way ahead of them!

It's hard to explain the sense of foreboding that I felt at this point.

'Don't be so sure about being ahead of the Russians, Graham,' I said.

I told Southgate about my visit to Radio Rothera and about how Sparks and I had listened in to the transmissions from Druzhnaya.

'Something's up,' I said. 'Your decoy plan may not have been as effective as you hoped.'

Southgate looked at me intently.

'The Russians don't have the falconite,' he said. 'They don't even know accurately where it is. They could be looking for a needle in a haystack. But we *do* know where it is. We had better be bloody sure we get to that nunatak before they do!'

'You could be wrong about that too,' I interrupted quietly. 'I think Kalinin's already here. I'm pretty sure I heard his voice over the air when I was up in the radio shack.'

'That's nonsense!' Southgate exclaimed. 'Kalinin's still in Cambridge.'

'Even if he is,' I said, 'he could have seen the sledging journals. He could have worked things out. That could mean the Russians know more than we think!'

I happened to glance across to Harry at that moment to see a smug look on his face. What the hell had he got to smile about, I wondered?

Southgate looked shocked. 'I'm going to get onto Cambridge straightway. Find out if Kalinin's still around.'

When Graham went back to his computer, Harry and I finally decided to turn in. It was well after midnight although, judging by the brightness outside, it could easily have been midday. We pulled down the blinds, but still the light streamed in.

I couldn't actually remember the last time Harry and I had slept in the same room together. Probably not since we were children. In spite of everything, there was still something companionable about sharing that cramped space with him in the BAS hut at Rothera.

Looking back, I'm sure it was precisely this feeling of cosiness, of solidarity, that resulted in my temporarily lowering my guard. That and being half asleep. Of course, I should have known better. The one thing you don't ever do when Harry is around is expose your chin. If you do, he'll sock you on the jaw.

'What I don't understand,' Harry said softly from the top bunk, 'is why, after you'd filed your story that morning in your Reuters office, you took off for the rest of the day. Went down to Kent, or whatever. Of course, it was marvellous from our point of view. You couldn't be forced to put out a correction because you simply weren't there. Gave us a whole day to trade. But still it was odd. We hadn't expected to have so much time. Why did you do it?'

I heard the question only distantly. I was already half-asleep. As a result I let myself be drawn into an answer whose consequences I hadn't bothered to assess. Not at that particular moment anyway.

'To tell you the truth, Harry,' I murmured, 'I think it was my subconscious which kept me away from my desk that day.'

'How so?' Harry suddenly seemed crisp and alert. Much more alert than I was.

'I mean that I think I had instinctively realised that something strange was going on. And that I had better leave the coast clear for a while.'

'You mean you knew what I was up to? You knew I was still alive?'

'Not quite that,' I replied slowly. 'But I think deep down I knew that *something* wasn't right.'

'How did you know?' Harry was like a terrier worrying a bone. The tension that emanated from the bunk above me was almost palpable.

I'm not sure that I had even worked it out for myself until Harry pressed the point. Lying there, in the narrow confines of the two-man unit, with the sounds of the skuas and snow pigeons still clearly audible outside, I tried to assess in my mind just what it was that had set up that first tingle of doubt.

Finally I said, 'Actually, Harry, I think it was the photograph.'

'What photograph?'

'The one of you and Alvarez.'

'Where did you see it?' He barked out the question.

I hesitated. I had actually seen two copies of the photograph. One hanging on the wall in Harry's office, the other in Nasreen's bedroom. 'The one in your office,' I said.

There was a long pause. Then Harry said, 'Ah yes, the one in my office. What about it?'

'I didn't realise it at the time,' I said, 'it was only after I met Alvarez in Belo Horizonte that I saw how odd it was.'

Harry was sounding pretty icy by now. 'What was odd?'

'In the photograph, Alvarez has his arm round you. You are both on his yacht. You are both in shirtsleeves on some kind of drinking spree.'

There was another pause, then Harry said slowly, 'I don't follow you.'

I knew then that I was digging myself deeper into the mire. My only hope was that Harry himself didn't know just how deep I was going.

'Alvarez wrote you a letter inviting you to a meeting with him. Nasreen showed me the letter. Why would he write to you in formal terms - "*Dear Mr Hodson*", and so forth - if you're already drinking buddies? I guess that's what my subconscious cottoned on to.'

Harry burst into a roar of laughter. 'You're a genius, Charles. You're a fucking genius!'

After that, there was total silence from the upper bunk.

It was at least another hour before I went to sleep. Harry's uproarious laughter sounded convincing enough, but I wasn't entirely happy. Frankly, I wasn't sure whether I had blown it or not. If I had, I knew there would be hell to pay. Harry was like that.

The Scott Memorial expedition had suddenly taken on a whole new dimension. Or, more precisely, several new dimensions. At one level, the fate of the globe itself might, literally, depend on it. At another level, my own personal future seemed to have become inextricably intertwined with whatever was going to happen out there on the ice of the Beardmore Glacier.

XIX

Beardmore Glacier, Antarctica I

THE NEXT DAY dawned fine and clear. Except it didn't dawn. I woke up at six o'clock and the light was still streaming in through the blinds, just as it had been when I had finally fallen asleep.

Our estimated time of departure was eight o'clock, but Harry and I were ready long before that. Wearing woolly hats and fur-lined anoraks, as well as the statutory super-strength sunglasses to protect against snow-blindness, we waited by the Sno-Cat for Steve Munro, Graham Southgate and Gary Lawson, the pilot, to join us. Colin, the Fid who had shown us around the base the previous day, drove us up the ramp to the airstrip.

The Scott Memorial Project Twotter was still parked where we had last seen it the previous day, but all the seats except four had been removed from the cabin. Four skidoos, as well as four pairs of skis, had been loaded on.

'We probably won't need the skis,' Munro said, 'but we like to have them on board as a safety measure.'

The Twotter was also carrying a forty-five gallon drum of aviation fuel.

'We've put depots where we need them,' said Munro, 'but we always like to carry a reserve. We can refuel in midair if we have to.'

I didn't find Munro's observation particularly comforting and I don't think Harry did either. Once or twice I stole a sideways glance at him. This morning he had a tense, calculating look on his face. I wasn't sure what to make of it.

The British Antarctic Survey research station at Rothera is, as I've already mentioned, situated at 67°34'S, 68°08'W. We were aiming for the upper end of the Beardmore Glacier, at more or less the point where the 85° circle of latitude intersected the 162°E meridian. When we took off, at around half past eight, we flew south along the panhandle, stopping after a couple of hours to refuel at one of the depots they had set up for us earlier.

I was surprised that the fuel hadn't frozen, left out in the open in drums like that. But Munro explained that aviation fuel only froze at –56°C.

'If it's got water in it, of course, that's another story.'

'Why should it have water in it?' I asked.

'Down here, you have to be prepared for anything.'

It's hard to describe what it's like to fly over the Antarctic continent in a small plane for the first time in one's life. At eight thousand feet, I could see every feature of the landscape below. I don't think I've ever experienced such awesome beauty. The farther south we flew, the more solid the ice below us became. The leads which had opened up around Adelaide Island disappeared as we reached the Bellingshausen Sea. On the starboard wing, I could see a great white sheet stretching out unbroken to the horizon, indeed to the very edge of the world. Straight ahead loomed the

Ellsworth Mountains and beyond them the beginning of that vast range of mountains which effectively spans half a continent: the Transantarctic Mountains.

We refuelled for a second time at a depot just west of the Vinson Massif in the Ellsworth Mountains, at around 80°S. While the pilot supervised the refuelling operation, Munro spread out a large chart on top of one of the skidoos.

'We're on the last leg now,' he said. 'We have enough fuel to land on the Beardmore Glacier. When we've found the nunatak, we'll have to drop down to the American base at McMurdo and refuel there.'

I studied the map carefully. Working from the coordinates Scott had given for the Upper Glacier depôt, as faxed to me by Southgate and estimating from that Scott's line of March, Munro had marked the area where we hoped to find the nunatak. I saw that he had drawn a large X to the west of Mount Buckley.

I was a bit puzzled by this. I'd done some research of my own the previous day in the Rothera library. Intrigued by Dame Pauline Fairweather's reference, I had glanced through the account by Roger Mear and Robert Swan of the journey they made in the mid-eighties in the footsteps of Scott. Their aim - in which they succeeded - was to manhaul their sledges just as Scott had done across the Ross Ice Shelf, up the Beardmore Glacier and over the Polar Plateau to the South Pole.

'I thought Scott kept to the *east* of Mount Buckley,' I said. 'That's what Mear and Swan did anyway.'

'We're talking about Scott's *return* journey,' Munro said. 'That's when he found the nunatak. He went up the Beardmore Glacier on the eastern side of Mount Buckley, but he came back the *western* side. Mear and Swan never followed Scott's return route. Their supply ship was crushed in the ice. They had to cut things short. The Americans flew them out from the Pole.'

Munro rolled up the chart, the pilot climbed back into his seat and we took off once again. Something was niggling me but I wasn't sure what it was.

Two hours later, as we flew over the snowcapped range of the eastern Transantarctic Mountains, we had our first view of the mighty Beardmore Glacier.

'There it is.' Munro pointed to the great river of ice carving its way through the mountains. 'Look, there's the Cloudmaker.' He gestured towards a mighty peak rising straight ahead of us. Shackleton's description of the mountain was apt enough, I thought. Even now, on this clear day, the summit of the Cloudmaker was wrapped in mist.

The pilot banked to port and lost altitude. We flew low over the ice.

Munro went up to the cockpit. 'Let's get as close to Mount Buckley as we can,' he shouted above the roar of the engine.

'Roger,' Gary shouted back.

Looking down, I could see that the surface of the glacier was badly crevassed in places, although there were also long stretches where the ice was smooth and unbroken. A few minutes later, as we saw the brown core of Mount Buckley rising from the middle of the glacier, like a great rock splitting the flow of a river, I felt a surge of excitement. We had come so far and now we were almost there.

'This is it, Harry.' I could feel the buzz as I spoke.

Harry still had that strange glint in his eye. I don't think he heard me.

The pilot put the plane down on a clear stretch of ice to the west of Mount Buckley, but kept the throttle open. The skis touched down and we roared along the surface of the glacier under full power, before taking off again and circling.

'What are we doing?' I asked Southgate.

'The pilot does a dummy run first. Then he takes a good look at the surface below us, checking for any crevasses or collapsed snow bridges.'

Gary Lawson obviously concluded from his careful inspection that the landing area was safe, because a few seconds later he brought the Twotter down smoothly and safely onto the blue-white sheen of the glacier.

The wind hit us when we slid the door back. It whistled around the plane and whipped our faces as we unloaded the skidoos. I reckoned that the temperature up there almost at the top of the glacier must have been ten or fifteen degrees colder than at Rothera.

To be on the safe side, Gary left the plane's engine running. There's nothing worse, he told us, than finding you can't restart a frozen engine when you're parked on the top of a glacier.

The fact that, minute by minute, second by second, the fuel gauge on the Twotter was dropping imparted an extra sense of urgency to our mission. We lost no time in climbing onto our skidoos. Munro and Southgate led the way; Harry and I brought up the rear. We headed straight for Mount Buckley. Once there, we had agreed that the two skidoo teams would split up to explore any rocky outcrops between Buckley and the western edge of the glacier. All of us, I believe, had a pretty clear idea of what we were looking for. Edward Wilson's own sketch of the 'pear-shaped' nunatak was still clearly imprinted on our minds.

Munro and Southgate set off at a cracking pace. Harry and I, skidoos roped together in the approved fashion, brought up the rear. Twenty minutes later, we reached the ice-free rock-face of Mount Buckley. We paused momentarily.

'Let's synchronise watches,' Munro shouted, looking at his own.

'How much time do we have?' I shouted back.

'Let's RV back here in an hour. Absolute maximum.'

It was a long hour, one of the longest in my life. I felt so sure we were going to find what we were looking for. Twice we came to rocky outcrops, two or three miles west of Buckley, but these were low-lying scattered formations which bore absolutely no resemblance to Wilson's sketch. For the rest, we skidded hither and yon across the surface of the glacier. I am sure our search could have been more systematic but, however systematic we made it, it would not have been able to turn up something which simply wasn't there.

We had to keep an eye on the time, of course. With twenty minutes left before we had to return to the rendezvous, I pulled up alongside Harry's skidoo.

'Where the hell is that nunatak?' I shouted.

'I don't think it's here,' he shouted back.

'Maybe Munro and Southgate have had better luck.'

'Maybe.' Harry seemed strangely unmoved.

Fortunately the terrain to the west of Mount Buckley was perfect. All the time we were out on the ice we didn't have to cross a single snowbridge. We didn't even see a crevasse. It was odd to know that beneath us the glacier was moving all the time - at its snail's speed of three feet a day - carrying its great load of ice from the plateau to the coast. Here at least one had no sense of movement or even stress. No cracks or fissures in the ice disturbed its smooth surface.

That, at least, was something to be grateful for, I reflected, as I brought up the rear, carefully aiming the nose of my skidoo along Harry's tracks. If the weather had suddenly taken a turn for the worse, if the terrain had been heavily crevassed, if one or other of us had suddenly become disoriented owing to poor visibility, it might have been a different story . . .

It was clear, when we met up with them, that Munro and Southgate were as disappointed as we were. Southgate in particular was almost beside himself with frustration.

'I don't know where we've gone wrong,' he kept saying. 'Dammit, I really don't know.'

LESS THAN TWO hours later, our de Havilland Twin Otter was on its final approach to the Williams ski-way on the McMurdo Sound between Ross Island and the mainland of Antarctica. Ahead of us, more or less in the centre of Ross Island, loomed the twelve thousand foot summit of Mount Erebus. However disappointed we might have been by the afternoon's failure, it was hard not to be awed and uplifted by the spectacular sight. Every inch of the mountain was covered with ice or snow, so that it seemed to be wearing a giant white cape. From the very top, wisps of cloud emerged. It was on the slopes of Mount Erebus, I recalled, that a few years back a DC10 had crashed, with the loss of all 257 people on board.

While our pilot wisely gave the mountain a wide berth, Munro briefed us. '*De facto* if not *de jure* this is the US sector of Antarctica. The United States' official policy is not to welcome private expeditions to Antarctica and, remember, that's what we are.' He nodded briefly in Harry's direction, an acknowledgment of Harry's role as the Scott Memorial Project's cash cow. 'However,' he continued, 'we may be able to talk them into a little traditional Antarctic hospitality!'

Munro's attempt at a joke served to lighten the atmosphere further, and when he suggested that we should be ready to have another crack at finding Scott's nunatak the following day, after refuelling at McMurdo, we all cheered up noticeably.

Seen from the air, McMurdo looks like a small mining town. It is the only settlement of any size on the whole Antarctic continent. All US activities on Antarctica are coordinated by the NSF - the National Science Foundation. In summer as many as a thousand people - many of them scientists - are to be found in or operating out of McMurdo. From the air, you see a sprawl of prefabricated buildings, Nissen huts and wooden sheds, which house the workshops and laboratories. There's a church, a fire station, a hospital, even a liquor store.

Gary Lawson had radioed McMurdo while we were still over the Ross Ice Shelf to tell them we were on our way in. A USAP Sno-Cat, blue and white logo emblazoned on the bonnet, was waiting for us on the ski-way as we touched down. Leaving our diminutive Twotter parked alongside the giant Hercules which USAP uses to resupply their Amundsen-Scott South Pole Station, we were escorted without further ado to the base commander's office.

Lieutenant-Commander Ed Parker was a forty-year old black American. He had a lean fit fiery look about him.

'What the hell are you guys doing?' he exploded as we were shown in. 'You know that US government policy is not to sponsor or encourage any private expeditions in Antarctica. We'll refuel you at cost, but that's all we can do.'

The rest of us kept quiet while Munro did the talking. Munro explained that, though the Scott Memorial Project was indeed a privately-financed expedition, he himself was base commander at Rothera on the Antarctic Peninsula and BAS was sufficiently interested in the objectives of the Scott Memorial Project to make certain facilities available to it, including, for example, his own time and expertise.

At the mention of the British Antarctic Survey, Lieutenant-Commander Parker appeared mollified.

'Of course, that changes the picture,' he said.

At this point we shook hands all round. A steward brought in a tray of drinks. Parker lifted a glass of bourbon. 'You Brits talk about the sun going down over the yardarm, I understand. Well, the sun doesn't go down at all at this time of year at McMurdo. When we have visitors, we offer them a drink, no matter what time of day or night it is!'

After that, it was all sweetness and light. In a bluff good-natured way, Parker probed into the Scott Memorial Project's precise objectives.

'You're looking to set up a memorial for Scott on the Beardmore Glacier then, are you?' he asked.

'Exactly,' Munro said. 'We think that's a fitting location. We didn't quite find the kind of place we are looking for today, so we thought we'd go back tomorrow. Then, when we've located the spot, we'll put things in hand.'

'A monument to a great man and to science?' Parker asked.

'Exactly.'

'Very fitting,' Parker agreed.

Parker had invited us to explore the base at our leisure before joining him for dinner later. While the others went off to find the quarters they had been allocated, I headed for the library. The niggling sense of unease that I had felt earlier in the day over the question of Scott's precise route had grown into full-blown anxiety. We had wasted one whole day already. We could not afford to waste another.

XX

McMurdo, Ross Island, Antarctica

THE BAS LIBRARY at Rothera had seemed comprehensive enough, as far as I was concerned, but McMurdo's collection of Antarctic literature was exceptional. That's the thing about the Americans; they never do things by halves. They'd build a library on the moon if they had to. Located at one end of the Crary Lab, with a magnificent view of the Transantarctic Mountains, the McMurdo library contained virtually every book about Antarctic exploration ever written.

To my amazement, the library actually had two copies of the famous two-volume account of Scott's last expedition, published in London in 1913 by Smith, Elder and Company, 15 Waterloo Place, London. I removed one of the sets from the shelf.

'I'm afraid you can't take that one out of the room,' the librarian - a grey-haired, middle-aged woman, who looked as though she could have come from a small town in Iowa - warned me, 'but you're welcome to read it here.'

'Thanks,' I said.

There are different ways of reading a book. One way is to concentrate on the printed word. Another is to try to absorb the material through your fingertips, as it were. To get the feel of it, to let it grow on you. Then you can look at the text. I tried the second way.

For a while, I just sat there in the library, thinking myself back into the heroic age of Antarctic exploration. Less than a mile from where I sat, on the tip of Hut Point Peninsula, the base-hut of Scott's *Discovery* expedition of 1901–04 could still be visited. And a few miles to the north, at Cape Evans, Scott had built a second hut to serve as the base for his ill-fated expedition with the *Terra Nova*, 1910–13.

This was the place, I said to myself, where it all began. And it was here, too, that it ended. For this was the anchorage the rescue vessel used when, over a year later, Scott's possessions, including the diaries and the rocks, were eventually shipped back to England. McMurdo might be a bustling town today - Big Mac, they call it - but if you're an Antarctic buff you know you're standing at the very gateway of history.

A splendid picture of Captain Robert F Scott CVO, RN, taken from a portrait, served as the frontispiece of the first volume. Wearing full naval dress, including ceremonial sword, he held my eye with his steady level gaze. Towards the end of the book - page 486 to be precise - there was another portrait. This one was a black and white photograph of Scott in his Antarctic gear, including fur gloves and balaclava helmet. The picture was captioned '*Scott wearing the wallet in which he carried the sledging journals*'. A third picture showed the party at the South Pole - Oates, Bowers, Scott, Wilson and P. O. Evans. You can see the string which he pulled to take the photograph, running out from Bowers' feet towards the camera.

The volume I had open in front of me, the first volume of the two-volume publication, contained the full text of Scott's diaries on that second expedition to Antarctica. (The second volume contained related material). I had seen the facsimile version in Cambridge, but now there was a chance to look at the whole thing in printed form.

The question which had been gnawing at the back of my mind, ever since our fruitless expedition to the top of the Beardmore Glacier earlier that day, was one of logistics, of practicality, of common sense. We had been looking for the nunatak in the area to the west of Mount Buckley. *But why the hell had Scott and his party made that detour*? They had gone up the Beardmore to the east of Mount Buckley. Why had they gone to the *west* on the way down?

Sitting there, reading the diaries word by word as Scott had written them, I experienced once again the same kind of overpowering emotion which I had felt that afternoon in Cambridge. The fact that a few hours earlier we had ourselves been up on the Beardmore Glacier, walking (or more accurately skidooing) in the footsteps of the great man, only served to add to the poignancy.

I made notes as I read, jotting down details of Scott's slow but steady progress up the Beardmore. Camp 44 had been on December 21, 1911, at around 7,100 feet with the temperature at –5 and the barometer at 22.3. Camp 45, on December 22, had been at 7,750 feet, with the temperature at –3° and the barometer at 21.61. Hugging the eastern edge of the glacier as they approached Mount Buckley, Scott - as he narrated it - ran into a heavily-crevassed area. '*The most extraordinary surface - narrow crevasses ran in all directions. They were quite invisible, being covered with a thin crust of hardened névé without a sign of a crack in it . . . we all fell in one after another and sometimes two together . . . how a hardened crust can form over cracks is a real puzzle; it seems to argue extremely slow movement.*'

Most days, at least on the journey south, Scott included a note of the camp's location. Camp 45 for example had been pitched at latitude 85°13½, longitude 161°55. More than once Scott referred to Evans' navigational skills. On December 23, for example, he wrote, '*Evans has just found the latitude.*' The camp that night was pitched at 86°55 minutes 47 seconds S, 165°5 minutes 48 seconds, E, demonstrating that Evans had in effect produced what in today's terms would be equivalent to a twelve figure map reference.

I read on for a few more minutes, drawn by Scott's description of the final approach to the South Pole. Of course I knew the story. Every schoolboy knows the story. But to read that story in Scott's own words, to read it in the very place from which the explorer had set out across the ice with such high hopes, that was something else again.

On Wednesday January 17, at Camp 69, the temperature was –22° at the start. Amundsen's black flag was flying at the Pole. Scott's disappointment is palpable. '*Great God!*' he writes. '*This is an awful place and terrible enough for us to have laboured to it without reward of priority.*'

Christ, I said to myself, how could he have handled that disappointment? How could Oates and Evans and Wilson have endured it? How could anyone have endured it?

I didn't quite know what I was looking for but I somehow felt sure that the text in front of me would yield the necessary clues if only I were able to recognise them. I found the first detailed confirmation of my suspicion in the entry for January 25, 1912. Scott and his party were almost two hundred miles into their return journey and Scott makes it clear that, wherever they can, *they try to follow the tracks made on the outward journey.* He wrote (on page 550 of the volume I had before me), '*the old tracks show so remarkably well that we can follow them without much difficulty, a great piece of luck.*'

It was clear to me as I read on that this 'piece of luck' was all the more important because by now the health and fitness of the party was deteriorating. '*Oates suffers from a very cold foot,*' Scott wrote, '*Evans' fingers and nose are in a bad state and tonight Wilson is suffering tortures from his eyes.*'

I think it was that last paragraph more than anything else that convinced me I was right. At a time when Oates and Evans were suffering severely from frostbite and when Wilson was enduring the agonies of snowblindness; at a time, moreover, when the marks of the outward journey were still clearly visible as a guide for their return - at such a time, I asked myself, why in heaven's name would Scott - whatever the scientific objectives of the expedition might be - have insisted on passing *to the west* of Mount Buckley? I remembered the passage from Huntford's book which Southgate had shown me in Cambridge. Huntford, of course, was convinced that Scott had made a detour. 'Geology cost him six or seven miles' - but Huntford had seemed determined to demolish Scott's reputation. Maybe Huntford was wrong in this, as in other, respects?

I flipped on through the book to try to find the full printed text of the long passage, whose manuscript version I had copied down from the Cambridge facsimile and which I had read out to

Harry that evening we sat in the hotel bar together in Willemstad, Curaçao. Because what Scott wrote on February 8, 1912 is so crucial to my own story, I'm repeating the entry here virtually in its entirety. Anyone who has followed this story so far will be spared the trouble of having to dig out the earlier citation.

Here then, once again, is the vital text.

'***Thursday, February 8*** *- R 22. Height 6260. Start Temp −11°; Lunch Temp −5°; Supper, zero. 9.2 miles. Started from the depot rather late owing to weighing biscuit, etc., and rearranging matters. Had a beastly morning. Wind very strong and cold. Steered in for Mt Darwin to visit rock. Sent Bowers on, on ski, as Wilson can't wear his at present. He obtained several specimens, all of much the same type, a close-grained granite rock which weathers red. Hence the pink limestone. After he rejoined we skidded downhill pretty fast, leaders on ski, Oates and Wilson on foot alongside sledge - Evans detached. We lunched at 2 well down towards Mt Buckley, the wind half a gale and everybody very cold and cheerless. However, better things were to follow. We decided to steer for the moraine under Mt Buckley and, pulling with crampons, we crossed some very irregular steep slopes with big crevasses and slid down towards the rocks. The moraine was obviously so interesting that when we had advanced some miles and got out of the wind, I decided to camp and spend the rest of the day geologising. It has been extremely interesting. We found ourselves under perpendicular cliffs of Beacon sandstone, weathering rapidly and carrying veritable coal seams. From the last Wilson, with his sharp eyes, has picked several plant impressions, the last a piece of coal with beautifully traced leaves in layers, also some excellently preserved impression of thick stems, showing cellular structure. In one place, we saw the cast of small waves on the sand. Tonight Bill has got a specimen of limestone with archeocy-*

athus - the trouble is one cannot imagine where the stone comes from; it is evidently rare, as few specimens occur in the moraine. There is a good deal of pure white quartz. Altogether we have had a most interesting afternoon, and the relief of being out of the wind and in a warmer temperature is inexpressible.'

I knew as I read and reread the passage that there was something wrong. Finally, I worked out what it was. Scott wrote that they had '*started from the depôt*'. That meant the previous night they had camped at the depôt which, as the entry for the previous day - February 7 - makes clear, is the Mount Darwin or Upper Glacier depôt. They had travelled altogether a distance of 9.2 miles before making camp again (R22, where R was the return journey and 22 the number of camps to date). During the course of that day's march, they had '*steered for the moraine under Mt Buckley*'. They had encountered some '*very irregular steep slopes with big crevasses*'.

None of this description as far as I could see tallied with the area we had visited that day. With a growing sense of excitement, I pulled from a pocket the facsimile Southgate had sent us from Cambridge. The manuscript version of the journal entry for Thursday, December 21 (1911) clearly showed 85 7°'S as the latitude for the Upper Glacier depôt, with 166°32'E as the longitude. Yet the printed text gave *85°1'S* as the latitude.

As I jotted the figures down, I remembered that I had myself first noticed the discrepancy when the fax from Southgate had come through to the hotel in Curaçao. I had thought at the time that I had simply made a mistake with the transcription. Now I wasn't so sure. Would the venerable firm of Elder and Co, 15 Waterloo Place, have permitted the typographical error? Was it not possible that, in between the time I had first noted down the coordinates and the time Southgate had sent me the fax, the manuscript in the Scott Polar Research Institute in Cambridge had somehow been altered?

The facsimile of Scott's Journal had been in a loose-leaf binder in an unlocked case in an ill-guarded Museum which was open to the public. While Southgate and his backers, whoever they were, were all busy trying to set up the decoy for Russians in Brazil, had the Russians worked out the truth about the location of the falconite for themselves? Having done so, had someone simply wandered into the Museum of the Scott Polar Research Institute in Cambridge and quietly, when no one was looking, changed a '1' into a '7'?

How to prove it, though - that was the question. The addition of a simple ink stroke would be hard to detect, particularly if the perpetrator of the forgery had actually photocopied the whole page once he had made the alteration, taking care to use similar or identical copier paper. Alternatively, could we track down the original of Scott's diaries at the British Museum in London to verify precisely what the original geographical coordinates were?

Given time, I was sure that this kind of detective work was feasible. But how much time did we have? If someone had gone out of their way to falsify the evidence, that someone was probably well ahead of the game.

I swore out loud, causing the librarian to shoot a warning glance in my direction. *Up until now we had been assuming that we knew the location of the falconite and the Russians didn't.* But it was obvious now that the reverse could be true.

What happened next put the matter beyond any shadow of doubt. No need for faxes to Cambridge or the British Museum. No need for any Hercule Poirot stuff. As I picked up the book to return it to the shelf, a piece of vellum fell out of a pocket at the back. Smith and Elder had included for the edification of the Edwardian book-buying public a reproduction of Scott's famous last '*Message to the Public*', the brief treatise which he penned during those lonely last hours in the tent when his companions were probably already lying dead beside him.

Almost casually, I began to read the text. For a man who was literally at the end of his tether, and who probably only had hours to live, the orthography was remarkably clear; the pencil strokes still bold; the letters well-formed and legible. '*The causes of the disaster*,' I read, '*are not due to faulty organisation, but to misfortune in all the risks which had to be undertaken.*

'*1. The loss of pony transport in March 1911 obliged me to start later than I had intended, and obliged the limits of stuff transported to be narrowed . . .*'

I noted how Scott wrote the 1 in '1911'; a clear, short, more or less upright stroke.

In the fifth paragraph of the '*Message to the Public*' I read, '*Every detail of our food supplies, clothing and depots made on the interior icesheet and over that long stretch of 700 miles to the Pole and back, worked out to perfection . . .*'

This time I noted that Scott used a sloping hand to write the 7 in '700'. I could clearly see now that in the fax Southgate had sent me the upward stroke of the 7 was in fact far too upright, a 1 to which someone had simply added a cross-stroke.

For a second I didn't see the clincher. Sometimes your eyes see what you're looking for, not what's really there. Then it hit me. Whoever had perpetrated that forgery in Cambridge had decided to make assurance doubly sure. Continentals, including the French and the Italians, actually write their 1s as though they were 7s, in other words they use a cross-stroke at the top of the upright. These same Continentals, to avoid the possibility of confusion between their 1s and their 7s, therefore put a cross stroke through the middle of the 7.

That was precisely what our Cambridge forger had done! He had produced a continental 7. Quite why I hadn't spotted that glaring solecism before, I couldn't fathom. No way could Captain Robert Falcon Scott RN CVO have written a continental 7 - then or ever!

I thrust the piece of vellum back into the pouch, slammed the book shut, handed it back to the librarian with some quick muttered thanks and bolted for the door.

I found the rest of the team - Munro, Southgate and Harry - deep in discussion in a small meeting room at the far end of the Crary Lab. Bursting to tell them my news, I didn't wait to find out what they were talking about.

'I've found it!' I proclaimed triumphantly, in the manner of Archimedes.

'Found what?' Munro and Southgate asked in unison.

'The true coordinates of the Upper Glacier depôt We've been using the wrong starting point!'

I took them through my reasoning step by step and I could see that they were convinced. They knew what I said made sense.

'Who the hell could have changed the map reference back in Cambridge? Who would have wanted or needed to do that?' Harry seemed genuinely puzzled.

'Someone who worked out the true location of the falconite deposit,' I replied. 'Someone who was in Cambridge between the time of my visit and the time Graham faxed me the copy of the diary entry.'

Suddenly I remembered the large shambling figure of Professor Boris Kalinin, the Russian academician specialising in global warming, whom I had met at diner in Churchill College the evening I was in Cambridge. I had been convinced that I had recognised Kalinin's voice on the air when we were at the BAS base at Rothera. Southgate had pooh-poohed the idea but I was still convinced I was right and that Kalinin was involved up to his neck in the Russian quest for falconite. Could Kalinin himself, during his Cambridge visit, have changed the critical map reference to send us miles in the wrong direction?

I turned to Southgate. 'Did you hear back from Cambridge, Graham?' I asked. 'Has Kalinin been seen in college recently?'

Southgate shook his head. 'Apparently, the Professor hasn't been seen for days. He said something about having urgent business in Moscow.'

I could tell from the grim expressions on Munro and Southgate's faces that my suspicions were probably well-founded.

'Damn it!' Munro exploded, pounding the table. 'When we removed the facsimile journals from the exhibition *it was already too late!*'

If it hadn't all been so real, I could have laughed. It was 'the Russians are coming' all over again.

'What's the worst possible scenario?' I asked.

Munro thought about that one for a moment. 'The worst possible scenario,' he replied at last, 'is that the Russians are days if not weeks, ahead of us, just as Amundsen was ahead of Scott. The worst possible scenario is that they have already found the nunatak and extracted the deposit. They may already have flown the material to Druzhnaya, on the Ronne Ice Shelf, and loaded it on the *Leningrad.* The worst possible scenario is that the Russians won't simply be trying to deprive the West of a substance which could slow down global warming. They won't be looking to blackmail us into paying an extortionate price for it. On the contrary, given Russia's immediate interest in an acceleration of global warming for all the reasons we know, they may already be preparing *to overdose the ocean down here in the Antarctic,* thereby triggering possibly irreversible climate changes of a kind which, while potentially of great benefit to Russia, could be catastrophic for the West. And the timing could be absolutely perfect for them! They could catch the onset of the phytoplankton bloom which happens in the Weddell Sea at the beginning of each Antarctic spring. If you're going to zap the plankton this is the place to do it and now is the moment!'

'Are you implying,' I asked, 'that we could already have run out of time? That if the Russians have already loaded the material on the *Leningrad* it's too late?'

'Not quite,' Munro interrupted. 'Before we left Rothera, we had a report in from our skidoo team out there on the Ronne Ice Shelf. The *Leningrad* hasn't left Druzhnaya yet, but it may only be a matter of hours before she does.'

Harry finally said something. He looked distinctly unhappy at the turn the discussion had taken.

'Now that we know the true location of the nunatak,' he said, 'shouldn't we first try to check whether the falconite is still there? This is all good James Bond stuff. I understand that. But we don't want to trigger a major international incident, do we? Are we going to stop and search a possibly innocent Russian vessel on the high seas? Shouldn't we establish the facts? Munro says the *Leningrad* is still at Druzhnaya. As I understand it, it would have to push its way out through the ice of the Ronne Ice Shelf before reaching the open water of the Weddell Sea! There's no point in sprinkling the stuff on the packice, as I understand. That won't do the trick. The Russians will know that, surely?'

He turned to Munro. 'You're the Antarctic wallah. Don't we have a couple of days at least? If they're going to dump the stuff in the ocean, to coincide with the phytoplankton bloom, they have to reach clear water first, don't they?'

Munro looked at Southgate and then they both looked at Harry. They seemed to be weighing up what Harry had just said. Momentarily I had the impression that Southgate winked, but he put his hand to his eye and I realised it must have been a twitch.

'I guess you could be right,' Munro said at last. 'Maybe it's not the Cuban missile crisis all over again. Not yet anyway. Maybe we still have some time.'

He looked at his watch. 'I'm going to get in touch with Rothera. Sparks will still be on duty. If the skidoo party out on the Ronne Ice Shelf confirms that the *Leningrad* is still at Druzhnaya, we'll follow the course Mr, er, Brokke suggests. We'll go back up to the Beardmore in the morning and see what there is to see. If we find the nunatak and the falconite has gone, we can call in the cavalry then.'

'Amen to that,' said Harry. I could tell he was pleased the decision had gone his way.

XXI

Beardmore Glacier, Antarctica

One of the problems with twenty-four hour daylight is that the internal clock, and the biological rhythms associated with it, go haywire. If we had taken a snap vote on it, I suspect we would have disregarded the need to eat and sleep and headed off for the Beardmore then and there on the grounds that the sun was still shining and there was still work to be done.

In the event, wiser counsel prevailed. Munro went off to find Gary Lawson, our pilot, located him in the bar and came back with the news that we were cleared for a 6.00 a.m. take-off. He suggested that the rest of us should have dinner together and turn in early.

When we arrived in the canteen, Lieutenant-Commander Parker was already seated at a large round table in the middle of the room. Dinner was a self-service affair, so we filled up our plates at a copious buffet and carried our trays over to join him.

'Good to see you again,' Parker said. He motioned to two women sitting at the same table. 'Let me present Dr Tanya Kuznetsov and Captain Ivana Popov. These two ladies,' Parker explained, 'are based at the Russian station, Vostok - latitude 78°S, 106°E. Russia and the United States operate a joint programme over there.'

In their very different ways, the two Russian women were stunning. Dr Tanya Kuznetsov was a tall striking redhead; Captain Ivana Popov was a petite brunette. Both, I suspected, had steel backbones.

'Life can be pretty bleak up at Vostok,' Parker explained. 'The base is situated at the Pole of Relative Inaccessibility. It's the farthest away point you can get to on this continent. And it's probably the coldest too. The temperature can hit minus 80° centigrade, if you can imagine that. If you take a kettle of water outside, the water literally explodes! So we like to invite the Vostok personnel down to McMurdo from time to time for a bit of R and R. Watch a movie. Unfreeze the toes. That kind of thing. Isn't that so, ladies?'

Parker was clearly in an expansive mood. He raised his glass. 'To your good health,' he said. 'To all of us. Long may the spirit of international cooperation reign in Antarctica!'

The redhead raised her own glass in turn. 'We have much enjoyed our stay, Commander. Thank you for your hospitality. As you know, we return to Vostok tomorrow morning. We shall take away happy memories of our time here.'

It was a friendly enough tribute. Soon after that the Russians left the table, saying they had to prepare for their departure.

'I'm sorry they didn't stay,' Parker chuckled. 'I told them you were coming to join me. They seemed pretty interested in your plans, I must say.'

'Which plans in particular?' Munro asked sharply.

'The plans to build a memorial to Scott on the Beardmore

Glacier, of course. The plans you described to me this afternoon, Mr Munro.'

I saw a look of dismay flash momentarily across Munro's craggy features. Could the American, unwittingly, have compromised our mission?

'You didn't tell them precisely where we were headed, Commander, I hope?'

Parker managed to look astonished. 'Why ever not? Are you afraid the Russians are going to get in first and build a memorial to Scott before you fellas do?'

'Good heavens, no!' Munro laughed heartily as though the idea of being pipped at the post by the Russians was furthest from his mind.

Soon after that, Munro and Southgate left the table and Harry and I followed suit a bit later. The facilities at McMurdo being as spacious as they were, at least compared to Rothera, we had each been allocated separate rooms in what was clearly the USAP guest wing.

Harry's room was at one end of the corridor; mine at the other. Harry walked down the corridor with me. As we did so, a door opened and one of the Russian women we had met earlier that evening emerged, with toilet kit in hand, presumably en route to the communal bathroom.

Harry, whose mood had been so sombre during the day, perked up visibly.

'*Spokoynoy nochy, tovarisha*,' he called out cheerfully.

Tanya Kuznetzov turned round and smiled at us. '*Spokoynoy nochy*,' she replied.

I said good night to Harry at the door of my room. 'I didn't know you spoke Russian, Harry,' I said.

'There's a lot you don't know about me, Charles.'

I slept fitfully that night. Even though I had drawn the blinds, the sun still shone through the cracks. Once, as I lay there trying to sleep, I thought I heard whispers in the corridor and the creak of a door.

By the time we reached the Williams ski-way at 5.45 the next morning, the Russians had already left. There was no sign of the little Tupolev 114 which we had seen parked at the end of the runway when we flew in to McMurdo the previous afternoon. Which of them was the pilot, I wondered? Or maybe they took it in turns.

Munro, I could tell, was still uneasy about our encounter with Dr Tanya Kuznetzov and Captain Ivana Popov and I had no intention of making matters worse by telling him, in jest or otherwise, that I suspected Harry had been fraternising the night before. I think at this point Munro wanted to put the Russians out of his mind and get on with the job. The reality was that BAS was operating very much at the edge of its capability down here in the Ross Sea area. We had been refuelled over night by the Americans, but otherwise we were on our own, with little or no backup to speak of. Things were complicated enough from the logistical and practical point of view without adding the political dimension.

To make matters worse, the weather had gone from 'dingle', i.e. fine, to 'manky', i.e. dubious. The clouds were low on Mount Erebus, behind the American base, and though the runway at sea-level was clear of fog we would be climbing to at least 9,000 feet on the glacier.

'Visibility could be bad up there today, Gary,' Munro warned. 'You may have difficulty landing.'

'I'm not worried about landing,' Gary scoffed. 'I'm worried

about all of you wandering around on your skidoos in a white-out.'

None of us, of course, wanted to turn back. Certainly not then, with so much riding on this second expedition to the Beardmore. I think the katabatic winds - the winds which blow down off the Polar Plateau to the coast - would have had to have been blowing at hurricane force to keep us away. Or else a fog thicker than the proverbial pea-souper of Nineteenth century London would have had to have descended on the glacier. Twenty minutes later, we were airborne.

Gary decided to go under the weather. We flew low across the ice, aiming for the break in the Transantarctic Mountains made by the Beardmore Glacier as it cuts through to the coast, an area known on the map as The Gap. After that, it was a matter of hugging the eastern edge of the glacier and keeping the nose well above the ground as we climbed.

The previous day there had been an element of fun in the trial touchdown, with the pilot holding the throttle open as the skis trailed on the ice, then climbing and banking to come round a second time. Now it was a different story. Visibility was getting worse by the minute. We knew, moreover, that the eastern edge of the Beardmore was heavily crevassed. Gary touched down once, flew round, wasn't satisfied, touched down again, still wasn't satisfied, so roared away for a third time of asking. When at last we slid to a halt without tumbling nose-first into a crevasse, I think all of us - even Antarctic veterans like Southgate and Munro - heaved a sigh of relief. Our satisfaction was all the greater when we realised that Gary's navigation had been spot on. Through the mist we could make out the bulk of Mount Buckley, jutting out blackly from the surface of the glacier as an island juts out from the surrounding sea.

As before, we divided into two teams. The same two teams. I couldn't help wondering whether it wouldn't have been better for me to go with Munro and Harry with Southgate, or vice versa. That way Harry and I would both have benefited from the practical Antarctic experience of our colleagues, particularly given the obviously difficult conditions. Actually, I was going to suggest a new alignment, but Munro was in such a hurry to unpack the skidoos and get going that I thought better of it. They obviously reckoned we could manage and I didn't feel able to insist.

Anyway, Harry was already on his skidoo and impatiently beckoning me to follow him. 'Buck up, Charles,' he shouted. 'We haven't got all day.'

Harry and I headed north, more or less. Munro and Southgate headed east. I saw Munro lift a gloved hand and wave as he and Southgate disappeared from sight.

I wouldn't say I enjoyed the next hour. In the first place, I wasn't happy with Harry's driving. He roared across a couple of snow bridges which, to my way of thinking, looked pretty dodgy. What's more, it had begun to snow. Not heavily, it was probably too cold for that, but still the thin powdery flakes were enough to clog up one's goggles.

We tried to make our search as systematic as we could, but I'm not sure we succeeded. I had a sense that in practice we dashed every which way, attracted by anything that looked like a rocky outcrop or nunatak.

I shouted to Harry. 'I think we should turn back.' But he shook his head violently, pointing to a dark outline ahead.

I saw at once why Harry was excited. The shape of the nunatak which now loomed up through the mist was precisely the one Wilson had sketched. Or rather, it would have been if a great hole had not been gouged out of its side. The 'pear' had virtually been sliced in half from top to bottom.

'What the hell?' I exclaimed as we brought our machines to a halt.

All around the nunatak, the ice had been crumpled and trampled. Whoever had quarried that rock had made a thorough job of it.

I think I know now what Scott must have felt like when he saw Amundsen's black flag flying at the Pole. The sense of disappointment, of frustration, was overwhelming.

'Oh God!' I said. 'They've beaten us to it.'

There was no way of proving that it was the Russians, of course. Not at that moment anyway. They hadn't left any calling cards. We didn't find any red star cap badges lying conveniently in the snow. But neither Harry nor I had the slightest doubt that Ivan and Co had got to Scott's nunatak first and, moreover, had removed every last ounce of the falconite deposit.

I took a series of photographs of the nunatak from all sides, cataloguing the devastation. I didn't know what we could use the photographs for - the Russians were never going to admit to this act of piracy - but it seemed the right thing to do anyway. For the hell of it, I also took a picture of Harry in front of the devastated nunatak, and then he took one of me.

'We'd better get back,' I said to Harry as we stood there. 'They'll want to move quickly. The Russians must be days ahead of us.'

Disaster struck on the way back. Obviously conscious of the

pressure of time, Harry set off at a fair lick. About half a mile from the nunatak, he drove his own skidoo over a snow bridge and then, suddenly and without warning, swung to the right along the lip of the crevasse just as I was about to cross it.

If our two skidoos hadn't still been roped together, it wouldn't have mattered. As it was, there was absolutely nothing I could do to save myself. My skidoo was jerked abruptly off the middle of the snow bridge.

'Jesus, Harry, what the fuck are you doing?' I shouted as I saw what was about to happen.

It's surprising how quickly you fall. There are no slow-motion effects. They may slow things down in the movies, showing the graceful parabola carved by the falling object, the spray of debris, snow and ice or whatever. In reality it's nothing like that. One moment I was in the driver's seat on the skidoo; the next I was dangling thirty feet down a crevasse. Fifteen feet above me I could see my skidoo, precariously wedged across the gap. I could just glimpse the opening at the top where Harry's own skidoo, safely anchored - or so I hoped - was taking the strain of the rope.

I didn't look down. As my skidoo tumbled into the crevasse, the skis I was carrying had come loose. Whereas my own fall had been halted by the rope which clipped me onto the vehicle, the skis had hurtled on down. I hadn't heard them hit the bottom of the crevasse. I suspected that the bottom, if there was one, was a very long way beneath me.

I could hear Harry shouting, 'Are you all right, Charles?'

'I think so,' I called back. 'Get me out of here.'

'You'll have to climb back up the rope.'

It's easier said than done. Climbing up a rope with the temperature ten degrees below zero and a full-laden skidoo teetering above you ready to crash down on your head is not, repeat not, a piece of cake.

The fact that the walls of the crevasse were relatively narrow helped. Using my feet and shoulders, I was able to brace myself against the sides. It took me ten minutes to get back onto the skidoo. Ten minutes of excruciating agony, mental as much as physical.

I think it was anger, as much as anything else, that saw me through it. I was so furious with Harry, so livid with rage at his typical unpardonable slapdash carelessness, that I couldn't wait to climb back out of that hole and clock him one on the nose. As it was, I cursed out loud every second of the climb.

The skidoo lurched dangerously as I dragged myself onto it, but the rope held. The sledge was at an angle, so I stood on the seat and grasped the rope. Ten feet to go. You can manage that, I said to myself. You're not a wimp. Go for it!

Harry was leaning down into the crevasse above me. He had taken his goggles off and I could see the expression on his face. I don't think I've ever seen anyone look so cruel and so vindictive.

'You shouldn't have done it, Charles,' he shouted, a wild staring look in his eyes. 'You had no right to. She was my wife. I loved her.'

'What the hell are you talking about?' I shouted back. One foot was still on the skidoo, but I was already beginning to climb. The sledge lurched beneath me and slipped a couple of feet.

'I'm talking about the photo, you bastard.'

Deep down, I knew then that there was no point in dissembling. My instincts had been right. When I had blurted out like an idiot that I had seen the photograph of Harry and Alvarez together, I had pretended that I was talking about the photo in the office not the one in Nasreen's bedroom. But Harry had picked up on the hesitation in my voice. When you've grown up with somebody, you get to know these things.

Still, I tried to bluff it out. My feet were well clear of the skidoo now. I guess I was less than five feet from the lip of the crevasse.

'What photo, for Christ's sake?' I called through clenched teeth.

There was a sudden snap as one of the strands of the rope parted. I heard Harry shout, 'It's not going to hold.'

There was a second snap as another strand parted, and then the whole rope gave way. As I fell back onto the skidoo I hit my head a terrific crack against the wall of the crevasse. Then I blacked out.

THE FIRST THING that struck me when I came to was the change in the light. I seemed to be in a dull blue-white cavern. I was still miraculously astride the skidoo, but the skidoo itself must have slipped twenty feet farther down the crevasse. Daylight was now a distant glimmer, a white square miles above me.

The second thing that struck me was the silence. The total mind-baffling silence. If you ever want to understand what is meant by a complete absence of noise, try hanging your head fifty feet down a crevasse in Antarctica. You might as well be in a soundproof room. A gale could have been blowing up there on the surface, but where I was there was not the faintest whisper.

'Harry, are you there?' I called once or twice.

I might as well have been shouting at the moon.

The third thing that struck me was the cold. When I had been struggling to climb up the rope the physical exertion itself had kept me warm. Now, with nothing to do but sit and wait, I could really feel the deep and icy chill. There was no sunlight down here to take the edge off. It was like being shut inside a refrigerator. I could feel the marrow in my bones congealing.

I tried to work out how long it would take Harry to fetch Munro and Southgate. How long would it take them to get a rope and drag me back to the surface? Would I even have the strength to grab a rope if they threw one down?

Anger was still my ally. It helped me fight. I'm sure of that. Anger at Harry for driving so bloody badly. Anger at BAS for having such lousy ropes. How the hell had that rope snapped? Wasn't all equipment tested against specifications? Anger, finally, at the bloody Russians. They had got to the nunatak first and by now it might be too late to stop them. And what if Harry lost his way back to the Twotter? How would the message about the Russians get through? If we both perished on the ice, it would be game set and match to the other side.

My mind began to wander. A kaleidoscope of images passed before my eyes. Images of my childhood, schooldays, Cambridge, even Reuters. Sometimes, Harry was there, sometimes Nasreen. Southgate made a walk-on appearance. They say a drowning man sees his whole life pass before his eyes. Speaking from personal experience, I'd say freezing has the edge over drowning.

At one stage, I remember thinking about Captain Scott in his tent on the Ross Ice Barrier, waiting for death. Scott had kept up his diary to the very end. Trying to follow his example, I somehow managed to remove a pen from my pocket with a view to scribbling some last message in case my body was ever found. But the pen slipped from my grasp and fell into the void below.

XXII

Weddell Sea, Antarctica

THE HOMING BEACON, activated the instant I fell from the skidoo, saved me. They would never have found me if the satellite hadn't beamed my position to BAS headquarters in Cambridge. Cambridge picked up the signal and immediately bounced a message back to Rothera, where Sparks, operating at the limit of her radio range, managed to get the news through to Gary Lawson in the Twotter. Gary in turn contacted Munro and Southgate who were still out on the glacier on their skidoos.

They were, I learned later, already looking for us. When neither Harry nor I showed up at the Twotter by the agreed deadline, Munro and Southgate became anxious. They started off by trying to follow our skidoo tracks, but that proved impossible. As I've already said, Harry and I had scooted around in all directions in our search for the nunatak and our tracks must have resembled the movements of a demented water beetle. The fresh snow would have made matters worse, obliterating most of the traces of our passage.

As soon as they had my coordinates from Sparks, it was another story. It took them twenty minutes to reach me, and another twenty minutes to heave me to the surface.

I was unconscious at the time, hypothermia having already set in, but I heard later that it was Munro who climbed down into the crevasse to fix the hook to my belt, while Southgate winched us up. I also heard that once they got me back to the Twotter they had to take a snap decision - should they fly me back instantly to McMurdo or should they carry on the search for Harry?

I should explain. If I had fallen down a crevasse (which was bad enough), Harry had disappeared completely. There hadn't been a peep out of him. When a few hours later I had recovered sufficiently to be able to talk, I reported that the last sight I had had of Harry was of his face leering maniacally down at me from the lip of the crevasse as the rope snapped and I plunged to what looked like certain death.

Of course, I didn't put it exactly like that. I may have hinted that faulty navigation on Harry's part had put me in the path of disaster, but I certainly gave no indication of the fraught nature of our final conversation. That was all part of a bad dream as far as I was concerned and I had no wish to relive the experience in any way. It was certainly no one else's business.

The BAS team had followed the rules. Stick to the bird in hand. If you can save one life, save it. They weren't actually sure that flying me to McMurdo and thawing me out would do the trick - apparently I was pretty far gone - but they were completely sure that if they didn't get me somewhere warm immediately I would not survive.

So they made the assumption - to my mind the correct assumption - that Harry too had fallen foul of a crevasse. No longer paired with another skidoo, his own vehicle would have plunged unhindered into the icy depths. The fact that Harry's own homing beacon had not been activated in the fall was by no means unheard of. There could have been a number of explanations. Harry might have unclipped the rope which attached him to the skidoo for some reason (looking at a nunatak? having a pee?) and failed to connect it again. Or else he could have fallen into a crevasse so deep that the beacon simply couldn't be picked up.

I have to say that the American medics at McMurdo were about as professional as you could get. They knew their job. They had had to defrost people in the past and they would have to do so again in the future. Objectively speaking, I am not sure which is worse - freezing or thawing. As far as the pain is concerned, I suspect thawing takes the cake, but of course there are compensations. Like surviving.

And I did indeed survive. That is the long and short of it. Though I dimly remember the journey back in the Twotter to McMurdo and being rushed across the ice to the sickbay, I relapsed into unconsciousness soon after and it took another twenty-four hours before I was even half-alert.

Lieutenant-Commander Ed Parker visited me in the sickbay almost as soon as I had my eyes open. He spent some time explaining what had happened that day, how Munro and Southgate had rescued me, how the Twotter had brought me back from the glacier, how they had rushed me to hospital, how the Americans had sent out a party to look (unsuccessfully) for Harry.

'I'm sorry about Mr Brokke,' Parker said.

I was pretty sure that Parker knew of the connection between us, but since Harry had wanted to maintain his alias for reasons best known to himself, I saw no reason to divulge his identity now.

Parker might know most of it but he didn't necessarily know everything.

'Yes, I'm sorry too,' I tried to sound nonchalant. 'I guess these things happen down here in Antarctica.' I stared at the tubes sticking out of my arm. It turned out I'd been dehydrated as well as frozen. 'Antarctica's not a risk-free environment, is it?'

'You can say that again,' said Parker.

I said it again and Parker laughed. As a matter of fact, I laughed too. I had mourned Harry for dead once and I wasn't really ready to mourn him a second time now, not after what happened out there on the glacier.

I think I knew from the start that it wasn't just a social call. Parker spread a set of blown-up photographs on my bed. 'Excellent work,' he said. 'You found it.'

'We didn't find it,' I said. 'The Russians found it. At least they found it first.'

As I talked, I tried - groggily - to work out how on earth Parker knew what we had been looking for up there on the glacier. Had he somehow been in the loop all along? Did the Americans know what the Scott Memorial Project was all about? If they did know, had they worked it out for themselves or had someone told them and, if so, why? When Southgate had spoken about the 'authorities', that night we had a drink together in the Upland Goose in Stanley, had he been referring to the Americans as well as the British?

For the time being, I knew I wasn't going to get the answers. I didn't even have the strength to ask the questions. So I concentrated instead on examining the pictures.

The team which rescued me from the crevasse had obviously

recovered my camera and developed the film. All the shots I had taken of the ravaged nunatak were there, as well as the photographs of Harry and me.

After a while I pushed the photographs aside and Parker gathered them up and slipped them back in the envelope.

'Munro and Southgate have already gone back, have they?' I asked.

'They have indeed. They have work to do. We all have work to do. You provided us with the confirmation we needed. We have to take advantage of the opportunity. We don't have much time.'

'When does the balloon go up?' I asked.

'About twenty-four hours from now. Dosing the Weddell Sea with falconite could be a bit like sprinkling pepper on a garden pond. In our estimate, the Russians will go for the point where they can have maximum impact - around 70°S and 50°W. That's where you're in the very heart of the Weddell Sea.'

'You're sure about that, are you?' I asked.

'Sure as we can be. They'll go for the area where the phytoplankton bloom is at its peak.'

I wasn't going to argue with him. They were the experts; I wasn't.

'How can we stop them?' I asked.

It was then that Parker dropped his bombshell.

'That's where you come in,' he said.

I'VE ALREADY EXPLAINED that I'm a general news reporter. However, I need to nuance that, as they say. One of the buzz phrases in Reuters nowadays is 'multimedia capability'. The agency, increasingly, is offering television news reports as well as the traditional wire services. Even old hands like me have had to undergo some pretty intensive retraining to ensure that we know how to perform in front of a camera.

'It's your story. You've got an exclusive. All the majors have agreed to pooling arrangements.'

'What about Reuters?' I asked.

'They're part of the pool, but that's all. They're claiming you're their special Southern Oceans correspondent and that this is a Reuters story but we told them it was the pool or nothing.'

'You did right,' I said. 'Stuff Arne van Meert.'

I told Parker about my Dutch nemesis and he laughed. I liked Parker. He seemed amazingly capable and confident. And, of course, I was thrilled to have a solid professional job to do again. At that particular moment, it was the best possible tonic anyone could have administered. I hadn't admitted to anyone, not even to myself, how much it hurt when I was told to clear my desk that night in London. We all gripe and whine at times, but Reuters had been my life.

Things happened very fast after that. I was staggered at how well prepared they all were. I had a second, more detailed, briefing session with Parker before I left - this time in his office. He explained that, as I had begun to suspect, the Americans and the British had been liaising at a high level. The US was ready to offer any necessary assistance, but the decision had been taken to entrust the actual interception to the British.

'If you look at the map,' Parker said, 'the Weddell Sea clearly falls within British Antarctic Territory. Dosing the ocean with illegally-mined minerals is a clear violation of the Antarctic Treaty which forbids all mineral exploitation. No reason why the Brits shouldn't intervene to prevent a treaty violation. You've got the legal right. And you've got the logistical support. That's why you fought the Falklands War, isn't it? To make sure you had a presence in Antarctica when you needed one.'

'You could be right about that,' I said.

'Like hell I'm right,' said Lieutenant-Commander Parker.

The Americans laid on a C130 for the flight to the Weddell Sea. It's a long haul, but well within the capability of that versatile aircraft.

'We'll fly you there, then we'll turn around and fly right back to McMurdo,' said Lieutenant-Commander Parker. When I asked him how the plane was going to land in the middle of the ocean - did it have floats like an old-fashioned Catalina flying-boat? - he replied curtly, 'It doesn't land. It drops you.'

And that is precisely what happened. On the morning of Monday November 10, I was unceremoniously pushed out of the cargo door of the C130 as it flew over the Weddell Sea at a height of around two thousand feet.

It's hard to describe what it felt like. One moment the wind was roaring in my ears as I tumbled through the slipstream; the next, I was swinging from my parachute in a well of silence. The Hercules had disappeared; the ocean beneath me, flecked with ice, seemed as vast and forbidding as eternity.

I splashed down virtually into the arms of a waiting Zodiac. They had given me a wet suit just in case but, frankly, I didn't need it. I was hauled aboard the rubber craft the moment I splashed down. I barely got my feet wet.

Getting aboard the *Albatross* was a different story. The *Albatross* was a British frigate normally engaged on fishery protection duties off the Falklands. Having received instructions to steam full speed south to and across the 69th parallel, then to continue on deep into the Weddell Sea so as to intercept the *Leningrad*, it was doing precisely that.

If the captain of the *Albatross* slackened speed at all when the Zodiac came alongside, it could not have been more than fractionally. Catching hold of a dangling rope ladder under those circumstances was, it seemed to me, hazardous enough even for a professional. Leaning out over the side of the Zodiac with a couple of sailors holding me steady, I made two desperate but unsuccessful lunges. Only on the third attempt was I able to grasp hold of one of the rungs of the ladder and bridge the foaming gap with my body.

I hauled myself up, breathing heavily from the exertion, then flopped like a stranded fish on the deck.

Moments later, a strong arm was hauling me to my feet.

I didn't recognise him at first. Major Willoughby was in combat dress, Antarctic duties version. He was heavily armed, his head covered by a thick navy-blue Balaclava helmet so that he looked a bit like one of those Abu Nidal terrorists.

'Good heavens, Major!' I exclaimed. I knew as I said it that it sounded like a line from a James Bond film, but I couldn't help adding: 'Fancy seeing you here.'

'Welcome on board, Mr Hodson,' Willoughby said.

'Good to be here,' I panted.

Behind Willoughby, a squad of Royal Marines came to attention.

'I'm glad you've brought the boarding party with you,' I said with as such nonchalance as I could muster.

'When we've winched in the Zodiac,' Willoughby said, 'I'll take you to your quarters.'

They had rigged up a studio for me in the wardroom. After I had changed from the wet suit into my 'normal' Antarctic gear - thick trousers, thick shirt, waterproof sweater - Willoughby showed me around.

'I think you'll find you've got everything you need. Most of the transmission will be live of course, but we'll probably cut in some background footage, as well as other film.'

One of the Marines had escorted us to the studio. Willoughby now introduced him as Corporal Cuthbertson. 'Cuthbertson was a cameraman with Independent Television News before he joined up. He's going to act as your film crew.'

Corporal Cuthbertson saluted. 'Yes, sir,' he shouted. Funny the way soldiers shout. I suppose they don't even think about it.

Willoughby and I sat down to watch while Cuthbertson fed in the tapes. There was, as Willoughby had indicated, some background material: general interest stuff on Antarctica; shots of Antarctic wildlife - seals, penguins and other bird life; scenic vistas of mountains and glaciers; majestic icebergs; that kind of thing.

'You'll probably want to record your own commentary,' Willoughby said. 'And of course you can edit this any way you like.' He waved his hand towards some expensive looking electronic items which stood on a table to one side of the studio. 'I'm told they've given you the latest editing equipment. Cuthbertson will give you any help you need.'

Willoughby turned to the soldier-technician. 'I expect Mr Hodson will want to see the other film as well. He'll need to cut that in too.'

He glanced at his watch and stood up. 'I'm going to leave you to it. You haven't got a great deal of time. Our estimated RV with the *Leningrad* is six hours from now. You'll want to get started. I'll have the galley send some food along. Don't want you to go hungry.'

As he left, he said, 'We're counting on you, Mr Hodson.'

'Major Willoughby,' I replied. 'I don't think I know everything. I'm pretty sure I don't know everything. But I expect I know enough. I'll do my best.'

The Major thrust out his hand and shook mine vigorously. 'Go for it,' he said. 'There's a lot hanging on this.'

After Willoughby had gone, Cuthbertson and I got down to work. We wanted the story to go out live, in real time, over all the networks. But we also wanted to be on air with the background even before the confrontation happened. People had to know what the issues were.

I don't think I've ever worked harder in my life than I did over the next six hours. From time to time I looked out of the window towards the grey-green expanse of ocean. Once I saw a great black-browed albatross swooping low to starboard and a humpback whale spouting in the middle distance. But on the whole, I kept my nose to the grindstone, or rather editing machine. I wouldn't have two bites at this cherry. I wanted to get the story right first time.

The estimated RV with the *Leningrad* was 12 noon South Atlantic time. At 11.45 a.m., I went up on deck. Cuthbertson followed with the camera and boom mike strung over his shoulder. He knew when to cue in the segments of tape we had already edited.

Looking back, I think it was that first minute or two of satellite film which more than anything else gave us our audience. In its own way, it was the equivalent of the pictures - back in 1961 - of the missiles on the Soviet ships heading for Cuba. Adlai Stevenson held the photographs up in front of the United Nations Security Council. We did better. We had moving, not still, shots - real time coverage, *in flagrante* stuff - and we banged those shots right into people's living rooms and boardrooms and bedrooms and breakfast rooms all the way around the world.

I was able to listen, through the earpiece, to the commentary I had recorded earlier.

'What we are seeing now,' I said, 'is illegal Russian mining activity in the very heart of Antarctica. These are satellite films taken earlier this week on the Beardmore Glacier. The Russians flew in a special mechanical excavator - probably using one of the supply helicopters from their nearby Vostok base - and you can actually see the machine at work.'

When I had reviewed the tapes earlier in the day I had been amazed at how clear the definition was. No question these were Russians. They hadn't bothered to disguise the fact. The satellite had even picked up the sable collars on their anoraks.

There must have been a dozen of them altogether. Except for one, the faces didn't mean anything to me. But one of the group was unmistakable. Kalinin seemed to tower head and shoulders over his colleagues. The satellite didn't of course pick up the words as the Russians shouted to each other, but Kalinin was clearly in charge. He seemed to know exactly what he was looking for, directing the movements of the excavator with precise economical gestures.

Cuthbertson had told me that the transmission had been received and downloaded only that morning. The timing could not have been better. It was exactly the starter I had needed before turning to face the camera myself.

As my prerecorded introduction came to an end, I positioned myself so that Cuthbertson could film over my shoulder to catch the unfolding drama as - for the first time ever - a British naval vessel intercepted a Russian flag-carrier in seas claimed by Britain as part of British Antarctic Territory.

The *Albatross*, in a splendid piece of seamanship, came within forty feet of the *Leningrad*, with all our guns run out and the gun crews standing by. I kept up a running commentary.

'The *Leningrad* has been ordered to heave to,' I shouted, trying to make myself heard above the roar of the wind and swell. 'It looks as though that order has been obeyed.'

Cuthbertson pushed the boom mike away from me to pick up the voice of Major Willoughby bellowing through the loud hailer.

'Stand by to be boarded,' he shouted, as the sides of the two ships came together and the grappling hooks were thrown across.

I could see, even as I spoke to the camera, that it was magnificent theatre. There was ice all around, great bergy bits, as the Fids would say, which you didn't want to argue with if you could help it. We were pitching and yawing with the waves. And all the time, we were staring at the Russian sailors eyeball to eyeball. You felt as though you could actually smell the vodka on their breath.

Willoughby was superb. As the ships touched, he leaped across the gap and a dozen Marines followed him, weapons at the ready. They didn't waste any time arguing the toss. They knew precisely what they were looking for. They headed straight for the forward hold.

I hesitated for a moment. Then Cuthbertson shouted. 'What are you waiting for, man? Get over there!'

How Cuthbertson managed to film in a coherent manner

while jumping from ship to ship and running down the deck in the wake of the marines, I shall never know. And it was a minor miracle that we managed to stay together.

'While the Marines search the ship for illegally-mined minerals,' I shouted into the mike, 'Major Willoughby is presenting his credentials as a duly-accredited officer of her Majesty's Customs and Excise. Make no mistake about it. Her Britannic Majesty's writ runs here in British Antarctic Territory just as it runs in South Georgia and the Falklands.'

I allowed Cuthbertson to cover for a moment the obviously heated confrontation between Willoughby and the captain of the *Leningrad*. When, seconds later, the burly figure of Boris Kalinin emerged to join in the row, I knew we had hit the jackpot.

'Professor Boris Kalinin,' I explained to the world's viewers, 'is probably the mastermind behind this illegal operation to change the world's climate. He must know now that he has been caught red-handed.'

Out of the corner of my eye I could see one of the Marines gesticulating urgently. Willoughby broke off his conversation with the Russians and strode over. Cuthbertson and I followed him.

The Marines had the cover of the forward hold open.

'Over there,' I pointed towards the bow of the ship, 'is a cache of the rarest - and in the wrong hands potentially the most dangerous - mineral in the world. The forward hold which we are looking at now is loaded with at least twenty tonnes of a mineral known to science as falconite already ground into powder and ready for sprinkling on the ocean.'

I motioned to Cuthbertson to bring the camera round, so I could look full-face at the lens. In the brief time I had had to prepare my presentation I had worked out in my mind the best way to seem solemn without being portentous; how to sound the note of alarm without being shrill or over-emphatic.

The wind had got up and I had to raise my voice to be heard.

'There is more than one way of achieving Armageddon,' I put my lips close to the mike. 'Thoughtlessly attempting to modify the world's climate could be as good a way as any. Thankfully, owing to prompt action today on the waters of the Southern Ocean, that damage has been averted.'

Out of the corner of my eye I could see the Marines abseiling down into the hold. What the hell were they doing, I wondered? The hold was meant to be full. I walked briskly over to peer down into the cavity. The Marines were sniffing around like tracker dogs but as far as I could see - and I had a bird's eye view - the cupboard was bare.

As you can imagine, I had to change tack pretty quickly after that. Through the earpiece I could hear Willoughby telling me that it was too late after all. The *Albatross* had been steaming at full speed; we'd intercepted the *Leningrad* right on the button. We were bang in the middle of the phytoplankton bloom. Except for one crucial aspect everything had gone to plan: the Russians had already injected the falconite powder into the sea!

'We're getting word from various sources which I won't go into now,' Willoughby informed me, 'that a wide area of the Southern Ocean some two hundred miles due south of where we are now has already been seeded with falconite in what could be a toxic or lethal dose as far as the plankton is concerned!'

I took my cue from Willoughby. Reporters often repeat parrot-like the messages they are hearing through their ear-pieces and I was no exception. I more or less reproduced word for word what

Willoughby had told me, adding a few embellishments of my own.

'We may have been premature in reporting an end to the current crisis,' I said. 'It seems clear that the *Albatross* has in fact arrived at the scene too late. The illicit material which the *Leningrad* was transporting has now been disposed of with possibly incalculable consequences for the environment of the Southern Ocean. However, there is one thing we may be sure of. Those responsible will be brought to book. This is Charles Hodson, reporting from the Weddell Sea, Antarctica . . .'

I have to say that Kalinin put up a command performance. Confronted with the charge not only of illegal exploitation of Antarctic minerals but of equally unacceptable interference with marine ecosystems, the Professor blustered magnificently, claiming that no substances of any kind had been mined by the Russians in Antarctica and even if substances had been mined, the Russians had no intention of trying to interfere with the global climatic balance by dosing the southern ocean.

With the cameras still rolling, Willoughby arrested Kalinin and the *Leningrad*'s Russian captain on the spot. He was well within his legal rights. HM Customs and Excise officers have draconian enforcement powers. Dawn raids are meat and drink to them and they are probably the only branch of government which doesn't have to produce a search warrant when they go about their business.

By now our side had rigged up a proper gangplank between the ships and the two Russians were frog-marched across.

In the studio, Willoughby played the tapes for the benefit of the still protesting Russians. He showed them, first, the footage of the Russian party surveying the nunatak on the Beardmore Glacier and the scenes where the excavator was being used to hack out the material. When he reached the part where Kalinin himself was clearly visible directing operations, Willoughby froze the tape. With the closeup of Kalinin's craggy features dominating the makeshift studio, Willoughby turned to the Russian and asked him straight out:

'Well, Professor, what do you say now?'

When Kalinin kept silent, Willoughby went on to show the film of the Russian helicopter hauling the rock away and other pictures of a Tupolev landing at Druzhnaya. We even saw the stuff being loaded on board the *Leningrad.*

The clincher came when Willoughby, in full view of Kalinin, went over to a cupboard, unlocked it and removed fragments of falconite which I myself had picked up that drama-filled day on the Beardmore Glacier and which I had brought with me, packed in a special pouch of my wetsuit, when they dropped me from the C130 into the Weddell Sea. There was no sleight of hand involved. No way Willoughby could have cheated.

'You're a scientist, Professor Kalinin,' Willoughby said. 'We know what you've taken from the Beardmore. We know precisely where you took it from. If you analyse this sample, which Mr Hodson here kindly collected for us the other day from the nunatak which you and your people have desecrated, you will be able to confirm that it is *exactly* the same composition as the substance you were carrying in the forward hold of the *Leningrad*, traces of which my men have found during their recent inspection.'

If Kalinin recognised me, he showed no sign of it. Instead he gave a loud bitter laugh.

'I'm afraid you're too late anyway, gentlemen. Far too late. Yes, I admit we have dosed the ocean with falconite. *Yes, I admit that we aim not to slow but to accelerate global warming.* We are acting in our own legitimate national interest. Had you mined the nunatak ahead of us, you would have done exactly the same. Except you would have chosen a different dosage rate, designed to increase, not reduce, carbon uptake. Why don't you admit it, gentlemen, instead of standing there like a bunch of hypocrites?'

Of course, Kalinin said all this in his *basso profundo* voice. Far from being a picture of contrition, he was virtually shaking his fist at us as he spoke, challenging us to contradict him.

Willoughby looked around the room. 'I think we had better patch the rest of the team in. Are you ready, Cuthbertson?'

I don't know how or when Graham Southgate made it back to England - presumably sometime while I was in the sickbay at McMurdo. At all events, when Cuthbertson switched on the video-conferencing unit, there Southgate was large as life standing in front of those four large seawater tanks in BAS's Cambridge laboratory.

'We'll need to know the exact dosage rates you used, Professor, as well as the speed and course of the *Leningrad* at the time injection took place. We need to know it *now*.' Southgate gestured to the tanks behind him. 'The clock may be ticking but it can still be turned back. Our best estimate is that we have a window of approximately twelve hours to counteract the effect of a falconite overdose. After that the plankton chain reaction effect may take over and it may be too late.'

Kalinin faced the screen as he replied. I wasn't sure whether Southgate could see the Russian or whether he could only hear his voice. Either way, Kalinin's message could not have been misunderstood.

'Captain Borosov,' Kalinin indicated the *Leningrad's* senior officer who up to this point in the proceedings had remained silent, 'is perfectly aware of the position, speed and course of his vessel. We know the dosage rates used. But can you tell us one good reason why we should now or at any other time divulge this information?'

As Kalinin spoke, the screen split into two. Southgate continued to occupy the left-hand side while the right-hand side now showed Lieutenant-Commander Edward Parker, sitting behind his desk in his office at the US Antarctic Program headquarters on McMurdo Sound. Behind Parker, the US flag and a framed photograph of Lowell Harmer, the incumbent President of the United States, was clearly visible.

'I'll give you one good reason, Professor Kalinin,' Parker interjected. 'Your President and my President have been talking to each other on the hotline and I think you'll find they have come to an agreement. Why don't you guys turn on the satellite television channel?'

Parker pointed to a television set off to the left of his desk, just past the furled American flag. Whoever was controlling the videoconferencing link managed at precisely that moment to zoom in on the picture being transmitted on the TV and we caught a glimpse of President Harmer in the White House press room giving a press conference. Seconds later Cuthbertson, a technological wizard if ever there was one, found the right channel on the *Albatross's* own satellite TV system and suddenly the voice of the most powerful man in the world filled the room.

President Harmer had some notes in front of him, but he didn't appear to be reading them. Instead he looked straight at a leggy blonde woman sitting in the front row of his audience.

'Thank you, Jane,' we heard Harmer say in solemn tones. 'I can tell you that the President of the Russian Federation, Vladimir

Cherniavsky, has given me the most categorical assurances that any interference with the ecosystem of the Weddell Sea which may have been carried out by elements operating in or from the Russian vessel, the *Leningrad*, is totally and utterly unauthorised as far as the Government of the Russian Federation and its President are concerned. These unauthorised actions appear to have been carried out by renegade hard line factions intent on achieving short-term economic and political advantage for the Russian Federation through the deliberate modification of the global climate.'

A large screen had been mounted in the White House press room behind the presidential podium and, as the President was speaking, we could see the image of Russian President Cherniavsky addressing the Russian people from his Kremlin office. Cherniavsky appeared to be in a foul temper. Though we could not at first hear the words, we could see that he was most of the time scowling ferociously and twice he banged his fist on the desk so hard that the glass of clear liquid in front of him (water or, more probably, vodka) spilled its contents onto the polished wood surface. After a minute or two, by some miracle of communication, they were able to run the sound and the picture together as President Cherniavsky ranted on. Kalinin listened carefully, nodding his head. Once I thought he smiled.

Suddenly, we were back in the White House again with President Lowell Harmer. He appeared to be wrapping things up.

'In view of all the circumstances,' President Harmer concluded, 'I have this morning authorised the immediate commencement of OPERATION ICECAP. In my judgement, and in the judgement of my scientific advisers, ICECAP represents our best hope of reversing a potential global ecological catastrophe. That is all for this morning, ladies and gentlemen . . .'

Willoughby nodded at Cuthbertson, who turned off the television leaving only the video-link in operation.

Lieutenant-Commander Parker was speaking again.

'Professor Kalinin, we have our own best estimates as to the information we need and, believe me, if that is what we have to use, that is what we will use. But it would certainly make our lives a lot easier at this point if you and Captain Borosov showed a readiness to cooperate.'

I was watching Kalinin closely. I heard him talking quickly to Borosov in Russian. Borosov, who still looked nonplussed by the recent turn of events, was nodding his head like an automaton and saying '*Da, da*'.

Well, I knew that *da, da* was a great deal better than *nyet, nyet* and I had a strong feeling that matters were at last moving in our direction, a feeling which was confirmed when Kalinin stood up abruptly and said, 'You will have all the information you need within the next five minutes.'

Down at McMurdo, Lieutenant-Commander Parker reacted immediately. 'Thank you, Professor,' he said. 'You will not regret your decision.'

Kalinin gave a last peremptory nod at the video-screen and strode from the room, followed by Borosov. Quite where they were going, I had no idea. Technically, I knew, they were under arrest but you wouldn't have known it. Kalinin's sheer physical presence, the magnetic force of his personality, dominated the wardroom of the *Albatross* just as it had dominated Churchill College's High Table.

When the Russians had left the room, Willougby spoke again to Southgate and Parker who were still on screen.

'I hope that was helpful, gentlemen. Dr Southgate?'

'Most helpful,' Southgate said.

'Commander Parker? Do you wish to add anything at this stage?' Willoughby asked.

We could see Parker tapping at the keyboard of the computer on his desk.

'We're just running the new data Kalinin has provided. It looks good,' Parker said. 'We're feeding it in now.'

The video-screen went blank.

'Well, gentlemen,' Major Willoughby picked up his Abu Nidal balaclava. 'All we can do now is wait. And pray.'

We were already on deck when we heard the distant sound of the planes. Cuthbertson and his crew had their cameras rigged and ready to go and we caught the first of the giant B16 bombers as it popped up over the grey-green horizon flying so low that we could clearly see the USAF decals and markings on the wings and fuselage. I counted thirty planes altogether in the first wave. The noise as they passed overhead was so tremendous that I had to shout to make myself heard.

'This morning,' I bawled into the mike, 'Russian President Vladimir Cherniavsky denied all knowledge of action by renegade Russian scientists to interfere with the marine ecosystem of the Southern Ocean and thereby accelerate global warming. President Cherniavsky has pledged his full support and cooperation in attempts to stem the potential disaster. What we are witnessing at this very moment is the onset of OPERATION ICECAP involving, so I am told, at least three and possibly more squadrons of US Bomber Command. I do not know what antidote the Americans are planning to use in the Weddell Sea but whatever it is it is clear from the number of planes involved that we are talking in terms of very considerable quantities of material.'

As Cuthbertson panned upwards to catch the undersides of the low-flying bombers, I continued:

'I have been told that instead of bombs, each one of the planes is carrying eighty 400-pound canisters of the antidote material. As they reach the drop zone due south of here, the bombers will release their loads in a precisely coordinated pattern to ensure full coverage of the designated area. The world has not witnessed such a massive display of airborne firepower since the allies bombed Dresden at the end of the World War Two. Today, however, this operation is being pursued for wholly peaceful ends. This is Charles Hodson . . .'

Suddenly, it was over. The last plane had passed out of sight. All we could hear was the distant dying rumble of their engines as they flew towards the epicentre of the Weddell Sea. Where had they taken off from, these mighty bombers, I wondered? Had they flown nonstop from their bases in Texas and Arkansas or wherever? Had they stopped overnight somewhere? The Falklands?

From the logistical point of view, if from no other, OPERATION ICECAP seemed little short of a miracle. Thank God for the Yanks, I found myself saying, long after the camera had stopped rolling.

Later that day I asked Willoughby what had happened to Kalinin and Borosov.

'I'd like to do an interview with Kalinin,' I said.

Willougby had been diplomatically evasive. He told me that Professor Kalinin was in custody on board the *Albatross*, but that no further communication with him was permitted. In order to avoid an escalation of the crisis, Captain Borosov had been allowed back on board the *Leningrad* and the Russian ship had been authorised to proceed. I didn't press the point because, quite frankly,

I didn't expect to get anywhere with it. The Weddell Sea incident, as I thought of it, had moved into the area of high politics. Willoughby himself was probably just carrying out instructions.

In any case, even if I had had the inclination, it wasn't really possible to search the *Albatross*, from top to toe, trying to find out what they had done with Kalinin. Willoughby's marines were still very much in evidence and I didn't suppose that freelance reconnaissance would take me very far. And, frankly, I just didn't have the time. For the next three days as we steamed north towards the Falklands, I was still broadcasting at regular intervals from the onboard studio.

One of the things I pointed out to my various audiences, was that there was no way of telling at this early stage whether ICECAP had been successful. All the experts appeared to agree that a full assessment of the situation would have to wait until the next Antarctic spring. We would know at that time whether the Southern Ocean was experiencing a normal plankton bloom, a superbloom, or no bloom at all. Until then, all we could do was wait.

Linked in to CNN, Fox, the BBC World Service - you name it - I made the most of my opportunity. The more the editors asked for, the more I gave them. It was the high point of my life. No question about that. I was Walter Cronkite, Dan Rather and Jeremy Paxman all rolled into one.

In spite of all the action, there were some quiet moments. I found myself pacing the deck of the *Albatross*, staring out at the waves as we pushed our way north. How strange it was, I thought: my face had probably been seen all over the world in the course of the last few days. Had Nasreen been part of that audience? Did she know what had happened down there on the Beardmore Glacier? Had someone told her about Harry?

The Albatross had a ship-to-shore telephone and more than once I felt the urge to put a call through to Rio. It would have been so good to have heard her voice again.

But something held me back. There was too much which I still didn't understand. I didn't expect to know the whole truth, or even most of it, but I definitely wanted to know more, much more, before I spoke to Nasreen again.

I didn't have long to wait.

XXIII

Falklands - Return Visit

'I OWE YOU an explanation,' Dame Pauline Fairweather told me as she pushed the decanter of claret towards me across the polished surface of the dining-table. The message inviting me to Government House had come over the radio as the *Albatross* was coming into the harbour at Stanley. I had just had time to change and smarten up my appearance before hopping into the Governor's official transport, the maroon London taxi with the emblazoned coat of arms, which I had seen on my last visit to the Falklands and which was waiting for me at the quayside.

I was the Governor's only guest that day. We had gone in to lunch as soon as I arrived.

'Yes,' Dame Pauline repeated, 'I most definitely owe you an explanation. Off the record, mind you,' she said. 'Can you agree to that?'

I thought about that for a moment. 'Yes,' I replied. I gave her a clear level gaze across the table. Man to man as it were. I've always found that it's best to look the other fellow straight in the eye. 'Not a word will pass my lips,' I said.

I thought she was going to whip out a copy of the Official Secrets Act and get me to sign it on the spot. But she didn't. She launched instead into an analysis of the breakdown of the Russian economy, telling me how the leadership in the Kremlin was weak and divided and how, some months previously, western intelligence had learned that certain hard-line elements in Moscow, possibly including President Cherniavsky himself, were planning a dramatic intervention to change the global climate - in Russia's favour.

'The Cold War revisited?' I asked.

'Exactly so. But with new weapons and over new terrain.'

The Governor pushed her glass aside and fixed me with a beady gaze.

'I won't tell you how we knew what the Russians had in mind. As you can imagine, we have our sources. What I will say is that from a scientific point of view it was at least theoretically plausible. The Americans looked at it. Our own people looked at it. We have worked closely with Washington at every stage. In the intelligence field at least the special relationship between Britain and the United States still works very well. We set up a special joint committee, with experts from both nations. I chaired that committee. Dr Southgate, whom you know, was one of the UK representatives. Lieutenant-Commander Edward Parker, whom you have also met, was one of the American representatives. You don't need to know the names of the other participants. Suffice it to say that our report was unanimous. We concluded, first, that it was probably *technically* possible to influence the rate of global warming by intervening in the atmosphere-ocean carbon cycle and that, secondly, *an acceleration in the rate of global warming could bring enormous benefits to Russia while being potentially devastating to the west.* Siberia would become productive as the Arctic warmed, a year-round shipping route from St Petersburg to Vladivostok would open up, while in the US the great wheat-belt which feeds so much of the world would turn into a dust-bowl.'

I had heard this before from Southgate. I even recognised some of Southgate's terminology. 'What was the time-scale?' I asked.

'Dramatically short,' Dame Pauline replied. 'The committee I chaired estimated that some interventions in the ocean-atmosphere carbon cycle could achieve an increase in global mean temperature of *over five degrees centigrade within a decade. The world hasn't seen temperatures like that since the dinosaur age.* The analysis was sensitive of course to other assumptions, such as the rate of increase in anthropogenic greenhouse emissions.'

'Of course,' I said. It was the first time I had come across the word 'anthropogenic' and I wasn't sure I liked the sound of it at all. I imagined it meant man-made but I wasn't going to demonstrate my ignorance by asking.

Dame Pauline leaned towards me.

'We had to assume the worst, i.e. that the hard-liners would win the argument inside the Kremlin. Don't forget Russia is in a state of almost total disarray. The economy is falling apart. The military haven't been paid for months. Climatic intervention along the lines I've described would have seemed to offer an almost miraculous solution.

'Of course none of us on the committee were sure how soon the Russians would be ready. We were fairly confident that they did not for the time being possess the necessary tools. In other words, though they might be aware of the physical, chemical and biological characteristics necessary if a substance was going to be used to interfere with the global carbon cycle, *they had not yet located that substance.* Nor had they been able to synthesise it, though that surely was just a matter of time. On the other hand we knew from our intelligence sources that they were devoting massive resources to the project. It was, if you like, a last mad throw of dice. And there was a risk, a very real risk, that they might succeed in coming up with something.'

Dame Pauline retrieved her glass and took a mouthful of wine before continuing. 'We had to find a way of stopping them, don't you see? On the surface, it's all lovey-dovey between us now. *They've* pulled back from Eastern Europe; *we're* thinking of letting them into NATO. But in its way their plan was *as great a threat to our security and prosperity as the thermonuclear bomb.* Perhaps greater. I know it may sound cynical, but the effects of a bomb, even a nuclear bomb, can be contained. The kind of climatic shift I'm talking about would be on a global scale and the impact would be permanent.'

I began to see a glimmer of light. 'Who came up with the idea first?' I asked quietly.

'I did,' Dame Pauline replied firmly. 'I chaired the committee. I had the necessary overview. I knew Dr Southgate had recently completed an analysis of the geological samples Scott had brought back from the glacier. Southgate told the committee that he had identified a mineral he proposed to call falconite in one or two of the samples and that this was a unique geological phenomenon. He also suggested that this mineral could be of critical importance for global warming. After that, it was just a matter of linking the two things together.'

'What do you mean?'

'The Russians had somehow to be made aware of the immense geopolitical significance of falconite. If they believed that the mineral could be used as a brake on global warming, their main objective would be to deprive us of access to the material. They have no interest in slowing down the rate of global warming. On the other hand, if the Russians believed that falconite at certain dosage rates and in certain key areas of the ocean could potentially be used as an *accelerator* of global warming, then it would be even more vital for them to get their hands on it.

'We agreed on a plan with the Americans. I told Southgate he should somehow ensure that the Russians knew precisely what he had discovered and that is just what he did, partly through accidental-on-purpose confessions to Boris Kalinin who, most conveniently for us, happened to be a Visiting Fellow at Churchill College in Cambridge and partly through the judicious dissemination of messages on the Internet and through other scientific outlets such as the *Journal of Geological Studies*. At the same time we had to make it seem that we were desperately trying to keep the secret to ourselves. If the Russians thought we were trying to tip them off, they would most definitely have smelt a rat. That was why we needed you.'

'I don't follow you.'

'I'm talking about the decoy plan,' Dame Pauline said. 'Dr Southgate had known you and your brother Harry for years. You had all been up at Cambridge together. You were a Reuters journalist. You could get a story out onto the wires and that story would carry credibility. Harry was working in Brazil in the minerals business. He was in financial difficulties. He was greedy. He needed money. He had worked out his financial scam and was only too happy when Southgate, who of course had his own reasons for doing so, decided to participate. We never really expected the Russians to fall for the decoy. We didn't *want* them to fall for it. We wanted them to believe that our side had set up this elaborate smokescreen with the specific aim of diverting attention from the real location of the mineral in Antarctica itself - on the Beardmore Glacier. If the Russians were to be persuaded to race us to the Pole - or at least to the glacier - they had to believe we would do anything to stop them, including pretending that the falconite deposit was in a different part of the world altogether.'

'What Southgate and Harry and Alvarez did was illegal, at least in terms of stock-market rules,' I said. 'What's more they used me unscrupulously into the bargain. They destroyed my professional reputation.'

'Oh, come now!' Dame Pauline tut-tutted. 'You have just enjoyed the scoop of a lifetime. Your television reports on the Weddell Sea incident were beamed around the world. You're famous.'

'For fifteen minutes at least.' I sounded sarcastic and I meant to.

Dame Pauline's tone softened. 'Don't let's talk about illegality,' she said. 'We were confronted with a crisis. The CMG business served a double purpose. First, it convinced the Russians we were serious - why should we set up an elaborate ploy in Brazil if not to buy time in Antarctica? Second, it generated funds. Your brother Harry, as you know - no doubt against his better judgement - has made a major financial contribution to our success. I'm not saying that the financial aspect was overwhelming. But it certainly helped us with the Treasury to be able to say we had some private sector co-financing! And that goes for the Americans too. Even the CIA isn't as flush with funds as it used to be.'

I laughed out loud then. Talk about the Iran-Contra scandal!

Here was a very senior official of the British Government conniving at a major financial scam in part at least to generate money for a highly speculative covert operation.

'Did MI6 do some quiet trading on its own account in CMG shares that day? I wouldn't be surprised.'

Dame Pauline Fairweather had the grace to looked shocked. 'What an idea!' she exclaimed.

I had to let that one pass.

'How much did Harry know at the time?' I asked.

'Harry knew part of it,' the Governor replied quietly. 'When Southgate told you Harry approached him with the idea of pretending there was a massive deposit of falconite in Brazil in order to make a killing on the Stock Exchange, that was true. Southgate told me of Harry's approach and between us we worked out how to play it. We planned every detail. *Harry faked his own death because we told him to.* We went over every element of the false trail together - the Internet website, the business about the golden lion tamarin, the trip around the museum in Ouro Preto. Alvarez played his part too, of course. Those samples in his outer office weren't falconite. Of course they weren't. Theoretically, I suppose we could have chipped a bit off the falconite samples in Cambridge. But we didn't need to. You were determined to be convinced. Alvarez just stuck a label on some plausible-looking mineral. Alvarez, of course, made even more money than Harry. We've made sure that, like Harry, he provides some helpful funding for useful causes, but he's done well enough anyway.'

I was still trying to hack my way through the thicket.

'What if I hadn't rung Southgate that night from Curaçao?' I asked. 'Are you telling me that your precious committee had already worked out that the most probable location of the falconite was precisely where Scott had discovered it - on the Beardmore Glacier?'

It was Dame Pauline's turn to laugh. 'What do you take us for?' she asked. 'Dunderheads? Of course we knew that's where the deposit was if it was anywhere. We made sure the Russians knew it too. When we noticed that the entry in Scott's diary had been manipulated so as to conceal the geographical coordinates, we knew the Russians had swallowed the bait hook, line and sinker. We knew the way to keep them hooked was to set up a race for the glacier, like Scott and Amundsen, and that was precisely what we succeeded in doing. We wanted the Russians to throw caution to the winds and they did. Of course, we had some help we didn't expect to have.'

'What do you mean?'

Dame Pauline pursed her lips. 'Southgate told Harry enough to make sure the "decoy" part of our plans worked properly. As it did. But your brother is no fool. He suspected we had set up the decoy business with CMG so that we could ourselves grab the deposit before the Russians got to it. So, in the time-honoured role of double agent, he decided to play both sides. He took it on himself to keep the Russians well informed. We had his office in Willemstad bugged and we know he contacted the Russians from Curaçao the morning you left to fly down here. We're pretty sure Harry made contact with them in Stanley as well. We think he used the cathedral here as a dead-letter drop.'

As Dame Pauline spoke, I suddenly remembered the occasion when Southgate and I had seen Harry emerging furtively from the cathedral along the harbour front in Stanley. How easy it would be to slip a message in a hymn book - a drawing of a nunatak? - in, say, the fourth pew in the centre aisle, for subsequent collection by visiting Russian 'sailors'!

'Oh God,' I groaned. 'What a stupid bastard!'

'I'll come back to Harry later,' Dame Pauline said. 'All I'm saying at the moment is that we're convinced for a variety of reasons that Harry kept the Russians fully informed of the progress of the so-called Scott Memorial Project. No doubt he negotiated himself some financial rewards which could more than compensate for his own somewhat reluctant contribution to the venture. At all events, in order to make sure the Russians were every bit as keen on getting to the Beardmore as we wanted them to be, we had to be seen to go flat out ourselves.'

'Not totally flat out, surely,' I commented. 'As I recall, we hung around for a few days in Stanley before we headed off to Rothera. You blamed the weather at the time. It wasn't the weather, was it?'

'No, it wasn't the weather,' Dame Pauline admitted. 'We wanted to be sure the Russians had a head start. Not too much of a head start, but enough.

'Of course, having a traitor in our midst, if you'll forgive the expression, was a two-edged sword. Southgate and Munro had to keep up the pretence to the bitter end. If Harry had suspected what our *real objectives* were, he could have found a way of tipping the Russians off and then the whole thing would have gone up the spout. That's why you actually had to get out there on the glacier and look for the nunatak. Of course, we already knew from the satellite photographs that the Russians had been there ahead of us. But we couldn't possibly have allowed them to know we knew that. The Americans arranged for the two Russians from Vostok to be visiting McMurdo when you arrived. That was just a precaution. It was vital to ensure that the Kremlin didn't suspect a trap. We knew the Russian visitors to McMurdo would pass on the message that a British team had arrived with clearly spurious credentials and nefarious intentions. It was a sheer bonus that Harry was there to make doubly sure the Russians knew precisely where we were and what we were doing.'

My head was beginning to swim. I decided to ask what seemed to me at least to be the obvious question.

'Dame Pauline, I'm sorry to sound naive,' I said, 'but what exactly have you been trying to achieve all along and why are you so confident that you have succeeded?'

'I'll tell you what we were trying to achieve,' Dame Pauline replied. 'By catching the Russians red-handed and by making sure the whole world knew precisely what they were up to, *we wanted to ensure that neither they nor anyone else ever again tries to interfere with the global climate in this way.* As you will know, over the last few days, in fact since you first went on the air with that television broadcast from the deck of HMS *Albatross* in the Weddell Sea, the world has witnessed a tremendous outpouring of anger and indignation. There have been marches in the street in a dozen capitals around the world. World leaders have gone on television to denounce all irresponsible interference with the climate. The President of the United States and the British Prime Minister, on behalf of the European Union, have jointly appealed for a new protocol to be added to the United Nations Law of the Sea Treaty outlawing the dumping, injection or insertion into the seas or oceans of any substance likely to or intended to affect or alter the key elements of the ocean-atmosphere interface. The Secretary General of the United Nations has responded urgently to that appeal and we expect that within a matter of months a draft protocol will be ready for signature.'

'You've probably written it already, haven't you?' I said.

'We have made certain preparations,' Dame Pauline admitted, smiling modestly.

I had to hand it to her. She had thought it all out. 'And the Russians?' I asked. 'Will they sign up?'

'They'll not only sign up. They've given copper-bottomed guarantees of compliance. I suspect that over the last few days some messages have been exchanged between the White House and the Kremlin which even I don't know about. What's more, the Russians have agreed finally to ratify the Protocol banning all mineral exploitation in Antarctica. When you think of what that great pristine wilderness means to mankind, that surely is something worth having.'

I needed time to absorb it. I gazed out of the window at the water of the sound. Half a mile away, I could see HMS *Albatross* rolling with the swell as she rode at anchor.

'So that's what it was all about, was it? Ensuring the world gets a new international treaty to save the environment, in its present admittedly imperfect state, for future generations. Am I right?'

'Spot on,' replied Dame Pauline. 'Absolutely spot on.'

The smug complacent look on the Governor's face riled me.

'I'm sure your objectives were impeccable,' I commented acidly. 'But I almost died down there in the crevasse. Was that part of a wider plan? Did you leave us novices roped together on our skidoos, against common sense, because, frankly, by then we were expendable and because it might actually have been more convenient to you if we had suffered an unfortunate accident out there on the glacier?'

'Good heavens!' For once, Dame Pauline seemed genuinely shocked. 'What ever made you think of that?'

'The rope. That's what made me think of it. Why did the rope break? Those ropes aren't meant to break.'

I think Dame Pauline must have pressed a bell beneath the table at that point, because Willoughby entered and saluted smartly.

'Sit down, Major.'

Willoughby looked fit and full of enthusiasm. The Weddell Sea incident had probably been the most exciting thing to happen to him since his tour of the Falklands began. He had been one of the stars of the show. I felt sure the fan mail would have been piling up waiting for his return to base.

It struck me then, in the light of what Dame Pauline Fairweather had just told me, that Willoughby's posting to the Falklands, like that of the Governor herself, was almost certainly not a coincidence. The powers that be would have realised that any intervention in British Antarctic Territory would have to be backstopped from the Falklands. Perhaps Dame Pauline had suggested that she herself be posted to the Falklands - it was an odd place for a high flier, otherwise. Perhaps she had handpicked Willoughby for the job. At least two safe pairs of hands would be available when the need arose.

'Tell him about the rope, Major,' Dame Pauline said.

Willoughby looked at me in a friendly manner. We would never be bosom pals or anything like that. Our worlds were too far apart. Let's face it; he was a soldier and I was a hack.

'The rope didn't just break. It was deliberately cut, three-quarters of the way through at least.'

'Christ!' I exclaimed. 'Who could have done that? The Russians?'

I suddenly remembered our departure that morning from the Williams ski-way at McMurdo. Early though we had been, the two Russian women had been still earlier. Our Twotter had been parked next to their Tupolev. Could one of the Russians have tampered with our equipment? Had we left the Twotter unlocked? I couldn't remember.

'It could have been the Russians,' Willoughby agreed. 'But somehow we don't think so.' Then he asked me the question straight out. 'Did you and your brother have a quarrel, a fight, up there on the glacier? We think your brother may have cut the rope. We think he may have left you out there deliberately. As a matter of fact, we think he drove his skidoo round to the other side of Mount Buckley and the Russians came in from Vostok or wherever they were and picked him up. We think he had it all planned. Unfortunately the weather that day was too bad for the satellite imaging to be of any help. Even the best technology has its limitations.'

As Willoughby spoke, I could see Harry leaning out over the crevasse, watching me struggle up the rope. He had taken his goggles off. He had seemed to be laughing, I felt sure of it. I experienced an overwhelming sense of gloom. Goddammit, the man was my brother. Flesh of my flesh, blood of my blood.

'He's dead,' I said with grim finality. 'I'm sure he went down a crevasse. The place was full of crevasses. Anyway, how would the Russians have known where to pick him up?'

'The skidoo had a radio.'

'How would he have known his position?'

'To the nearest ten metres, actually,' Willoughby said. 'Harry was carrying a GPS device - a Global Positioning System device. A GPS device is only the size of a pocket calculator. The Russians could have left it for him in the cathedral here when they exchanged messages as we suspect they did. Or they could have given it to him at McMurdo. You and the Russians were quartered in the guest wing together, weren't you?'

I nodded. I recalled the location of our rooms that night at McMurdo. Harry's had been right next to the Russians!

'I'm sure he didn't have a GPS device.' Somehow, I preferred to believe that Harry was dead than to think he had deliberately tried to kill me, and then defected.

'Take a look at this.' Willoughby slid a large glossy colour photograph towards me across the table. I could see at once that it was a blowup of the picture I had taken of Harry in front of the nunatak on the Beardmore.

Willoughby pointed at the left-hand breast pocket of Harry's anorak. I noticed a flat oblong object, a bit like one of those personal organisers marketed by Sharp or Psion, sticking out.

The Major passed another picture across. This time an enlargement of the object in question. 'That's a GPS device all right,' he said. 'I think Harry placed it in his pocket like that deliberately before you took the picture. His little joke. He wasn't expecting either you or the photograph to survive.'

'You mean he deliberately tried to murder me?' I protested. 'I don't believe any of this. I don't think Harry planned my murder. Maybe one of the skidoos ran over the rope and cut it. And I don't believe Harry defected for heaven's sake. This is all a load of rubbish.'

Willoughby waited for me to calm down. 'The GPS system is different from a homing beacon,' he explained partially. 'It doesn't tell other people where you are. It tells *you* where you are. US pilots shot down in Bosnia used it to find out their position, then they used their emergency signalling equipment to let their rescuers know where to find them. Authorised users are guaranteed

22 metre horizontal accuracy, 27.7 metre vertical accuracy, 100 nanosecond time accuracy - that's known as the Precise Positioning System. Civil users world wide use the Standard Positioning System. SPS accuracy is intentionally degraded by the US Department of Defence, but it still gives you 100 metre horizontal accuracy, 156 metre vertical accuracy and 340 nanoseconds time accuracy. Even farmers use GPS nowadays to make sure their tractors are correctly positioned in the field. The system is that good.'

'I still don't believe Harry used it.'

Dame Pauline intervened at this point.

'I know it's painful, Mr Hodson, but you must face the facts. The GPS Operational Constellation consists of twenty-four satellites in twelve-hour orbits. That's twenty-one navigational Space Vehicles and three active spares. The orbits are arranged so as to provide the user with between five and eight SVs visible from any point on the earth. The GPS Master Control and Monitor Network is located at Falcon Air Force Base in Colorado. The Americans have a total monopoly of the GPS system, Mr Hodson. There is no Russian equivalent. The Russian space programme has virtually collapsed. They can't keep their existing satellites functioning, let alone put up new ones.'

'So you have a record of Harry's signal, asking to know his precise location?' I said.

'We do,' Dame Pauline nodded. 'The time, the date, the duration.'

'And the response? You have a record of that too?'

'The Americans have been very helpful.'

Dame Pauline wouldn't say more than that. I suspected that there were some aspects of the GPS system that even she didn't know about, and even if she did she certainly wasn't going to share her knowledge with someone like me. I had heard enough anyway. I didn't need any more convincing. My brother was guilty as hell. On both counts. Attempted murder and treason. That was the long and short of it.

'I don't think I need to know any more.' I stood up. 'I think I had better be on my way.'

It was such a bittersweet moment. What I had learned about Harry in the last few minutes had been enough to change my whole perspective on recent events. I could no longer work up any enthusiasm for Dame Pauline's grandiose conceptions, her geopolitical machinations, her ploys and counter-ploys. Operation ICECAP might have been a top priority for the allies; working up a new international regime on the oceans might have been an immensely desirable outcome in itself, but somehow these macro-considerations no longer interested me. When you learn, from incontrovertible evidence, that your own brother has left you dangling in a crevasse on the end of a rope, when you know for a fact that he's actually sawed the rope through to ensure that you plummet to your death, when you hear that he's defected like a coward to the other side, it's the *micro* not the *macro* view that tends to prevail.

They didn't try to stop me leaving. On the contrary, the Governor assured me that her car was at my disposal to take me to the airfield.

'We're laying on a plane for you,' she said. 'It's the least we can do in the circumstances.'

We shook hands all round.

'Goodbye,' said Dame Pauline.

'Goodbye,' said Major Willoughby.

I felt a bit like Captain Oates heading off into the blizzard.

When I reached the door, Dame Pauline called after me. 'Be careful, Mr Hodson. Be very careful. He's still out there somewhere. And if he's been watching television, wherever he is, he certainly knows you're still alive and kicking.'

As I rode in the Governor's car along the road to the Mount Pleasant airfield, her words echoed in my ears.

XXIV

Rio de Janeiro, Brazil - Return Visit

You would have thought, after so many years, that they would have organised by now some regular links from the Falklands to the South American continent. I could understand a reluctance to restart the local air service between Stanley and Ushuaia in Argentina, but surely some enterprising operator could lay on a weekly or even monthly flight to Montevideo?

As it was, I hitched a ride on the BAS Dash-7 as it made one of its regular re-supply runs to Rio.

'There'll be plenty of connecting flights to London,' the pilot told me as I climbed on board. 'You won't even need to spend the night in town.'

It wasn't a long flight; just a couple of hours. But it was long enough for me to agonise over what to say to Nasreen, or indeed whether to see her at all. I hadn't after all expected to be returning from the Antarctic via Rio. Nasreen certainly didn't know I was coming. I wasn't even sure that I wanted to see her. Harry had vehemently maintained that Nasreen played no part in the original deception. He had led me to believe that when Nasreen had telephoned me that evening from Rio to report Harry's disappearance she had done so in good faith. But now I was not so sure. Harry had lied about so many things. He could easily have lied about this as well. Besides, what was I going to tell Nasreen? That her husband was a murderous, treacherous bastard who once again might or might not be dead?

In the event, those were the exact words I used.

'Harry's a murderous, treacherous bastard, who - once again - may or may not be dead,' I said when she opened the door of her Ipanema apartment to me around seven that evening.

It was as good an opening line as any I have used. It rocked her. I could see that.

'You'd better explain,' she said.

I noticed that her hand was shaking when she poured me a Scotch.

I didn't hold anything back. I told her everything that had happened since we had last met, everything I knew or suspected. I know Dame Pauline had spoken to me off the record but, damn it, I felt that Nasreen at least had a right to know. So I told her about ICECAP, as Dame Pauline had explained it to me, and the fact that the Russians, with total cynicism, had attempted to manipulate the world's climate to their own advantage. I told her about the part Harry and Graham and Alvarez and Oliveira and even Letitia had played.

'Harry may have come up with the idea in the first place for reasons of his own,' I said, 'but as far as people like Pauline Fairweather are concerned, the whole CMG affair, the whole business with falconite being discovered up in the forest, was crucial in convincing the Russians we were in practice trying to conceal a major find in Antarctica. These are the kind of games the Russians expect us to play.'

Nasreen shook her head at that point in astonishment. I don't think she had ever had much time for schoolboy antics, certainly not when performed by grown men who should have known better. ICECAP didn't ring a lot of bells with her. In her own way, she was the antithesis of Dame Pauline Fairweather.

When I came to the part about the crevasse and the way the rope snapped and Harry's involvement, she burst out, 'I can't believe Harry could have done that! You're his brother.'

I hesitated then. I could see that Nasreen did not and would not accept what I was saying.

'Harry knew about us,' I said quietly.

'What about us?'

'That we slept together that night before I left Rio. In this flat. In your room. In your bed.'

I tried to sound as prosaic, as matter-of-fact as I could. It was one way of dealing with the situation.

'I never told him. I promise you,' Nasreen protested.

Frankly I wasn't sure whether I believed her or not. 'You didn't need to.' I told her about the photograph of Alvarez and Harry together, the one in the bedroom. 'It wasn't what I said. He just knew. He could tell it from the way I spoke. I hesitated when I shouldn't have done. Christ, Harry has known me long enough. "Thou shalt not covet thy brother's wife." It's the primal sin.'

As I spoke I remembered the evening we had sat out on the terrace after I came back from the forest. I remembered how she taken me by the hand and guided me to her room and to her bed.

'You knew,' I said quietly. 'You knew all along that Harry wasn't dead, didn't you?'

Nasreen sighed. 'How did you guess?'

'I didn't guess. I just worked it out. So many things didn't make sense. Why didn't you come with me up into the forest to look for Harry? Surely any loyal loving wife would have done that? I know I tried to talk you out of it but why did you agree? How did Scarface know where I was staying in Belo Horizonte? Scarface must have followed me from the hotel to the restaurant that evening. You were the only person who knew what hotel I was staying in because I called you when I arrived. How come the bank in Luxembourg had a cheque for one hundred thousand pounds waiting for me, if not because I'd told you that night we had dinner in Rio, when we were chatting away about this and that, one hundred thousand pounds was what I needed to buy the freehold of my place in London?'

I went on hammering my points home. 'Why didn't you insist that Harry return immediately when he first contacted you, from Curaçao or wherever? *Because you knew all along that Harry was alive.* That day I met Harry in Curaçao, he pretended that he called you for the first time since his disappearance. Rubbish! You were in regular contact, weren't you?'

She didn't pretend she didn't understand what I was talking about.

'I slept with you because I wanted to, Charles,' she said. 'Not because I was playing a part. I don't know what Harry told you, but if he told you I loved you, it's true.'

'Harry used me,' I wanted to drive the points home. 'But *you* used me even more. The night you rang me in London - even then, you knew Harry hadn't disappeared, that he wasn't dead. The two of you set it up between you. You needed the money and the CMG scam was a way of getting it. You exploited me, abused me. Worst still, you exploited the feelings you know I had - have - for you. Southgate and the others may have had plans of their own. But that doesn't change things. That was sheer opportunism on their part.'

For a while she said nothing, just sat there dabbing at her eyes with a handkerchief. At last she seemed to get her thoughts together.

'Yes, it's true I was playing a part,' she said, 'but there was more to it than that. Things are not what you think. It wasn't a question of money, not as far as I was concerned anyway. One day perhaps you'll know the whole story. I can't tell you now.'

'What do you mean?'

'I'm not free to speak.' Nasreen shook her head. 'Don't press me, Charles. Not now. I'll just say one thing. I slept with you that night because I wanted to. I don't know what Harry told you, but if he told you that I loved you, it's true.'

It was good to hear her say that. God it was good!

'I should never have left you,' Nasreen went on. 'I've always loved you, you know. Somehow, Harry just swept me off my feet. Oh God, Charles, what are we going to do now?'

I put my arm round her shoulder.

'Nobody knows where Harry is at the moment,' I said. 'They think he's in Moscow, but no one knows for sure. *He could have seen me arrive here at the flat.*'

What happened after that will be fixed in my memory as long as I live. The extraordinary thing about it was that it all occurred so quickly.

I still had my arm around Nasreen when I heard the door of the apartment open. A second later Harry burst into the room. He had a gun in his hand.

'For Christ's sake, Harry. Put that gun down!' I shouted.

I think he had been drinking. The gun wavered between us, one moment covering me, the next Nasreen.

'Put it down, Harry,' Nasreen pleaded.

He fired once. I'm sure he was aiming at me but he missed. The bullet passed over my left shoulder and smashed a china vase behind me. Almost simultaneously, I heard another shot fired and Harry fell to the ground clutching his heart.

I could see he was dead. He lay on his side with his neck twisted round so that his wide-open eyes stared at the ceiling.

'Oh God, I've killed him!' Nasreen shrieked. She had a gun in her hand, a small snub-nosed Beretta.

'I had to do it!' She was virtually hysterical now. 'He would have shot both of us. I'll call the police. I'll call them straight away.' She picked up the phone.

'Put the phone down,' I snapped.

As she did so, I removed the gun from her hand. I felt strangely calm and in control.

'What are you going to do?' I asked. 'Report Harry dead? The police already believe that Harry's dead. Everyone else believes he's dead. He's been living under an alias since he disappeared. People who met him in Curaçao didn't know him as Harry Hodson. They knew him as a Dutchman, Cornelius Brokke. Okay, Graham Southgate and I knew Harry didn't die in the forest, Dame Pauline Fairweather knows and so does Major Willoughby. But that's the extent of it. They're not going to rock the boat. That wouldn't suit their book. Harry was dead long before you shot him. Lost in the rainforest weeks ago. The case is closed. Why reopen it? You shot Harry in self-defence. You know that, I know it. But will other people see it that way?'

I don't think Nasreen understood immediately what I was suggesting. She was too shaken. To tell the truth, I hadn't worked it all out myself at the time. The only thing I knew for sure at that moment was that it would have been madness, utter madness, to bring the police in. Nasreen had reacted in the heat of the moment. That was clear to me. But the authorities might take a different view.

I don't think anyone heard the shots. What with the noise of the evening traffic along the sea front and the roar of the breakers beyond, a couple of small reports from inside an apartment block could easily pass unnoticed. I poked my head out of the door and looked around. There was only one other apartment on Nasreen's floor and I could see no sign of movement in the hallway.

We waited till well after midnight before hauling Harry's body down in the lift to the block's basement level garage. We stretched him out on the back seat of his Mazda, covered him with a rug and drove north out of town. There was surprisingly little blood.

'Where are we going?' Nasreen asked. She still seemed to be in a state of shock.

'To the forest.'

'Do you know the way?'

'Yes, I know the way.'

Before we left, I found a coil of rope and a torch and put them in the boot.

There was very little traffic on the road. Even the Cariocas have to go to bed sometime. We reached the turnoff in less than four hours.

'Are you sure this is the right place?' she asked.

'Yes, I'm sure.'

As I drove, I felt a strange mixture of emotions; anger, hatred, love - all of these, and something more. I felt an urgent need to do the right thing - by Nasreen, by myself and even for Harry's own sake. Poor bugger, I thought. Heaven only knew what pressure he'd been under. He'd been caught between Scylla and Charybdis, between the devil and the deep blue sea, between a rock and a hard place. Hold up the appropriate cliché and take your pick. Except we weren't just playing with words. ICECAP had offered Harry the way out of his financial nightmare. It must have seemed like a godsend to him when Southgate had jumped at his crazy proposal. Just set up a false trail or two, Harry old boy, and then play possum for a while. Nasreen will call Charles and Charles will root around and before you can say *Cornelius Brokke* we'll have the Russkis where we want them (except we can't tell you that . . .). You'll be a rich man, Harry, you and Alvarez. You can pay off your debts and still be ahead of the game. Nasreen won't have to use that nice little revolver you gave her. Not against your 'business friends' anyway . . .

Poor bugger! Poor benighted bugger, I thought. He had tried to kill me. Why not? I had slept with his wife. In the old days that was the kind of thing you *did* kill chaps for. And in the end Nasreen had killed him. Cleanly, competently, almost clinically. She had shrieked and sobbed later but at the crucial moment she had been steady in her aim.

I couldn't help glancing across at Nasreen as I drove. Except for the occasional query about the route we were taking, she was virtually silent. I had no idea what she was thinking.

I had spent almost a week looking for Harry, so I knew my way around. The track into the forest once we left the Rio to Belo Horizonte highway looked the same as it had when Oliveira and I took it. We drove into the trees as far as we could, the car's headlights lighting up the rough path in front of us.

When we found the clearing, we parked the car almost exactly where Harry had parked it when he first 'disappeared'.

'I'll get the rope and torch out of the boot,' I said.

'What for?' Nasreen asked. She still seemed to be in a daze.

'So we don't get lost.'

I tied one end of the rope to the bumper of the car and held the other in my hand, paying out the coils as I walked into the forest. Nasreen walked just behind me, shining the torch.

When we had gone far enough, we went back to fetch the body, always being sure to keep one hand on the rope at all times.

It took us half-an-hour to drag Harry's body through the trees. When we reached the end of the rope, we propped him against a treetrunk. In so many ways, it was the worst day of my life.

As we stood there together, Nasreen clasped my hand tightly.

We must have waited there ten, fifteen, minutes, each of us lost in our own thoughts. Nasreen turned off the torch. Through the thick canopy of trees I could just glimpse the stars of the southern hemisphere.

How ironic it all was, I thought. I had mourned Harry a few weeks earlier in this very spot, thinking he was dead. Now I *really* mourned him.

'What's that?' Nasreen whispered suddenly.

I listened. We both listened. We could hear a rustling among the undergrowth which was not the rustling of the wind. Nasreen switched on the torch.

Sitting upright in front of the tree where we had propped Harry's body was the most beautiful creature I have ever seen.

'Oh my God!' I exclaimed. 'It's a tamarin. A golden lion tamarin. They really *are* here!'

By the light of the torch I could see the ghost of a smile cross Nasreen's face. 'That's typical of Harry,' she said. 'You never knew how much to believe. Sometimes when you were convinced he was lying he turned out to be telling the truth.'

We wanted to get well clear of the area before dawn. I doubted if Harry would ever be found, but if he was then it would be found in precisely the area he had been reported missing.

His body, I knew, would rot quickly, or else it would be consumed by wild animals. In the event that his corpse was discovered in a fit state for an autopsy, it would no doubt be established that he died of a bullet through the heart. There was no way, though, that the bullet could be traced to Nasreen's Beretta. There is no registry of handguns in Brazil. This is the wild west as far as personal weapons are concerned. Nasreen told me her gun had been bought for her by Harry over two years previously on the black market. All her friends had them. They stuffed them down the side of the chairs when they were at home or in their jacket pockets when they were out shopping. Some of them even took their guns to the beach along with their swimsuits and sunscreen lotion.

To make assurance doubly sure, I wiped the gun clean (after all my own prints were on it as well as Nasreen's) and hurled it far into the forest. For good measure, I threw Harry's own gun after it. Speaking personally, I don't like having guns around.

I remembered there was an all-night bar-cum-restaurant-cum-rest stop a couple of miles past the turn-off on the road to Belo Horizonte.

Around three in the morning, when the stars had gone in and it was pitch dark outside, we got out of the car and walked over to the still brightly lit building. We went inside and bought two *cafesinhos.*

Those little cups of dark coffee are really so sweet that you don't need to add any sugar. But Nasreen took a couple of sachets anyway and busied herself tearing the paper and tipping the contents into the cup.

I looked at her across the grubby little table.

'I'm going away to think about things,' I said. 'About us. If there is to be an "us".'

I took her hand across the table. 'I'd love to stay but it wouldn't be right. I feel too raw, too bruised. I need to sort it all out in my mind.'

I saw her hesitate, as though there was something that she wished to say but couldn't, something which even at that late hour could have cleared the air between us and made things right. Then she sighed and shook her head.

'Will you call me?'

'I promise I'll call,' I said.

'Where are you going?'

'To Manaus.'

'That's a hell of a long way.'

'I need to go a long way away.'

'How are you going?'

'By bus.'

'When?'

'Now.'

I could see the long-distance coach pulling into the rest stop as I spoke. The board on the front didn't actually say 'Manaus'; it said Belo Horizonte, but I knew that in the city I would find another bus going further north - to Brasilia, maybe - and then another one after that, deep into the heart of the Amazon region.

She clung to me as I said goodbye. 'What am I going to do now?' she asked.

'Drive back home and go to sleep.' I remembered my own trip to Rio a few weeks earlier. 'Watch out on the bends,' I added. 'Don't let anyone get too close behind you.'

She managed a weak smile at that. 'Do you promise you'll ring?'

'I'm not sure there'll be a telephone where I'm going.'

XXV

Manaus, Brazil - Cambridge

It turned out I was wrong about the telephone. Lord's Hotel, Manaus, situated on the banks of the Rio Negro a few miles from its confluence with the Amazon, is as well endowed with telephones as any other five-star hotel.

Christ knows how Reuters found out where I was staying but somehow they did. A few days after I reached Manaus I got a call from Arne Van Meert. I was sitting on the terrace with a beer in my hand watching some river dolphins playing in the water forty yards off shore. One of the waiters brought the telephone out to me.

Arne didn't waste any time reviewing the circumstances of our last encounter. He could hardly have sounded more cordial.

'Reuters wants you back, Charles,' he began. 'The MD liked the way you performed down there in the Antarctic. We all did. We want to put you on the new multimedia team. You'll be leading for us on Reuters television news as well as having a roving assignment for the wire services. You can write your own ticket. You're going to be one of the stars.'

'I need some time, Arne.' Christ, it was good to hear him grovel!

'How much do you need?'

'A week or two, maybe a month.'

'What on earth for?'

'I'm thinking of writing a book. I'm working on the outline. May even rough out a chapter or two.'

Arne groaned at that but I knew he would agree. I wasn't just playing hard to get. I really did need the time.

As a matter of fact, Lord's Hotel, Manaus, turned out to be a marvelous environment for my particular purposes. For several hours a day I sat at my desk in my hotel room looking out at the vast expanse of water. There was a lot of traffic on the river; tourist craft, seagoing vessels, river-boats, natives in canoes - all that kind of thing.

When I was hungry or needed a break, there were splendid meals to be had in the hotel diningroom. In the evening, I watched the sun go down sipping a *caipirinha* on the verandah. One evening, when I felt I needed a spot of culture, I was lucky enough to catch a performance of *Cosi fan tutti* at the Opera, a splendid baroque masterpiece constructed in the Brazilian rubber boom of the 1890s. The great Caruso himself once sang here to an enraptured audience, or so I was told.

As I say, it was a perfect place to gather one's thoughts. I scribbled away like mad - in longhand, would you believe it? - in a series of school exercise books which I bought at a newsstand near the hotel. I know I solemnly promised Dame Pauline Fairweather that not a word would pass my lips, but I didn't say anything about writing things down, did I?

By the time I had finished, I think I had sorted most of it out. However, there were still some unanswered questions. On my last day in Manaus, I tried to list the most important of them on paper in chronological order.

1. Was it purely coincidence that Harry read Southgate's article in the *Journal of Geological Studies?*
2. How could Dame Pauline Fairweather and company have known that the Russians would swallow the bait and go looking for the nunatak? Could they have anticipated that Harry would - helpfully - keep the Russians in the picture about our side's activities?
3. Why did the *Albatross* not attempt to intercept the *Leningrad* earlier, before the falconite had been dispersed in the Weddell Sea?
4. How had the complicated logistics of OPERATION ICECAP, including assembling very large quantities of the 'antidote', been worked out at such short notice?
5. What precisely *was* the antidote used?
6. How could the Americans have been sure that Kalinin had given them the right coordinates so that their bombers were able to drop the antidote in the correct place?
7. What ever happened to Kalinin?
8. What about the golden lion tamarin? Was there really a tribe or colony of them up there in the forest north of Rio or had Nasreen and I suffered an optical illusion the night we disposed of Harry's body deep among the trees?
9. Why was Nasreen's Beretta so conveniently stuffed down the side of the sofa when Harry walked in on us?
10. Was the signing of some new United Nations Treaty the real

goal of ICECAP, as Dame Pauline had suggested? Weren't there lots of UN Treaties and weren't most of them pretty useless documents? In that case, was there some other, far more vital, objective?

One evening after I had been in Manaus for about five days I was clearing the dresser table in my hotel room when I came across the ticket from my evening at the Manaus Opera. I'm not on the whole a collector of souvenirs when I travel but it had been such a memorable occasion sitting there in the gilded splendour of the old Opera house in the steaming heart of the jungle a thousand miles from anywhere that I couldn't resist taking out my wallet to put the ticket inside. As I did so I dislodged another scrap of paper. When I picked it up from the floor I saw it was the paper napkin on which Southgate, back in that café in Cambridge, had drawn the molecular structure of the mineral he was proposing to call falconite.

I stood there stock-still as I looked at the diagram. I knew now why it had seemed familiar to me when Southgate first drew it. Oh my God! I said to myself. I just don't believe it. I looked at my neat little list of unanswered questions and I suddenly realised that I had the answer to most, if not all, of them.

I settled up my hotel bill on the spot, made a couple of telephone calls, then took a taxi to the airport to catch an internal Cruzeiro flight to Recife in north-east Brazil with an onward overnight connection to London. I hired a car at Heathrow and drove straight to Cambridge.

When I called him from Brazil, Southgate had told me he would be waiting for me in the BAS Research Laboratory on the outskirts of the science park and he was as good as his word. He was sitting at a long work-bench in front of the four big seawater tanks which I had seen on the previous visit. His lap-top was open in front of him and he was tapping away at the keys.

This time no technicians were in evidence and the four seawater tanks were clearly empty. The murky liquid which had once filled those containers had been drained away. Someone had even polished the glass of the tanks, inside and outside, as though to demonstrate that whatever experiment was being conducted had now been terminated.

Southgate looked up with a cautious smile as I walked over to his table as though half-anticipating fireworks on my part. He started to say something but I cut him short.

'I can't believe you took the risk,' I said.

I knew he knew what I was talking about but he pretended not to understand.

'What risk?' he said.

He was clearly on the defensive because he started patting his pocket as though looking for his pipe even though there were signs all over the lab saying No Smoking.

I didn't want to lose my advantage. 'What if the *Albatross* hadn't intercepted the *Leningrad* in time? What if the Russians hadn't loaded the falconite onto the *Leningrad* at all? What if they had flown the falconite out of Antarctica and sprinkled it somewhere else? What if Kalinin and Borosov gave you duff information and it turns out you've spread the antidote in the *wrong* part of the ocean? You and your clever committee actually led the Russians towards the great prize; you sign-posted the way for them. Wasn't that absolutely crazy given the potential for disaster?'

'Oh dear,' Graham Southgate sighed. 'I rather hoped Dame Pauline Fairweather had cleared things up.'

'Well, she didn't,' I said. 'Dame Pauline Fairweather told me part of the truth but a lot of it was eyewash.'

I pulled up a chair and sat down opposite him. 'How could you have taken the risk?' I repeated. 'You didn't have to publish the article about falconite. You could have kept quiet about your computer-modelling exercise which told you that falconite was the one substance you needed to deal with global warming. Okay, I understand some clever chaps in Whitehall or Washington or wherever decided they would try to entice, to entrap, the Russians into some unwise actions down there in the Antarctic, to catch them with their hands dirty or whatever. But don't tell me that getting some UN treaty signed was worth the risk, the appalling risk, you ran!'

Southgate let me rant on for a while. When I had finally run out of steam, he said quietly:

'There never was any risk. It's true I analysed the samples Scott brought back. It's true I wrote a report in the *Journal* citing falconite as a key component of one of the samples. It's true I spoke to Harry and to you - and to Kalinin too - about falconite's potential as far as global warming was concerned. But don't think for one moment that I believed that's what the samples contained. When I analysed the samples I found them to be precisely what Edward Wilson, Scott's naturalist, described - lumps of coal full of organic remains. Some of the samples, admittedly, contained iron pyrites and to that extent might have been of marginal interest. But there was no falconite there. Not the faintest trace. It was just a convenient, plausible and, I have to say, highly imaginative peg to hang a story on. For generations now, people have been hoping that Scott's heroic sacrifice was not in vain. Well, I can tell you now that sacrifice was not in vain. Far from it.'

'You lied to me,' I interrupted. 'You told me the nunatak contained falconite. Loads of it. And you told me falconite could be a key factor in global warming.'

'Of course I lied to you. You had to believe in the importance of the race to the glacier. Ends and means. It wasn't all lies. I told you Scott's samples had languished for decades in the basement of the Scott Polar Research Institute in Cambridge. That part was true enough. But the rest, I admit, was fabrication, deliberate disinformation, a lure to draw the Russians.'

'And yet the *Journal of Geological Studies* accepted your article for publication?'

Southgate shook his head sadly. 'I'm afraid standards aren't as high as they used to be, even in the academic world.'

'But you leant on the editor?'

'The editor didn't raise any queries. The piece was plausible. Besides, I *am* the editor.'

I didn't want to laugh, but I couldn't help it. 'Okay, but why didn't the Russians do their own analysis?'

'Where were they going to get the material from? Raid the museum in Cambridge on a dark night? No, *the Russians believed us because they wanted to believe us.* We came up with precisely what they were looking for.'

'The Russians had twenty tonnes of the material on board the *Leningrad* - quite enough for them to analyse and discover you tricked them.'

'Why should they have done so? They suspected nothing. Anyway I doubt whether they had the time, or the facilities.'

'What about OPERATION ICECAP?' I asked. 'What was the point of all those American bombers dumping a so-called antidote in the ocean if the material the Russians quarried from the nunatak was totally inert anyway?'

Southgate smiled complacently. 'Ah, that was the beauty of the whole thing! Remember I told you last time you were here about the Scripps Institute project, how a team of scientists took a ship out into the Pacific in 1990 to fertilise the equatorial ocean with a special cocktail?'

'It was iron or iron fillings, wasn't it?' I said. 'As I recall, you told me that the results were interesting, they showed you could influence carbon-uptake in marine plankton, but the sheer volume of iron which would be needed made the whole idea unworkable.'

'Correct. It also turned out that the increases in carbon uptake we achieved were only temporary. The carbon wasn't taken out of circulation for good. The plankton stayed near the surface and eventually the carbon was released into the atmosphere again. What we've learned since 1990 is that we were dosing the oceans *in the wrong place.* Work which the British Antarctic Survey and the United States Antarctic Program have been jointly undertaking over the last few months, including lab tests up here in Cambridge, has proved conclusively that the place to achieve maximum carbon absorption is in *Antarctic* not equatorial waters. Have you heard of the Weddell Sea gyre?'

'I'm afraid not.'

'Let me explain then.'

Southgate got up from the table and walked over to a blackboard. He pulled down a fresh sheet of paper, picked up a felt-tip pen and drew a rough diagram.

'What you see here,' he explained, 'is a map of the Weddell Sea.

Round about latitude 50°W and longitude 75°S a peculiar kind of ice tongue often develops in the course of the Antarctic winter.'

As he spoke, Southgate sketched a tongue-shaped profusion jutting out in an easterly direction from the Antarctic peninsula, then curling to the north, towards the Sandwich Islands and South Georgia.

'We're talking about a very major feature,' he continued. 'At its maximum extent, the ice-tongue could cover an area of around 200,000 square kilometers, which is greater than the surface area of England. Norwegian sealers first named and mapped the feature in the 19th century. The Weddell sea-ice tongue has occurred almost every year since records were kept.'

I wasn't sure that I understood what he was driving at.

'What's the significance of this, er, ice-tongue feature?' I asked. 'How is it linked to global warming? Or to ICECAP, for that matter?'

'Let me continue.' Southgate looked at me, the light of excitement in his eyes. This was the kind of thing he enjoyed.

'I've been studying the Weddell Sea ice-tongue feature for over a decade now,' he said. 'I've visited the area a dozen times on different vessels. I've even been down there in a submarine to see what the underneath side of the ice looks like. The phenomenon is unique. It's hard to explain exactly what happens to turn the Weddell Sea ice-tongue into a gigantic carbon-sink, but I'll try.'

Southgate reverted once more to the flip-chart and drew what appeared to be a series of huge water lilies.

'The ice-tongue is not pack ice in the traditional sense,' he said. 'It's basically frazil and pancake ice. Some of the pancakes are less than 50 centimetres in diameter, the largest run to seven or eight metres in diameter. We've tried to measure them over the years. You could probably put the average size of the ice-pancake at around two or three metres. Most of them have raised edges. That's why they look like water lilies, as you may have observed from my sketch. Because of the pancake structure you have a very high volume of ice relative to the surface area. That means you have a very high rate of salt expulsion to the ocean, because sea water freezing into ice expels salt. And this in turn means that your seawater in the ice-tongue area has abnormal salinity and it sinks to the bottom. We call it the mid-gyre convection.'

He pointed again to the diagram.

'The ice-tongue grows eastwards from the Antarctic peninsula or panhandle. It curves round to the north-east until it reaches the 20°W meridian. In its curvature it embraces a bay of open water at about 30°W and 70°S. This is the heart of the gyre. Think of it, if you like, as a kind of giant planetary plughole.'

This time Southgate used the stem of his otherwise inactive pipe to jab at the blackboard..

'The heart of the gyre is here,' he repeated, digging the pipe into the paper. 'I mean the heart of the deep or mid-water convection process. The super-saline water sinks, down through all the intervening layers, down, down, down to the bottom of the ocean. *It's the only place in the world where convection happens on such a scale.* Take any other ocean and you'll find that the different layers of water seldom mix. And what makes the Weddell Sea gyre so supremely important is that *as the water sinks it drags down with it vast quantities of carbon from the atmosphere.* We're talking gigatonnes here. Billions of tonnes of carbon. *And that carbon is taken permanently out of the system.* It's neutralised. It's consumed by the phytoplankton, and the phytoplankton are consumed by the zooplankton and the zooplankton are eaten by god knows what else - I'm a geologist not a marine biologist. Anyway, the central point is that the carbon is gone for good, bound up in various shell-like structures on the bottom of the ocean.'

I was beginning to comprehend the enormous significance of the work in which Southgate, and the scientists working with him, were involved.

'What you're telling me,' I said, 'is that there is already operating in the world a gigantic natural biological pump sucking the carbon out of the atmosphere. You're saying that if we dose the ocean down there in the Weddell Sea rather than in equatorial waters you can achieve maximum carbon absorption because of the Weddell Sea gyre effect. The carbon absorbed by the super-voracious plankton in this area of the ocean will be taken out of circulation permanently.'

'Precisely,' said Southgate. He was still enjoying himself. 'So what do you think we need for our magic ingredient? Remember we're not talking about an antidote to falconite or any other substance. We're talking about a basic plankton growth-enhancer whose introduction into the marine environment would be timed to coincide exactly with the Antarctic spring phytoplankton bloom in the Weddell Sea gyre.'

I thought about the answer. I wasn't sure what to say but I hazarded a guess anyway.

'The same iron cocktail as before - but this time used in the right place?'

'Exactly,' Southgate nodded with pleasure, acknowledging that I had scored a direct hit. 'Don't forget there is plenty of iron around in the world. That is one mineral we are not short of!'

'Plenty of bombers too,' I commented. 'Things must have been quite busy when you were setting it all up.'

As I spoke I could visualise the great lumbering planes with their iron-cocktail 'bombs' taking off at dawn from Mount Pleasant airfield in the Falklands heading south for the Weddell Sea gyre.

Southgate resumed his seat at the table opposite me. 'It's one thing to know the theoretical solution to global warming. It's quite another to put it into practice. Dame Pauline's Committee looked at the problem from all the different angles. One thing was clear to us right from the start. We couldn't just go in there out of the blue and bomb the Weddell Sea gyre with thousands of tons of iron filings. It wasn't just realistic politically. The Weddell Sea may notionally fall within British Antarctic Territory but remember all those sovereignty claims have been frozen under the Antarctic Treaty rules and even if it was in some sense a British sea, we could never have got away with unilateral action. Besides, it was quite clear we would need the Americans. The iron filings had to be delivered over a wide area and within a very short timeframe. That meant a massive aerial bombardment was the only option. Imagine going to the UN Security Council to ask for permission! Even if the Russians and the others had agreed, think what a price they would have screwed out of us! We're looking for a cheap and effective way out of the problems presented by global warming. We want to be able to continue with our gas-guzzling cars, our polluting factories, our extravagant production and consumption patterns. Don't think our Third World friends in the UN wouldn't have made us pay for the privilege. And don't forget about the environmentalists either. The last thing some of them want to see is a quick technical solution to global warming. They see global warming as a chance to get rid of the car and a host of other things they don't like.

'Let me summarise it,' Southgate continued. 'We worked out at an early stage that the only way we could go ahead with ICECAP was by representing it as being a *response* to actions already taken by others. That's why we set up the whole business with CMG, the red herrings of Scott's samples, the hectic dash to the Beardmore Glacier. We've told the world that ICECAP was undertaken in order to counter a Russian initiative which threatened the future of the planet. I have to say your broadcasts were superb. I watched most of them. *Chapeau!* But of course it was nothing of the kind. As I say, the whole purpose of ICECAP was to introduce several hundred thousand tonnes of iron filings into the Weddell Sea - at precisely the right point and at precisely the right time. If our scientists have got it right, we could have solved global warming for good. We will have set up a unique biological carbon pump down there in the Southern Ocean which will take care of the rise in atmospheric carbon-dioxide without the need for further action on our part.'

'Won't you have to dose the seas every year?' I asked.

'We don't believe so,' Southgate replied. 'Of course, we'll monitor the carbon-uptake rate in the marine plankton communities pretty carefully. I'm sure that if we find it's tapering off, we'll find a way of giving it a boost. But we're fairly confident we've got it right.'

I saw Southgate glance in the direction of the now empty seawater tanks.

'You never had any falconite in those tanks, did you?' I said.

'No,' Southgate agreed. 'We had iron filings. Four different dose rates, four different results. All tending to increase carbon absorption. No toxic effects observed. No overdose level. Of course, our able technicians printed out some very different results.'

'And carelessly left them lying around the lab? Disinformation for the benefit of the Russians?'

'You can call it that.'

'What if your clever biological pump down there in the Weddell Sea takes *too much* carbon out of the atmosphere? What if you end up with a temperature decrease of 5 degrees, rather than an equivalent increase? If you've got it wrong, couldn't the world flip over into a new Ice Age?'

Southgate seemed to find the idea hilariously funny. 'Then we'll freeze instead of drown! Or else we'll have to adjust the pump again.'

It took him a long time to stop laughing.

'By the way,' he said, when he had finally got a grip on himself, 'you'd already guessed most of what I just told you, hadn't you? I could tell. As a matter of fact, when you rang me from Manaus, I realised at once from your tone of voice that you had already sorted most of it out.'

'You're right,' I nodded. 'But I wanted to hear your own version anyway.'

'How did you guess?'

I took out my wallet, removed the now somewhat frayed paper napkin and spread it out on the table.

'Lend me your felttip pen, would you?'

Southgate watched as with a few strokes of the pen I converted the long-tailed, short-bodied molecule into a golden lion tamarin.

'Fully-grown,' I said, 'the golden lion tamarin is 8 to 14 inches long; its tail can be 16 inches long. You had the proportions exactly right. You even had the head and legs in the right place. So, even now, you're still lying to me, aren't you, Graham?' I said.

'What do you mean?'

By now I felt a certain sense of weariness. Why did people have to dissemble so much? Why did the truth have to be squeezed out of them, drop by painful drop? Who was being protected from what?

'I'll tell you what I mean. You tell me if I'm wrong. You told me, Graham, that Harry just happened to see your article in the *Journal of Geological Studies*, with its account of how falconite was first discovered, with your analysis of the substance and your diagram of its molecular structure. That's what you said, didn't you?'

'Yes, that's what I said.'

'Then how was it that long before Harry thought about this scam with CMG and the monkeys, you had already used the image of the golden lion tamarin, *Leontopithecus Rosalia*, as the basis for your description of the falconite molecule?'

'It must have been unconscious plagiarism,' Graham spluttered. He tried to make light of the matter. 'Even the best academics are guilty of it sometimes.'

Southgate obviously decided that attack was the best form of defence. 'Anyway, how are you so sure what a golden lion tamarin looks like. Have you seen one?'

'As a matter of fact I have. And not only on the Internet. I've seen one in real life too. Or I think I have.'

I knew I had won when Southgate suddenly gathered up his papers, looked at his watch and said: 'It's opening time. Let's go to a pub.'

He paused. 'Of course you're right. Falconite was an invention right from the start. There's no such mineral. Not in Antarctica. Not anywhere else. Basing the so-called "falconite" molecule on that monkey was my idea of a joke.'

'Some joke,' I said.

XXVI

Cambridge, London

WE WENT TO a quiet hostelry in a side street with a garden looking out onto the river. We sat in the bow window with a view across the meadow towards the sublime Cambridge skyline.

We talked a long time that evening. Southgate told me things which, on reflection, he probably shouldn't have. But I guess he reckoned that since I had obviously worked most of it out anyway by now, it probably wouldn't hurt to tell me the rest. I suspect he'd received some kind of authorisation anyway. Some old buffer in one of the Whitehall clubs Southgate visited when he went to London would have said: 'if you can't fend him off, tell him enough to keep him quiet!' or words to that effect. They must have known I wasn't a threat.

'I guess it's the old story,' he said, sipping his beer, 'but this time with a twist.'

'What do you mean?'

'I mean that Cambridge men in the past have been rather

notorious in working for the enemy. Philby, Blunt, Burgess, Maclean - they were all Cambridge men. They were recruited by the other side during their undergraduate days and they just carried on from there. This time we did a bit better. We got in first.'

'I still don't follow,' I said.

'Oh, come now!' Southgate blew a cloud of smoke at the ceiling. 'You've already worked out that, consciously or unconsciously, I based my conception of the falconite molecule on the image of the golden lion tamarin. That was because Nasreen had already come up with the brilliant idea of linking the discovery of falconite in the *mata Atlantica* with the threat to the tamarin. Of course, Harry subscribed to the *Journal of Geological Studies* but Nasreen made certain he read my piece about falconite when the magazine arrived at their home in Rio.'

'Nasreen?' I knew the answer to my question even before I asked it. 'She was working for you all along?'

'When you are an Oxford or Cambridge don, you're a talent-spotter for the intelligence community,' Southgate replied. 'Some of us are anyway. That's the way it works. Always has. How else do you think MI5 and MI6 get their people? I had Nasreen marked down as potential material the moment she first came up to Cambridge. She was Iranian. She was beautiful. She had a first-rate mind. Of course, we knew it might be years before we needed her or could use her, a classic sleeper, if you like. But we felt sure that one day the time would come. You have to be ready to play a long hand.'

I could feel a great burden being lifted from my shoulders. In the context, so many of Nasreen's actions seemed understandable, forgivable.

'Did you keep in touch with her even after she went to Brazil with Harry?' I asked.

'Of course, we did. Nasreen not only made sure that Harry saw my piece about falconite in *Nature.* She even suggested the CMG scam to Harry, how to use the map in Ouro Preto, how to pretend there was a falconite deposit up there in the forests of Minas Gerais, how to exploit the possible presence of the golden lion tamarin to add plausibility to the tale. Our people helped to work out the details, of course, but Nasreen persuaded Harry it could work.'

'Did she specify the part I was to play? Was I just an optional extra?'

'Nasreen *insisted* on you, old boy. The fact that you were Harry's brother, the fact that you were so deeply involved, so determined to find out why he had died and if possible expose his murderers meant that, quite understandably, you went beyond the bounds of journalistic propriety. You filed a story you should never have filed - but of course it was just what we hoped for. And then you went one better. Maybe you were trying, subconsciously, to make amends, to wash the dirt off your hands if you like. Anyway, the way you went after the Antarctic angle was, again, precisely what we needed.'

'What if I hadn't rung you that night from Curaçao?'

Southgate smiled complacently. 'I never doubted but that I'd hear from you. You had the bit between your teeth. Right from the start, when I was reading you that piece from Huntford's book about how Scott and his team went off to look for minerals on the glacier, I knew you were hooked. I knew you'd go back to the museum and start nosing around, looking for the map references. You're a bloody good journalist, Charles, and it was the obvious thing to do. And, anyway, if you hadn't rung me, I would have called you on some pretext, filled you in on the background and offered you the chance to join the Scott Memorial Expedition, with or without Harry.'

Thinking about Harry, I remembered what Harry's secretary, Letitia, had told me about Harry's clients in Brazil.

'Did Nasreen know that Harry was in touch with the Russian intelligence even while he was in Rio?'

'Nasreen was the person who tipped us off. That was her job. To keep an eye on things out there for us. If that included keeping an eye on Harry as well, so be it. Nasreen's a professional. You don't make exceptions for the family. She knew that Harry had a list of business clients which included several interesting gentlemen from Moscow. We worked out the rest. From our point of view it was ideal having Harry in some sense as a double agent. We always estimated that Harry would try to maximise his profits, no matter what. He was that kind of man, even if that meant dealing - or double-dealing - with the Russians. We reckoned that if Harry wanted to get in touch with the Russians in a hurry, he would know where to turn. And we were right. He was able to contact them in Curaçao, in the Falklands, even in Antarctica. That was a great help. It meant that the Russians were fully aware of what we were doing. They knew we were taking the falconite business very seriously indeed. They knew they were under pressure. They had to go for it otherwise we would get there first. They couldn't sit around trying to work out whether we had some ulterior motive.'

I took a deep breath, trying to keep my anger under control. 'Let's get it clear: Harry used me; you used Harry; Nasreen operating under instructions as an agent of Western intelligence used us both. What about Kalinin?' I said. 'Did you "turn" him too? Was he one of ours? With Kalinin occupying the position he did as Chairman of the Russian National Scientific Academy, you could have been even more certain of ensuring that the Russians swallowed the "falconite" story, launched their own smash-and-grab raid on the nunatak, dumping a load of perfectly harmless minerals in the Southern Ocean but nevertheless providing you with just the excuse you needed for ICECAP. More subtle perhaps than the Gulf of Tongking incident which brought the Americans into full-scale war with North Vietnam, but just as efficient!'

'I'm not prepared to speculate about Professor Kalinin,' Southgate commented tartly. 'And I would suggest you don't do so either.'

As soon as Southgate opened his mouth to reprimand me, I knew I had got it right. If Kalinin had all along been on our side, it all made sense, didn't it? Why did the Russians accept without question the thesis about falconite and global warming? *First, because it was inherently plausible.* The idea of intervening in the ocean-atmosphere carbon cycle to affect global warming rates was very much in the air. Among the people who follow these things - and that included the intelligence community around the world - the Scripps Institute project back in 1990 must have caused quite a stir of interest. Even if Southgate hadn't been the editor of the *Journal*, his piece could quite easily have appeared in it. As a matter of fact, even if Southgate had sent it off to *Nature*, the world's foremost scientific magazine, I bet they would have printed it.

The second reason, as I saw it, why the Russians had swallowed the bait, hook line and sinker, was that Kalinin himself, with his immense scientific stature and authority, had given it the nod. And Kalinin could have led the Russian mission to the glacier and supervised the dumping of the minerals from the

Leningrad, knowing full well that the whole operation was a charade. The fact that Moscow was receiving, independently, messages which appeared to confirm that the charade was real (my own reports on the Reuters tapes, for examples, as well as Harry's own secret communications) must - from Kalinin's point of view - been an additional bonus.

I wondered whether Kalinin knew the full story about ICECAP.

'Graham,' I spoke, taking a flyer. 'It was Kalinin who really thought of ICECAP in the first place, wasn't it? I mean ICECAP as a scientific intervention designed to reverse current global warming trends and save the planet for future generations?'

I was expecting another great performance with pipe and tobacco while Southgate worked out how to put me off the scent without seeming to prevaricate but to do him credit, he just looked at me and nodded.

'I'm going beyond my brief now, Charles,' he said. 'But I've known you a long time. Your own contribution to the success of ICECAP has been immense. Even though it's not in the script, you deserve to hear what I'm going to say.

'You're right about Kalinin,' he continued. 'Boris Kalinin is possibly the greatest climatologist the world has ever known. He is a man of outstanding authority and, as you know, a dominant personality. Of course, he is perfectly aware, as he told you at dinner that night in Churchill, that under certain hypotheses there could be some short term advantages for Russia from an *increase* in global warming but he is far too big a man to be influenced by such a petty nationalistic consideration. He sees the broad picture. For some time now, he has been convinced that global warming is the greatest single threat facing the planet. He knows what the rise in sea-level will do to coastal communities around the globe, hundreds of millions of peoples. He knows what the impact of desertification will be as fertile lands dry out. He's ready to put the planet first. He believes that the only way the world has a chance to deal with global warming is through direct physical intervention in the ocean-atmosphere carbon cycle. He simply doesn't believe that the political systems exist in the world to bring about through voluntary means the kind of emissions-reductions programmes which would otherwise be required.

'Kalinin came to us some time ago. I won't say when. I won't say where. We started talking about the problem. At one stage we actually suggested that the West and Russia might cooperate on ICECAP. Our cosmonauts have worked together. Why shouldn't our climate people? Why shouldn't we save the world together? Kalinin just laughed at us. He said the hardliners in the Kremlin just wouldn't wear it. The thawing of the Siberian permafrost and the opening up of the northern sea-route was more and more being touted as the definitive answer to Russia's economic problems. What's more, a lot of Russian businessmen, and not a few Russian politicians, including perhaps President Cherniavsky himself, were looking to make a great deal of money from the new developments.'

I nodded. I could see the point. You didn't have to be Richard Branson to see the profits to be made on the new all-season Murmansk to Vladivostok sea-route, to take just one example.

'So he came up with a different idea, did he?' I said. 'Draw the Russians into an illicit Southern Ocean operation and then use that as the excuse for ICECAP. Make sure the Russians were convinced that we were convinced of the importance of falconite by setting up a race for the nunatak except that our side, of course, knows it's not really a race at all.'

I felt myself blushing as I remembered those tense conferences out there on the ice or at the US base at McMurdo as we tried to work out precisely what route Scott would have taken on his way back down the Beardmore Glacier. And all the while they were pretending: Southgate, Munro, Lawson, Parker - the whole bloody lot of them!

'Did Kalinin himself change that "1" into a "7"?' I asked, 'while he was still here in Cambridge or did he ask you to do it one lunchbreak?'

Southgate ignored the note of sarcasm in my voice.

'For Christ's sake,' he said, 'what does it matter which of us engineered that particular forgery? The main thing is that Kalinin totally saw the point of setting up a race to the nunatak like that. It added to the credibility of the whole operation. We wanted the Russians to go full tilt for the great prize. "Relocating" the nunatak like that so that our side - ostensibly - headed off in the wrong direction was all part of the game.

'But, of course,' Southgate continued, 'for Kalinin, it wasn't really a game at all. ICECAP was a deadly serious and desperately important exercise. Apart from anything else, Kalinin is a scientific genius. He knew about the Scripps Institute project, of course and Professor Martin's work. We all knew. But it took Kalinin to point out the possibility of using iron, not in equatorial waters where it was wasted, but in the southern oceans and specifically in the Weddell Sea. And it needed a genius to work out that the one place down there in the Antarctic where you could achieve a permanent impact with an ocean-dosing programme would be not at the epicentre of the Weddell Sea, even though that's where the spring phytoplankton bloom is at its greatest, but hundreds of miles further south, where the ice is still thick on the water, in the very heart of the gyre. It's counter-intuitive, if you like, but Kalinin realised it was the only way.'

'So he actually gave us the correct coordinates, did he?' I asked. 'The *Leningrad* actually sprinkled the falconite in the gyre?'

'Of course it did. Kalinin knew all along that the substance they dug up out of the nunatak was totally inert, totally inactive. But he couldn't afford to give any sign that he knew. When President Cherniavsky, presumably under pressure from President Harmer, instructed him to spill the beans, Kalinin split the beans. Cherniavsky denied any involvement, he talked of renegade elements. Bullshit. The whole Kremlin was behind this one.'

'Cherniavsky didn't know Kalinin was on our side,' I said. 'What if Cherniavsky refused to let Kalinin tell us the coordinates of the dumping zone? What if he had instructed Kalinin to stay silent or else to tell us the wrong coordinates?'

'It wouldn't have mattered since the stuff the Russians dug out of the nunatak was chemically inert. They could have injected that material anywhere they liked in the southern ocean and it wouldn't have made any difference. What mattered was that we knew where we had to go and we knew what we had to do. The bombers had the target zone of the gyre all lined up in their onboard computers before they even left the United States. All that stuff with Parker and me on the video was bluff, pure bluff. We had to make it look convincing and I believe we did!'

For a few moments I sat there quietly, absorbing what Southgate had said. It made sense. By Christ, it made sense. Deep-down I had always known that this idea of Kalinin as a cardboard cutout villain was implausible.

'How did you spirit him off the *Albatross*?' I asked. 'I'm sure he wasn't still on board when we docked in the Falklands.'

'No, he wasn't,' Southgate agreed. 'The US Navy had a submarine standing by. When you reach the higher latitudes, the sun dips beneath the horizon and you get a couple of hours of darkness. Apart from Willoughby and a couple of the marines, I don't think anybody saw Kalinin leave. We've told the Russians Kalinin is wanted for questioning. They're not going to complain. They've already decided to make Kalinin a scapegoat.'

'Where is Kalinin now?' I asked.

'He's lying low for the time being,' Southgate said, 'but he'll resurface. You may be sure of that.'

'Some American University will presumably make him an offer he can't refuse,' I suggested. 'Harvard, MIT, Berkeley - they'll all be falling over themselves to get him.'

Southgate smiled. 'Don't forget about Cambridge, Charles. I rather fancy we might be in with a shout. The claret's probably better over this side of the Atlantic! Or maybe the academic life won't tempt him at all. Maybe he'll go back to Moscow and enter politics when the current fuss has died down. Cherniavsky won't last for ever. Kalinin would have some powerful backers if he ever decided to throw his "shapka" into the ring.'

'Our man in Moscow?'

'Kalinin's his own man,' Southgate said. 'Always was. Always will be. That's what makes him what he is.'

All the time we had been talking, I knew I had to tell Southgate about Harry but the moment never seemed to be right. But I saw Southgate checking his watch. Time was passing. I knew I had to do it.

'Nasreen shot Harry,' I said. 'I saw her with my own eyes.'

Southgate looked at me blankly. 'I don't know what you're talking about, old boy. Harry died in the forest looking for monkeys.'

'Harry's body is in the forest,' I corrected Graham. 'He didn't die there.'

Southgate drained his beer. There was a steely note in his voice, an edge to it which I hadn't noticed before.

'Don't push it, Charles,' he warned. 'Don't forget you were in the apartment that afternoon too. You could be implicated. Better to stick to the story you worked out at the time. It's a good story. It will see you through. No one's going to question it, not from our side anyway, I can assure you. Sticking to Harry's alias like that was a fine idea. Whoever disappeared in Antarctica wasn't Harry Hodson. If anyone disappeared, it was the mysterious Cornelius Brokke. Better let sleeping dogs lie.'

'Jesus Christ, Graham!' I exploded. 'How the hell do you know where I was when Harry died?'

And then it came to me. Nasreen must have told him. That was the only possibility. Whether, in the classic parlance of espionage, Southgate was actually 'running' Nasreen, I didn't know but he was clearly still in touch with her. Nasreen must have filed her latest report presumably while I was busy making notes and watching the river in Manaus. Not content with spying on him, could Nasreen, Harry's lawful wedded wife, conceivably, have eliminated Harry on instructions, Southgate's or someone else's? I put the idea out of my mind. It just didn't bear thinking about. I knew what I saw that day in the apartment off Ipanema beach. It was best to leave it at that.

Southgate once again looked at his watch. 'Good heavens! You had better get going! Otherwise you'll be late for your appointment.'

'What appointment?'

'Trinity Great Court. 6 p.m. sharp. I'll walk with you if you like. It's on my way.'

Southgate let me off at Trinity Lodge and I went in alone.

Nasreen was standing with her back to me looking up at the window of the room I used to occupy. She turned round when she heard my footstep on the gravel.

'I'm sorry. I couldn't tell you myself, Charles. I wanted to tell you but Graham said no. He said rules are rules. He said he'd ask for clearance and, if he got it, he'd give you all the briefing you needed.'

'He did tell me,' I said.

I took her in my arms and held her a long time.

We had dinner that night at Oliver's, a little restaurant in Thriplow, a few miles outside Cambridge. Years ago, before Harry intervened, I had brought Nasreen there. There had been some changes since our last visit - a new menu, music in the bar, that kind of thing - but the place still had a lot of charm.

'What I don't understand,' I said when we had finished ordering, 'was how you knew I was back in England?'

'Graham rang me as soon as you called him from Manaus. So I just jumped on the first plane from Rio. We must have arrived at Heathrow at about the same time. Sorry I missed you!'

I laughed. It all seemed so bizarre.

It was clear to me, as we talked, that Nasreen had come to some kind of decision. She said that Harry, somewhat to her surprise, had left her a lot of money. Which means, I suppose, that, even allowing for his generous support of the Scott Memorial Project, he had still made a handy profit on that business with the CMG shares. In the circumstances, she told me that she had cleared out the apartment in Ipanema and planned to leave Brazil.

'Where are you going to go?' I asked.

'I want to go back to Iran,' she said quietly. 'I want to see my parents again before they get too old. They've given us our old house back up in the mountains by the Caspian. I want to go there again. I miss it. It has been so many years.'

I still wonder whether the talk of Teheran wasn't just a gambit, a way of trying to force my hand. I think she was tired of waiting for me to 'sort things out', as I had put it. I don't think she thought there was much to sort out. Either I was ready to understand that she had had a job to do or I wasn't: I had a feeling that for her Harry was history. She spoke of returning to Iran, it seemed to me, as a way of pushing me in the direction of a decision.

I could sense her anticipation. For me it was one of those crucial defining moments, the fork in the road where you have inevitably to make a decision even though you are not sure, not entirely sure anyway, which path to take.

It is true that I hesitated at that moment. My dealings with Nasreen over the years had not been easy. New scars had been added when the old scars had barely healed. I did not for a moment suppose that if I threw in my lot with her now this would be some magic formula for instant and permanent happiness. She said she loved me and I believed her, but would that love last? How could I be sure of that? How could I be sure of anything?

But then I suddenly realised as I sat there that there wasn't, after all, any decision to take. You don't fall in love twice in your life, not the way I fell in love with Nasreen anyway. We had a chance to start again. How many people get a second chance?

'I'll come with you,' I said. 'I'd like to see your parents again. I could finish my book in Iran just as well as here. After that, we can buy a house in London if you like. I'm a high-flyer now.'

'In my country,' Nasreen said deadpan, 'people get married before they start living together.'

'Is that a "yes"?' I asked.

'Yes, it's "yes".'

'Last time "yes" meant "no".'

She leaned over the table to kiss me. 'I meant it last time,' she said. 'Things just got into a muddle.'

'That's one way of putting it,' I said.

As I sat there wondering whether Nasreen would insist on a white wedding, I couldn't help asking myself what Harry would have made of the latest turn of events. In my mind's eye, I could see him even now standing unrepentant on Trinity's hallowed turf and flourishing his colourful boater as he bowed theatrically in front of Nasreen.

'Here's to Harry!' I raised my glass.

'Here's to Harry!' Nasreen raised hers too.

In Hollywood movies, Harry would have burst through the door at this point, miraculously resurrected for a second time. In real life, it doesn't work that way. I think we both had tears in our eyes when we put our glasses down.

The Greeks had a word for it, you know. They called it 'hamartia' - the fatal flaw. Read the last lines of Marlowe's *Faustus*. 'Bent is the branch that might have grown full straight.' The odd thing, of course, is that the quirks in Harry's character, his charm, his flair, his venality, were precisely the ingredients needed to help make ICECAP the success it was. There was a moral here, I felt sure, though I couldn't work out what it was.

For the record, Nasreen and I were married a month later in Marylebone Register Office in London. For the time being we live in my flat in Little Venice, having acquired the freehold thanks to one hundred thousand pounds sterling wired to me at my request by Mr Jan Visser of Luxembourg's Banque de Graaf.

My career as a journalist goes from strength to strength. Though, as I mentioned at the outset, I am not used to thinking of myself as a 'high-flyer', Reuters top brass have told me that the sky is the limit. Arne van Meert clearly expects me to take his job in the near future but frankly I'm not sure I want it. I'll see how things pan out.

In the meantime, we plan to visit Iran soon to see Nasreen's parents and to spend time in the country which Nasreen hasn't seen for more than a decade. I have absolutely no idea what Nasreen's status vis á vis MI6 is at the present time. I don't propose to ask her and I'm sure she won't tell me.

However, I picked up a fairly strong hint the other day.

On December 28, *The Times* reported:

> *'Conservationists are winning the battle to save the golden lion tamarin. Eight hundred of the rare, squirrel-sized monkeys are now alive in the wild. Paulo Oliveira, director of Brazil's wildlife group SOS Mata Atlantica, said yesterday that the monkeys, which have a reddish-gold coat, were the wildlife success story of the 1990s.*
>
> *'He added: "Now we have a new challenge, to double the size of the tamarin's habitat during the next 30 years in order to ensure the long term viability of this species in the wild."*
>
> *'Mr Oliveira said scientists put at 2000 the number of wild golden lion tamarins needed to sustain the species' survival into the 21st century.'*

I've quoted the article here because, just by itself, I found it to be of consuming interest. Here were the Oliveiras hand in glove with Harry and Nasreen pretending that nonexistent tamarins were threatened by CMG and the tamarins turned out not to be nonexistent after all!

Another reason I've mentioned the article was Nasreen's reaction. As soon as I had read it I cut it out and showed it to her. 'The monkeys were there after all,' I said. 'We saw one that night in the forest, didn't we?'

Nasreen looked right through me. 'What night? What forest?'

'The night we said goodbye to Harry,' I said.

She was really angry then, the first time I've ever seen her angry. 'For Christ's sake, Charles, either you're professional or you're not.'

As you can imagine, I am a little uneasy at the idea of being married to a 'spy' or an 'intelligence operative', assuming that Nasreen is still on the active list. But I shall have to learn to live with that. A lot of women know or suspect that their husbands work for the CIA or MI6 and they don't freak out. You've just got to get used to it. That said, without being impolite or seeming wimpish, I shall try to insist that the time we spend in Iran is as brief as possible. My own view is that Nasreen has done her bit for the West already and she doesn't need to run any risks with the mullahs even if they are slightly less fanatical than before.

One thing at least will help ensure a relatively rapid return to England. Both Nasreen and I want the baby to be born in England and the doctor has warned her against flying back late in her pregnancy, particularly since this is her first child.

Nasreen is delighted by the news that she is expecting a baby though she is a little vague as to precisely when the event is to take place. From the evidence of her swelling abdomen, it seems to me that it could be sooner rather than later.

Of course, I am thrilled too, though I didn't expect to become a father quite so soon. If I *am* the father . . . Speaking strictly within these four walls I have to admit that I sometimes have a nagging doubt. I'm not an expert in these matters but it does seem possible in terms of timing that either Harry or I could be progenitor of this particular offspring. I know that Nasreen and I made love that night in Rio after I came back from the forest. How could I forget it? But how often did Harry see Nasreen after he first 'disappeared'? Might he even have visited her in Rio *after* he got back from Antarctica? And if Nasreen *did* see Harry that fatal day in Rio, went to bed with him, even conceived his child, didn't that mean she knew for sure he was in town and could even have had her little gun ready and waiting for him when he returned later?

I suppose I could insist on a DNA test after the child is born but I'm not sure what it would prove. Harry and I may not be identical twins but I'm sure we share enough of the same DNA to make the results of any such tests inconclusive . . .

As you can imagine these and other related questions preoccupied me somewhat when we first learned about the baby. On reflection, however, I have decided to look on the bright side. The baby may not be born until well after the summer in which case Harry certainly can't be the father. And even if Harry, typically, somehow manages to have the last laugh, will that really be such a disaster? I love Nasreen, Nasreen loves me. We both, in our way, loved Harry and Harry - God bless him! - in his way loved both of us. If it's his baby, not mine, well, so be it . . .

I told Nasreen the other day that I thought we should call the child Harry.

She burst into tears, flung her arms around me and cried, 'Oh, darling, I'm so glad you understand.'

I'm still not quite sure what she meant.

On Saturday morning, a few days later, just after I had finished taking Nasreen her breakfast tray, another of these thick cream-coloured envelopes dropped through the letterbox of my flat. The envelope bore the inscription 'On Her Majesty's Service' and was marked URGENT and PERSONAL. There was a coat of arms on the back.

Inside was a single sheet of paper, headed '10 Downing Street. From the Principal Private Secretary. *In Confidence*'.

' "Sir," ' I read, ' "The Prime Minister has asked me to inform you in strict confidence that he has it in mind on the occasion of the forthcoming list of Birthday Honours to submit your name to the Queen with a recommendation that Her Majesty may be graciously pleased to approve that you be appointed an Officer of the Order of the British Empire.

' "Before doing so, the Prime Minister would be glad to be assured that this would be agreeable to you . . ." '

I took the letter into the bedroom and showed it to Nasreen. 'That's one in the eye for Arne,' I said.

I think I've already mentioned that Nasreen, in spite of her Iranian origins, has a perfect grasp of the English language. Sometimes almost too perfect.

'Oh, Charles,' she said affectionately. 'You're such a prat. Who gives a toss about an OBE? Don't let them buy your silence with a gong. They all used you, exploited you. Now it's your turn. Publish and be damned, that's what I say!'

'Won't that compromise you?' I asked

'We'll cross that bridge when we come to it,' she replied.

Maybe it was the effect of pregnancy, maybe she was just happy, but I don't think I've ever seen Nasreen looking so beautiful.

She held out her arms. 'Come back to bed,' she said.

About the Author

STANLEY JOHNSON is a British politician and author, and a noted expert on environmental and population issues.